AN ARMADA THREE-IN-ONE

THREE ENID BLYTON MYSTERY AND ADVENTURE COLLECTIONS

THE MYSTERY THAT NEVER WAS
MYSTERY STORIES
ADVENTURE STORIES

ENID BLYTON

ILLUSTRATED BY RODNEY SUTTON

ARMADA

This Armada *Enid Blyton Mystery and Adventure Three-in-One* was
first published in the UK in Armada in 1989
by William Collins Sons & Co. Ltd

Armada is an imprint of
the Children's Division, part of
the Collins Publishing Group,
8 Grafton Street, London W1X 3LA

Printed and bound in Great Britain by
William Collins Sons & Co. Ltd, Glasgow

ENID BLYTON

The Mystery That Never Was

Illustrated by
Rodney Sutton

The Mystery That Never Was was first published
in a single volume in hardback in 1976
by William Collins Sons & Co. Ltd
and in Armada in 1983

CONTENTS

CHAPTER 1

News At Breakfast Time

Nicky Fraser came down the stairs at top speed, his dog Punch at his heels barking in excitement. The little terrier flung himself against the dining room door and it flew open, crashing against the wall.

The family were at breakfast. Nicky's father gave a roar of anger. "NICKY! What's the matter with you this morning? Take that dog out of the room!"

Mrs Fraser put down the coffee jug and fended off Punch who was leaping up joyfully at her. Grandma smiled at Nicky, and tapped his father on the hand.

"*Just* like you used to be when you were his age!" she said.

"Hallo, family!" said Nicky, beaming round as he went to the sideboard to help himself to scrambled eggs. "I can see you've forgotten what day this is!"

"I told you to take that dog out of the room," said his father.

"Day? Well, what particular day *is* it?" said Grandma. "Not a birthday – that I do know!"

"No, Granny! It's the first day of the hols! Ha – four glorious long weeks to do just what I like in!" He began to sing loudly. "Hey derry, hey derry ho, hey . . ."

"Stop that row," said his father. "And take that . . ."

"Dog out of the room!" finished Nicky. He put his plate down on the table and turned to give his father a sudden hug. "Oh, Dad – it's the first day of the hols. Come on, Dad – I bet *you* used to sing for joy, too!"

"Sit down," said his father. "*I'll* sing for joy – I hope – when I see your report. Punch, get off my feet."

Punch removed himself and went to sit on Grandma's feet. He gave her leg a loving lick. He loved her very much. She *never* shouted at him!

"I suppose you and Kenneth have plenty of plans for these holidays?" said the old lady. "It's lucky he lives next door."

"Jolly lucky!" said Nicky, buttering his toast. "Actually we haven't any *definite* plans. We thought we'd teach Punch a few more tricks – like fetching shoes or slippers for people. Granny, wouldn't you be pleased if Punch fetched you your slippers to put on, when you came in from a walk?"

"Good heavens!" said his father. "Don't tell me we're going to find slippers strewn about all over the place!"

"What's that dog eating?" said Mrs Fraser, as a loud crunching noise came from under the table. "Oh *Nicky* – you've given him a piece of toast again."

"I bet it was Grandma who gave it to him," said Nicky. "Punch, stop eating so rudely. Dad – are you going to give me my usual ten shillings if my report's good? And a pound if it's super?"

"Yes, yes, yes," said his father. "Now be quiet. I want to read the paper, and your mother hasn't even read her letters yet."

Mrs Fraser was reading a short letter. Nicky's sharp eyes recognized the handwriting.

"I bet that's from Uncle Bob!" he said. "Isn't it, Mother? Has he had any exciting jobs lately?"

"Yes – it *is* from my brother Bob," said his mother, putting down the letter. "He's coming to stay with us for a while, and . . ."

"CHEERS!" cried Nicky, putting his cup down with a thump. "Did you hear that, Punch?"

Punch barked joyfully, and came out from under the table, his tail thumping against Mr Fraser's leg. He was promptly pushed back again.

"Mother! I say, Mother, he isn't coming down here on a *job*, is he?" asked Nicky, his eyes shining.

"I bet he is! Mother, will he do some sleuthing here? I'll help him, if so. So will Ken. What's the job? Is it something we . . .?"

"Nicky! Don't get so excited!" said his mother. "No. Uncle Bob is coming down here because he's been ill and wants a rest."

"Oh, blow! I thought he might be hunting a murderer or a swindler or a – a kidnapper or something," said Nicky, disappointed. "You know, Mother, I'm the only boy at school whose uncle is a detective!"

"A private investigator," his mother corrected him. "His work is . . ."

"Oooh, I know all about his *work*," said Nicky, taking another piece of toast. "They've got plenty of investigators on television. Last week one had a frightfully difficult case to solve. It ended up in an aeroplane chase, and . . ."

"You watch television too much," said his father, gathering up his letters. "And now listen to me – if your Uncle Bob is coming here for a rest, he will NOT want hordes of gaping schoolboys coming here to listen to his adventures! Bob is not supposed to talk about them, anyway – they are private. Nobody is to be told that he's the uncle you've been boasting about."

"Oh Dad – can't I even tell *Ken*?" said Nicky, in dismay.

"Well, I suppose you can't *possibly* keep anything from Kenneth," said his father, going out of the room. "But ONLY Kenneth, mind!"

"I shall tell him immediately after breakfast!" said Nicky, passing another bit of toast under the table. "Did you hear the news, Punch? Whoops – we'll have some fun with Uncle Bob. Mother, have you ever seen him in any of his disguises? Can I telephone him and ask him to come in disguise tomorrow, to see if Ken and I can spot him?"

"Oh don't be so ridiculous, Nicky," said his mother. "And listen – there's no going over to Ken's until you have tidied up your room. All your school books seem to be spread over the floor!"

"Right, Mother!" said Nicky. "Gosh, to think it's only the *first* day of the hols! Come on, Punch! You're going to be busy the next few weeks, learning a whole lot of new tricks! That's the time to learn, you know – when you're young! And you're hardly a year old yet. Scram!"

Punch scrammed. He shot out into the hall, sending the mat flying, and up the stairs, barking. He thought it must be a Saturday as Nicky was not going to school. He raced into Nicky's room and raced round and round the bed at top speed, barking madly. Oh what joy to have Nicky all day long!

Nicky picked up all his scattered books, and decided to stack them in the fireplace, out of the way.

"All my bookshelves are full," he told Punch. "So the fireplace is the obvious place. They'll go half-way up the chimney, I expect. Then I'll slip downstairs and phone Uncle Bob. Shut up barking now, Punch – you'll have Mother shouting up to us."

He slipped downstairs to the study after his bout of tidying. No one seemed to be about. He went in, shut the door and sat down by the telephone. He rang his uncle's number and waited impatiently, Punch sitting as close to him as possible.

His uncle's secretary answered. "Oh, is that you, Mr Hewitt?" said Nicky. "Well, listen. Uncle Bob's coming to stay with us tomorrow. Tell him I'll meet him with my friend Kenneth – and we'd like him to come in disguise just to see if we can spot him. You won't forget, will you?"

"I'll tell him," said the voice at the other end of the phone. "That's if I see him before he leaves but it may be that I . . ."

Nicky heard footsteps approaching along the hall, said goodbye hurriedly, and put down the receiver. He couldn't help feeling that his father would consider it a waste of the telephone to ask Uncle Bob such a thing. Luckily the footsteps passed the study door, and Nicky crept out unseen.

"Come on, Punch! We'll go and find Ken and tell him Uncle Bob's coming!" he said to the excited dog. "Race you out into the garden – GO!"

CHAPTER 2

Down In The Shed

Punch took the short cut that the boys always used – out of the back door, through the yard, down the garden to the hole in the hedge. Mrs Hawes, the women who came in to help each day, shook her broom at Punch as he flew past, almost tripping her up.

"You and that boy!" she said. "Sixty miles an hour and no brakes! Give me a cat any time!"

Punch and Nicky squeezed through the hole in the yew hedge, and Nicky gave a piercing whistle. It was immediately answered by Kenneth, who was down in his garden shed. Punch arrived there before Nicky, and flung himself on Kenneth, whom, next to Nicky, he adored with all his heart. He licked him from top to toe, giving little whines all the time.

"You'll wear your tongue out, Punch," said Kenneth. "Stop it now. I've already washed twice this morning. What a dog! Hello, Nicky! I see Punch is his usual fat-headed self. Hope you are too!"

Nicky grinned. "Hello, Ken! I say, isn't it grand, no school this morning! First thing I thought of when I woke. How are your guinea pigs?"

"Fine. I've just finished feeding them," said Ken. "Look at this tiddler – the youngest of the lot, and the cutest. Get down, Punch. He's an awfully *nosy* dog, isn't he, Nicky? Nosy would be a much better name for him than Punch."

"Listen, Ken – I've a bit of news," said Nicky, pulling Punch away from the guinea pig cage. "Wait a minute though – where's that nosy sister of yours? She's not anywhere about, is she?"

"She might be," said Ken, cautiously, and went to the door of the shed to see if his sister Penelope was in sight. "No – all clear," he said, and came back.

"Penny's just about as nosy as old Punch here," said Nicky. "Listen, Ken – you know my Uncle Bob – the one who's a sort of detective?"

"Yes. What about him? Has he solved some mystery or other?" said Ken, interested at once. "I say, did you see that detective play on TV last night – where nobody could make out who stole the . . .?"

"No, I didn't. Do listen, Ken. Uncle Bob is coming this morning – and I phoned him and asked him to come in disguise, so that we could show him how good we are at tracking people and seeing through any disguise. Uncle Bob's a wow at disguising himself – he showed me his Special Wardrobe once – bung full of all kinds of different clothes – and hats! You should have seen them!"

"Gosh!" said Ken. "I say – do you think he's come down to do a spot of detective work here in our town? Can we help him? We're pretty good at disguises ourselves, aren't we? Do you remember that time when you dressed up as a guy and I wheeled you down-town on Guy Fawkes Day? If you hadn't had a coughing fit nobody would ever have seen through *that* disguise!"

"My mother says he hasn't come to do any sleuthing here," said Nicky, mournfully. "But, of course, he might *not* have told her, if anything was up. He's supposed to be coming because he needs a rest."

"*That's* a likely story, I *don't* think!" said Ken, scornfully. "I never in my life saw anyone so bursting with health as your Uncle Bob. The way he made us walk for miles, too – do you remember? Personally I'm quite glad to hear he needs a rest!"

"Well, anyway, he's coming today," said Nicky. "And, as I said, I asked if he'd come in disguise. He's always one for a game, you know – so what disguise do you think he'll wear?"

There was a pause. Ken scratched his head. "Well – he might dress up as an old man," he said.

"Yes, he might," said Nicky. "Or as a postman. I saw a postman's uniform in his wardrobe. Anyway, there's one thing he *can't* disguise, and that's his big feet!"

"Would he disguise himself as a *woman*?" asked Ken.

"I don't *think* so – the voice would be difficult," said Nicky, considering the matter. "And the walk, too. Uncle Bob's got a proper man's walk."

"Well, so has Penny's riding mistress," pointed out

Ken. "And her voice is jolly deep. Like this!" And to Punch's alarmed surprise he suddenly spoke in a curious, deep-down, hoarse voice. Punch growled at once.

"It's all right, Punch," grinned Nicky, patting him. "That was a jolly good effort, Ken. Well, what we'll do is this – go to the station and meet the London train with old Punch here, and . . ."

"But that wouldn't be fair," objected Ken. "Punch would recognise him at once by his smell. We'd better leave him behind. He'd do what he always does when he sees or smells anyone he knows – go round them in circles, barking his head off."

"Yes, you're right. We won't take old Punch then," said Nicky. "He'll howl the place down," said Ken. "Lock him in *yours*."

"Right," said Nicky. "Do you hear that, Punch, old thing? In the shed for you, see, while we go walky-walkies – and if you don't make a sound, I'll give you a great big bone."

"Wuff!" said Punch, wagging his tail violently at the word "bone." The boys patted him, and he rolled over on his back, doing his favourite bicycling act with all four legs in the air.

"Ass," said Nicky. "What shall we do till midday, Ken? The London train comes in about five past twelve."

"Sh!" said Ken, as the sound of someone singing came on the air. "There's Penny. Pretend to be tidying up the shed in case she wants us to do anything."

At once the two boys began to pull boxes about feverishly, and straighten up things on the dirty shelves. A face peered in at the door.

"Oh, so there you are," said Penny, and came right

into the shed. "*You've* been a long time feeding your guinea pigs, Ken! Mother wondered what you were up to."

"You mean *you* did!" said Ken, busily brushing a great deal of dust off a shelf, all over Penny. "Look out! We're busy, as you can see. Like to help – though it's a pretty dirty job, cleaning out this shed."

"*Well*! I've never seen you clean out this shed before!" said Penny, sneezing as the dust flew around. "I wondered if you'd like to mend my bicycle brake for me. It's gone again."

"Penny – we're BUSY!" said Ken. "I'll do it tonight. Or you can ask Gardener. He's good at bikes."

"Well, I certainly don't want to stay here in *this* mess and muddle!" said Penny. "Get down, Punch. *Now* look how he's dirtied me with his paws!"

"Oh, for goodness' sake, go away," said Ken, and swished another cloud of dust from a nearby shelf. Penny sneezed and hurried out. Nicky looked at Ken.

"Shall *I* go and mend her brake?" he said. "She just *might* have an accident, you know. We've plenty of time."

"I can hear her asking Gardener," said Ken, climbing down from the box he was standing on. "She's a Nosy Parker – only came down to see what we were doing! Why *are* girls so nosy? You're lucky not to have a sister."

"Oh, I wouldn't mind a *little* one," said Nicky. "It's not much fun being an 'only', you know. It's a lucky thing for me that you live next door. Still – I've got old Punch!"

"Wuff!" said Punch, and licked his hand. Ken looked round the shed. "We might as well clean it up properly now," he said. "We've nothing to do till midday, when the London train comes in. Shan't we get filthy!"

They worked hard, and quite enjoyed themselves. "My word – we're a sight!" said Nicky. "I'd better go in and change – and hope I shan't bump into Mother on the way! Meet you outside my gate in a quarter of an hour – and then we'll just show Uncle Bob that we can see through *any* disguise he's put on! Come on, Punch – you've got to be locked up, old fellow, till we come back!"

CHAPTER 3

Which Is Uncle Bob?

The two boys left a very angry Punch locked up in Nicky's shed. "Hope Penny won't hear him howling and let him out," said Ken. "I say, I'd better come in with you while you put on something clean, and give myself a brush. I'm pretty filthy too – but if I go into my own house and Mum sees me I might be sent on all kinds of errands."

"Well, come on in, then," said Nicky. "Back way, then we'll only see Mrs Hawes, our daily woman."

Mrs Hawes stared at them in surprise, as they tiptoed through the kitchen. "Well, there now – I never knew the Missis had ordered two sweeps for the chimneys this morning!" she said, as they went by her, grinning cheekily.

Nicky put on a clean sweater and washed his face, while Ken brushed himself vigorously, sending black clouds of dust all over the bedroom. Through the open window came woeful howls from the garden shed. Poor Punch!

"Now to slip out without Mother seeing me," said Nicky. "I don't want to have to stop and do odd jobs just as we're off to meet the train."

They crept down the stairs and made for the kitchen again. An astonished voice called after them. "Oh! *There* you are, Nicky! Where have you been all morning? I wanted you to . . ."

"Sorry, Mother – we're off to meet the London train!" shouted Nicky. "Uncle Bob, you know!"

"Yes, but wait, Nicky, you silly boy, you won't be . . ."

began his mother, coming out of the sitting room after them. But the boys had disappeared, and the kitchen door banged.

"Narrow escape!" panted Nicky, racing round to the front gate. "Come on! We'll just get to the station in time."

The train was signalled as they ran on to the platform. "Now you keep a watch on the people coming from the back of the train, and I'll watch the front," said Nicky. "And remember to look for BIG FEET!"

Ken remembered quite well what Nicky's Uncle Bob looked like – an upstanding fellow with keen eyes, determined mouth, and clean-shaven.

"Still, he might wear a false moustache or a beard this morning," thought Ken. "And stand bent over like an old man." He stood waiting as the train came in by him and pulled to a stop.

Six people stepped down from the carriages. Two were women, both small. They could be ruled out at once. One was a boy, who went whistling down the platform. That left three. Nicky and Ken looked at them closely.

An oldish man with a beard – shuffling along, head bent forward – glasses on his nose – and large feet! Nicky brightened at once. "Might quite well be Uncle Bob!" he thought, and fell in behind him at once.

Of the other two, one was a postman with a large bag. He too had large feet, and was bent under the weight of his heavy bag. He had a small moustache, and mopped his face with a handkerchief as he went, giving a large sneeze as he passed the boys. They nudged one another.

"Bet that's him!" whispered Ken. "You follow him

and I'll follow the old chap – just in case! I don't think that other person's any good. Small feet!"

Nicky nodded. He followed close behind the postman, wishing he could get a better look at his face. Gosh – he certainly had large feet! Nicky tried to peer into his face as he walked past him, but the man was still mopping his nose. He slung his bag from one shoulder to the other, and it knocked against Nicky.

"Hey!" said Nicky, almost bowled over by the weight of the bag. "Got a cold, Uncle Bob?"

"What you following me about for?" growled the postman. "Think you're being funny calling me your uncle? Clear off!"

His voice was not deep, but rather hoarse as if he had a bad cold. Nicky decided that it was decidedly a false voice. He gave the postman a nudge with his arm. "Come on, Uncle Bob! Own up! I'd know your voice anywhere, even though you're making it as croaky as an old crow's. But it's a jolly good disguise!"

The postman put his bag down with a thump and glared at Nicky. "Now if I have any more funny business from *you*, me lad, I'll talk to that policeman over there, see?"

The postman was now staring straight at Nicky, and he could see the man's whole face very clearly – good gracious, it was nothing like his Uncle Bob's face – and the little moustache was certainly real! Nicky began to feel most uncomfortable.

"Sorry!" he said, awkwardly. "I just thought you were – er – in disguise, you know. I was looking for someone else!"

"Now you clear off, see? And if my voice sounds like an old crow's, so would yours with a cold like mine,"

"Come on, Uncle Bob! Own up!"

said the angry postman, and sneezed again so violently that his postman's cap almost flew off.

"It was a mistake," said poor Nicky, red in the face. "I apologise!" And he raced off after Ken, who was still following the old man. Ken was lucky, thought Nicky – *that* must be Uncle Bob, shuffling along, pulling at his beard and mumbling to himself.

He caught up with Ken and raised his eyebrows, muttering, "Any luck?"

Ken nodded. "I think so. Haven't said anything yet, though. Look at his feet!"

Nicky looked. Yes – they were just about the same size as Uncle Bob's – and so were his hands. That beard was clever – hid half the face! The old man suddenly stopped, pulled out a cigarette case and lit a cigarette, holding the match with trembling fingers. He flipped the match away with finger and thumb. "Just like Uncle Bob always does!" thought Nicky. "Aha, Uncle Bob! I'll have a little fun with you!"

So he fell into step beside the old man and began to talk. "Do you know the way to Mr Fraser's house?" he asked, and Ken gave a grin, for that, of course, was Nicky's home. "I'll take you there myself, if you like."

"Don't play the fool," grunted the old man in a husky voice. "What are you two boys following me for?"

"What big feet you've got, Uncle Bob!" said Nicky. "And do let me feel your nice thick beard!"

The old man looked angry and a little frightened. He walked on, saying nothing, then suddenly crossed the road to where the town policeman stood, stolid and burly.

"Constable, will you take these boys' names, and tell their fathers they have been molesting me?" said the old man. The policeman stared in astonishment at Nicky and Ken, whom he knew well.

"Now what have you two been doing to old Mr Holdsworth?" he demanded. Then he turned back to the old man. "All right, sir," he said. "I'll deal with this for you. Young rascals!"

"I say, Constable – is he *really* an old man?" said Nicky, taken aback, as he watched the old fellow go off, mumbling. "I thought he was my Uncle Bob in disguise. Is he *really* a Mr Holdsworth?"

"Now look here, Nicky Fraser, *you* know he's an old man all right, and no more your Uncle Bob than *I* am!" said the policeman. "Don't you start getting into trouble like some of the youngsters in this town! Playing the fool and making fun of old people isn't the sort of thing your parents would like to hear about."

"It was a mistake, really it was," stammered poor Nicky, and Ken nodded his head too, scared. "You see . . ."

"Go home," said the policeman, impatiently. "I've no time to waste on silly kids that don't act their age. *Next* time I'll deal with you properly."

He marched out into the road, and began sorting out a small traffic jam. The two boys, red in the face, hurried home. They felt very foolish indeed.

Nicky saw his mother in the front garden and yelled to her. "Mother! We went to meet Uncle Bob, and he wasn't on the train."

"Well, no wonder!" said his mother. "Didn't you hear what I called out to you, when you left in such a hurry? I said he was coming by *car*!"

"BLOW!" said both boys at once. Nicky groaned. "Gosh – what asses we've been! What time *is* Uncle Bob arriving, then?"

At that very moment a sports car drew up in front of the house, and the horn was blown loudly. The boys swung round.

"It's Uncle Bob! Goodness, Uncle Bob, we've been meeting several of you at the station! What a smashing car! Come on in, you're just in time for dinner!"

CHAPTER 4

Good Old Uncle Bob!

Uncle Bob was just the same as ever, except that he was a bit thinner, and rather pale. Nicky's mother, his sister, made a fuss of him.

"Oh Bob, dear! Whatever have you been doing to yourself? You've gone as thin as a rake!"

"Now Lucy, don't exaggerate!" said Uncle Bob, and gave her such a bear hug that she gasped. "I'm a bit overdone, that's all! If you can put up with me for a week or two I'll soon be as fit as a fiddle! Hello, boys – what's this about meeting several of me at the station?"

The boys told him, and he roared with laughter. "You're a couple of idiots! I can see you need a few lessons in detective work! Come on in and help me to unpack my bag."

It was grand to have Uncle Bob staying with them again. Punch was thrilled too. When the boys let him out of the shed, giving him a bone as they had promised, he ignored the bone completely, and tore up the garden, barking loudly. He had already heard Uncle Bob's voice, and not even a juicy bone could tempt him! He flung himself on Uncle Bob, and licked every bit of him that he could.

"Here – be careful of Uncle Bob – he's rather frail at the moment," said Nicky, grinning. "Isn't he pleased to see you, Uncle! You've come on a good day – it's the first day of the Easter hols!"

"Good for you!" said Uncle Bob, clapping Nicky on

the back. "You'll be able to take me for some walks – and maybe we can do some bird-sleuthing together – you're still keen on birds, I suppose?"

"Oh *yes*," said Nicky, pleased. "Ken and I mean to go out bird-watching as usual. We've heard there's a sparrow hawk somewhere on the hills, and we'd like to find his nest. Not to take the eggs," he added hastily, knowing his Uncle's strict ideas about egg-collecting. "Ken's got an old pair of field-glasses. Wish *I* had!"

"Well – I might lend you *my* pair," said his uncle, who was by this time up in his room, opening his bag. "I always have a pair with me – useful in my work, you know – and as I shan't be needing them this time, I'll lend them to you. That's if you'll promise to care for them as if they were made of gold! They're jolly fine ones."

"Oh, Uncle Bob! Thanks most awfully!" said Nicky, overjoyed. "It's not much fun sharing a pair, you know. Ken always wants to use them when *I'm* longing to – but it's jolly decent of him to lend them to me, anyhow. Now we'll each have a pair. I *say* – are these the ones you use? What *magnificent* field-glasses! I bet Mother'll say you're not to lend them to me!"

Everyone liked Uncle Bob, and as for Mrs Hawes, she was, as Nicky said, "quite potty on him."

"We always get smashing cakes when *you* come, Uncle," said Nicky, at tea time, when a grand new fruit cake appeared on the table. "And I bet we'll get heaps of rissoles now, because Uncle Bob likes them. Shan't we, Mother?"

"Bob always was spoilt," said his mother.

"I wish *I* was," said Nicky. "How did you manage to get spoilt. Uncle Bob?"

"Let's change the conversation," said his Uncle. "Actually, when we were kids, *I* always thought your mother was the spoilt one. Well – what sort of a report did you get for last term, youngster?"

"It hasn't come yet," said Nicky. "Two of the teachers were ill at end of term, so the reports are held up. Horrible! It means I have to shiver in my shoes longer than I need. Don't let's talk about reports! Let's talk about Punch. We're going to teach him a lot of new tricks, Uncle. Will you help?"

"You bet!" said Uncle Bob, helping himself to a second piece of the fruit cake. "My word, Lucy, if Mrs Hawes goes on cooking and baking like this, I shall get so fat I'll have to buy new clothes!"

Punch was sitting as close to Uncle Bob as he could. He liked his smell. He liked his voice. He liked the firm way in which Uncle Bob patted his head. How wonderful to have his two best friends together – Uncle Bob *and* Nicky!

"I thought I'd teach Punch to fetch people's slippers for them, Uncle," said Nicky. "Think how pleased Dad would be to find his slippers by his armchair each night! And I could teach him to fetch you your outdoor shoes, Granny! Then you wouldn't have to go and look for them."

"Hm!" said Granny. "If Punch is going to be as clever as that, he *will* be a busybody! I think it would be better to teach him to wipe his feet on the mat when he comes in from a walk – that really *would* be something!"

"Wuff!" said Punch, sitting up straight, proud that he was being talked about. He gave Nicky's hand a lick, and then Uncle Bob's. He did so like this family of his!

He gave a happy sigh, and laid his head down on Uncle Bob's foot.

"He's getting a bit soppy," said Nicky, amused. "Biscuit, Punch?"

Punch stopped being "soppy" at once, and sat up, barking. "Beg, then; beg properly!" ordered Nicky, and waited for Punch to sit up on his hind legs, front paws waving in the air.

"Not very steady, are you?" said Nicky, and gave him a biscuit.

It really was good to have Uncle Bob in the house. He was always ready for a joke, always ready to give a hand with anything, and full of funny stories about his work,

though, of course, he never gave any secrets away. He took Punch for long walks, he went shopping for Nicky's mother, and was quite one of the family.

But there were times when he sat silent by the window, drawing on his pipe, hardly answering anyone who spoke to him. He puzzled Nicky and Ken one rainy morning. They were full of high spirits, and wanted him to join in the fun – but he seemed somehow far away, and didn't even notice when Punch tried to leap on to his knee.

Nicky went to his Mother. "Mother – is Uncle Bob all right today? He's hardly spoken a word."

"Well, I told you he's been overworking," said his mother. "He's been forbidden to do any of his work for some time – and the days must sometimes seem empty to him now that he has no puzzling cases or problems to work out. With a brain like his, he must often be bored to death, not being able to use it. I only wish something interesting would happen, so that he could have something to think about."

"What sort of thing do you mean?" asked Nicky. "Burglaries – or kidnappings – something like that? I bet our policeman would be proud to have Uncle Bob's help if anything happened here. But nothing ever does – unless you count things like Mrs Lane's washing being stolen off her line – or somebody breaking the grocer's window!

"No, of course I don't mean things like that," said his mother. "I don't really know what I *do* mean – except that Bob needs something to take his mind off himself. It's not like him to sit and mope at times. I think the doctor's wrong. Bob doesn't need time on his hands like this – he wants something to *do* – something to set those brains of his working again, instead of rusting."

This was a long speech for his mother to make. Nicky

stared at her, worried. "Would he like to go bird-watching with us?" he said, hopefully. "Or shall I ask him to help me to teach tricks to Punch? He'd do anything for Uncle Bob."

"Well – you ask him. See what *you* can do," said his mother. "He can't bear me or Granny to fuss round him – and *I* can't bear to see him sitting there not taking any notice of anything, as he's doing today! Maybe you and Ken can help him more than anyone else can."

Nicky went off with Punch, looking thoughtful. Poor Uncle Bob! He certainly must miss the exciting life he usually had – tracking down criminals – perhaps hunting a murderer – finding stolen goods! But what *could* he and Ken do to help?

"Come on, Punch – we'll find Ken, and see if he's got any good ideas," said Nicky. Off they went to Ken's shed, little knowing what good ideas Ken would have – and what extraordinary things would come of them!

CHAPTER 5

Ken Has An Idea

Ken was down in his guinea pig shed as usual. Penelope was there too, cleaning some garden tools. "Hello Ken!" said Nicky. "Hello, Penny!"

Penny didn't answer. "She wants to be called Penelope now," explained Ken. "She won't answer to Penny."

"Oh," said Nicky, astonished. "But, why?" Penelope is rather a silly sort of name – Penny's much nicer."

"Well, if that's what you think, I'll go," said Penny huffily, and promptly threw down the hoe she was cleaning, and went.

"Good!" said Ken, with a sigh of relief. "She's been reading an old Greek story about some wonderful person called Penelope, and she rather fancies herself now. Any news?"

"Yes. A bit," said Nicky. "I want your help, Ken. Stop messing about with those guinea pigs."

Ken looked solemn at once, and shut the door of the cage. "What on earth's up?" he said. "You look as solemn as Penny!"

Nicky began to explain about his uncle. "Mother thinks he's moping now," he said. "You know – misses his work. Hasn't anything to sharpen his brains on. She said that perhaps you and I could think of something interesting to brighten him up."

"He might like my guinea pigs," said Ken at once.

"They're *really* interesting. This one, now, he washes his whiskers just as if . . ."

"Don't be an ass, Ken. Who wants to sit and watch guinea pigs washing their whiskers? I'd go potty if I'd nothing better to do than that! No – I mean something really *exciting* – something to take the place of all the interesting and thrilling puzzles and problems that Uncle Bob has to solve for people, when he's in London."

"Well, let's make up a few for him," said Ken, half-joking. "Let's see now – the 'Mystery of the Lights in the Empty House!' or 'Who is the Prisoner in the Cave?' or 'What made those strange Noises in the Night?' It would be a bit of fun for all of us! We'd lead him properly up the garden path!"

"You really are rather a fat head, Ken," said Nicky. "You *know* we couldn't do things like that." He drummed his heels against the side of the box on which he was sitting. Then he suddenly stopped, and sat up straight. He gave Ken a delighted punch, and stared at him with bright eyes.

"*Now* what's up?" said Ken, quite surprised. "Well – it's just that I think you've got hold of a good idea," said Nicky. "It sounded too silly for words when you said all that – but, you know, there *is* something in it!"

"Wuff!" said Punch, feeling Nicky's sudden excitement, putting his paw up on the boy's knee.

"You don't mean we *could* make up a mystery for your uncle to solve, do you?" said Ken, disbelievingly. "He'd be wild when he found out! Anyway, he'd never believe in it. He'd smell a rat at once."

"Wuff!" said Punch again, hearing the word "rat".

Penelope was there too . . .

"Don't interrupt, Punch," said Nicky, feeling more and more excited. "Ken, it would be *fun*! We'll work out something between us. Let me see – how could it be done? I'll have to think."

"Look – we can't deceive your uncle like that," said Ken, really alarmed now. "He'd be furious. Anyway, he's so jolly clever he'd see through it at once. We can't pit our brains against *his*!"

"We can try!" said Nicky, red with excitement. "Look – something like this, Ken. We'll get him to come out bird-watching with us – taking our field glasses, of course. And we'll put clues here and there, see, for him to find."

"You're barmy," said Ken, disgusted.

"I'm not. We could let a piece of paper blow in the wind, and when he picks it up, it's a message in code! Ha – very mysterious! And we could get him to train his field glasses on something peculiar, and . . ."

"Peculiar? What do you mean, *peculiar*?" asked Ken, puzzled.

"Oh – someone signalling out of a window or out of that old tower up on the hills!" said Nicky. "I'm sure Uncle Bob would think that peculiar, and he'd want to find out what was going on."

"Yes. But actually there wouldn't *be* anything going on," said Ken. "And he'd soon find that out."

"Oh shut up finding fault with everything I say," said Nicky, drumming his heels angrily against the box, and making Punch bark again. "I thought you'd be glad to help. Mother said we might think of something together – and here you've come up with a perfectly splendid idea, that would be fun for all of us – and now you pooh-pooh it! I only wish *I'd* thought of it!"

Ken began to think he must have been very clever after all. He stopped making difficulties. "Oh well – if you *really* think I've had a brainwave, I'll help. But it's all got to be worked out carefully, mind – this pretend mystery, whatever it is. And what will your uncle say when he finds it's all a hoax?"

"He'll laugh like anything," said Nicky. "He's got a terrific sense of humour, and he never minds a joke against himself. We'll be giving him a bit of excitement, something to puzzle him and take him out of himself, as Mother says. And what's more, *we* shall enjoy it too! Shan't we, Punch, old thing?"

Punch hadn't the faintest idea what the boys were talking about, but he heartily agreed with everything. He ran round the shed, barking loudly, and nosed excitedly into every corner.

"He's looking for a deep, dark secret, a hidden mystery that only Uncle Bob can solve," said Nicky, in a hollow, dramatic voice that made Ken laugh, and Punch look up in surprise.

"All right," said Ken. "You think up the clues. I thought of the idea, so I've done my bit. Is all this to happen in the daytime or night-time? I'm quite game to wander about at night, if you want me to. Only it's no good asking Mum if I can – she'd say 'no'."

"For goodness' sake! You mustn't say *anything* about this to your mother!" said Nicky, in horror. "She'd go and tell *my* mother at once, and that would be the end of it. We're doing this to help my Uncle Bob, remember, and NOBODY except you and me must know about it. And Punch, of course."

"When will you think out the clues we're to spread around?"

"I think I'd better think about them in bed tonight," said Nicky, sliding off the box. "That's when I get my best ideas. What a laugh we'll have! By the way – I'm teaching Punch some tricks. Like to come and help? I'm teaching him to fetch people's slippers for them. He's already got the hang of it."

"*Really*? Isn't he a marvellous dog?" said Ken, twiddling one of Punch's alert ears. "Yes, I'll come. And listen, Nicky – don't say a word of our plan in front of Penny – Penelope, I mean – you know how snoopy she is."

"As if I would!" said Nicky, scornfully. "Come on, Punch. Come and show what a clever dog you are!"

And, for the next half-hour, Nicky's house echoed to sounds of "Fetch it, then, boy! Grandma's shoes! Up the stairs, Punch! That's right. He's gone to get one, Ken! Buck up, Punch! GRANDMA'S SHOES!"

Down the stairs came Punch at top speed, carrying one of Uncle Bob's bedroom slippers in his mouth. He put it down at Nicky's feet with a look of pride, his tail wagging nineteen to the dozen.

"Ass!" said Nicky. "I said 'GRANDMA'S' not Uncle Bob's. Try again." And up the stairs went Punch, tail down now. He appeared in a few seconds with one of Nicky's football boots, tripping over the laces as he came.

"He's not really very clever, is he?" said Ken. Nicky was puzzled. "I don't understand him. He fetched Grandma's shoes after breakfast all right."

A voice came down the stairs – Grandma's. "Nicky! Please STOP Punch scratching at my door. He can't have my shoes – I'm wearing them!"

"There!" said Nicky, relieved. "I *knew* there was a

good reason why he didn't bring them. Good dog, Punch. You shall help us with our secret plan! You're as clever as a bagful of monkeys!"

CHAPTER 6

Nicky Makes Some Plans

For once in a way Nicky went off to bed without voicing his usual strong objections. He really was longing to think up some wonderful mystery for his Uncle Bob! His Granny was surprised when he kissed her so early in the evening.

"My, Nicky – you're going early tonight!" she said. "Are you feeling all right?"

"Yes. I'm fine," said Nicky. "I just want to think out something in bed, that's all. 'Night, Mother, 'night, Dad. Come on, Punch."

Punch leapt up, gave everyone a goodnight lick, and disappeared out of the door with Nicky.

"Well! *They're* early to roost tonight!" said Grandma. "Nicky must be tired."

He wasn't! He was very wide awake indeed, and his mind was already busily thinking out plans, as he undressed. Punch was surprised that Nicky said nothing to him, for usually he was very talkative. He whined, wondering if he was in disgrace for something, but still Nicky took no notice!

Punch wondered what to do. Why didn't Nicky talk to him as he usually did? Was he in disgrace? The little terrier suddenly barked and ran out of the room, his tail wagging. *He* knew how to please Nicky and make him talk to him, he was sure he did! He came back with a shoe of Uncle Bob's. Nicky didn't even notice! Punch ran out again, and came back with Mrs Fraser's bedroom slippers, and set them down beside the shoe. Then off he went again for more!

But Nicky was still lost in thought. He had cleaned his teeth, washed, done his hair – and then by mistake he cleaned his teeth again without even noticing! That really did surprise Punch!

Nicky leapt into bed, and was just about to put out his bedside lamp when he caught sight of the seven or eight slippers and shoes that Punch had been fetching to try to please him. There they were, all set out on the bedside rug, Punch lying forlornly with his head on two of them.

"Oh *poor* old Punch!" said Nicky. "I've not said a word to you for ages! I've been thinking hard, Punch, and all the time you've been rushing about fetching shoes to please me. *Dear* Punch! Did you think I was cross with you, or something? Well, I'm not. I think you're the best dog in the world!"

Punch went quite mad with joy. He tore round and round the room, sending the shoes flying, barking madly – and then with one final enormous leap he landed on top of Nicky, and licked every inch of his face.

"Oooh, Punch – that was my tummy you jumped on!" groaned Nicky. "Lie down, you ass. No, you can't get into bed beside me. You know Mother would find you when she came up, and you'd get a smack. Gosh, look at all those slippers and shoes – honestly, you're a mutt. Now just you take them back!"

But that was a trick that Punch had not yet learnt, and he lay still, licking Nicky's hand every now and again, glad to find that his beloved master was not angry with him after all.

"Now just keep absolutely *quiet*," said Nicky. "I'm going to have one of my THINKS, and I'll push you off the bed if you so much as wriggle your tail."

Punch lay so still that Nicky forgot all about him, and was soon lost in thought. Now then – a smashing mystery was what he wanted – complete with clues, strange goings-on, and all the rest of it – a mystery in which he could make Uncle Bob so interested that he would forget all about being bored and miserable.

Where should the mystery *be*? That was the first thing to think out. At once a picture of an old burnt-out building up on Skylark Hill came into Nicky's mind. Yes – that would be a fine eerie sort of place for a mystery. He thought about it, remembering the blackened, half-fallen walls – the one old tower still standing – the curious spiral stairway of stone that led down into the old cellars, which he and Ken had so often longed to explore.

"My word, yes – *that's* the place for a pretend mystery," thought Nicky, beginning to feel excitement welling up inside him. "Now, what next? – yes, clues. They'd better be in code – an easy code, so that Uncle Bob can decipher it and read the message. And there shall be lights flashing from the tower at night – I'll make Ken go up there with his torch and flash it – and what about noises? If I can get Uncle up to the burnt house, Ken can hide and make awful groans. Gosh, this is going to be super. If only I could tell Ken this very minute!"

He debated whether to put on his clothes again and slip over to Ken's. No – he'd probably be in bed, and if he was asleep nothing in the world would wake him, not even stones rattling against his window!

Nicky became so excited as he thought of the wonderful Mystery that was lying in wait for Uncle Bob, that he couldn't keep still. He turned over and over in bed, and Punch was soon tired of continually being bumped, and leapt down to the rug, landing on the slippers and shoes.

"We'll begin the Mystery tomorrow," thought Nicky, sticking his hot feet out of bed to cool them. "Ow – stop it, Punch – those are my toes you're biting! Sh – here comes Mother. Get under the bed."

Punch disappeared at once. Mrs Fraser opened the bedroom door, and the landing light shone into the room, showing her Punch's surprising collection of shoes. "So *that's* where my slippers went to!" she thought, and picked them up. "Good gracious – this is quite a shoe-shop! I'll have to stop this new trick of Punch's, I can see!"

She laid her hand gently on Nicky's forehead, for she still felt puzzled about his going off to bed so early. But it was quite cool – Nicky was obviously all right! Picking up a few more shoes she crept out of the room.

Punch came out from under the bed, and climbed carefully up beside Nicky. He gave his face the tiniest lick, heaved an enormous sigh of love, and settled down to sleep.

Nicky gave Punch a pat, and then slid off into his Mystery once more. But now he was getting sleepy, and his thoughts became muddled. He was at the old burnt house – he was climbing up to the tower – a light was flashing there – good gracious, *two* lights – but no, they weren't lights after all – they were the brilliant green eyes of Ken's cat – and now the cat grew simply enormous, and Nicky fled down to the cellar, where immediately some frightful, bloodcurdling noises began that made poor Nicky's hair stand on end!

He was so scared that he tried to scream – and immediately found himself sitting up in bed clutching at a growling, most surprised Punch.

"Oh, it was a *dream*, thank goodness!" said Nicky, thankfully. "I suppose those awful noises I heard in my dream were you snoring or something, Punch. Gosh, I was scared! If our Mystery's going to be anything like as thrilling as my dream about it, we're going to have some fun! Get off my feet, Punch. No wonder I found it difficult to climb up to the tower in my dream – you must have been lying on my feet all the time!"

Punch obligingly slid off Nicky's feet, and lay at the bottom of the bed. His ears twitched as an owl hooted somewhere in the trees at the bottom of the garden. They twitched again, and a small growl came from him when he heard a cat miaowing below the window. Nicky turned over and buried his head in the pillow. He felt wide awake again, and longed for tomorrow to come so that he might tell Ken all his plans.

"Ha, Uncle Bob – you don't know what thrills I've got in store for you!" he murmured. "I'll write out that code message first thing tomorrow and show it to Ken – I bet *he* won't be able to decipher it! And we'll go up to that old burnt-out house and snoop round. I wonder what will come of my Plan for a Mystery – I DO hope it will be a success!"

Success, Nicky? Well, you're certainly going to be *surprised*! It's a wonderful plan of yours – but it may not work out in quite the way you think. So watch out, Nicky, watch out, Ken!

CHAPTER 7

A Mysterious Message

As soon as Nicky woke up the next morning he remembered his wonderful plan of the night before. He sat up in bed, excited, and Punch began to pull off the blankets and sheet, trying to make his master get up and dress.

"All right, all right, Punch – I'm in just as much a hurry as you are!" said Nicky. "If Ken's up I could go and tell him my plans before breakfast. No – *don't* drag the pillow on to the floor. Bring me my shoes – SHOES, idiot, not boots."

Nicky was soon dressed, and leapt down the stairs with Punch just in front. They almost bowled over Mrs Hawes, who was sweeping the hall.

"Are you two catching a train or something?" she demanded. "Stop it, Punch – leave my broom alone! Nicky, he's got my duster now – if he goes off with it, I'll . . ."

"Bad dog," said Nicky, sternly. "Drop it, sir! There – see how obedient he is, Mrs Hawes. What's for breakfast? I've got time to go and see Ken, haven't I?"

"It's kippers for breakfast, and you've about ten minutes," said Mrs Hawes. "Bless that dog – he's gone off with my floor cloth now!"

Nicky grinned and shot off at top speed after Punch. He ordered him to take back the floor cloth.

"And then come down to Ken's shed," he said. "But DON'T bring any shoes with you. I'm sorry I taught you that trick now."

He squeezed through the hedge and went across to Ken's shed. He could hear him chanting his favourite tune – good – he was there then. He whistled piercingly and Ken at once appeared at the shed door, holding one of his smallest guinea pigs.

"Hello! *You're* early!" he said. "Anything up? Get down, Punch, you are *not* going to have guinea pigs for breakfast."

"Ken! I've thought out a smashing mystery!" said Nicky. "Where's Penny? Not in hearing distance, I hope?"

"No. She's with Winnie – our cousin, you know. She's come to stay again."

"Not that Winnie who wants to tag on to *us* all the time?" said Nicky, in dismay.

"The very same," said Ken, gloomily. "She arrived last night, fat as ever. We'll have to look out, or we'll have the girls spying on us all the time – especially Winnie. But I say – why are you up so early?"

"Because I wanted to tell you about the Mystery I've thought out – the one we're going to pretend is a real one, so that Uncle Bob can have something exciting to think about," said Nicky. "Honestly, Ken, it's really *good* – I tell you, we're going to have some fun. Shut the door, and listen. Punch, sit by the door and bark like mad if you hear footsteps or whispering."

Punch at once sat down by the door, and cocked his ears. "Now we're safe," said Nicky. "Listen, Ken."

And he told his surprised friend all that he had thought of during the night. Ken listened, gaping, taking in all the details, but when Nicky came to the bit where he, Ken, was to go to the old burnt-out house at night and flash a torch, he shook his head firmly.

"No. If anyone's to do that, *you* can. I'd be scared to do that on my own."

"Oh don't make things difficult," said Nicky. "Anyway, we can decide all the details later on. I just HAD to let you know what I'd planned. The first thing to do is to write out a secret message – in code, of course. Then we'll take Uncle Bob for a walk up the hills – and let him find the paper with the message on – and – oh BLOW, there's the breakfast gong. You be thinking out a good secret message. I'll be back after breakfast."

He tore off with Punch barking at his heels, and just managed to be sitting down at the breakfast table before his father arrived.

"You seem out of breath," said his mother, surprised. "Have you been for a walk?"

"No. Just to see Ken about something important," said Nicky. "Do you want me to do anything this morning, Mother? I thought I'd ask Uncle Bob if he'd like to go for a walk up on Skylark Hill with me and Ken. We want to go bird-spotting, and Uncle Bob said he'd lend me his field glasses."

"I'm sure he'd *love* to go with you," said his mother pleased. "It's such a beautiful morning, it will do him good – and he's always been so fond of birds."

Uncle Bob arrived down a few minutes later, looking rather gloomy.

"Hello, everyone!" he said. "No, no kipper for me, thanks. I don't feel too good. Couldn't get a wink of sleep because of the owls hooting all night."

"I never heard them," said his sister. "Poor old Bob – you do look washed out."

"Uncle – come for a walk up Skylark Hill this morning!" said Nicky, eagerly. "Ken's going too – bird-spotting. We might see the sparrow hawk. You said you'd lend me your field glasses, remember?"

"Right. I'll come with you," said Uncle Bob. "Do me good to stretch my legs. What time do you want to start?"

"Er – would ten o'clock do?" asked Nicky, remembering that he must leave himself enough time to work out a message in code, so that he could plant it somewhere for his uncle to find.

"That'll suit me fine," said Uncle Bob. "I'll unpack my field glasses after breakfast – they're still in one of my cases. Is Punch coming with us? I hope he won't race about and scare all the birds for miles."

"Of course he's coming," said Nicky, feeling a sudden little paw on his knee. He bent down to Punch, who was as usual under the table. "You heard what Uncle Bob said, didn't you, Punch? No racing about and barking – but plenty of sit, sit, sit, when you're told. Got that?"

"Wuff," said Punch, quite understanding, and lay down again.

Nicky hurriedly finished his breakfast, trying to think out what message he should write on a piece of paper.

"Please excuse me, Mother," he said. "I've a few things to do before we go."

"Well, remember that one of them is to make your bed, please," said his mother, as Nicky raced off with Punch just behind him.

He went to his bedroom and hurriedly pulled together his sheets and blankets. Then he tore a piece of paper from an old writing pad, sat down and chewed the end of his pencil. What should the message be? Perhaps he had better go and see if Ken had thought of one.

Soon he was down in Ken's shed. "Ken – I *can't* think

of a message!" he said. "And Uncle Bob will be ready to go with us at ten. What shall . . .?"

"Don't worry. *I've* thought of one," said Ken, proudly, and showed Nicky a piece of dirty, torn paper. On it he had written a most mysterious-looking message, which looked like this:-

UFMM KJN XFSF SFBEZ. NFFU JO DFM-MBST. TUVGG IJEEFO PO TLZMBSL IJMM. MPPL PVU GPS TJHOBM GSPN UPXFS. IBSSZ.

"What on earth does *that* mean?" said Nicky.

"It means '*Tell Jim we're ready. Meet in cellars. Stuff hidden on Skylark Hill. Look out for signal from tower. Harry.*'" said Ken, proudly. "It's an awfully simple code –all I've done is to use the next letter to the real one each time – B for A, C for B, D for C and so on. This first

word UFMM, for instance. All you've got to do is to think of the letter before . . ."

"Oh, *I* see – for the letter U the one before would be T – and for F it would be E, and for MM it would be LL," said Nicky. "The word 'tell' – and so on. Isn't it too simple?"

"No. Don't you think it's an *exciting* message?" said Ken. "I mean – when your uncle picks up this old dirty-looking bit of paper with such a strange code message on it, he's bound to prick up his ears! I rubbed it on the floor of the shed to make it look dirty."

Nicky began to feel excited. "Yes! It's fine!" he said "I don't know how you thought of such an exciting message. Jolly good, Ken. Look now – when Uncle Bob is training his field glasses on some bird or other, you drop the bit of paper nearby, and maybe he'll see it and pick it up. If he doesn't I'll pick it up, and pretend to be very puzzled, because of the code. I bet Uncle will decipher it at once."

"And then the fun will begin!" said Ken, his eyes shining. "We'll go exploring the cellars – we'll hunt on the hill for the stuff that's supposed to be hidden there. We'll . . ."

"We'd jolly well better buck up!" said Nicky. "It's almost ten, and I'm not ready yet. Meet me at your front gate as soon as you can. This is going to be fun! I *bet* Uncle Bob will prick up his ears and forget to be mopey, once he gets going on our mystery!"

CHAPTER 8

Up On Skylark Hill

Nicky and Punch raced off to see if Uncle Bob was ready to go for his walk up Skylark Hill. Yes – there he was, waiting impatiently in the front garden, his field glasses slung over his shoulder.

"Oh, there you are," he said. "Where's Ken?"

"Just coming – he'll be at his front gate," said Nicky. "Shall I go in and get my bird book, Uncle?"

"No. I can tell you anything you want to know," said his uncle. "For goodness' sake let's start while it's fine! Come along."

They picked up Ken at his front gate and set out happily, Ken with his glasses slung round his shoulder just like Uncle Bob. They came to Skylark Hill, and at first took an ordinary path, Punch running ahead as usual, sniffing about for rabbits.

The birds were singing madly. "There's the chaffinch, with his 'chip-chip-cherry-erry-erry-chippy-oo-EEE-ar' song," said Uncle Bob, standing to listen. "And you can hear that greenfinch – and the hedge-sparrow – and what's that now, singing so VERY loudly?"

"The wren – look, it's over there!" said Ken, pointing. "Seems funny that such a *little* bird should have such a very loud voice!"

It was lovely up on the hill. It was quite a wild part where they were now wandering, no paths at all, except for those made by the rabbits. Uncle Bob suddenly stopped.

"Listen – there's a nightingale singing in that bush over there – see, at the top of that hawthorn bush."

"I thought nightingales only sang at night," said Nicky, astonished.

"Oh no – you can hear them in the daytime too," said Uncle Bob, "though no one notices them much then, with so many other birds singing. We really ought to come up here at night-time to hear them at their best."

Nicky at once gave Ken a violent nudge. What a wonderful excuse for coming out at night! Perhaps he could make Ken go up unseen to the old tower and flash his torch, while he and Uncle Bob were listening to nightingales! Uncle Bob would never guess that the flashing light was a put-up job – he would be sure to think there was something funny going on in that old burnt out place! He'd smell a mystery at once!

They went on a little way, and soon Nicky thought it was about time that Ken dropped his dirty bit of paper with the code message on it. He nudged him again, and Ken put his hand in his pocket, and nodded.

He went on some way in front, and suddenly spotted a chaffinch's nest in a bush. Ah – now he could perhaps make Nicky's uncle find the paper for himself! That would be very much better than either he or Nicky pretending to find it. He cautiously parted the twigs, and dropped the note into the bushy part below the nest. Then he called to Nicky.

"I say – here's a nest, just newly-built. No eggs yet, though. Ask your uncle what kind of nest it is – looks like a chaffinch's to me."

"Don't disturb the bird if it's on the nest," called Uncle Bob, as he and Nicky came up the steep little rabbit path. He peered into the bush. "Yes – that's a chaffinch's nest – see how neat it is. The bird has even woven tiny bits of torn paper into it. I wonder it didn't take *this* old bit of paper too, below the nest."

And, much to the boys' delight, he picked up the note that Ken had just dropped into the bush! He saw that something was written on it and glanced idly at it, as he was about to screw it up.

"Hello – what's this? It's a note written in code!" he said, in surprise.

"I *say*!" said both boys at once, pretending to be astonished. "Code! What's it say?"

"Don't know, unless I can break the code," said Uncle Bob. "It looks a fairly simple one. See what *you* can make of it. I don't feel too bright this morning."

The boys didn't know whether to decipher it or not. Wouldn't Uncle Bob think they were a bit too clever if they did? They sat down and put their heads together, pretending to puzzle over the queer message.

"Look at that first word," said Uncle Bob. "'UFMM'! A double-letter at the end. Now what letters can be doubled at the end of words? S can, for instance. There are plenty of four letter words ending in double S – fuss, boss, toss, hiss and so on – or in double F – such as huff, muff, etc."

"Or double L," said Nicky. "Such as ball, call, toll, er . . ."

"Or TELL!" said Ken, as if he had just that very minute thought of it. "It might be 'tell', mightn't it?"

"I should think it's more likely to be 'TELL' than anything else," said Uncle Bob, taking back the paper. "Now, let's see what the next word would be, if the first is TELL – it will mean that the letters of each code word must be replaced by the *preceding* letters of the alphabet. All right – the next code-word is KJN. We'll replace those three letters by the alphabet letters immediately before – that is, K would be J, J would be I, and N would be M – making the word J-I-M- – Jim!"

"Aha!" said Ken, "that would make the first two words 'TELL JIM'! You've broken the code already! We shall be able to decipher the whole message now!"

He looked so excited that Nicky stared at him in surprise. Goodness – how clever Ken was at acting! No one would ever think that it was he himself who had actually made up the message and put it into code.

Uncle Bob looked rather startled. He stared at the message again, and stood frowning over it.

"Queer!" he said at last. "That's the code all right – a very simple one, too – listen – I'll decode the whole message."

The boys felt a great desire to giggle. This was marvellous! Dear old Uncle Bob was well and truly taken in! They listened as he slowly read the decoded message.

"Tell – Jim – we're – ready. Meet – in – cellars. Stuff – hidden – on – Skylark – Hill. Look – out – for – signal – from – tower. Harry."

He frowned down at the paper again. "Why did the writer of this message, whoever he is, use such an easily deciphered code?" he wondered. "He might just as well have written it in plain English! I wonder if it *could* be a joke – but if so, how did it come to be in that bush?"

"Perhaps the wind blew it there," suggested Nicky. "Oh Uncle Bob – it's awfully exciting, isn't it?"

Uncle Bob put the paper into his pocket. "Something funny about it," he said. "Funny and phoney! I'll have to think about it."

"Should we try and find whatever stuff it is that's supposed to be hidden on the hill?" said Ken, feeling nervous in case Uncle Bob should decide it *was* a hoax. "We might find something interesting. Stolen goods – or – or hidden money, perhaps."

"And what about looking in the cellars of that old burnt-out house?" suggested Nicky. "It says something about cellars in that note, doesn't it, Uncle Bob? It might mean the old cellars up in that place on the top of the hill. And it's got a tower, too – a fine tower to signal from!"

"Yes – anyone on the hillside waiting for a signal could easily see flashes from that tower!" said Ken, backing up Nicky valiantly. "I *say*! We can see that tower from our back gardens, you know – we ought to watch out at night, in case someone *does* signal!"

"Well – I must say it all sounds rather queer – and, as I say, I can't help feeling there's something wrong – something phoney about that note," said Uncle Bob, frowning. "It's too easy a code. I'll think about it. In the meantime, what about a little more bird-spotting."

"Let's go up to the old burnt house," suggested Nicky. "It's quite interesting, Uncle. The tower is still all right – and the cellars too, though an awful lot of walls have fallen."

"Well – we'll have a quick look round," said his uncle. "But I'm pretty certain that note doesn't mean a thing – probably some silly schoolboy joke. Still, I can see you're longing to do a little exploring, so come along!"

The two boys fell behind Uncle Bob, as he went up the hill. "Do you think he suspects us!" said Nicky, in a low voice. "You heard what he said about 'schoolboy joke'."

"Yes – but I don't believe he thinks *we* wrote that message," answered Ken. "Come along – we're going up to the old cellars – you'll love sniffing round those! You might even find a *rat*!"

Rat? Ah, that made Punch leave his rabbit hole at once, and tear after Nicky. He hadn't any interest in birds – and there didn't seem to be any rabbits about – but maybe a nice big rat would turn up in those old cellars. Wuff!

CHAPTER 9

"Loomy and Gloomy, Glowering and Towering!"

Nicky led the way up to the top of Skylark Hill, following the overgrown path that had once been used by the people who had lived in the great old building at the summit. They came to a gateway, where broken gates hung all askew on their hinges and the old drive that had led to the house was now a mass of strong-growing weeds.

"What a miserable-looking place!" said Uncle Bob. "It gives me the creeps."

"Wait till you get a good view of the burnt-out building," said Nicky. "That'll give you nightmares!"

They went up the thickly-weeded drive and past a great clump of pines. Behind these, sheltered from the prevailing wind, stood the great, blackened hulk that had once been a grand mansion, overlooking the countryside with majestic splendour.

Uncle Bob stopped. From the bottom of the hill the old building had merely looked a poor old ruin, its one remaining tower outlined against the sky – but here, at close quarters, it was rather frightening.

"It sort of *looms* at you!" said Ken.

"Yes – I know exactly what you mean," said Uncle Bob. "It frowns – and glowers – and, as you so rightly say – looms."

"It's loomy and gloomy and glowering and towering, and sulky and hulky," said Nicky, most unexpectedly.

Uncle Bob and Ken stared at him in amazed surprise. "Why, that's poetry!" said Ken. "Surely you didn't say that out of your own head?"

"Well, I did," said Nicky, almost as surprised as the others.

"Whether it came out of your own head or not, it just about describes this brooding, blackened old place," said Uncle Bob. "You might give us warning when you're going to break out into verse again, Nicky. I feel almost as surprised as if Punch had suddenly burst into song!"

"Wuff!" said Punch, pleased at hearing himself talked about. He ran on in front of them, his tail wagging. He had been here before, and thought it was a most exciting place.

They all went up the curving drive, and came to the great building itself. It was a sorry sight. The fire that had devoured it had swept it from top to bottom, and had left only one tower untouched, though blackened with smoke.

"Birds build in the tower now," said Ken, as they went towards the fallen archway that had once framed the great front entrance. "And once I saw a badger coming out of a hole in the wall."

"Who lived here?" asked Uncle Bob. "It must have been a wonderful place."

"Somebody foreign," said Nicky, trying to remember. "A prince from the East somewhere."

"It had a magnificent view!" said Uncle Bob. "I wonder what caused the fire."

"Nobody knows," said Ken. "All the people down in the valley awoke one night to see flames reaching up into the sky – and not a single fire engine could get up this hill to do anything to help. It just burnt to a shell. Everyone in it escaped, and went back to their own country – they were nearly all foreigners. The prince never came back."

"So there it is – just a hulk of a place!" said Nicky. "Most people are scared of coming up here to it. Like to see the cellars?"

"Yes – we'd better, as the writer of that peculiar message – what was the name he signed now – Harry – mentioned something about cellars, didn't he?" said Uncle Bob. He walked into what must once have been a great hall. The floor was still paved with stone, though it was now cracked and blackened, and weeds grew up in the crevices. Nicky pointed to a burnt mass of wood hanging from one of the walls.

"That was the staircase – or one of them," he said. "But the tower had a stone stairway, so it wasn't burnt. A good many of the stone stairs have got broken, though – perhaps the heat cracked them, or something. Some of them are missing, so you have to be careful in climbing up."

He led his Uncle to a far corner of the old hall, and in at a small stone-arched doorway. "Here's the tower!" he said. "And that's the stone stair up to it, going round and round the walls – not very safe, is it?"

"Have you ever been up?" asked Uncle Bob, going up the first few steps.

"Oh, yes!" said Nicky. "There used to be an iron rail fixed into the wall – there's still some of it left – so you can hang on to that when you come to the broken-away bits."

Uncle Bob began to ascend the narrow stone stair. He went very gingerly indeed, for much of the stone was breaking away, and he didn't want to plunge downwards. The boys followed.

When they came at last to the top, and were able to look through one of the great square stone windows through which the wind blew cold and strong, Uncle Bob gave a low whistle.

"My word! WHAT a view! All round the hill, and down into the valleys for miles and miles."

"What a place to signal from, too!" said Ken, giving Nicky a nudge. "Flashes from this tower could be seen for a long way, couldn't they?"

"Oh – you're thinking of that code message," said Uncle Bob. "What was it now – 'look out for signal from tower' or something. Yes – certainly this would be a good signalling place. But I don't imagine that anyone would want to come all the way up to this windy tower to do a spot of signalling that hundreds of people could see – if they happened to be looking!"

"I say – look – there's a dead match on the floor here," said Nicky, suddenly, and picked one up. "Would that belong to some signaller, do you think?"

Uncle Bob laughed. "No! To some innocent sightseer like ourselves, ass! Anyone would think you really did believe that message! I tell you, I'm pretty sure it's phoney – just a silly schoolboy joke."

"Where's Punch?" said Ken, hurriedly changing the subject. "Didn't he come up with us?"

"No – he doesn't much like the noise of the wind up here," said Nicky. "Don't you remember how scared he was before, when we brought him up, and the wind whistled all round him! He shot down again so fast that he rolled down the last dozen steps, and then sped off down the hill at sixty miles an hour! Let's go down and find him. He'll be lonely."

So they left the magnificent view and went carefully

down the stone stairway, calling to Punch as they came near the bottom. But no answering bark came, no patter of eager feet.

"PUNCH!" yelled Nicky. "Where are you? Surely you haven't gone home without us?"

Not a sound was to be heard, except for the hoarse croaks of crows flying round the tower. Punch was nowhere to be seen!

"Where on earth has the idiot gone?" said Nicky, puzzled. "Can he have gone down the spiral stairway to the cellars? Not without us, surely?"

"Where *is* this spiral stairway?" asked Uncle Bob, looking all round.

"In the kitchen part of the building," said Ken, and led the way through a great doorway, one side of which had fallen in, through a passage, and into what must have been the kitchen.

The boys called loudly as they went. "Punch! PUNCH! Where are you?"

"Here's the cellar door," said Ken. "At least here is where it *used* to be before it was burnt off its hinges!"

A narrow stone doorway led into an equally narrow passage. Nicky produced a torch, and shone it before him. "Better go carefully, Uncle," he said. "These steps are pretty steep – and slimy, too, because they're rather damp. See how they go round and round in a spiral?"

It was indeed a curious spiral stairway, and dangerous too. Uncle Bob wished there was a handrail to hold on to! At last, after treading warily down what seemed to be at least fifty curving stone steps, they reached the bottom.

"What a horrible place!" said Uncle Bob, shivering. It was pitch-black, cold, and rather smelly. "Surely Punch didn't come down here?"

But he *was* down there! From what seemed to be a great distance, his bark came echoing up to them, sounding weird and hollow – and scared!

"PUNCH! Come here! PUNCH!" shouted Nicky.

But Punch didn't come. Only his bark came to their ears, a frightened, pleading bark. Whatever was the matter?

"Come on – I'm going to find him!" said Nicky, and flashed his torch around, to see which was the best way to go. "Something's happened to old Punch. He sounds quite lost. I simply MUST go to him!"

CHAPTER 10

A Bit Of Excitement

"Wait a minute!" said Uncle Bob. "Do you know your way about these cellars? It seems a pretty vast place down here to me, from what I can see by the light of your torch. Passages leading off everywhere! We might easily get lost."

"Once we find Punch he'll lead us back to the spiral stairway all right," said Nicky. "Listen – he's barking again."

They went along a dark, low-roofed passage and came into yet another cellar, heaped with old rubbish.

The fire had not reached down into the cellars, so the old boxes and junk had not been burnt. And then, just at that moment, Nicky's torch went out! They were in complete darkness.

"Battery's gone," said Nicky, in disgust. "If only Punch would come to us, and show us the way back! PUNCH! COME HERE!"

But no Punch came – and what was almost worse, he stopped barking! Not a sound came up the dark passages, and Nicky felt scared. What could have happened to make Punch stop barking?

Uncle Bob took matters in hand at once. He took Nicky firmly by the arm, and pushed him back towards the way they had come. "No more nonsense," he said. "If we go down there any farther in complete darkness, we shall lose our way, and not know how to get back."

"But I CAN'T leave Punch by himself," protested Nicky, trying to wriggle away from his uncle's firm hand.

"If he went down there, he can come up again," said Uncle Bob. "Anyway, we are ALL going back at once! I'm a bit afraid we shall miss our way even the short distance we came, it's so dark. Ken – are you there? Keep close to us."

"I'm just behind, sir," said Ken, who felt only too thankful to be going back.

At last they were up in the kitchen again, having found the spiral stairway very difficult indeed to climb in total darkness. "Whew!" said Uncle Bob, sitting down hard on the wide windowsill that ran round the great kitchen. "Whew! I don't particularly want to go down *there* again!"

Nicky was almost in tears over Punch. He spoke sullenly to his uncle.

"I think we're cowards, leaving Punch down there. What are we going to do about it?

"We'll wait here for a bit and see if he comes back by himself," said Uncle Bob. "If he doesn't we'll go home and get lanterns or more powerful torches. But I don't think we need worry. Punch will appear soon."

Uncle Bob lighted a cigarette and wandered about a little. The boys sat sulkily on the old stone sill, ears open for Punch, eyes on the entrance to the cellars.

Suddenly Nicky leapt to his feet. "I can hear Punch barking! Listen!"

Sure enough a barking was to be heard in the distance. Nicky ran to the cellar entrance – but the barking wasn't coming from there! It came nearer and nearer. Ken looked out of the open window arch, and gave a shout.

"He's coming up the drive. Look, there he is, absolutely filthy! Punch! PUNCH! Here we are!"

Punch gave a delighted volley of barks, raced into the old building, and hurled himself on Nicky, smothering him with dirt and licks. Nicky hugged him.

"Where have you been, you dirty little dog? We thought you were down in the cellars."

"He *was*," said Uncle Bob. "And as he certainly didn't return up the spiral stairway, as *we* did, how on earth did he get out?"

"Down a rabbit hole?" suggested Ken. "I never heard of any *secret* way out of the cellars. Must have been a rabbit hole! You rascal, Punch! We almost got lost for good down those cellars because of you!"

Punch was hungry. He barked and tugged at Nicky's sleeve, trying to pull him along. Nicky patted him.

"All right, all right, we're all coming. I'm as hungry as you are! What about you, Uncle Bob?"

"Well, yes – I must say that for the first time since I came to stay with you, I feel really hungry!" said Uncle Bob. "We've certainly had an interesting morning – and what with that rather strange coded message – and all the birds we saw – and exploring this gloomy old building – I feel that life has become quite exciting again"

The boys were pleased. They looked closely at Uncle Bob, and decided that he already looked more like the cheerful, amusing man he had always seemed to be.

"Our trick worked, didn't it?" said Ken, in a low voice to Nicky, as they went back down Skylark Hill. "But I wish your uncle believed more in that message of ours – don't want our plan to come to a sudden end. I'ts been fun so far."

"The thing that puzzles *me* is how Punch got out of those cellars," said Nicky. "I suppose he *did* find a rabbit warren and went through it and found a hole into the open air. But usually he's too big for any rabbit hole."

"Well, what else could he have done?" said Ken. "I didn't much like going so far down those cellars. I couldn't help being glad there wasn't *really* any mysterious "Harry" waiting down there to meet his men."

"Harry? Harry who?" said Nicky, and then remembered the made-up message, and laughed. "Oh, of course – the Harry who was supposed to sign that message! Well, Punch would have given him a bit of a fright, wouldn't he?"

Penny and her friend Winnie were standing at Ken's front gate as he and Nicky and Uncle Bob came up. "Hello, hello!" said Uncle Bob. "And what have you two girls been up to this morning? You ought to have come with *us*. My word, we've had an exciting time, what with finding a strange message in code, hidden in a bush – and exploring that great burnt building – and seeing Punch disappear down into the cellars, and . . ."

"Oh PLEASE, Uncle Bob – don't give away our secrets," said Nicky, in a low voice, horrified to think that Penny and Winnie should be told all this. They were both agog at once, of course, and to the boys' despair and disgust Uncle Bob actually took out the coded message and showed it to the two excited girls.

"Oooh!" said Winnie, her eyes big with amazement. "Is it a *real* message? Not just one made up by the boys? Once Ken did a message rather like this, and . . ."

"Shut up!" hissed Ken, and gave poor Winnie such a hard pinch that she screamed and ran straight in through the gate, holding her arm. Uncle Bob stared after her in amazement.

"What's the matter with your friend all of a sudden?" he asked, but Penny seeing Ken's grim look, decided not to say anything about the pinch. Fortunately the sound of a gong being violently struck by Mrs Hawes in Nicky's hall, brought such delicious thoughts of dinner that Nicky and his uncle at once walked smartly to the front gate, and up the path, followed by an even more hungry Punch.

"It was *mean* of you to show the girls that secret message," Nicky couldn't help saying to his uncle.

"What on earth's *secret* about it?" said his uncle, astonished. "Anyone might have found it! Anyway it's probably a hoax, so cheer up. There *won't* be any meeting in the cellars – there *won't* be any flashing of signals in the tower. There are *no* goods hidden on the hill."

Nicky frowned and set his teeth. "Oh, won't there!" he thought. "You just wait and see, Uncle Bob! You'll be surprised! And very soon too! I'll just pay you out for showing our secret message to those girls! You just wait!"

It was a pity Uncle Bob couldn't read Nicky's angry thoughts. He didn't even know that the boy felt so angry, or he would have been gentler to him. Poor Nicky! He had only thought of the mystery just because he wanted to *help* his uncle, and now everything had gone wrong – and those GIRLS knew about the message!

He sat rather silent at dinner time, pondering what to do next. Could he possibly persuade Ken to go and signal from the tower at night – and then he, Nicky, could wake his uncle and tell him to look at the flashes. *That* would make him sit up and take notice! "It's no good *me* going to the tower," thought Nicky. "Because someone has got to tell Uncle about the signalling – and he'd think it funny if Ken came to him in the middle of the night – and I wasn't anywhere to be found. Oh blow! I do hope this plan isn't going wrong. Ken will simply HAVE to go and do the signalling. He can take old Punch with him, if he's afraid. Yes – that's a *good* idea."

"You're very quiet this meal time, Nicky," said his mother. "What are you thinking about so deeply?"

"He's pondering over a very strange message, I expect!" said Uncle Bob, laughing. "Am I right, Nicky?"

"NO!" said Nicky, so fiercely that everyone jumped, and Punch began to bark. "You wait and see, Uncle – I bet that message was right. You just wait and see!"

CHAPTER 11

Quite A Few Things Happen!

After dinner was over Nicky disappeared. "Where's he gone?" said his mother. "He seems rather down in the dumps. What happened this morning,Bob?"

"Oh nothing much," said Uncle Bob. "We did some bird-spotting and found a strange message in a bush – and explored that old burnt-out place – and almost lost Punch in the cellars. Nicky seemed a bit cross because when we met Penelope, Ken's sister, and her friend, I told them what we'd been doing."

"How silly of Nicky to be cross about that!" said Mrs Fraser. "But he and Ken can't bear the girls knowing about their doings. Penny is a bit of a snooper, from what I hear."

Nicky was certainly feeling cross. After all their trouble in making up a super mystery, Uncle Bob had laughed at it, and almost given it away! He made up his mind to go across to Ken's and find out whether the girls had wormed anything out of him. Ken wasn't very clever at keeping things from Penny!

Ken wasn't in the shed – but *somebody* was! Nicky shushed Punch, afraid he would bark, and went to peep in at the window. Penny and her friend Winnie were there, poring over a piece of paper, and giggling.

What could be so amusing about it? Nicky longed to know. Then a horrid thought struck him. Had the two girls found the first rough copy of that coded message? Had they looked in the drawer of the old table in the shed, where Ken kept his things? He ran up to the house to find Ken, and ask him where he had left the copy. If the girls knew all about their mystery, he and Ken might as well give up their little joke on Uncle Bob.

Ken was in his room, reading. He was very pleased to see Nicky and Punch. "Hello! Anything up? You look upset," he said.

Nicky told him what he had just seen. "Those *tiresome* girls!" said Ken, in a rage. "I thought they were going for a walk, so I didn't bother to hide that first rough copy of the coded message. I felt sure they'd do a bit of snooping sometime – but they *said* they were going for a walk, so I didn't rush down to the shed to hide my things!"

"Well, we'd better give up the whole idea," said Nicky, very angry. "And I jolly well hope you'll knock their silly heads together when they come in."

"What's Punch doing under my bed?" said Ken. "He's chewing my new slippers! Come on out, Punch, and behave yourself. Go on down and chase the girls out of the shed."

Almost as if he understood what Ken had said Punch ran to the door, pushed it open with his nose and disappeared. All right – if he couldn't play with Ken's slippers, he'd go and find someone else's. *He* wasn't going down to the shed! He slipped into the room that the two girls shared and was faced with a most wonderful array of shoes of all kinds! He sniffed at a pair of fur boots, and settled down to chew them in peace and quiet.

The boys began to play a game of cards, but after a few minutes the thought of the two girls messing about in his shed was too much for Ken. "Let's go and give them a fright and turn them out," he said. "Come on." So down the stairs they went, and out into the garden. When they came to the shed it was empty!

"Blow them! Where have they gone?" said Ken. Here it is in my drawer – they'll pretend they never found it or read it!"

Punch arrived at that moment, carrying the fur boot he had been chewing. "Where did you get that, Punch?" said Nicky, sternly. Punch ran out into the garden with it, and Nicky was just going after him when the two girls came running up to the shed, pretending to be very excited.

"Ken! Nicky! What do you think we've found! A note! A secret message – just like the one you found up on the hills. See what it says – let's decode it, quickly."

"We found it under a bush," said Winnie. "Who *could* have put it there!"

"Idiots!" said Ken, angrily. "You can't spoof *us*!"

"It says we're to watch out for a man with a limp," said Penny. "And it's . . ."

"You made it all up yourselves and hid it, so don't tell such whopping stories," said Ken.

"Was *your* message true then?" asked Winnie, giggling. "Go on – do tell us. We're certain you made *yours* up!"

Penny gave a sudden shriek, and pointed at Punch. "Winnie! He's got one of your best fur boots! He's chewing it! Drop it, Punch, drop it!"

She made a dart at Punch, who picked up the fur boot and danced away with it, out of the shed. This was a lovely game! The two girls chased him up the garden and round the pond. Punch suddenly stopped and very neatly dropped the boot into the water, where it bobbed for a few seconds and then sank.

Winnie angrily picked up a stick and ran after Punch, who at once disappeared through the hedge. "If you bring that dog of yours here again I'll–I'll put him in the dustbin!" she shouted. "He's *ruined* my new boot!"

The boys decided to leave the two angry girls to themselves. They went through the hedge, grinning at one another. "Clever old Punch! The way he dropped Winnie's boot into the water – splash! Just as if he were saying, 'Sucks to you! There goes your boot!'" said Ken. "I vote we give him a jolly good bone or something."

"There are some sausages in the larder," said Nicky. "I'll get him one if Mrs Hawes is out of the way."

And a little later, a most surprised Punch was eating a really delicious sausage, and being patted and petted. Well! If dropping people's shoes into the pond produced sausages to eat, Punch was quite willing to drop any amount into all the ponds in the district!

Winnie and Penny were quite determined not to make up their quarrel with the boys. "We'll just ignore them," said Penny. "Letting Punch drop your boot into the pond like that! They'll be telling him to drop in our hats next and goodness knows what. He's a most annoying dog!"

So, much to Ken's relief, the girls ignored him and said nothing to him at all. They played a game of cards by themselves after tea, watched television until supper, and then went up to their room to read.

But that night something happened to make the girls change their minds about not speaking to Ken. They were both in bed, and had been asleep for some time, when a screech owl suddenly screamed outside. They both woke up with a jump.

"Blow that owl! It *will* sit in that tree at night below our window and screech its head off!" said Penny, crossly. She jumped out of bed to frighten it away, and it flew off on silent white wings. Penny glanced idly out into the night. Her room was at the back of the house, and looked across the fields to Skylark Hill. Penny was just about to turn back to bed when something caught her eye. What was that flashing on the top of Skylark Hill? It must be a light in the old tower!

"It's those boys!" she thought. "Ken and Nicky must be up there, playing a silly trick. That was one of the things in the silly secret message we found in Ken's drawer – signals from the old tower! Winnie – are you awake? There's a light flashing from the tower – those two boys must actually have gone up there to do what that silly message said!"

"But what on earth *for*?" said Winnie, astonished. "Anyway, it's surely too late for the boys to be out, Penelope! It's half-past eleven!"

"I'll see if Ken's in bed," said Penny and went to the room across the passage, where Ken slept. She pushed open the door and switched on the light. To her amazement Ken was in bed and asleep! Could it be *Nicky* up in the tower, then, all alone? She shook Ken awake.

"What is it? What's up? Penny, what's the matter?" mumbled Ken, sitting up, rubbing his eyes.

"Ken – there's a light signalling from the old tower on Skylark Hill," said Penny, fearfully. "Just like you said it would in your secret message. Ken, can Nicky be up there, all alone? If not – who is it?"

Ken shot out of bed and went into Penny's room. He looked through the window – and had a real shock when he saw the flashes coming from the old tower up on the hill. He stared as if he couldn't believe his eyes!

"It *can't* be Nicky!" he said, quite dazed. "He would have told me if he'd planned to do anything like that. Penny, there's something strange about this. There is really."

"That's what *I* think," said Penny. "You'll have to tell Uncle Bob in the morning. But I bet he won't believe you. *He* didn't believe that silly message of yours. It *was* a made-up one, wasn't it – all pretence?"

"Oh shut up!" said poor Ken. "I'm going to dress and go over to Nicky's. I'll throw some stones at his window and see if I can wake him. If he doesn't come I'll climb up the tree just outside and see if he's in bed. If he's not – well – he must be up in that tower. Whew! Better him than me! I'd be scared stiff. Get back to bed, Penny. I'll just drag on a few clothes, and I'll be off to Nicky's."

In a few minutes' time, Ken was letting himself quietly out of the back door, and running down the garden to creep through the hedge. Would he find Nicky in bed – or not? and if he *were* in bed, what in the world was happening up on Skylark Hill?

CHAPTER 12

An Adventurous Night

Ken was soon under Nicky's bedroom window, which was at the front of the house. He scraped about in the gravel path there, and gathered a few small stones. He threw them up one by one, missing the window with all but two, which hit the glass with a sharp click. Nicky was fast asleep, and didn't stir. As a rule not even a thunderstorm would wake him!

But someone else stirred – someone who pricked up his ears at the very first sound! Punch was on Nicky's bed as usual, and he growled when he heard the soft sound of footsteps outside. He growled even more when a stone struck the window! Then he gave a sharp bark, and tugged at the blanket which was tucked in round Nicky's neck.

Nicky awoke. "Shut up, Punch! What do you think your're doing?" he said, sleepily. Punch tugged at his sleeve as he sat up, rubbing his eyes.

Click! That was another small stone against the window. Punch growled again and ran across the room, standing up with his paws on the sill.

"Is there somebody about?" said Nicky, waking up properly now. He leapt out of bed and joined Punch at the window. "Anybody there?" he called.

"Sh!" said Ken's voice from below. "It's me, Ken. I'm coming up the tree, Nicky. Give me a hand at the top, will you? I've some startling news!"

He climbed the tree carefully. It wasn't easy in the dark. Nicky took his torch and shone it down the tree to give him a little light. Ken was most relieved when he was at last on the sill.

"What's up?" asked Nicky.

"There's someone up at the old tower – flashing lights," said Ken. "Penny's bedroom faces that way, and she saw them and came to wake me. At first she thought it might be us up there on the hill – carrying out what we'd said in that code message! Who on earth can it be? I did think for a moment it might be you – but you wouldn't go without telling me, of course!"

"Ken! This is *extraordinary*!" said Nicky. "I mean – we go and make up a mystery – and put in signals from the tower – and it comes true! Look – are you *sure* that you saw flashes? I mean – you might have been half-asleep or something."

"Well, I wasn't," said Ken. "Nor were the girls. Look – let's go into a room where we get a view of Skylark Hill and the tower – we can't see them from your window."

"Wuff!" said Punch, annoyed because Ken and Nicky were taking absolutely no notice of him. He was delighted to see Ken in the middle of the night, but neither of the boys had even patted his head! They were too puzzled and excited to fuss over Punch!

"Now you be quiet, Punch, and don't growl or whine or *anything*," ordered Nicky, in a low voice. "Stay here for a minute. We'll be back soon."

He and Ken stole across the passage to an empty room at the back of the house – but alas, a tree was just in front!

"Blow!" said Nicky.

"Well, let's go into another room," said Ken.

"They're all occupied," said Nicky. "Uncle Bob's got the spare room. We might steal into his if he's asleep. I daren't wake up Dad."

"Come on, then," said Ken. So Nicky led him down a passage to another door. They listened outside. To their delight little snores came from inside – yes, Uncle Bob was well and truly asleep!

They turned the door handle carefully, and crept in. A lamp in the street outside gave a faint light to the room, which had its curtains pulled right back. The boys avoided some clothes on the floor and tiptoed to the window, glad that the curtains were drawn back. They pressed their noses to the glass, and looked towards Skylark Hill. Faintly outlined against the night-sky was the old tower – and as the two boys watched, they saw a sudden sharp flick of light, then another and another.

"There you are!" said Ken, in excitement. "See that –

and that! If that's not someone signalling I'd jolly well like to know *what* it is!"

The light from the street lamp caught some glassy surface in the room, and Nicky realized what it was.

"Look – Uncle's field glasses are over there in that corner – let's borrow them and see if we can focus them on the tower and see more clearly what's going on!"

In his haste to get the field glasses Nicky fell over some shoes on the floor, and knocked against the bed. Uncle Bob awoke at once – the bed creaked as he sat up in alarm.

"Who's there? What is it?"

"It's all right, Uncle Bob – it's only us – me and Ken," said Nicky.

Uncle Bob switched on his bedside light and stared at the boys in the greatest astonishment.

"What in the world are you doing?" he asked. "And what's *Ken* here for, in the middle of the night? Or am I dreaming?"

"Uncle Bob, listen!" said Nicky, keeping his voice low. "Someone's signalling from the tower on Skylark Hill – it looks as if he's signalling with a powerful torch."

"Now look here, my boy – don't let's have any more of this silly nonsense," said Uncle Bob, annoyed. "I'm pretty certain you and Ken made up that coded message – the look on your faces gave you away! I didn't mind playing along with you for a joke – but when it comes to you both invading my bedroom in the middle of the night, talking about someone signalling from the tower, it's just TOO MUCH!"

"Didn't you believe our message then?" said Nicky, feeling very small.

"Look – I'm a private detective in real life, as you very well know!" said Uncle Bob. "And I'm not likely to be taken in by a joke invented by a couple of silly schoolboys. Clear out of my bedroom, and don't let's hear any more of this nonsense."

"But *listen*, Uncle Bob," said Nicky, desperately. "We DID see lights in the tower – so did the two girls. Look, you get your field glasses and focus them on the tower. I bet you'll get as much of a surprise as we did."

"I simply don't believe a word of it," said Uncle Bob, reaching for his field glasses. "And I very much resent you two boys invading my bedroom in the middle of the night and telling me fairy tales!"

He got out of bed with the field glasses, and went to the window. He focussed the glasses carefully on the tower and stared for so long that the boys felt impatient.

"Can you see lights flashing?" asked Nicky, at last.

Uncle Bob lowered the glasses and turned on the two anxious boys.

"NO!" he said. "There's not a thing to be seen. Just as I thought! You both deserve a good hiding for coming into my room like this at night – you really must think I'm a bit of a fool to play such idiotic tricks on me. Now, clear out, and be your age!"

"But Uncle *Bob*," began Nicky, desperately. "I tell you we did see some . . ."

"Oh shut up and go away," said Uncle Bob, and gave the boys a hard push. Ken wriggled away and went to the window for a quick look at the tower. Alas – Uncle Bob was right – all was darkness there now. Whoever had been signalling had stopped flashing his torch or lantern. What bad luck!

"Come on, Nicky," said Ken, and the two boys went

out of the room, dismayed and angry. Whoever would have thought that Uncle Bob would treat them like that?

The boys sat on Nicky's bed, an excited Punch between them, and talked sorrowfully about Uncle Bob's utter disbelief.

"Anyway, there *is* something going on up there," said Ken. "And *we'll* go and find out what it's all about. We made up a mystery – and it seems to be coming true! That's strange – but strange things do happen."

"All right. We'll keep Uncle Bob out of it all," said Nicky. "We'll solve everything ourselves. We'll take Punch up to the tower tomorrow and scout round for all we're worth! We'll show Uncle Bob we're better detectives than he is! But gosh – I hope he doesn't tell Dad about all this. I'd get into trouble, I bet I would."

"Cheer up – he won't say a word," said Ken, comfortingly. "He's angry with us – but he's not mean enough to get us into trouble! I rather wish we hadn't made up that mystery now!"

"Well, *I'm* not," said Nicky. "If we hadn't thought of it, we'd never be solving this one, would we? You go back home now, Ken – we'll talk about this tomorrow."

"We'll have to tell the girls, you know, Nicky," said Ken. "I mean – it was they who saw the lights flashing from the tower. We can't keep them out of things now."

"Oh blow it!" said Nicky. "I suppose we can't. But they're not to come up to the tower with us, Ken. I won't have that! What we do, we do on our own."

"All right," said Ken, climbing out of the window. "I'll leave *you* to argue with them about that. So long, Nicky! Sleep well!"

And down the tree he went. What a truly adventurous night!

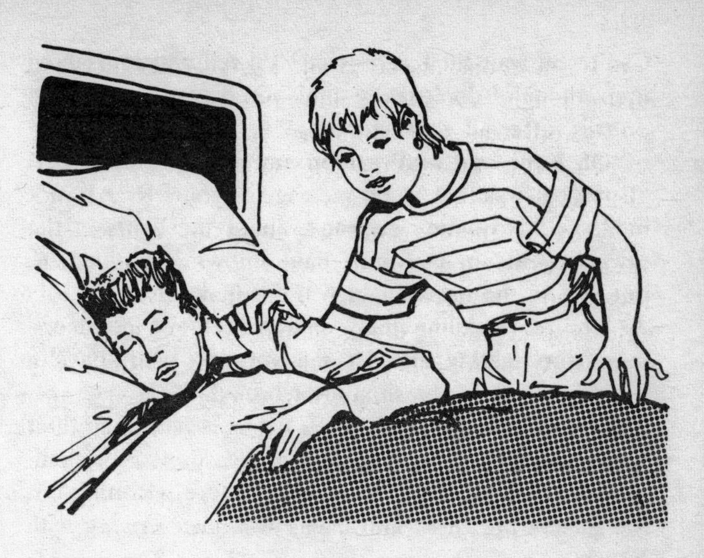

CHAPTER 13

Exciting Plans

The girls were both fast asleep when Ken crept back into the room, so he didn't disturb them – he was, in fact, very thankful not to have to explain what had happened.

He jumped into bed, puzzled about the lights in the tower for a few seconds, and then fell into a deep sleep. Penny woke him up in the morning by shaking him violently, and demanded to know whether it was Nicky who had been up to the tower and was playing about there in the night.

"No, it wasn't," said Ken. "And get out of my room.

Can't you wait till I'm dressed? I'll tell you everything then, though I don't really think you deserve to come in on this, after all your snooping."

"Oh Ken – we won't snoop any more," said Penny. "But Ken, was that secret message of yours REAL, not made-up? How did you know about the lights in the tower – I mean, you must have known *something*, to put that in the message, if you did make it up."

"You're muddling me," said Ken. "For goodness' sake stop talking and let me get up. We'll have a meeting down in the shed after breakfast."

And so, at ten o'clock when the girls had done their household jobs, they went down the garden to the shed, to join the boys. Ken was already there, cleaning out the guinea pig cage, and Nicky was just arriving with Punch.

Nicky took charge at once, determined not to let the girls get out of hand.

"Now just listen, everyone," he said. "You two girls know that Ken and I made up a mystery to interest Uncle Bob and make him forget about being overworked. *We* wrote out that message, Ken put it into code – jolly clever of him – and we dropped it into a bush on Skylark Hill. That's where Uncle Bob found it – and he *seemed* to believe it, I must say."

"I bet he didn't really," said Winnie, with a giggle. "He wouldn't have shown it to *us*, if he'd *really* believed it."

"Shut up, Winnie," said Ken, sharply, and Winnie subsided, with a grin spreading over her plump face.

"Well," went on Nicky, "you two girls saw lights in the tower last night, and you told Ken, and he came over to me – and we *both* saw them, of course. We had to go in to Uncle Bob's room to see them, and he woke up, and . . ."

"Ooooh! Did *he* see them too?" asked Penny. "Whatever did he say? I bet he believed in your mystery then!"

"Will you PLEASE not interrupt?" said Nicky, exasperated. "He *didn't* see them! The beastly signals had stopped by the time he got to the window – and so he doesn't believe us – he thinks we made up the flashing signals, and he's so angry that he won't listen to a single word about any mystery now, real or otherwise!"

"Gosh!" said Penny. "What are we going to do, then? I mean – your pretend mystery's turned into a *real* one, hasn't it? *Someone* must have been up there in the tower last night – up to no good – and there are others in the mystery too – *the people he was flashing to*. And what was he signalling about, – and why – and . . .?"

"All right, all right, Penny," said Ken. "Just hold your tongue for a minute – if you *can* – and let Nicky get on. It's only because you saw the flashes last night, and were decent enough to tell me, that we're letting you come in on this."

"And what's more we're going to tell you any future plans we make," said Nicky. "You'll have to be in on this now that you know so much – BUT – you've got to take orders from *me*, and do as you are told, see?"

"Right," said Winnie, glowing with excitement. "Oooh, Nicky – you do sound grown up. I'll do exactly what you say! You will, too, won't you, Penny?"

"I don't know about *that*," said Penny. "I'll back up the boys – but I'm going to have *my* say in the matter, too."

"WUFF!" said Punch, sitting up straight as if he thoroughly agreed with all his.

"Now, don't *you* start airing your views, too," said Nicky, giving Punch a tap on the head. "It's bad enough coping with two girls without *you* entering into the argument as well!"

That made everyone laugh. Ken went to his cupboard and took out a packet of toffees.

"All this talk is making me hungry," he said. "Have some, girls? No, not you, Punch, old thing. Have you forgotten what happened to you last time you chewed up some toffees? You lost your bark for ages because your teeth got stuck together!"

Winnie giggled. "Oh I *wish* I'd seen him! Now do let's go on with your plans. What are you going to do about this mystery? What do you *think* is going on?"

"Well – I really haven't the faintest idea," confessed Nicky. "I've just thought of the usual things you know – thieves – or somebody captured and imprisoned up there, perhaps – or someone hiding there for some reason – perhaps an escaped prisoner . . ."

"Oooooh!" said Winnie, her eyes round with excitement. "Go on, Nicky!"

"Whatever it is, we're going to find out," said Ken, firmly. "And though we'll let you girls know what we're doing, you are NOT going to be mixed up in this."

"We'll see about that," said Penny.

Ken put the toffee bag well out of Punch's reach and sat down. "*I* think the first thing to do is to try and find out who was up there signalling last night – see if he left any traces – try to find where he was hiding – and that means that Nicky and I go up there for the day – take a picnic lunch, and do a bit of spying."

"We ought to go down into the cellars again and look round," said Nicky. "We couldn't look round properly yesteday because my torch battery went phut. There might be some very interesting clues down there!"

"Gracious – I hope you'll be careful!" said Penny. "Do you remember old Harriet, our daily woman? Well, her sister is caretaker at the local museum here, and one day when we were there, she showed us some old plans of that burnt-out place – plans made before it was destroyed, of course – and you should have seen the plans of the cellars – gosh, they seemed to go half down the hill!"

"REALLY!" said Nicky, sitting up at once. "Look, there's something you girls could do – go and have a look at the plans – perhaps copy them very simply – and see what else you can find out. There may be some secret hiding place, for instance, which might still be there. *Somebody* must be hiding up there, that's certain!"

"Right," said Penny, delighted. "We'll do that this very morning. We'll go now!"

She jumped up, and Winnie got up too. They felt very important. This was a REAL mystery now, not a silly made-up one – and they were in it!

"Right – you go straight away," said Nicky, pleased to think that the girls would not be able to track them up the hill, and follow them to the tower, as he had been half afraid they would. They would be safe in the museum. He stood up. "I'll go and get lunch packets for the two of us, Ken," he said. "Mrs Hawes will make some – she'll give us smashing sandwiches! And I'll take a bone and some biscuits for old Punch. That be all right for you, Punch, old chap?"

Punch danced round him, delighted to hear Nicky talking to him at last.

"Wuff, wuff!" he said, and Nicky patted him. Punch ran to Penny, and she patted him too. "You'd better not ask *Winnie* for a pat," she said. "She hasn't forgotten how you tried to drown her shoe yesterday!"

At the word "shoe" Punch was off like lightening. Nicky groaned. "*Why* did you mention the word 'shoe'? I thought he'd forgotten all about shoes today – he hasn't dragged any downstairs at all. Now he's gone to fetch some, I bet you anything you like!"

He and Ken went back through the hedge to find Mrs Hawes, who was very pleased to make them sandwiches.

"That dog of yours shot past me at sixty miles an hour just now," she said. "Up to some kind of mischief, I expect!"

And, sure enough, by the time the boys were ready to go, and the neat packets of sandwiches were on the kitchen table, Punch had raided all the bedrooms, and brought at least six pairs of shoes into the kitchen!

"You take them back!" ordered Mrs Hawes, pointing at them with the bread-knife. "If you think *I'm* going to trot up and down the stairs with all those shoes, you'd better think again!"

"Oh you *ass*, Punch!" said Nicky, gathering them up. "This trick isn't funny any more! Ken, take the packets of sandwiches and stick them into my shoulder bag, will you? And fetch some apples and bananas from the sideboard, and take a couple of ginger beers from the larder. I'll bring some chocolate – and biscuits and bone for Punch – though he jolly well doesn't deserve them, messing about with everyone's shoes like this!"

Mrs Hawes heaved a sigh of relief when all three were safely out of the house, Punch barking his head off with joy. He was off for the day with the boys – could anything be more exciting than that? Ah well, Punch – it may perhaps be a little more exciting than any of you imagine!

CHAPTER 14

The Cellars In The Hill

While the two boys set off to go up Skylark Hill, Penny and Winnie walked in the opposite direction to the little local meuseum.

"There's Harriet's sister, look," said Penny, nodding towards a plump little woman who was dusting the glass-fronted museum cases. "Hello, Miss Clewes! How's Harriet? I haven't seen her today."

"She's in bed with a cold, miss," said Miss Clewes. "Well, it's not often I see *you* here – last time I saw you was when you came with your school class to see some old documents about our village. What do you want to see this morning?"

"Well, Miss Clewes, we're rather interested in that great old place up on Skylark Hill," said Penny. "The one that was burnt down years ago. Are there any maps of it?

"Oh, yes – plenty!" said Miss Clewes, bustling over to a cupboard. "Funny you should come about that old place – there's been quite a lot of people looking at the old plans lately. But surely nobody would want to build that awful old building up again, would they?"

"What sort of people came?" asked Penny, surprised.

"Well – not very *nice* folks, miss," said Miss Clewes, getting some enormous stiff papers out of a cupboard. "Men, you know – off-hand like – almost rude – poring over them plans, and making notes. I says to them, "What's all the excitement about, all of a sudden? Thinking of rebuilding the old place and living there in style, like in the old days?"

"And what did they say to that?" asked Penny.

"Oh, they said maybe they *were* going to do that, and maybe they *weren't*," said little Miss Clewes.

"And that it wasn't none of *my* business! Quite rude, they were."

Penny and Winnie unrolled the enormous plans and studied them. They were not very clever at making out what the plans showed. They ignored the ones of the great house itself, because the fire had destroyed all the rooms, both upstairs and down, and only the stone walls were standing now.

"Are these the plans of the cellars?" asked Winnie, poring over a curious map that showed what looked like passages and caves.

"Yes – the plans of the house itself aren't much use to anyone now it's burnt," said Miss Clewes, "but the plans of the passages and caves that honeycomb the hill are still more or less correct, I should think. The folk who used to live in the old place used them as cellars – but they were *natural* cellars, if you know what I mean – not man-made. Saved them the trouble of digging out cellars for the goods or the food they wanted to store!"

"Are there any old stories – old legends about the place?" asked Winnie.

"Well – a few – but I wouldn't put much belief in them," said Miss Clewes, rolling up the plans the girls had finished with. "There's the story about the golden Statue, for instance. They do say it's got magic powers, and if its feet are kissed seven times, it will grant wishes."

"A nice story – but I'm afraid no statue could grant wishes!" said Penny. "Not even a golden one. What happened when the place was burnt down? Did the statue melt and disappear? It must have been worth a lot of money."

"Nobody knows what happened to it," said Miss Clewes. "I suppose it *might* have melted, the heat was so great. Or it might have been removed to safety, and taken by the family to wherever they went. Or it *might* be just a story, you know – all kinds of tales grow up about old places."

"Yes, that's true," said Penny. "Do you mind if I quickly trace the plan of the old passages and caves in the hill just near the burnt building – the ones used as cellars? We might go exploring there today."

"No – now don't you do that," said Miss Clewes. "Since we had a great storm and a cloudburst of rain five years since, those underground places have been dangerous – fallen in, you know, or full of water. You'd much better not go exploring there."

"Well, we'll see," said Penny, putting a piece of tracing paper over the map, and running her pencil here and there. "I'll let you know what happens if we *do* explore!"

The girls left the museum at last, taking with them a very well-traced copy of the passages and caves that made up the "Cellars" of the old building.

"I don't expect it will be of any use," said Penny. "But you never know! It wouldn't *really* matter if the boys got lost in the cellars, because Punch could easily take them out. A dog always knows the way! What shall we do now?"

"Well, I'm jolly hungry," said Winnie. "Let's go home, and get some sandwiches and apples, and go up on Skylark Hill. I know the boys don't want us spying on them, but we could just have a look round. We could sit and have our sandwiches on the hill, and hear the birds singing – especially the skylarks, of course!"

So back they went and made themselves some ham sandwiches, and took some apples from the larder. Then they set off to Skylark Hill and found a cosy place at the bottom, where they could sit and munch in peace.

"Let's have a good look at our map-tracing, too," said Penny. "I've an idea it might help us a lot. If only we could find the lower entrance to the cellars! That would save us going all the way up to the old building!"

It was very pleasant sitting in the sun, munching, and poring over the map. Penny rolled it up at last. "I wonder what the boys have been doing," she said. "How I'd like to know! Well – let's have a walk up the hill, and see if we can spot anything interesting. My word, we have been a time eating our lunch!"

The boys had had a most adventurous time. They had gone up to the old tower first of all, and examined it thoroughly, trying to find some traces of whoever had been signalling there the night before.

"Here's another match like the one we found before," announced Ken, picking one up from the stone sill. "This is the window-opening that the signaller must have used last night. And here's a second match on the floor – *and* a cigarette packet – empty! All clues, Nicky! I'll put them in my pocket."

"Well, at least we know some *real* person was here, said Nicky. "It wasn't just a ghost signalling!"

They made their way down the dangerous stairway, and Ken picked up yet another match – and then, down in the great old kitchen, they found an empty matchbox, thrown near the old iron stoves. They looked at the name on the matchbox.

"Ha – the signaller uses Quick-Lite Matches!" said Ken. "And we know he smokes Splendour Cigarettes, because he left the empty packet behind. He's not very careful, is he?"

"Why should he be?" said Nicky. "He's probably only using this place to signal from, because from here any flash can be seen for miles – and he's away long before daylight, I should think."

"He could hide quite well in those old cellars," suggested Ken.

"Maybe. Yes – that's quite a thought. Or somebody might be using them as a hiding place for goods of some sort – and perhaps the time has come for whatever's hidden to be fetched in safety. You know, I think we've hit on something!"

"You mean valuables may have been stored away in those old caves and passages – maybe stolen some time ago – and the robbers arranged for a signal to be given when it was safe for the stolen goods to be fetched. A signal from someone in the know?"

"Yes – something like that," said Nicky, feeling suddenly very excited. "Gosh, this is thrilling! We certainly MUST go and explore those cellars. Thank goodness we've brought strong torches – and Punch. He'll bark like anything if there's anyone down there."

"Perhaps that's why he barked the other day?" said Ken. "Maybe there was someone down here then."

"Yes. I say – isn't this getting EXCITING! What about going down now? There's nothing more to be seen here. I've got the matches – and the cigarette packet. Come on – we'll go down the cellar stairs very quietly, and tell Punch not even to growl!"

So once again the boys went underground down the curious spiral stairway, into pitch darkness, Punch at their heels. Nicky flashed his torch cautiously around. They were in the same dark, low-roofed passage they had found themselves in the day before. They went quietly down it and came to the cellar they had seen heaped with old junk. That was as far as they had gone yesterday, for it was here that Nicky's battery had given out, and they had been forced to go back.

But now their torches shone steadily and brilliantly before them, making a path through the darkness. They stood listening, and Nicky put his hand on Punch's collar to stop him running forward. Not a sound could be heard, and Punch gave a very small whine. He wanted to go on!

"All right, Punch – but go quietly and carefully," Nicky warned him. "We don't know what's down here – nor do we know who may be hiding – so walk *just* in front of us, see?"

They went silently through another passage whose roof became so low at one part that the boys had to bend double to get through. Punch was very good. He stopped whenever they did, walked very slowly, and kept his nose in the air, sniffing for smells of animals or humans, all the time.

They came to three caves, all running into one another,and then another passage, a wide one this time. And then, what a surprise – they came to a cave piled with tins, boxes and cartons of all sorts and sizes! Nicky shone his torch on them.

"Tins of meat – butter – bacon – cartons of cigarettes – packets – gracious, what's all this?" he whispered. "Someone's been living here for some time – look at all the empty tins and cartons – as well as the unopened ones. This must be where that signaller lives!"

"Better go carefully then," whispered Ken. "He may be near."

They went down another passage, so narrow that it was hard at times to squeeze through. And then Punch stood absolutely still and gave a very small, deep growl!

The two boys hardly dared to breathe. What was Punch growling at? Then they knew! A long drawn-out snore came to their ears – and then another! SOMEONE was there – someone fast asleep. Who was it? Be careful now, Nicky and Ken – this may be a very dangerous moment!

CHAPTER 15

Deep Underground

The two boys stood perfectly still, Punch just in front of them, still growling softly.

"Sh!" whispered Nicky, and Punch stopped growling at once. "Take hold of Punch's collar, Ken, while I go forward a little."

Ken held Punch's collar tightly while Nicky went cautiously forward. The passage curved just there, and Nicky felt sure the snorer was just round the bend. He put his head round – and there, in a little side-cave, was an enormous man, lying on his back, snoring. Beside him were the remains of a meal, taken out of tins.

Nicky stared at him. He was dark-skinned and wore a fine beard. Nicky thought he looked as if he came from the East – was he an Indian – or perhaps a Persian? He looked pretty fierce, anyway! What on earth was he doing in the underground cellars?

Then Nicky saw tools of all kinds – spades big and small – iron bars – buckets! He was astonished. Were the men excavating, then – digging out the caves – were they looking for something?

He crept back to Ken, and pulled him farther up the passage, so as to be out of the sleeping man's hearing, should he awake.

"Something's certainly going on down in these old cellars," he said. "There are all kinds of digging tools down there – and a big, foreign-looking man with a beard is snoring away near them! What is he digging for? Who would hide anything in these caves?"

"I don't know," said Ken, puzzled. "Maybe precious things were stored here when that great old building was lived in – or taken down here for safety when the fire began, and hidden – and then perhaps forgotten."

"Or they might have been *stolen* when the fire raged," said Nicky. "Maybe someone fired the old place on purpose, so that they could run off with some of the really valuable things. After all, it was a Prince who built that place – he must have been very rich and had some wonderful treasures."

"Yes – an Eastern Prince," said Ken. "You said that snoring fellow down there looks foreign? I bet it's someone who's been told where something is hidden – hidden in this hill."

"Goodness – that's just like we put in our coded message!" said Nicky, startled. "Don't you remember –

we put, 'Stuff hidden on Skylark Hill'! Little did we know how true that was!"

"And we put in about the signalling from the tower, too," said Ken. "That came true, as well! What was the other thing we put? Oh yes – 'Meet in cellars'! Gosh, it looks as if that's correct, too. I say – it's all a bit queer, isn't it?"

"It is rather," said Nicky. "I mean – we only thought of our silly message just as a joke – something to amuse Uncle Bob. I don't much like the way it's all coming true. It's just as if we'd foretold what was going to happen."

"Well – we can't stop it now," said Ken. "We'd better look out for this Cellar Meeting next! Perhaps someone is coming to talk to that snoring fellow. We might overhear something interesting."

Punch began to growl again, and Nicky tapped his head. "Shut up! No noise now, Punch. Someone else may be coming."

Nicky was right! The boys suddenly heard a scraping noise as if someone was coming up a passage to where the snoring man lay in the little side-cave. Then a man's voice spoke angrily.

"Hassan! Always you sleep! Why are you not working? Have you dug out the golden urns?"

The sleeping man had awakened with a jump. He growled something in a language that the boys did not understand. Then there came the sound of metal rubbing against metal, and the boys imagined that Hassan was showing the other man what he had dug out.

"Did you find the statue?" asked the visitor.

Apparently Hassan answered no, for the second man flew into a rage, and shouted a string of words that the boys couldn't understand. Punch couldn't help growling when he heard the angry shouts.

His growl must have been heard, for the two men suddenly fell silent.

"What was that?" said the second man, in English. "Could it be Harry coming down from the passages above? He was in the tower last night, signalling for the others to meet him here, and take the stuff."

Ken gave Nicky a sudden nudge. *Harry*! Good gracious, that was the name Ken had chosen when he had signed that secret message! This was really very weird. Harry! He must be the head of this gang. Would he come?

"Hope he won't come down this way," whispered Ken. "We'd be caught then, between Harry and the others. Golly – I don't much like this!"

He fell silent – and in the silence the two boys heard another noise. Someone *was* coming down from the old building above – coming down by the very same path that they themselves had taken. The boys hurriedly squeezed into a little side-cave, pulling Punch with them. If only this fellow would go by without seeing them!

He would have done, but for Punch, who simply could *not* resist another growl – rather a loud one this time. The man stopped at once.

"What's that? Who's there?" he called, roughly.

There was no answer, of course – and then, alas, Punch growled again, a deep, angry growl that rumbled all round the little cave. The man bent down and looked into the cave. He was an ugly fellow, with a black shade over one eye. He flashed a torch on the boys and the dog.

"What's this? Who are you? What on earth are you

doing here?" he shouted. Then he yelled to the other two men, who were looking extremely startled. "Look! There's a couple of kids here! Didn't I tell you to keep watch, and see that no one came down here? You idiots? Just when everything's almost ready! We've only got that statue to find now! I'll knock your heads together – didn't I TELL you that . . ."

"It's all right Harry," said the second man. "If it's only kids we can shut them up in a cave, and put a stone in front of it. We'll soon be out of here – by tomorrow at the latest."

"Tomorrow will be too late," shouted Harry. "Someone may come hunting for these two kids – just when we want to take out all the stuff. We'd better go and tell the other two men to come up and help tonight."

He turned to the two frightened boys. "Well, you've got mixed up in something you didn't expect," he said, in a voice the boys didn't like at all. "Well – we shan't hurt you – but you'll just have to stay imprisoned in a cave till we're ready to go. Come on out of there – we'll find another cave for you with an entrance we can easily block."

The boys made no move, and the man lost his temper. He dragged them both out roughly – and Punch went completely mad. He flew at the man and bit him hard on the left foot, right through his shoe! The man gave an anguished yell, and pulled off his shoe at once. His foot was bleeding through his thin sock.

The other two men came running up and one of them aimed a vicious kick at poor Punch. How he yelped! He ran to Nicky at once, but he ran on three legs, because one of his hind legs was badly hurt by the kick. Nicky picked him up and ran, Ken close behind him.

The men stumbled after them. "Look – let's get into that narrow passage running off to the left – the roof's so low that I don't think the men will be able to squeeze through after us," panted Nicky.

"Right," said Ken, and he squeezed in after Nicky, who found it very difficult with Punch in his arms. In fact he had to put him down at the end of the narrow passage, because there he had to crawl on hands and knees, the roof was so low!

The men stopped – and one of them laughed. "Couldn't be better! They'll be nicely boxed up in there. We only need to roll up a heavy stone, and they'll be imprisoned! Serve them right – and that dog, too!"

The boys heard the sound of the men tugging at a stone – and then – thud – it was right up against the opening to the narrow passage, completely blocking it.

But neither of the boys worried about that. It was poor, whining Punch they were upset about. They shone a torch on to his leg, fearing that it was broken.

Thank goodness it wasn't – although it was badly bruised and bleeding. Nicky hugged Punch lovingly.

"You brave little dog!" he said. "I'm *glad* you bit that man. Does your leg hurt very much? Poor old Punch – where's my hanky? I'll bind up your leg, and hope it will be all right."

Punch licked him, and gave a tiny whine as if to say, "Don't worry! We'll be all right!" But *would* they be all right? Did the men *really* mean to leave them imprisoned? And if so, how in the world would anyone ever find them?

CHAPTER 16

An Astonishing Find

The two boys sat silently for a while, with their arms round Punch. How sickening to be caught like this! Then Ken remembered the food they had brought with them in the bag. He brightened up at once.

"Let's have something to eat," he said. "It's about dinner time, and I bet Punch would like his bone! Sandwiches will cheer us up!"

They certainly did! After the boys had eaten half the sandwiches, they felt very much better. They had a banana each too, and Punch had a biscuit. Then they drank one of the bottles of ginger beer.

"Better not eat everything now," said Ken. "You just never know how long we'll be imprisoned here."

"*Not* a very nice thought," said Nicky. "Well, anyway the girls know we've come up here, so if we don't appear for some time, they'll tell Dad, and he'll organize a search party. Wait, though – what about trying to move that stone away that they've put at the entrance of this place? We *might* be able to."

They crawled down the passage to the entrance. It was well and truly blocked with a very heavy stone indeed. No amount of shoving would move it. Punch came along and looked, too. He began to scrape round the stone with his front paws, and managed to make a small space between the stone and the rocky entrance.

But, alas, it wasn't nearly big enough for either of the boys to squeeze through, try as they would. However,

Punch managed to wriggle out, and set off cautiously on three legs down the passage where the men had gone.

"Be careful, Punch!" called Nicky. "Come back before you get into any more trouble." Punch went on very cautiously, giving a little growl every now and again. If only he could find those men, what a fright he would give them!

He came to the cave where Hassan, the sleeping man, had been. No one was there. Punch sniffed round and came across one odd shoe. It was the shoe that Harry had removed from his swollen, bleeding foot, and thrown down in the cave when he limped away to help the others in their work of shifting some goods.

A shoe! Ah – Punch simply couldn't resist picking it up in his mouth and running off with it! Back he went to the boys' cave, shoe in mouth, proud of himself. Why, even down here he could show off his latest trick!

The boys couldn't help laughing when they saw Punch with the shoe in his mouth!

"Punch, you dear old idiot!" said Nicky. "Where did you get that? Oh, of course – it must be the shoe that fellow took off when you bit his foot. Put it down, old thing – he can jolly well go without it!"

"I say, Nicky – do you suppose we could get out of the *other* end of this cave?" Ken suddenly said, shining his torch towards the back. "There must have been a fall of earth at some time – so if we dig through with our hands, we may find a passage we can go up."

"Right. Let's try," said Nicky, bored with doing nothing. So he and Ken and Punch all dug hard with hands and paws. The earth was very loose, and it was soon obvious that part of the earthy roof *had* fallen in and blocked the passage.

"We're through the fall of earth!" said Ken, suddenly, as his hand went through the last layer of soil into nothing. "Quick – we'll soon have a hole big enough for us to squeeze through. Gracious – old Punch is through already. What's the other side, Punch?"

Punch began to growl. He was on the other side of the earth-fall, and the boys could not see what he was growling at.

"There surely can't be any of the men there!" said Ken. "Here, let *me* wriggle through the hole we've made and shine my torch to see what's the other side. Punch must be growling at *something*!"

So Ken wriggled a little more, and was then able to shine his torch into the space beyond. He was silent for so long that Nicky grew impatient.

"What is it? Can you see something?"

"Yes. Yes, I can certainly see something. But I can't believe it!" said Ken, in an awed voice. "Nicky – get beside me and look. I must be seeing things! It's – it's so strange!"

Nicky squeezed beside him and looked into the dark space lighted by Ken's torch. He caught his breath in wonder and fear. Something very beautiful was there – something that looked at them out of brilliantly shining eyes, and shone brightly from top to toe.

"What is it?" whispered Nicky.

"Well – can it be the statue that one of the men spoke about?" Ken whispered back. "Nicky – it's made of *gold* – pure, shining *gold*. And its eyes are precious stones. It's a statue from one of the far Eastern lands – it must have belonged to the prince who built that burnt-out mansion. Someone must have taken it down here for safety when the fire started."

"And stuffed it right at the back of the cave – and then a fall of earth came, and it was hidden from everyone's sight!" said Nicky. "No one has found it since! We heard the men talking about finding golden urns – you remember – they must have been hidden down here, too. And after all these years *somebody* has remembered them, and sent men here to look for them!"

"But that *statue*! Did you ever see anything like it?" said Ken, shining his torch on the strangely beautiful face. "I say – we mustn't let the men know it's here!"

"They're too big to get through that narrow low tunnel to it," said Nicky. "We could only just squeeze through it ourselves. This is *our* secret, Ken! My word – it's a wonder we didn't put a statue into our coded message, isn't it?"

"I do wish we could get out of here," said Ken. "There's rock behind that statue, so the passage must end there. Let's get back into the other part – there's more room. My *word* – what a find! Come back, Punch – look, Nicky, he's licking the statue's feet to see what it's made of! It's gold, Punch, gold!"

"What do you suppose the girls are doing?" said Nicky, when they were back through the hole they had made, sitting in the cave again. "I wish I knew where they were!"

At that very moment Penny and Winnie were walking up Skylark Hill, excited because they had such a good tracing of the underground cellars in their hands. They were about half-way up when Penny stopped.

"Look – there's a strange-looking man coming down the hill!" she said. "Foreign-looking – see his very black beard. Isn't he tall!"

"And look at the man with the black eye-shade," said Winnie, "He's limping! He's wearing only one shoe, and see, his foot's bleeding! And there's another man behind him. Where in the world can they have come from? They appeared so *very* suddenly!"

"Winnie – do you think they've come from the underground cellars?" said Penny, suddenly. "You know how far down the hill they stretch – and we do know there's an entrance at this lower end, as well as through the kitchen of the old place – and you remember that the boys told us that Punch must have found a way out, too? Well – *I* think those men have come from the same outlet Punch found, when the boys missed him the other day. There's simply nowhere else on this hill for them to have so suddenly appeared from!"

"Look – I think that one-eyed man is coming up to us," said Winnie, in a fright.

Sure enough the man with the eye-shade came right up and spoke to them.

"I need a doctor," he said. "My foot is bad. It has been bitten by a dog. Can you tell me of a doctor, please?"

"Er – well – there's one down in the town there," stammered Penny, frightened, pointing down the hill. "Anyone will tell you where he lives. Er – what kind of a dog bit you?"

The man didn't answer, but went back to the others, limping. They set off down the hill again.

"I *bet* it was Punch who bit him!" said Winnie. "I bet it was. Oh, Penny – you don't think anything's happened to the boys, do you? Hadn't we better go back home for help?"

"No – we'll try to find the place where the men came out of the hill," said Penny. "I feel as if we ought to look for the boys and make sure they're all right. Come on – this way. That's where we first saw the men appear, over there. Hurry, Winnie – the men may come back at any time."

There they go, the two of them, anxious and scared. There must be some way in, there must!

CHAPTER 17

The Girls Are Very Clever

Penny and Winnie made their way round the slope of the hill to where they had first seen the men appearing. They kept looking back over their shoulders to make sure that no one was following them.

"This is quite an adventure, Penny, isn't it?" said Winnie, in rather a trembly voice. Then she gave a loud exclamation. "OH! I *say* – I've thought of something."

"You made me jump!" said Penny, who was feeling just as scared as Winnie. "What have you thought of?"

"That tracing we made of the underground cellars!" said Winnie. "Let's have a look at it, and see if it will help us."

They sat down on the hillside and opened out the roll of tracing paper. They pored over it, frowning.

"Here's the old building, see," said Penny, her finger on the map. "And here's where the cellars begin. They go along here – down under the hill, of course – and spread out here and there – really underground passages, I suppose. But I don't see how we're going to tell where they *end* on this actual hill."

"Look – what's this on the tracing?" said Winnie, pointing to a little curving line. "Could it be a stream?"

"Well, I suppose it might," said Penny. "But what's the use of that? There's no stream here on the hill now, that I can see. It must have dried up years ago."

"But its *bed* will still be there – like a dried-up ditch!" said Winnie, jumping up. "Come on – if we can find that,

They pored over it, frowning.

and follow it up, we shall perhaps come across the bottom entrance to the cellars!"

The girls walked over to the place where they had first seen the three men appearing. They looked all round but at first saw nothing that could have been a stream-bed. Then Winnie gave a shout.

"Here you are! This must have once been a stream – the ditch running along this old hawthorn hedge."

"Yes – I think you're right," said Penny, excited. She looked at the traced map again. "Here it is on the map," she said. "And look – it seems to go curving up the hill, and swings off just by where the entrance to the cellars is marked. Let's follow it up the hill."

So the two girls went slowly up the hill, following the half-lost track of the old stream. But where could the entrance into the hill be found?

The old ditch took a sudden curve round – and Penny gave an exclamation.

"The entrance should be here – where the ditch curves – look on the map and see what I mean, Winnie. This is where we must hunt for the entrance, I'm sure!"

She was right. A great gorse bush barred their way, thick and prickly. The ditch curved round it – and Penny's quick eye saw a smooth patch of earth just under one side of the great bush.

"I think *that's* the way into the opening," she said. "See that worn patch of earth? The men may have gone in and out there. Good gracious – we shall be scratched to bits!"

They certainly did get well and truly scratched! Fortunately they both had coats, and were able to wrap them round their faces and shoulders as they crawled under the prickly bush. Someone had cut away the bush

in the thick middle part, so it was not so thorny there – and what a surprise they had!

A hole went down into the ground, almost under the middle of the bush – a hole that had rough steps cut in one side! The girls crouched under the bush, and looked down into the hole rather doubtfully.

"Do we go down?" said Penny. "We don't know what's down there – or who."

"Oh, come on – let's be brave!" said Winnie, who was not feeling brave in the least. "I'll go first."

And down she went, groping with her legs to find the rough steps. Soon she was in an underground passage. She switched on the torch she had brought.

"Well – that was very clever of us," said Penny, jumping down and joining her. "Now – where do we go from here?"

"Well – there's only one way – and that's *up*," said Winnie. "Thank goodness you took that tracing, Penny. Come on – I'll go first."

The two girls went slowly up the dark passage. They flashed their torches into little and big side-caves, marvelling at seeing so many. What a honeycombed hillside this was. There must have been many little underground streams at one time, rushing down to make such a number of caves and passages!

"Shall we shout and see if the boys answer?" said Penny. "There doesn't seem to be anyone here – no men, I mean. Let's shout."

So they shouted at the tops of their voices. "KEN! NICKY! PUNCH!"

The two boys were still far away from the girls, sitting in their tiny cave, and heard nothing. But Punch's ears were very sharp. He cocked them up and listened. What was that far-off noise? He growled.

"Oh, *don't* say the men are coming again," groaned Nicky. "I'm fed up with them. What's the matter, Punch?"

Punch heard the far-away voices once more, and stood up on three legs, holding up his hurt one. He didn't growl this time. Surely he recognized those voices! He put his head on one side and listened hard.

The girls shouted again as they came up the underground passages in the hillside – and this time Punch knew the voices. Why – that was Penny's voice – and that was Winnie's! WUFF-WUFF-WUFF!

Punch barked loudly and joyfully, almost deafening the two boys in that small place. They stared at him in astonishment.

"What's the matter, Punch, old thing?" said Nicky.

"You're barking *happily* – who's coming? It can't be the men or you'd be growling."

Punch gave Nicky a quick lick and then barked again. He could hear the girls coming nearer and nearer. They heard his bark, and knew they were near the boys. "We're coming, Nicky, we're coming, Ken. Where are you?" they yelled.

"Here! Here! Can you hear us?" shouted Nicky in delight, crawling as near as he could to the great stone that blocked the entrance. "Penny! Winnie! Here we are – imprisoned in this cave."

The girls at last came to where the boys were, and yelled to them.

"We're here! We came all the way up from the lower entrance – the one Punch must have found the other day. We saw the men – they spoke to us!"

"Gosh! Did they *see* you coming up here?" asked Nicky, as the two girls began to try and move the great stone from the entrance.

"No – they've gone down to the town to find a doctor!" shouted Winnie. "I hope it was Punch who bit that man with the black eye-shade."

"It was," answered Ken. "Look – we'll *push* this stone while you *pull*. It's such a weight that I doubt if even the four of us can move it."

To their enormous disappointment the great stone could not be moved even an inch! It had taken three strong men to put it there – and four children certainly would not be able to budge it. It was most disappointing.

Punch barked, and scrabbled frantically with his front paws, but it was no use. Everyone sat back to take a rest, and the boys told the girls about the wonderful golden statue they had discovered in the hole behind their cave.

"*Gracious*! Miss Clewes at the museum told us about that!" said Penny. "It's quite a legend, she said. And apparently anyone who wants a wish to come true has only to kiss the statue's feet seven times!"

"Well, *I'm* not going to kiss any statue's feet, not even to get free," said Nicky. "Gosh – what are we to do *now*? I don't like you girls hanging about in these passages in case those men come back. They'd make *you* prisoners too!"

"Would they?" said Winnie, in alarm. "Then hadn't we better go back straight away and get help? We could bring your Uncle Bob up here in no time, and your father, too!"

"Yes – I almost think you'd better do that," said Ken. "Don't you agree, Nicky? But I *bet* Uncle Bob won't believe you girls! Gosh, this mystery has come true in every detail in a most remarkable way! I'm never going to make up any more!"

"We'll go now," said Penny. "Cheer up, both of you – and pat old Punch for us. We'll be as quick as ever we can!"

And away went the two girls, very cautiously indeed. The boys sat silent, listening to the small noises made by the girls as they went down the passage. Punch listened, too, his head on one side.

"Can't hear them any more," said Ken, with a sigh. "I'm getting tired of this hole, aren't you, Nicky? Well – I just hope the men don't come back. I say – what do you suppose Uncle Bob will say when we show him the golden statue?"

"Oh – he simply won't believe it!" said Nicky, with a grin. "It's just part of the Mystery that Never Was. He – just – won't – believe it!"

CHAPTER 18

Uncle Bob To The Rescue

The two girls went down the dark passage, their ears open for any sound of the men coming back again. Penny thought she heard a noise and stopped in alarm.

"Do you think it would be wiser to go *up* the passages to the old kitchen, and get out that way – the way the boys told us about?" said Penny. "It would be so terrifying if we met the men."

"No. Let's go on down," said Winnie. "At least we *know* this way. The men won't be back yet. I expect they've not only gone to find a doctor but also to make plans for removing whatever they found in the old caves. I *am* glad that Punch bit one of them!"

They came safely to the opening under the old gorse bush. It seemed to be more difficult getting out than getting in, and the girls were in a very dirty, untidy state when at last they were safely out of the great bush, and standing on the hillside in the sun.

"My word – it's good to be out in the open air and sunshine again!" said Penny, breathing in deeply. "I'm sorry for the two boys, shut up in that horrid little cave. Buck up – let's get back as soon as ever we can, and tell everyone where the boys are. Nicky's father is home today, isn't he? He can help too, and Nicky's Uncle Bob and . . ."

"I wonder if his Uncle Bob will believe our story," said Winnie. "It does sound a bit peculiar, doesn't it – hidden men – caves – a golden statue – the boys made prisoners.

Still, strange things *do* happen – you see them in the papers every day."

"Well, I never thought an adventure like this would happen to *us*!" said Penny. "Usually adventures are things that happen to other people. Come on – we're nearly home."

"I've been lokking out for those men all the way back, but there hasn't been a sign of them," said Winnie. "I'd run for miles if I did meet them!"

"We're back at last! said Penny, as they came to Nicky's front gate. She ran into the house, calling for Nicky's mother and father. "Mr Fraser! Mrs Fraser! Are you in? Quick!"

"Nicky's Dad has gone to the bank, and his Mother's gone shopping, miss!" called Mrs Hawes from the kitchen. "But his Uncle's in the garden reading the paper, if you want him."

"Yes, we *do*!" said Penny, and flew out into the garden, with Winnie close behind. "Uncle Bob! UNCLE BOB!"

"Hello, hello – what's all the excitement for, Penny?" said Uncle Bob, in surprise. "And where are the boys this morning?"

"Uncle Bob, something's happened," panted Penny. "The boys went up to the old burnt building this morning to find out about that signalling, and . . ."

"Now listen – I don't want to hear any more fairy tales," said Uncle Bob, looking annoyed. "I'm TIRED of hearing what's in that silly message, I'm TIRED of the boys pretending that something's going on. The joke's OVER!"

"But Uncle Bob – the boys are prisoners in a horrid little cave," said Penny, almost in tears. "A cave with a beautiful golden statue at the end . . ."

"And if you kiss its feet and wish, your wish comes true!" said Winnie.

Uncle Bob threw down his paper in exasperation. "What next! Do you *really* expect me to believe in a golden statue that grants wishes? You must be mad. Go away."

"The men have pushed a great heavy stone in front of the boys' cave," said Penny, in a suddenly trembling voice. "And Punch is hurt. One of the men kicked him. Oh, where's Nicky's father? I MUST get someone to help Nicky and Ken. We saw those horrible men walking down the hillside, but I'm sure they'll soon be back. Winnie, let's go and find *my* Daddy. He'll tell the police, I'm sure he will."

Tears suddenly ran down her cheeks, and Uncle Bob looked at her in surprise. He took her hand. "Penny – listen to me – are you *really* telling the truth? This isn't just another idiotic bit of made-up mystery, is it? You remember the silly coded message I showed you, and told you of – about a meeting in cellars – and stuff hidden on Skylark Hill – and signals from the tower – signed Harry – that the boys made up between them? Well, are you *sure* this isn't another silly bit of nonsense?"

"It wasn't nonsense – it's all *true*!" wept Penny. "It *came* true, I don't know how, but it *did*. And 'Harry' is one of the men; Uncle Bob, if you won't come and help, I'll *have* to go and find Daddy."

"Well – this is about the queerest thing I've ever come across," said Uncle Bob. "How *could* a made-up mystery have any truth in it? All right all right, I'm coming, Penny. Stop crying. I believe you, dear, though I'm blessed if I understand what's happening. Come along – we'll all go back to Skylark Hill."

So, much to the girls' relief, Uncle Bob hurried off with them to Skylark Hill. The birds were singing there, just as they had been on the morning he had been there before, but none of them stayed to listen. The girls were anxious to get back to the boys before the men returned – and Uncle Bob was beginning to feel not only puzzled, but most disturbed. What in the world was going on?

The girls took him to the great gorse bush. "The entrance is right in the middle – there's a hole that goes underground," said Penny. "I saw the men coming from somewhere about here – and Winnie and I looked at a map we have, and it showed an entrance just about here, too – so we hunted till we found it. It's awfully prickly, Uncle Bob."

"Bless us all – what next!" said Uncle Bob, not at all liking the idea of creeping under the great thorny bush, and sliding down underground. "My word – I haven't brought a torch!"

"It's all right – we've one each," said Winnie. "Do hurry – I'm so afraid the men will be back. And they're HORRID, Uncle Bob!"

With many groans, Uncle Bob managed to get down the steps that led into the passage below. The girls switched on their torches, and at once beams of light cut through the darkness.

"This way," said Penny. "We can only go uphill. We pass lots of caves on the way."

Uncle Bob followed the two girls, wondering if he was dreaming! He saw the cave where the tools lay scattered about – he saw the hoard of tins, some opened and empty, some still untouched. And then, in the distance, he heard a noise. He stopped.

"Wait – what's that?" he said.

"It's all right – it's only Punch barking," said Penny. "We'll soon come to the cave where the boys are. Who would have thought that the hill was honeycombed with passages and caves like this, Uncle Bob?"

As soon as Punch began to bark the boys wondered who was coming. Was it the men again? Surely it couldn't be the girls back with help already?

"Wuff-wuff-wuff-wuff!" barked Punch madly, scraping with his paws at the big stone blocking the cave entrance. *He* knew who was coming – he knew those voices as soon as he heard them far away in the distance!

"Here's the cave – and there's the stone the men put in front, that we can't move," said Penny. "NICKY! KEN! We're here, and Uncle Bob's with us! You shove the stone and we'll tug it."

"Hallo, Uncle!" shouted Nicky, in delight. "Come on, now – all together!" And he and Ken shoved at the great stone with all their might, while Uncle tugged and pulled till he was out of breath. The stone moved!

"It's coming!" yelled Penny, doing her bit, too. "Shove again, boys! It's moving!"

The stone gave way so suddenly that the girls and Uncle Bob fell over. The boys crawled out at once, with Punch barking loudly, leaping round on three legs!

"Well!" said Uncle Bob, sitting on the ground, rubbing his grazed hands, for the stone was very rough and hard. "This *is* a do, isn't it! I could hardly believe the story that the girls came and told me. And what's all this about a golden statue?"

"Crawl into this cave, and you'll see a fall of earth near the end of it," said Nicky. "Poke my torch through the hole in the middle of the fall, and see what's beyond!"

Uncle Bob did as he was told, though with much

difficulty – and when he saw the gleaming beauty of the magnificent golden statue, he was so amazed that at first he couldn't say a word.

"Well – what do you think about our pretend mystery *now*?" said Nicky, triumphantly. "We didn't put a golden statue in it – but everything else has come true!"

"I certainly have an apology to make to you all," said Uncle Bob, wriggling out of the cave. "This is a most extraordinary find. I must get on to the police AT ONCE! Come along – let's get back to the town. We oughtn't to lose any time – those men may come back for the other things they found, though probably not till night-time."

Excited, chattering, thrilled to the core, the little party began to make its way down to the great gorse bush. They clambered up the hole one by one, and squeezed through the opening, pricked once more by the bush that guarded it.

And what should they see, as soon as they came into the open, but the three men straggling back up the hill! Harry had his foot bound up now, and was walking with a limp.

"There they are!" yelled Nicky. "LOOK!"

At his shout the men stopped in surprise – then turned tail and made off, Harry limping painfully down the hill. The boys were too stiff to go after them, and the girls too scared. Uncle Bob grabbed hold of Nicky in case he *should* take it into his head to chase them! Punch limped down the hill on three legs, barking, but soon came back.

"Let them go," said Uncle Bob. "The police will soon round them up! You've had enough for one day. My word, what a shock those men must have had, when they saw us all crawling out from their own private entrance!"

CHAPTER 19

An Exciting Finish!

Uncle Bob went down the hill at a quick pace, followed by the four jubilant children. Punch hopped along behind on three legs, his left hind one still very bruised and painful. Nicky turned round to make sure that he was following, and gave a sudden loud exclamation.

"Look! Look what Punch is carrying!"

They all turned – and how they laughed! Punch carried a shoe in his mouth – rather a large one – with a bite right through the leather!

"It's the shoe belonging to Harry, the man that Punch bit!" said Nicky. "Dear old Punch – you *had* to do your shoe trick didn't you – and bring a shoe along somehow? Drop it!"

"No," said Uncle Bob. "It might be useful. Let him carry it. Which man did it belong to?"

"Er – well, I'm afraid you'll think it's queer – but actually it belonged to a one-eyed man called Harry," said Ken. "The man whose name we put at the end of our secret message."

"How extraordinary!" said Uncle Bob. "I'm beginning to think that you and Nicky must be in league with this band of thieves – how else can you possibly know so much about them?"

Everyone laughed. Nicky turned to his uncle. "I say – we never came up at night to listen to the nightingales," he said. "What about it, Uncle? We might find something else peculiar to look into. I can hear a bird singing now – and I'm sure it's carolling something about a golden statue!"

"Ass!" said Uncle Bob. "But my word – that statue really is a marvellous find, you know. There'll probably be a fine reward for that – and you kids will get it!"

This was a most exciting thought! But there wasn't much time to consider it for they were now down in the town. Uncle Bob walked straight to the police station and asked for the superintendent. The children went with him, feeling VERY important.

The superintendent listened in amazement, for he knew Uncle Bob and his work very well. He took rapid notes, telephoned sharply to somebody, called in three of his men, and rapped out some orders.

The children listened in excitement, but couldn't quite understand what was happening. The superintendent turned to them at last, and smiled.

"You've done some very good work!" he said. "I congratulate you. We shall have to ask you to identify these men for us, I'm afraid, once we've caught them, but we will let you know when that happens."

"Yes, sir," said Nicky, thrilled. "And, er – what about the golden statue, sir?"

"Well – we'll see to that at once," said the superintendent, smiling. "I doubt if it's *gold*! I can't say I've ever heard of it myself. But there may be many other quite valuable things in those old cellars – or caves, whatever they are! There must be *something* – or those men wouldn't have gone to so much trouble, digging under the hill. It's likely that the big bearded man you heard called Hassan is one who knew about the cellars and what they might contain – he may even be a descendant of the family of the prince who built the old mansion up on Skylark Hill."

"He ought to have kissed the feet of the statue and wished for sucess," said Winnie. "Then he might have got everything he wanted! Only, of course, he wasn't lucky enough to *find* the statue!"

The superintendent laughed. "Did any of *you* kiss the statue's feet and wish?" he asked.

"NO!" said Nicky. "We're not so silly. But wait a bit – one of us *did!*"

"*Who?*" said the other three children, in astonishment.

"*Punch* did – I saw him licking the feet!" said Nicky. "That's his way of kissing. Punch – what did you wish for?"

"WUFF!" said Punch, at once.

"He says he wished for an enormous, meaty bone," said Nicky, in such a serious voice that the others all laughed. "All right, Punch – your wish will soon come true – granted by the magic power of the Golden Statue! We'll buy you a bone on the way home!"

"WUFF!" said Punch again, delighted.

"Well – I think that's about all for the moment," said the superintendent, smiling. "We'll let you know when we need you again – and that will be when we've rounded up the men."

"Look – Punch is still carrying that shoe he brought from the caves," said Ken, when they were outside the police station. "Uncle Bob – ought we to leave it with the police?"

"Well – let him take it home, and we'll wait till they ask us to go to the police station again," said Uncle Bob. "I don't expect it will be long before we get a call to go. I feel that the superintendent had a very good idea where to look for those men.

Uncle Bob was right. The police went at once to the

next town where they had reason to believe that a small colony of foreigners had made their headquarters a few weeks back. They looked for the men that Nicky and the others had described to them.

But no – not one of the men seemed to resemble the children's descriptions! There was no man with a long dark beard, no man with a dark shade over one eye – and all of them denied knowing anything at all about the old burnt mansion, or the caves in the hillside.

"Well – you will please come along with us for an hour or two, for questioning," said the police officer, and hustled the men into the police van. A car was at once sent to the children's homes, with a message for them to go to the police station, and Uncle Bob, too. They piled into the car in great excitement. Punch went with them, of course!

The men were paraded in front of the four children. But what a disappointment! Not one of them seemed to be like the men they had seen underground – or those the girls had met coming down the hill! Not one had a beard – or wore an eye-shade

But Punch recognized them! He growled and showed his teeth. He strained at the lead and tried to get at one of the scowling men.

"Sir!" cried Nicky to the superintendent, "I believe that man is the one called Harry that kicked Punch and hurt him. He must hav taken off the black eye-shade we saw him wearing. Punch bit right through his shoe, sir, and made his foot bleed – and he even carried home the shoe! The man couldn't wear it, because his bitten foot was bleeding and hurt him. We've brought the shoe with us – just in case it might be useful. Here it is!" And Nicky promptly placed it on the superintendent's table.

The superintendent snapped out a few words, and the man sullenly took off his right shoe and sock. The foot was red and swollen, and teethmarks could be plainly seen. Punch gave a blood-curdling growl, and the man edged away, scared.

"Put this other shoe on – the one the boy brought," ordered the superintendent. "See if it fits."

It did, of course, though the man pretended that he could not get it on!

"It's the same type of shoe that he's wearing now, sir," reported the sergeant who had been watching. "A foreign type, sir. Must be his!"

The man mumbled something angrily, and put on his other shoe again, easing it on gradually because the bite that Punch had given him was still painful. Nicky noticed that his hands were shaking.

One of his friends noticed this too, and took out a packet of cigarettes. He offered it to the big man, who took one thankfully. He was obviously in a state of panic.

Nicky stared at the cigarette packet, and so did Ken. It seemed somehow very familiar! Ken gave a sudden shout.

"*He's* one of the men too, sir – the one with the cigarettes."

"How do you know?" asked the superintendent, astonished.

"Well, look sir – the cigarettes are called Splendour Cigarettes – and we found an empty packet up in that old mansion!"

"Ah!" said the superintendent. "Got the empty packet with you?"

"Yes, sir," said Nicky, and took out the packet from

his pocket. "AND we found an empty match box, sir – and these dead matches. "Quick-Lite matches they're called. I kept them in case they were clues!"

"Well, well, WELL!" said the superintendent, surprised, and he took them from Nicky. "Search the pockets of these men, Sergeant, please."

The men stood sullenly while their pockets were turned out. Aha! Two of them had "Splendour" cigarette packets, and one had a box of "Quick-Lite" matches.

"There you are!" cried Nicky, thrilled. "This is the gang all right, sir. They were probably the signallers up in the tower – they smoked cigarettes and threw down the matches, and the empty box and packet. And the shoe belongs to *that* fellow – he's called Harry. And I'm sure that the biggest fellow is called Hassan. He has shaved off the black beard he wore!"

"You know, my boy, you should be of quite considerable help to your uncle, when you're a little older," said the superintendent, smiling broadly. "Take the men away, Sergeant. I'll deal with them later."

Uncle Bob, the children, and Punch went out feeling very jubilant. Uncle Bob stopped outside a shop.

"I think," he said, "that we should all go in here and celebrate the triumphs of that fine bunch of detectives, Nicky, Ken, Winnie and Penny – to say nothing of that remarkable sleuth, Punch, who knew when to turn a most annoying shoe-fetching trick into a wonderful CLUE. Punch – will you kindly lead the way? There cannot be another dog in the world who can catch a criminal by the simple method of stealing his shoe!"

Everyone laughed. They trooped into the shop, which sold the biggest and creamiest ice creams in the town. Uncle Bob promptly ordered two each.

"What – two for the dog as well?" said the shop girl in amazement.

"Certainly! And bring six bottles of ginger beer," said Uncle Bob.

"Ginger beer for the *dog*, too?" said the shop girl, quite dazed.

"Why not?" said Uncle Bob. "He likes ginger beer so why shouldn't he share in our celebrations? Don't you agree, children?"

"Oh, YES!" said everyone, delighted that their little dog should be honoured. Punch barked joyfully, and ran round giving everyone a loving lick. He had quite forgotten his bad leg.

The ice creams were delicious. The ginger beer fizzed and bubbled in the glasses. Uncle Bob raised his glass and spoke solemnly, with a twinkle in his eye.

"Here's to the 'Mystery-That-Never-Was,' which turned into the 'Mystery-That-Came-True'!" My congratulations to you all – and apologies for disbelieving you. And let's hope the Golden Statue brings you the good luck you all deserve!"

"Hear, hear!" said everyone. And Punch joined in too. "Wuff-wuff-wuff-wuff!" What a time he had had! *What* an adventure!

"All the same," said Ken, solemnly, "it's the very last time I'll *ever* invent a mystery. Honestly – I never *guessed* it would all come true! I'll be jolly careful in future, and so will Nicky!"

No – don't be careful, Ken! Invent another one, and do tell us what happens then!

ENID BLYTON

Mystery Stories

The Secret of Cliff Castle
and
Smuggler Ben

Illustrated by
Rodney Sutton

The Secret of Cliff Castle and *Smuggler Ben*
were first published separately
in 1947 and 1943 respectively
by T. Werner Laurie Ltd
First published in the UK in hardback
in 1976 by William Collins Sons & Co. Ltd
and in Armada in 1982

THE SECRET OF CLIFF CASTLE

CONTENTS

CHAPTER ONE

OFF FOR A HOLIDAY

Peter and Pam leaned out of the railway carriage together and waved goodbye to their mother as their train slowly left the long platform.

"Goodbye, Mother! Goodbye!"

"Be good!" called Mother. "Goodbye! Have a lovely holiday! Give my love to Auntie Hetty."

"I hope Brock will be at the station to meet us," said Peter. "Good old Brock. It will be lovely to see his round, smiling face again."

Brock was their cousin. They were going to stay with him for part of the summer holidays, down in the country village of Rockhurst. Usually they went to the sea, but this summer Mother thought it would be nice for them to be in the country. Then Auntie Hetty had written to invite them for three weeks, and the children had been thrilled.

"We can go to the farm and see all the new animals there," said Pam. "And we can go exploring in the woods and find exciting things there. I hope there are some woods near."

"There are always woods in the country," said Peter. "Anyway, Brock will know all the places to go to. It's fun going to a place we've never been to before!"

The train sped on. It soon left London behind, and green fields took the place of houses and streets. The train was an express, and stopped at very few stations. The children had sandwiches with them, and when Pam's wristwatch showed half-past twelve, Peter undid the parcel Mother had handed them, and took out the packets of food.

"I always feel so hungry in a train, somehow," said Pam. "Oooh – ham sandwiches. How lovely! What's in that other packet, Peter?"

"Biscuits, and two pieces of cake," said Peter, looking to see. "Oh, and two bars of chocolate as well. What a nice lunch. Mother's put in some lemonade, too – it's in that bag, Pam. Get it down."

Pam reached down the leather bag, in which Mother had squeezed a bottle of lemonade and two cardboard cups. Soon the two children were eating a lovely lunch, watching the scenery as it flew by the carriage window.

"We shall arrive at Rockhurst at half-past three," said Peter. "But we've got to change at Deane. We must look out for that."

It was quite easy to change at Deane. A porter came by, calling, "Change here for Rockhurst! Change here for Rockhurst," and out the children hopped with their suitcases. The little train for Rockhurst stood on the other side of the platform, and they simply got out of one train and into the other! It was fun.

"Shan't be long now," said Peter. "You know, Pam, I feel awfully excited. I feel as if we're going to have adventures!"

"I feel that too," said Pam. "But I usually do feel like that when I'm setting out on a holiday."

"So do I," said Peter. "But this time I feel we really are. Proper adventures, I mean. Sort of dangerous, you know!"

"Do you really?" said Pam, feeling all excited too. "Oooh, I hope we do have some. I'd like some. School was so dull last term that I could do with something exciting in the hols!"

"Goodness! Isn't it slow, after the express!" said Pam. "We could almost lean out of the window and pick flowers off the bank!"

Peter laughed. "Well, in another twenty minutes we shall be there," he said. "And then we'll see old Brock."

The time went by, and at exactly half-past three the little train drew in at a small country platform, where red geraniums flared in beds at the back. "Rockhurst!" shouted the one and only porter. "Rockhurst!"

Peter jumped out, and helped Pam down. She looked eagerly up and down the platform, whilst Peter dragged out the two suitcases and the big leather bag. Pam gave a shriek.

"Oh! There's Brock! Brock! Brock! Here we are! Hello!"

Brock came rushing up. He was a tall boy, with a strong body, and a red, smiling face. His eyes shone very blue in the sunshine as he greeted his cousins. He was twelve, the same age as Peter, but stronger and taller. Pam was eleven, smaller than either of the boys.

Brock clapped his cousins on the back, and grinned at them. "Hello! Glad to see you both! Welcome to Rockhurst!"

"Hello!" said Peter, smiling. "It's fine to see you, Brock. Golly, you've grown awfully tall since we saw you last year. You make me feel quite small."

"Come on," said Brock, taking one of the suitcases. "Mother's outside with the pony-cart. It'll just about take us all, though we'll have to put our feet on these cases."

They gave up their tickets, and went out of the station, chattering hard. Pam called out to her aunt, in delight, "Hello, Aunt Hetty! Here we are! It *is* nice of you to come and meet us."

"Hello, my dears," said their aunt. "Glad to see you. Climb into the cart. Brock, hand up the cases first, and I'll pack them under our feet."

Soon the four of them were driving swiftly along the country lanes. Sally, the pony, was a smart little beast, and cantered along merrily. The sun shone down, and everything looked gay and holiday-like. The children felt very happy.

They soon arrived at Brock's home. It was a comfortable-looking house, rather rambling, set in a nice big garden. The children liked the look of it very much.

"It's a friendly sort of house, isn't it?" said Pam. "Oh, Aunt Hetty, isn't the beginning of a holiday exciting?"

"Very exciting!" said their aunt. "Quite the most exciting part of a holiday, I always think."

"But it isn't going to be the most exciting part of *this* holiday!" said Peter, as the pony trotted in at the gate and came to a standstill in front of the house. "I've got a funny feeling about this holiday. It's going to be exciting all the way through!"

"What do you mean?" asked Brock in surprise.

"I don't exactly know," said Peter, jumping down, and helping his aunt out. "But I've got a feeling! You just wait and see!"

"Well, I hope your feeling is right!" said Brock, and they all went into the house.

CHAPTER TWO

A LITTLE EXPLORING

Tea was ready when they got indoors. The children washed their hands and brushed their hair. Peter was sharing Brock's little room, and Pam had a tiny room to herself up in the attic. She loved it because it had peculiar, slanting ceilings, and funny, uneven boards in the floor. She looked out of the window as she brushed her hair, humming a little tune to herself because she was so happy.

The countryside lay smiling in the afternoon sunshine. Cottages clustered together here and there, and cattle grazed in the fields. In the distance, a curious, steep hill caught her eye. It rose up very suddenly, and at the top was a strange building. It looked like a small, square castle, for it had towers at each end.

"I wonder if anyone lives there," thought Pam. "It looks sort of deserted, somehow. I'll ask Brock about it."

Downstairs, round the tea table, Brock and his cousins chattered nineteen to the dozen about everything, telling each other all their news. Aunt Hetty smiled as she listened, and handed round her plates of home-made scones with jam, and new ginger buns, and currant pasties.

"Anyone would think you hadn't had anything to eat since breakfast-time," she said, as one after another the plates were emptied.

"Well, we did have a good lunch on the train," said Peter, "but it seems ages ago now. I do like these buns, Aunt Hetty. They're the nicest I've ever tasted."

"Shall we go out and explore round a bit, after tea?" said Pam. "I'm longing to. I saw the farm not far off, Brock – and what is that strange sort of castle on the top of that very steep hill towards the west?"

"Oh, that's Cliff Castle," said Brock. "It's called that because it's built on that steep hill, which falls away behind the castle in a kind of cliff."

"Does anyone live there?" asked Peter.

"Not now," said Brock. "Mother, who lived there, years ago?"

"Oh, I don't really know," said Mother. "It belonged to a strange old man who wanted to live quite alone. So he built himself that castle, and lived there with two old servants, as strange as himself. He spent a fortune on the castle. When he died, he left a will which said the castle was to be left exactly as it was, cared for by the two old servants till they died. Then it was to go to some great-nephew, who has never bothered to live there – or even to go and visit the castle, as far as I know."

"Is it really a castle?" said Pam.

"No, not really," said Aunt Hetty. "But it's built to appear like one, as you see – and I believe the walls are almost as thick as a real old castle's would be. People do say that there are secret passages in it, but I don't believe that. What would a lonely old man want with secret passages! That's just make believe."

The children stared out of the window at the lonely castle on the top of the steep hill. It suddenly seemed very mysterious and exciting to them. It stood there, with the sinking sun behind it, and looked rather black and forbidding.

"Is it quite empty then, Aunt Hetty?" asked Pam.

"Quite," said her aunt. "It must be in a dreadful mess by now, too, I should think, for nobody has dusted it for years, or lighted a fire there to warm the place. The furniture must be mouldy and rotten. Not a nice place to visit at all!"

Peter and Pam looked at one another. It seemed to them that their aunt was quite wrong. It would be a wonderfully exciting place to visit! If only they could!

After tea, they spoke to Brock about it. "Brock! Will you take us to see Cliff Castle one day soon? Tomorrow, perhaps. It does sound so exciting – and it looks so strange and lonely. We'd simply love to explore round about it."

"We'll go tomorrow!" said Brock. "But come and see our garden now – and the farm. We've plenty of time."

So the three of them went over Brock's big garden, and admired the vegetables, the outdoor tomatoes, the peaches on the wall, and everything. They saw Brock's exciting playhouse in the garden, too, set all by itself out of sight of the house.

"Daddy had this built for me to take my friends to, when we wanted to play by ourselves," said Brock. "You know, Mother doesn't like a lot of noise, and boys can't help being rowdy, can they? So I just take my friends to my playhouse when we want a good old game – and we don't disturb Mother a bit! We can play out here on rainy days, too. It will be fun."

Peter and Pam liked Brock's playhouse. It was a small, sturdy, little wooden house with a red door, and windows each side. Inside there was one big room, and around it were spread all Brock's possessions – a small gramophone, a big meccano set, boxes and boxes of railway lines, engines, trucks, signals, and other things belonging to a railway – and on a bookshelf were scores of exciting-looking books.

"You *are* lucky, Brock!" said Peter, looking round. "This is a lovely place."

"Yes – we'll come here and talk when we want to be all by ourselves," said Brock. "Nobody can see us or hear us. It's our own private place."

They went to see the farm, too – and then the sun sank so low that it was time to go back home to supper. The strange castle on the hill showed up clearly as they went down the farm lane back to their house.

"Brock, do take us to Cliff Castle tomorrow," said Peter. "It would really be marvellous fun to explore it. Haven't you ever been there yourself?"

"I haven't been very near it," said Brock. "I somehow never liked the look of it very much, you know. I think it's got rather a wicked look!"

"It has, rather," said Peter. "Anyway, do let's go tomorrow!"

"All right," said Brock. "I shan't mind going with you – though I've never wanted to go alone!"

It was fun going to bed that night in a strange bedroom. The two boys talked till late, and Brock's mother had to go in twice to stop them. Pam could hear their voices as she lay in bed, and she wished she was with the two boys so that she might hear what they said.

She fell asleep, and did not wake until the house was all in a bustle with its early morning cleaning. She heard the two boys talking below in loud voices, and she jumped out of bed at once.

"It's holiday-time – and we're at Brock's – and we're going exploring today!" she hummed to herself, as she dressed quickly. She ran downstairs to breakfast feeling very hungry.

"What are you going to do today?" asked Aunt Hetty, pouring out the tea.

"We're going over to Cliff Castle," said Brock. "Can we take sandwiches, Mother, and have a picnic?"

"All right," said his mother. "You must all make your beds, and tidy your rooms, please, before you go. I'll get you some lunch ready whilst you do that."

It wasn't long after breakfast before the three children were ready to set out. Brock's mother had been very generous with the picnic lunch. She had cut them potted meat sandwiches, tomato sandwiches, and egg sandwiches, and had put some buttered scones, some ginger buns, and some boiled sweets into the packets, too.

"There's a tiny shop, not far from Cliff Castle, where you can buy yourselves something to drink," she said. "Here is some money for that. Now – off you go!"

They set off happily. Brock knew the way, though it was rather a roundabout one, down narrow little lanes, through a small wood, and then across some fields. It was eleven o'clock by the time they got to the little shop where they wanted to buy drinks.

"I'm so thirsty already that I could drink about twelve bottles of lemonade straight off!" said Peter.

"Well, don't let's drink all of it straightaway," said Brock. "The woman here has a well – look, there it is, with the bucket beside it. Let's ask her if we can have a drink of cold water – then we can save up the lemonade!"

The woman said that of course they could use her well water. "Have a whole bucketful, if you like!" she said. But they couldn't quite manage that. They sent down the bucket, and it came up filled with silvery water.

"It's absolutely ice-cold!" said Pam, gasping a little at the coldness. "But it's simply lovely."

"Where are you off to?" asked the woman, handing out three small bottles of lemonade.

"To explore round about Cliff Castle," said Peter.

"Oh, I wouldn't do that," said the woman. "Really, I wouldn't. It's a strange place. And people do say that funny lights have been seen there lately. Well, that's very strange, isn't it, in a place that's been empty for years?"

"Most peculiar," said Brock, staring at the woman, and feeling rather excited. "What sort of lights?"

"I don't know," said the woman. "I only know I wouldn't go near that place in the dark, or in the daytime either! There's always been something odd about it – and there is still!"

The children said goodbye and went out of the tiny,

dark shop. They stared up at the nearby hill, on the top of which stood Cliff Castle. It looked much bigger now that they were near it. It had funny little slit-like windows, just like very old castles had. It certainly was a peculiar place for anyone to build in days when castles were no longer of any use!

"Well, come on," said Brock, at last. "Don't let's be put off by silly village stories. Mother says stories always get made up about any deserted place."

"They certainly make it more exciting," said Peter, hitching his kitbag full of lunch over his other shoulder. "Well – up the hill we go!"

And up the hill they went. There was no proper road up the steep hill, only a small, narrow path that wound between jutting-out rocks, for it was a very rocky part of the countryside. Stunted bushes grew on the hillside, mostly of gorse. It was exposed to the east winds, and nothing very much grew there.

"Well – here we are!" said Brock, at last. "Cliff Castle! I wonder what we shall find there!"

CHAPTER THREE

CLIFF CASTLE

Now that the children were right up to the castle, it looked enormous! It rose up in front of them, square and sturdy, a tower at each end. Its small, slit-like windows had no glass in. The great front door was studded with big nails that had gone rusty. There was a large knocker, which the children longed to use – but which, of course, they dared not touch!

"Let's go all the way round the castle and see what we can see," said Pam.

So they went down the great flight of steps again, and began to make their way round the towering walls of the strange castle. It was difficult, because creepers, bushes and weeds grew high up the walls. Tall nettles stood in great patches, and the children had to make their way round them after Pam was badly stung on her bare legs.

"We'll find some dock leaves to help the stings," said Peter, and he found a patch of dark green dock leaves. He picked some and Pam pressed the cool leaves against her burning skin.

"That's better," she said. "Gracious, I shan't go near nettles again today!"

They went on their way round the great grey walls. The slit-like windows were placed at regular intervals. The children gazed up at them.

"You know, in the olden days, they had those funny narrow windows so that archers could shoot their arrows out without being hit themselves," said Brock rather learnedly. "I can't imagine why the old man should have built windows like that for himself, long after the time of bows and arrows had gone! It must make the rooms inside awfully dark."

"I wish we could see them, don't you?" said Pam excitedly. "Just imagine how strange they would look after all these years when nobody has been here – cobwebs all over the place – dust everywhere. Oooh – it would be awfully odd."

They could not go all round the castle, because, when they came to the side that faced due west, the hill fell away so steeply that it was impossible to go any farther. The walls of the castle were built almost sheer with the hillside, and there was a very big drop down to the bottom of the hills below.

"Let's have our lunch now," said Peter, all at once

feeling terribly hungry. "It's almost time. We can find a nice place out of the hot sun and sit down, can't we?"

"Rather!" said Brock, feeling hungry too. "Look – what about that shady bit over there, facing the castle? We can look at the castle whilst we're eating."

They sat down in the shady spot, and undid all they had to eat. It had seemed a lot when Brock's mother had packed it up – but it didn't seem nearly so much when three hungry children began to eat it. They unscrewed the tops of the lemonade bottles, and drank eagerly. Except that the lemonade tasted a little warm, it was delicious.

Pam finished her lunch first, because she did not want so much as the boys, and gave some of hers to them to finish up. She lay back against a tree and looked up at the silent grey castle.

She looked at the narrow windows and began to count them. When she came to the second row, she spoke out loud: "Look, Peter; look, Brock – there's a window in the second row up that is bigger than the others. I wonder why."

The boys looked up. Peter screwed up his eyes to see why the window should be bigger.

"I don't think it's meant to be bigger," he said, at last. "I think the weather has sort of eaten it away. It looks to me as if the bottom part of it has crumbled away. Perhaps a pipe comes out just there, and has leaked down the window and made the stone and brickwork rotten."

"Do you see the tree that grows up to that window?" said Brock, in sudden excitement. "I believe we could climb it and look in at that window! I wonder what we should see if we did!"

Peter and Pam stared at him, and then at the tree that grew up to the window. What fun it would be if they really could climb it and have a peep inside the castle!

"Well, let's see if we can peep inside any of the lower windows first," said Peter. "I don't think Aunt Hetty would be awfully pleased with us if we climbed trees in these clothes. We really want old clothes for that."

"Oh, bother our clothes!" said Brock, his red face shining with excitement. "I vote we climb up! But we'll have a peep in at one of the lower windows first. Peter, you come and give me a leg up."

It wasn't long before Peter was bending down, heaving Brock up to the narrow windowsill to see inside the slit-like window. Brock peered through, but could see nothing at all.

"It's so dark inside," he said. "It wouldn't be so bad if the sun wasn't so brilliant today – but my eyes just simply can't see a thing inside the darkness of the castle."

"Well, we'll climb the tree then!" cried Pam, running to it. She loved climbing trees as much as the boys did.

"Wait a bit, Pam," cried Brock. "Peter and I will go up first, and give you a hand. You're only a girl, you know."

It always made Pam cross to be told she was only a girl. "I'm as strong as you are, anyway!" she cried, and looked about for an easy way to climb.

But Brock was up the tree before either of the others. He was a country boy, used to climbing, and he saw at once the best way to go up. He was soon lost to sight among the greenery.

His voice came down to them: "Go up the way I did. It's not difficult."

Peter followed him, and then Pam. Pam had to have a hand from Peter every now and again, and she was glad of it. They were soon all of them up on a high branch beside Brock. He grinned at them.

"Good climbing!" he said. "Now, look – see this branch? It reaches right to that window. It's pretty strong, and I think it will bear us all. But we'd better go one at a time, in case it doesn't."

"You go first, then," said Peter. Brock edged his way along the branch, working carefully with his arms and legs. The bough bent beneath his weight and swung down below the windowsill. Brock came back.

"No good," he said. "We'll try the next branch. That looks a good deal stronger – and although it grows right above the window at its tip, our weight will bend it down till it rests almost on the windowsill, I should think."

They all climbed a little higher. Then Brock worked his way along the next branch. As he said, his weight bent it gradually down, and by the time he was at the end of it, its tip rested on the sill itself. Part of it even went right through the window-opening into the castle.

"Fine!" said Brock. He put one leg across the stone windowsill, and peered into the slit. He could see nothing but darkness. But certainly the weather had worn away the stone around that window, for the opening was almost big enough to take Brock's stout body!

"I believe I could get right inside!" he called to the others. He stood upright on the sill and tried to work his way in. It was a very tight fit, for Brock was not thin! He had to squeeze himself in till he almost burst.

He found that the wall was very thick – about a yard thick, before he had got right through the window. Then he jumped down to the floor inside and called out through the slit: "Come on! It's not very difficult! We'll be able to explore the castle from top to bottom, if you can get through!"

CHAPTER FOUR

INSIDE THE CASTLE

Pam felt a little nervous about going right into the castle, but she couldn't hold back if the boys thought it was all right. So she followed Peter when he squeezed himself through the slit in the stone walls, and held his hand tightly when he gave it to her to jump down into the darkness.

Two slit-like windows lighted the room they were in. It seemed as dark as night to the children when they first looked round – but their eyes soon grew accustomed to it, and they began to see quite well. Shafts of bright sunlight lighted up the room in two places – the rest seemed rather dark.

They stared round, and then Pam cried out in disappointment: "Oh – the room is empty! It's just like a prison cell! There's absolutely nothing here!"

She was right. There was nothing to see at all, except for bare walls, bare floor, and bare ceiling. At the far side was a closed door, big and strong. It had an iron handle. Brock went over to it.

"Well, we may be unlucky in this room, finding nothing to see," he said, "but maybe there will be plenty to see somewhere else! Let's open this door and explore!"

He pulled at the door by the great iron handle. It opened! Outside was a dark passage. Brock felt in his pockets, remembering that he had a torch somewhere. He found it, and switched it on.

The passage led from a narrow stone stairway, and seemed to wind round a corner. "Come on," said Brock. "This way! We'll open a few doors and see what there is to be seen."

He opened a door nearby. But again there was nothing to be seen but bareness. He shut the door, and the noise echoed through the stone castle in a very strange way. It sounded as though dozens of doors were being shut, one after another. Pam shivered.

"Oooh!" she said. "It's not nice to make a noise in this place. Even a little sound echoes round like thunder."

No room just there had anything in it at all. It was most disappointing. Brock then led the way to the stone staircase. It wound downwards in the heart of the castle, and as it came towards the bottom, grew a little wider.

It ended in a vast room with an enormous fireplace at one end. "This must be the kitchen," said Pam in surprise. "And I suppose those stairs we came down were the back stairs. There must be a bigger flight somewhere else. I did think they were very narrow stairs for such a huge castle."

The kitchen was furnished. There was a big wooden table, and around it were set stout wooden chairs. Pots and pans hung around the stove. There was an iron pot hanging over what had once been a fire. Brock peered into it. There was an evil-smelling, dark liquid in it.

"Something made by witches!" he said, in a deep, mournful voice that made Pam jump. Brock laughed. "It's all right," he said. "It's only some soup, or something gone bad after all these years!"

The kitchen was dark and dirty, and there was not much to be seen there. The children went out of it and came into a great hall from which four doors led off. Brock opened one.

And then, indeed, there was something to be seen! The big room beyond the door was furnished most magnificently! Great couches, carved chairs, cabinets, tables – all these stood about the room just as they had been left! But how mournful they looked, for they were adorned with great spiders' webs, and when the children walked into the room, clouds of fine grey dust flew up from their feet.

Sunlight came in long golden shafts through four of the slit-like windows, and divided the room into quarters. It made the whole room even stranger than it might have been, for the brilliance of the sunlight lay in sharp contrast to the blackness of the shadows in the far corners.

"Oooh! What an enormous spider!" said Pam, with a

shudder, as a great eight-legged spider ran out from under a table. The boys didn't mind spiders. They didn't even mind walking into the cobwebs that hung here and there from the enormous chandeliers that had once held dozens of candles to light the room. But Pam couldn't bear the strange, light touch of the webs on her hair, and longed to get out into the sunshine again.

"Isn't it odd, to have left everything just like this?" said Brock wonderingly. "Look at those curtains. They must once have been simply gorgeous – but now they are all faded and dusty."

He touched one – and it fell to pieces in his hand. It was almost as if someone had breathed on it and made it melt!

"The brocade on the furniture is all rotten, too," said Pam, as she felt it. It shredded away under her fingers. "Everything is moth-eaten. What a horrid, sad place this feels. I don't like it. Let's get away."

"No – we'll explore first," said Peter. "Don't be a spoilsport, Pam. Come with us. You'll be quite all right."

Pam didn't want to be a spoilsport, so she followed the boys rather unwillingly as they went out of the room and into the next.

The same things were found there – furniture and curtains, rotten and decayed. A musty smell hung over everything. It was most unpleasant. Pam began to feel sick.

"I hate this smell," she said, "and I hate walking into these horrid webs. I can't seem to see them and it's horrid to get them all round my head."

"Let's go upstairs again," said Brock. "And this time we'll go up by the main stairway – look, that great flight of steps over there – not by the little narrow back staircase we came down."

They mounted the enormous stone steps, and came to some big rooms furnished as bedrooms. Up they went again and came to more rooms. Leading out of one of them was a tiny staircase all on its own. It wound up into one of the stone towers that stood at the end of the castle.

"Let's go up this staircase!" cried Peter. "We shall get a marvellous view over the countryside!"

So up they went and came to the open door of a strange, square little room that seemed to be cut right out of the heart of the tower. A tiny slit on each side lighted it. A stone bench ran round the walls, but otherwise there was nothing in the room.

"What a wonderful view!" cried Pam, peering out of one of the slits. She saw the whole of the countryside to the east lying smiling in the hot August sun. It looked marvellous.

"I can see our house!" cried Brock. "Over there, beyond the farm. Oh, how tiny it looks! And how small the cows and horses look, too. Like animals on a toy farm."

So they did. It was fun to peer out and see everything from so high up. But soon the children grew tired of it and thought they would go downstairs again.

So down they went, and then paused on the first floor where they had first squeezed in through the window. But somehow they couldn't find the room they had climbed inside! It was strange. They opened door after door, but no, there wasn't a tree outside a window.

"I've lost my bearings," said Peter, at last. "I've no idea where that room was. Well, if we don't want to stay here all night we've got to get out somehow! I vote we go right downstairs into the hall, then make our way to the kitchen, and up that back stairway again. We know the room was somewhere near the top of that."

So down they went, into the hall, into the kitchen, and then towards the back stairway.

But just near the stairway was a small door, very low, set in the wall. The children stared at it. They hadn't noticed it before.

"Perhaps we could open this and get out by it," said Peter. "It would save us all that big climb down the tree. I tried the front door to see if we could get out by that, but it was much too heavy. The bolts had all rusted into the door, and I couldn't even turn the handle. Let's try this funny little door."

"It's so low we'll have to bend down to get out of it!" said Brock, with a laugh. They went to the little door and looked at it. It was latched on the inside, but not bolted or locked, though the key stood in the door. Peter lifted the latch.

After a push, the door opened a little way, and then stuck fast. The two boys together pushed hard. It opened just a little farther, and sunshine came through.

Peter put his head round the edge. "There's a great patch of nettles and a gorse bush preventing it from opening," he said. "Got a knife, Brock? I believe if I hacked away at this gorse bush a bit I could make the door open enough to let us out!"

Brock passed him a fierce-looking knife. Peter hacked at the bush, and cut off the pieces that were stopping the door from opening.

"Cut away the nettles, too," begged Pam. "My legs still sting from that other patch we went into."

. . . Just near the stairway was a small door

Peter did his best. Then he and Brock were able to push the door open just enough to let them squeeze through one by one. They were all rather glad to be standing out in the bright sunshine again, after the dim, musty darkness of the silent castle.

"I say – if we just push this door to, and leave it like that, not locked or bolted, we shall be able to get in whenever we want to!" said Peter. "We might find it rather fun to come and play smugglers or something here. We could pile weeds against the door so that nobody else would notice it."

"Good idea!" said Brock. So they shut the door gently, then forced the gorse bush back against it, and pulled pieces from a nearby hedge to throw against the door to hide it.

Pam got stung again by the nettles, and almost cried with the pain. Peter had to hunt for dock leaves again!

"Cheer up!" he said. "What do a few nettle-stings matter? We've had quite an adventure this afternoon! We'll come back here again soon and have a fine time."

Pam wasn't sure she wanted to. But she didn't say so! The boys talked eagerly about the afternoon's excitement on the way home – and by the time they reached the house, Pam had begun to think that nettle-stings or no nettle-stings, it had all been simply marvellous!

CHAPTER FIVE

IN THE MIDDLE OF THE NIGHT

The next day Aunt Hetty took Pam and Peter and their cousin Brock in the pony-cart to the sea, which was about three miles away. This was such fun that the three children forgot all about Cliff Castle for a day or two. And then something happened that reminded them of it.

It was something that happened in the middle of the night. Pam woke up and felt very thirsty. She remembered that Aunt Hetty had left a jug of water and a tumbler on the mantelpiece and she got up to get it.

She stood at the window, drinking the water. It was a moonlit night, but the moon kept going behind clouds.

It showed up Cliff Castle very clearly, when it shone down. But when it went behind the clouds the castle was just a black mass on the hill.

Then Pam saw something flickering quickly somewhere at the top of the castle. It caught her eye for a second and then disappeared. What could it be?

She stood watching the castle, forgetting to drink the cool water. Then the flicker came again, this time farther down the castle. Then it disappeared once more. It came for the third and last time at the bottom.

Pam felt excited. She remembered what the woman at the little shop had said about strange lights being seen in the castle. Now here they were again – and they were real, because Pam had seen them!

"I really must wake the boys and tell them!" she thought. "I know it isn't a dream now – but in the morning I might think it was, and not tell them. But it isn't a dream, I've seen the lights!"

She crept down the stairs and into the open door of the boys' room. They were both sleeping peacefully. Pam shook Peter and he woke up with a jump.

"What is it?" he said loudly, sitting up in bed, surprised to see that it was night.

"Sh!" said Pam. "It's me, Peter. Listen – I got up to get a drink of water – and I saw lights in Cliff Castle!"

"Golly!" said Peter, jumping out of bed and going to the window. "Did you really? I say – let's wake Brock."

But Brock was already awake, disturbed by the noise. He was soon told what the matter was, and went to the window, too. All three watched for a little time – and then, suddenly, a light flickered again, this time at the bottom of the castle.

"There it is!" said Pam, clutching Peter and making him jump almost out of his skin. "Did you see it?"

"Of course," said Peter. "And there it is again – the first floor somewhere this time – and there again, higher up – and now it's right at the very top. Somewhere in that tower, look. It's the very tower we were in the other day!"

Pam felt a bit frightened. Who could be in the castle so late at night? The children watched for a little longer and then went back to bed, puzzled and excited.

"I vote we go there tomorrow again, and see if there's anyone there," said Brock. Nothing ever frightened Brock, and nothing ever stopped him from smiling! He meant to find out the secret of Cliff Castle as soon as possible!

So the next day three excited children met in Brock's playhouse in the garden to discuss their plans. They all felt certain that somebody was living in, or visiting, the castle – someone who had no right to be there. Who could it be – and why did he go there?

"When can we go?" asked Peter eagerly.

"After dinner," said Brock. "We're going over to the market this morning, in the next town. We don't want to miss that. It's fun. Dad will take us in his car."

So it was not until after the three children had been to the market, and had come back and eaten a most enormous dinner that they set off to Cliff Castle once again.

They stopped at the little shop where once before they had bought lemonade. The woman served them again with sweet drinks, which they drank in the shop.

"Any more been heard about the lights in Cliff

Castle?" they asked the woman, when they paid her. She shook her head.

"Not that I know of," she said. "But don't you go wandering about there, my dears. It's a dangerous place."

They went off again, and soon came near the castle, which towered above them on its hill. They climbed the hill by the narrow rocky path and came to the big flight of overgrown stone steps.

"We won't go up the steps, in case there really is somebody in the castle, watching," said Peter. "We'll try and find that tiny little door. You know – the one we left latched."

So they made their way around nettle patches and other weeds until they came to where the little low door was set in the thick stone walls. The branches they had pulled from the nearby hedge were still against it. Nobody had disturbed them.

They pulled at the door, lifting the iron latch as they did so. It opened silently, and the children squeezed through, shutting it after them. They stood in the big kitchen, so dark and musty, shining their torches all around.

There was nothing new to be seen. They crossed the kitchen and went out into the hall – and here Brock gave a cry of surprise, and levelled his torch steadily on something on the ground.

The others looked. Pam couldn't make out why Brock was so excited, because all she saw were footprints crossing and recrossing the floor – and, after all, they had all walked there themselves last time!

"What's the matter?" she said.

"Can't you see, silly?" said Peter, pointing to a set of

footprints that went across the floor. "Look at those. Those are not our marks. None of us have feet as big as that, and certainly we don't wear boots studded with nails. You can see the mark the nails have made in the thick dust."

Pam and the others stared at the marks. Yes – it was quite plain that somebody grown-up had walked across that floor. Brock found another track and shone his torch on it.

"*Two* men have been here," he said thoughtfully. "Look – this set of prints shows a narrower foot than the other. Now, I wonder whatever two men were doing here?"

The children stared at one another. They couldn't imagine why men should visit the castle in the middle of the night. Perhaps they had come to steal something?

"Let's look in the rooms down here and see if anything has been disturbed," said Brock, at last. So they opened the nearest door and looked into the room there, still festooned with cobwebs, and still smelling of the same horrid, musty smell.

"Nothing has been moved," said Brock. "And there are only *our* footprints here. No one else's. Let's follow these other prints and see where they go. They show very clearly, don't they?"

They did show clearly in the thick dust. It was fairly easy to sort them out from the tracks the children themselves had made, for the men's prints were large and had made more impression in the dust. The children followed the prints up the big stairway to the first floor. There, neatly outlined in the dust, was something else!

"Look at that big oblong shape marked in the dust!"

said Brock. "It looks as if someone had put down a big box there, doesn't it?"

"Yes," said Peter. "And look – there's the mark of another box, or something, farther along. It looks as if the men had been carrying something very heavy up the stairs, and had put their load down for a rest before going on. See how their footprints are muddled here, too, as if they had picked up their load again and gone on carrying farther along."

"I feel rather like a detective!" said Pam excitedly. "Tracking things like this! I wonder where the men took their loads to! I expect that explains the lights we saw last night. The men had torches, and every time they passed one of those slit-like windows, the reflection shone out for a moment, like a flicker. I guess they didn't know that!"

"Come on," said Brock impatiently. "Let's follow on."

They went on, past many closed doors and up another flight of stone steps. This brought them to the second floor. The footprints still went on!

"I believe they're going up to that tower!" said Pam. "We saw the light flicker there, you know. Oh – I hope the men aren't hiding there!"

This made the boys stop hurriedly. They hadn't thought of that! Suppose somebody was up there in the tower? That wouldn't be very pleasant, because they would be sure to be angry to see children interfering.

"We'd better go very quietly indeed, and not speak a word!" said Brock in a whisper. "Come on."

So in complete silence, their hearts beating fast, the three children crept on and up until they came to the room where the little stone staircase led up into the tower. They mounted it quietly, seeing the men's foot-prints still on the steps.

They came to the wooden door that had been open the first time they had gone up the staircase. This time it was shut!

CHAPTER SIX

A PUZZLE

"It's shut!" whispered Brock. "Shall I try and open it?"

"No!" said Pam.

"Yes!" said Peter. Pam clutched Peter's hand. She didn't know what she expected to find behind that closed door, but she felt certain it wouldn't be nice! The boys felt that they really *must* push the door open. They were bursting with curiosity. Brock pushed. It didn't open. He took hold of the iron handle and tried to turn it. It turned – but still the door didn't open.

"Look through the keyhole and see if you can see anything," said Peter eagerly. "It's so big that maybe you can."

Brock put his eye to the keyhole. "It's all so dark," he said, "but I believe I can make out shapes of boxes and things. You take a peep, Peter."

So first Peter and then Pam peered through the keyhole, and they both agreed that certainly there were things there that hadn't been there before. They couldn't possibly see if they were boxes or trunks, or what they were, but there *were* things hidden there.

"If only we could get inside and see what's there!" said Brock longingly. "Something that ought not to be there, I'm sure!"

The castle was so silent and lonely, and the sound of their whispering voices was so peculiar, echoing down the stone stairway, that Pam felt nervous again. She pulled at Peter's arm.

"Let's go," she said. "We'll come back another time. Shall we tell anyone about what we know?"

"I don't think so," said Brock. "It's our own mystery. We've discovered it. Let's try and solve it ourselves. We often read about secrets and mysteries in books – it would be fun to try and keep this one all to ourselves."

They went downstairs again, puzzled to know what was in the tower, and why it was locked. When they got into the hall, Brock switched his torch towards the front door.

"I suppose the men came in at the front," he began – and then, he suddenly stopped. "Look!" he said. "There are no footsteps leading from the front door. Isn't that strange? How did the men get in, then?"

The three children stared in silence at the enormous door. Certainly the men had not used it. Then which door had they used? As far as the children knew there was only one other door, and that was the little low one they themselves had used. They felt quite certain that the men had not used the window above, where the tree touched, because it was as much as the three children could do to squeeze inside there. No grown-up could possibly manage it.

"Let's follow all the footprints and see where they lead from," said Brock. "If we follow them all, we are sure to come to where the men entered."

So, their torches directed on the ground, the children followed the tracks patiently, one after another. They couldn't understand one lot of tracks at all. They apparently led to, and came from, a room that had once been used as a study. The footprints went in and out of the door – there was a double-track, one going and one coming – and led across the room to the big fireplace, and back again.

"Why did the men come into this room, and out again?" said Pam, puzzled. "They don't seem to have touched anything here. Why did they come here?"

"Goodness knows," said Brock, switching off his torch. "Just idle curiosity, or something, I suppose. There doesn't seem anything for them to come for, here. I say – look at the time. We shall be awfully late for tea!"

"We'd better go, then," said Peter, who, although he wanted his tea, didn't want to leave the mystery unsolved like that. "Come on. We'll come back again soon."

They went into the kitchen and out of the little, low door. They pushed it to behind them, and piled the boughs against it, dragging the gorse bush round again. It hid the door well.

"I hope the men aren't as smart as we are!" said Brock, looking back at the castle. "We've left plenty of footprints there for them to see. They could easily tell that three children have been wandering about."

"I only wish I knew how the men got in and went out," said Peter, still worrying about that. "I feel sure there must be something in that room we last went into to account for their coming and going."

But it wasn't until late that night, when Peter was in bed, that he suddenly thought of something most exciting! Why ever hadn't he thought of it before? He sat up in bed and called Brock's name in such an urgent voice that Brock, half-asleep, woke up in a hurry.

"What's up?" he said. "More lights showing in Cliff Castle?"

"No," said Peter. "But I believe I know how the men got in and out, Brock!"

"You don't!" said Brock.

"Well, listen – you know that often there were secret ways made into and behind rooms through the big chimneys they had in the old days," said Peter. "Well, I believe there must be some kind of way into that room – and that's how the men got into the castle!"

"Crumbs!" said Brock, wide awake now. "I never thought of that. I wonder if you're right. Maybe there's a secret entrance, then!"

"We'll jolly well go tomorrow and find out!" said Peter, "even if we all get as black as sweeps exploring that chimney! What ho for a real adventure tomorrow!"

The two boys told Pam their idea in the morning, and the girl's eyes shone as she listened.

"Gracious! Do you really think there might be a secret way in and out of the castle through that big chimney-place? It's certainly enormous. I looked up it and it would take two or three men easily!"

To their great disappointment the children could not go that day to the castle, because Brock's mother had planned a picnic for them. She was surprised when the three children did not seem pleased about it.

Next day the three children set off once more to the castle. They knew the way very well now and took a few short cuts so that it did not take them very long to arrive at the bottom of the hill. They stared up at the great castle, and it seemed to look down on them with a frown.

"Frown all you like!" said Brock, with a grin. "We'll find out your secret one day!"

They made their way to the little low door they knew and pulled it open. Into the vast kitchen they went, quite silently. Brock switched on his torch to see if there were any more footsteps to be seen. But there were none. In the hall and up the stairs were the same sets of prints that had been there before – there were no new ones, so far as the children could see.

"The men haven't been here again," said Brock. "Come on – let's go into that room where the prints led to and from the fireplace."

So into it they went, and followed the sets of prints to the big, open chimneyplace. This was of stone, and the three children could easily stand upright in it!

"Now, we'll just have a hunt and see if, by any chance, there's a way out of the chimney itself," said Brock, and he switched his torch on to examine the stonework.

"Look!" cried Pam, pointing to something that ran up one side of the stone chimney. "A little iron ladder!"

The three of them stared at the little ladder. In the middle of each rung the rust had been worn away a little. "That's where the men went up and down!" cried Brock. "Come on – up we go! We're on to something here!"

CHAPTER SEVEN

A STRANGE PASSAGE

Brock went first up the little iron ladder. Peter followed, and then Pam. The ladder went up some way, and then ended.

"It's come to an end!" cried Brock. "But there's a broad ledge here. I'll give you a hand up, Peter."

He pulled Peter up on to the stone ledge, and then the two boys pulled Pam up beside them. The ledge was broad enough to hold all the children quite comfortably.

"This funny ledge seems to have been made about halfway up the chimney, just before it begins to get very narrow," said Brock, pointing his torch upwards, and showing the others how the chimney suddenly narrowed just above their head. "We couldn't have gone up much farther, even if there had been a ladder."

"Well, what did the men do?" said Pam, puzzled. "Surely they didn't just come to this ledge and go back?"

"Of course not!" said Brock. "This is where we use our brains a bit. Somewhere round about this ledge is the key to the secret passage that the men used. We've got to find it!"

"You don't mean a real key that turns, do you?" asked Pam, looking round and about with her torch, as if she expected to see a large iron key somewhere.

"Of course not," said Brock impatiently. "I don't exactly know what we're looking for, Pam – maybe a lever – or a handle of some sort – or a stone that moves when it's pushed. We just don't know till we try."

So they tried. They hunted for any small bit of iron that might serve as a handle to move a stone. But they could find nothing in the walls around. They pushed against every stone they could reach, but they all seemed as solid as could be. They knocked with their knuckles to see if any stone sounded hollower than the rest, but except for taking the skin off their knuckles, there was no other result!

It was terribly disappointing. The children looked at one another, after about twenty minutes, and wondered what else to do.

"I'm afraid we're beaten," said Peter, at last. "There doesn't seem a thing here that might show us where a secret passage is."

"There's only one place we haven't looked," said Pam, suddenly.

The boys stared at her. "We've looked simply everywhere!" said Brock. "You know we have, silly."

"Well, we haven't looked at the stones we're *standing* on!" said Pam. "We've looked at the stonework around and above us – but not beneath our feet!"

"Pam's right!" said Brock excitedly. "Good for you, Pam. You may be only a girl, but you get the right ideas sometimes!"

Pam felt pleased. She only hoped she was right in her idea! The three of them knelt down to examine the stonework under their feet.

It wasn't long before Peter gave a loud cry, which made the others jump. "Look! What's this in this stone?"

They all looked closely, shining their torches down. Set deep in a hole in the rough stone was a sunken iron handle. On the stone by the handle a rough arrow was carved, pointing towards the chimney hole.

"This is it!" cried Peter. "Brock, what do we do? Pull at the handle?"

"Wait," said Brock. "This arrow means something. See where it points to? Well, I think we have to pull in that direction. Get off the stone, Pam, and Peter and I will see what we can do."

Pam took her foot off the stone, and watched as the two boys took hold of the iron handle and heaved at it in the direction of the arrow. At first nothing happened at all – and then a very strange thing came to pass under their eyes!

As the boys heaved at the handle, the stone in which it was set began to move smoothly outwards as if it were on rollers! It moved towards the chimney hole, and then, when it seemed as if it really must overbalance and fall down the chimney, it stopped moving. In the space where it had been was a dark hole that led downwards!

"Look – there's something just a little way down,

coiled up on a big staple!" cried Peter, and he shone his torch on it. "It's a rope!"

Brock reached down and pulled it up. It wasn't a rope – it was a rope ladder. He saw that the top of it was firmly hitched to the staple, and the rest dropped down out of sight. He let go and the rope ladder swung back to its staple.

"Well, that's the way we go!" said Brock. He shone his torch on to Pam. "What do you feel about it?" he asked. "I know girls aren't so daring as boys. Would you like Peter to take you outside and leave you to wait in the sunshine somewhere, whilst we see where this goes to? It might be a bit dangerous."

"Brock, don't be so mean!" cried Pam indignantly. "I'm not a coward – and do you suppose I want to go away from here just when things are getting really thrilling? I'm coming with you, so that's that."

"Righto," said Brock, grinning. "I thought you would. Don't get all hot and bothered about it. I'll go first. Peter, shine your torch down, old man."

Peter shone his torch down the curious hole, and Brock let himself over the edge and felt about with his feet for the first rung of the rope ladder. Then down he went, very cautiously. After a bit, he shouted up: "The ladder has come to an end. There's a stone floor here, and a passage leading off. Come on down. Send Pam first, Peter, then you can give her a hand down."

So Pam went next, so thrilled that she could hardly feel for the rungs with her feet! She went down and down, and at last stood beside Brock, her feet safely on solid floor again. Then came Peter. They shone their torches into the passage that led off to the left of the strange hole.

"This is a real secret passage," said Brock in an excited voice. "A really proper one. Golly – isn't it fun!"

"Come on," said Peter. "Let's see where it leads to. I can hardly hold my torch still, my hand is shaking so!"

They went down the narrow winding stone passage. It was perfectly dry, rather airless, and very small. In places, the children had to bend their heads so as not to knock them against the roof of the passage.

The passage went steeply down, then at intervals turned right back on itself. "It must be made in the walls of the castle itself," said Brock wonderingly. "What a funny thing for anyone to have thought of making. Hello – what's this?"

A shaft of daylight had suddenly appeared in one side of the passage! It came from an iron grille set in the wall of the passage itself.

"A sort of air-hole, I suppose," said Peter, and he looked out. "I say, do you know where we are? We are at the west side of the castle – the side that goes sheer down with the steep cliff. I believe there must be a way cut down through the cliff itself, and the entrance to it is somewhere at the bottom of it!"

"Yes – you're right," said Brock, peering out too. "Well, if that's so, the passage will soon change from a stone one to an earth one – and let's hope it hasn't fallen in anywhere."

"Well, the men used it, didn't they?" said Peter.

Just as Brock said, the passage soon changed from a stone-walled one to one whose walls were made of earth, strengthened here and there by wood and stones. It zigzagged down, and at the steepest places steps were cut. It was not an easy way to take.

"This is a real secret passage," said Brock in an excited voice

"We must surely be nearly at the bottom!" said Brock, at last. "My legs are getting jolly tired."

There was still a little way to go – and then the secret passage ended abruptly in a small, low cave. The children crept into it, and then out into a larger cave. The entrance to this was set so closely about with gorse and blackberry bushes that it would have been quite impossible to see from the outside.

The children forced their way out, tearing their clothes and scratching their legs.

"You can see where the men got in and out," said Brock. "Just there, where sprays of bramble are broken."

They looked round and about. They were now at the very bottom of the steep side of the cliff, where few people came. It was quite impossible to see the cave from where they stood, although they were only a few feet from it.

"Do you think we'd better climb back and swing that moving stone back into its place." said Peter, suddenly. "If the men come again, as it's pretty certain they will, they'll see that stone is moved, and suspect someone has been after them."

Brock looked at his watch. "We haven't time to do it," he said in dismay. "Golly, Mother will be angry with us – it's half an hour past dinnertime already!"

"But, Brock – suppose the men see the stone is moved?" said Peter anxiously.

"We'll come back another time and put it into its place," said Brock. "Maybe the men won't be back for some time now. They don't come every night. Come on, now – we'll have to *race* back!"

And race back they did – but it didn't prevent them from being well scolded by Brock's mother!

CHAPTER EIGHT

BROCK'S ADVENTURE

The children went to Brock's playhouse that afternoon, and talked and talked about their discoveries in the castle. They couldn't say enough about the finding of the strange secret passage. When they remembered that long dark climb downwards through the walls of the castle, and then down the cliff itself, they felt more and more thrilled.

But Peter also went on feeling uncomfortable about the stone in the chimney. He kept saying that the men might come back and discover it.

"Perhaps you're right," said Brock, at last. "I'll slip

off this evening, after tea, by myself, and put it back. It won't take me long now I know all the short cuts."

"All right," said Peter. But it was not to be, for Brock's mother wanted him to drive the pony-cart over to the farm and collect a crate of chickens for her.

"Oh, Mother! Won't it do tomorrow?" said Brock in dismay. "I've got something I want to do this evening."

"Well, I'm afraid *that* must keep till tomorrow," said his mother. "I've arranged with the farmer to send over for the chickens this evening and he'll have them all ready. Take Peter and Pam with you. It's a nice drive."

So Brock had to go off with his cousins in the pony-cart. "Just after I'd really made up my mind to go and do that at the castle," he grumbled. "I hate changing my plans. I really do feel you're right about that stone now, Peter."

"So do I," said Peter gloomily. "It would be just our luck if the men came tonight!"

"I'll tell you what I'll do!" said Brock, suddenly. "I'll go as soon as we're in bed! It will just be getting dark then, but the moon will be up early tonight, and I'll be able to see my way back beautifully."

"Oooh, Brock! You surely don't want to go to the castle at night-time!" cried Pam in horror. She felt quite nervous enough in the daytime, and she knew she would never be brave enough to go at night!

"Why not?" said Brock with a laugh. "You don't think I'm frightened, surely? It would take more than Cliff Castle to make *me* afraid!"

"Shall I come with you?" said Peter. He didn't really want to, but he felt he ought to make the offer.

"No, thanks," said Brock. "I think it would be best for just one of us to go."

All Brock's family were early bedders, and it was about half-past ten when the boy got cautiously out of bed and began to dress himself. Twilight still hung about the fields, but would soon disappear. Then the moon would come up.

"Good luck, Brock!" whispered Peter. "Do you think your father and mother are asleep?"

"I don't know," said Brock. "I'm not going to risk going downstairs and opening any of the doors. They are sure to creak!"

"Well, how are you going, then?" asked Peter, in astonishment.

"Down my old apple tree!" whispered Brock, and Peter saw the flash of his white teeth as he grinned.

He went to the window and put a leg across. He caught hold of a strong branch, and in a moment had worked his way down it to the trunk. Then down he slid and Peter heard the soft thud of his feet on the ground below. He watched the boy's shadowy figure as he ran down the garden and out into the lane. "I hope he won't be too long," thought Peter, as he curled up in bed again. "I shall keep awake till he comes back. Then I'll pop up and wake Pam, and she can come down and hear what Brock has to say."

But Peter didn't keep awake. By the time that half-past eleven had struck downstairs, he was fast asleep!

But Brock was wide awake, running like a hare over the fields. He met nobody, for no one was out so late at night in the country. Grazing sheep lifted their heads to look at him and a startled rabbit skipped out of his way.

Brock saw the moon coming up slowly. It lighted up the castle on the hill, and made it look silvery and unreal.

"It's like a castle out of some old story," thought the boy. "It will be fun to get inside at night-time!"

Brock was quite fearless. He enjoyed this kind of adventure, and was quite glad to be on his own without the others to bother about. He ran round to where the little, low door was set at the bottom of the castle. He pulled at it and it opened.

He slipped inside. He waited a moment in the great dark kitchen to see if anyone else was about by any chance, but everything was still and silent. The boy switched his torch on, and went into the hall to see if there were any more footprints. But there were none. So the men hadn't yet been – but, after all, it wasn't many hours since Brock had left, and it didn't leave much time for anyone to come.

The boy made his way to the room where the iron ladder led up the chimney. He climbed up the ladder, and soon came to the ledge. The stone that had moved out to disclose the secret passage was still swung out over the chimney hole. Brock wondered how to get it back.

"I suppose I must heave on the iron handle in the opposite direction," he thought. He took hold of it – and then almost fell down the hole in astonishment. He had heard voices!

"Golly!" thought the boy, sitting quite still on the ledge, "somebody is coming – two people at least. But where do the voices come from?"

Brock couldn't distinguish any words, he could only hear the murmur of voices, talking and answering. They came up from the hole, and were getting louder.

"My goodness, someone is coming up through the secret passage!" thought the boy, in a fright for the moment. "It must be those men. I must get the stone back into place as quickly as I can!"

With the sound of voices came other sounds, rather like something being bumped against the wall. Brock felt sure the men were carrying something again. He took hold of the iron handle sunk in the stone and heaved hard at it. At first the stone would not move – then, slowly and gradually, it gave way to Brock's stout pulling, and rolled back into its place.

It made a slight grinding noise as it did so, and Brock hoped that the men below were talking loudly enough to drown the sound. He climbed quickly down the iron ladder and ran into the kitchen, meaning to get out of the little low door.

Then he stopped. "No," he said to himself. "This is a big chance for me to find out exactly what the men are up to. I'll hide somewhere, and listen and follow. Golly, what an adventure!"

He darted behind a big cupboard in the hall, and waited to see what happened. After some while he heard sounds coming from the room he had left. The men were climbing down the iron ladder in the chimneyplace, dragging something heavy with them.

Then came the sound of voices, quite clearly echoing weirdly through the silent castle.

"We ought to be paid double for bringing the goods up that narrow way!" grumbled one voice. "I'd be willing to risk the front door, but Galli won't hear of it. Come on – we've got to take the things up to the tower now. Then we'll get away quickly. I don't like this wretched moon, showing us up so clearly when we walk outside."

From his hiding place Brock could see two men, each

carrying large and heavy boxes on their shoulders. They were half-bent beneath the weight, and the boy marvelled that they could possibly have carried them all the way up the secret passage, up the rope ladder, and then down the iron one!

"They must be very strong," thought the boy. They were. They had broad shoulders, and when they were caught in a shaft of bright moonlight, Brock saw that they looked rather foreign. He had thought that their voices sounded a little foreign, too. They were very dark and swarthy, and one man wore gold earrings in his ears.

They came into the hall, carrying the boxes, and then went up the broad flight of stairs. They put the boxes down for a rest when they came to the top, and again Brock heard the murmur of their voices as they spoke together. The boy crept out from his hiding place and went to the foot of the stairs.

He followed the men silently up and up until they went into the room from which the little stone staircase led into the tower room. One of the men unlocked the door at the top. Brock heard them put down their loads and sigh with relief.

"I could do with a drink now," said one man. "Is there a well in the kitchen – or somewhere we can get water?"

"We'll look," said the other. He locked the door, and the men came down the narrow staircase again. Brock saw that they had left the key in the door and his eyes gleamed. Maybe he could slip up and take it out before they remembered it – and then he and the others could come and find out what was in those boxes! Something exciting, he was sure!

He slipped out before the men, and ran into one of the nearby rooms. It was furnished, and the boy pulled some curtains around him to hide himself. But the things were quite rotten and fell away as he touched them. Thin grey dust flew all around, and before Brock could stop himself, he sneezed!

CHAPTER NINE

BROCK IN TROUBLE

Now when Brock sneezed, everyone knew it, for he sneezed heartily and well. In the silence of the castle his sneeze made a most tremendous noise! It echoed all round and about, and startled poor Brock just as much as it startled the two men.

"There's someone here!" said one. "In that room. Quick – we'll get him!"

They darted into the room where Brock had tried to hide. Luckily for him they missed him and he was able to dart out and elude their outstretched hands. He ran down the stairs at top speed, his boots making a tremendous clatter as he went.

The men ran after him. Down and down went Brock, meaning to make for the little low door in the kitchen. But when he got there, it was so dark he could not see where he was going and he fell over a stool. He crashed to the floor, and had no time to make for the door. Instead, he rolled quickly under a big oak seat in the fireplace and lay there, hardly daring to breathe. The men switched on their torches, and one of them gave an exclamation.

"Look here – here's a little door, ajar!"

"That's where the boy came in!" said the other man. "Well, he didn't have time to get out, that's certain. He's somewhere here. But first I think we'll shut and lock the door. Then our friend won't be able to escape quite so easily as he hoped!"

Poor Brock heard the door being shut and locked. He felt certain that the man had put the key in his pocket. He couldn't think what to do. He wondered if the men knew of the little back staircase. If he could run up that he might be able to find the room where the big tree touched the windowsill. Then he'd be out in a jiffy and the men couldn't follow him!

"Let's shut the kitchen door, and have a good hunt round," said one man. "He's here somewhere."

Now was Brock's chance. The big kitchen door was at the far end of the kitchen. He stood up quietly, and then made a dash for the little back staircase, which was quite nearby. The men gave a shout when they heard him, and switched their torches round to the noise.

"There's a stairway there!" cried one. "He's gone up. Come on – after him!"

The men tore up the narrow stairway after Brock. "If only I could remember which room that tree touched!"

thought the boy desperately. "But we couldn't find it again before. There are so many rooms here, all exactly the same!"

He ran on till he came to a room and then he darted inside. He took off his boots quickly, because he knew that the noise they made gave him away and made him easy to follow.

The men passed the room, flashing their torches ahead of them. Brock ran to the window. Alas, it was not the right one. It was far too narrow to squeeze through.

Brock ran to the door and peered out. The men had gone to the other end of the stone landing and were looking into each of the rooms as they came back. Brock ran into the one next to his. Again he was disappointed. It was not the right one. He went into a third, his heart beating fast, for the men were now coming back. But again he was unlucky.

He did not dare to go into another room. The only thing he could do was to run back to the staircase and go down it, hoping to hide himself so well somewhere that he would not be found.

As he ran to the staircase the men saw him in a shaft of moonlight and raced after him. Brock almost fell down the stairs, and raced across the kitchen into the hall. Then he tore into one of the big, furnished rooms, meaning to hide behind some furniture.

The men saw him. They went into the room after him, and in a few moments they had found Brock and dragged him out from behind a big dusty couch that smelt so mouldy that the boy was almost sick.

"Well, we've got you now!" said the man. He shone his torch into Brock's face. "What are you doing here, spying on us? You're doing a dangerous thing. We can't let you go, because you've found our secret, and we daren't risk your telling it till we've finished our job and are safe."

Brock said nothing. His red, round face looked surly. The men looked at one another.

"What are we to do with him?" said one. "He's only a kid. We'd better lock him up somewhere and tell Galli. Then he can put him away till it's safe to let him go. Well, youngster, you'll be sorry for youself when Galli gets hold of you. He won't be gentle with a nastly little boy who spies on him!"

Still Brock said nothing. One of the men gave him a shake. "He's lost his tongue," he said to the other. "Come on – let's lock him up in the tower room with the boxes. He'll be safe there."

So Brock was dragged up to the tower room, and put there among the big boxes. The men locked the door behind them, and Brock heard their footsteps going down the stairs. He felt sure they would go out by the little low door instead of the difficult way down the secret passage. And they would lock the door behind them, so that Peter and Pam couldn't get in if they came to look for him.

"I've made a mess of things," said Brock, looking at the big boxes. "I wonder what's in those boxes. How I'd like to know!"

He shone his torch on to one, but soon saw that it was so well fastened and nailed down that it would need strong tools to open it. His bare hands and pocketknife would be no good at all! He went to a window and looked out gloomily on the countryside. A ray of moonlight came through the slit. Far away, Brock could see his own house.

As he looked at it, he saw a light moving in one of the windows. He tried to reckon out which it was, and soon came to the conclusion that it was his own window. Then Peter must be awake. That must have been his torch shining!

In a trice Brock took out his own torch again, and pushed it as far as he could through the slit. He pressed the knob of the torch up and down, so that it flashed regularly and continually.

"If only Peter sees it, he may guess it's me," thought the boy. "Oh, I do hope he sees it! I don't want to be kept a prisoner here for days!"

CHAPTER TEN

PETER AND PAM TO THE RESCUE!

Peter slept soundly till half-past one. Then he woke up with a jump. He remembered at once that Brock had gone to Cliff Castle, and he sat up in bed to see if the boy was back.

He stared at Brock's empty bed, and then switched on his torch to look at his watch. Half-past one! Whatever could Brock be doing?

As he sat wondering, he heard a sound at the door, and almost jumped out of his skin as a white figure came into the room. It was Pam in her nightdress.

"Peter! Is Brock back? You said you'd come up and wake me when he came back, but it's awfully late."

Peter shone his torch on to Brock's empty bed. Pam felt scared.

"Golly! Where is he?" She went to the window and stared out at the big black mass of Cliff Castle. The moon had gone in for a moment, and it looked very dark and forbidding. Then she suddenly caught sight of a bright little light winking and blinking in the top tower to the right.

"That's funny," she said to Peter. "Look at that light, flashing every other moment, Peter, just as if it were a signal. Those men wouldn't do that, would they, because they wouldn't want to give themselves away. But who else would be signalling like that?"

Peter looked, and as soon as he saw the winking light he guessed that it was Brock. "It's old Brock!" he said. "I'm quite sure it is! What's he doing in the tower room – it was locked, wasn't it? He must have got in somehow and wants us to go and see what the treasure is in those boxes!"

"Or do you think he's been captured?" said Pam slowly. "He might have been, you know. Maybe he's locked up in the tower."

"We'd better go and see," said Peter, beginning to dress hurriedly. "We won't tell Aunt Hetty, or Uncle, Pam, in case Brock wants us to go and see the treasure with him without anyone knowing. We don't want to give the secret away unless we have to! Hurry and dress now!"

It wasn't long before the two children were climbing down the old apple tree and sliding to the ground below. Then they made their way to Cliff Castle, panting as they ran.

They got there safely, and went to where the little,

low door was set in the kitchen wall. Peter pulled at it, expecting it to open. But it didn't. It remained tightly shut.

"I say! It's locked or something!" he said to Pam. "Here, help me to pull."

But pulling was no use at all. The little wooden door wouldn't budge!

"Well, Brock wouldn't have locked it, that's certain," said Peter, speaking in a whisper. "Someone else must have. I say – I rather think old Brock's been captured!"

"How shall we get in, then?" she whispered. "Up that tree? But, Peter, surely we can't climb it in the dark."

"We'll have to try," said Peter. "Look, the moon will be out for some time now – we'll climb whilst it gives us a bright light. I'll help you. Or would you rather stay on the ground whilst I climb?"

"No, I'll climb, too," said Pam bravely. So they made their way to the tree and Peter shinned up it first. But Pam couldn't climb it because her legs trembled so. "I'll just have to stay here," she whispered up to him. "I shall fall if I climb up, Peter. Isn't it sickening?"

"Never mind, old girl," said Peter. "You stay down below and warn me if anyone comes. I'll go in and see if I can rescue Brock."

Pam couldn't see Peter climbing the tree because it was full of dark shadows, flecked by moonlight. She heard the rustling, though, and knew when Peter had reached the bough that led to the window because of the sudden swinging of the tree.

Peter didn't find it so easy to climb the tree in the dark as in the light, but he managed to slide down the branch to the window, and then squeezed himself through. He jumped down on the floor. His boots made a noise, and he took them off. He ran on tiptoe to the door, not making a sound. When he got there he looked out, and suddenly remembered how hard it had been to find that room again. He took one of his boots and made a big cross with it in the dust of the floor. Now he had only to pop his head in at the door to see the cross and know it was the room with the tree outside.

"I feel quite clever!" said the boy to himself. He ran to the little stone staircase and went lightly down it. The moon was now high and shone in at every slit-like window, so that it was fairly easy to see, though the shadows were as black as could be.

Across the kitchen went the boy, and into the dark hall. Then up the broad flight of stairs on the other side, and on to the first landing. He paused there in the shadows to listen. Was there anyone about? After all, if Brock had been captured, someone must have captured him – and it was quite likely they might still be somewhere in the castle. This was rather a weird thought, and the boy felt a shiver down his back.

"I won't get into a fright!" he thought to himself. "I'm rescuing Brock, and I'm not afraid of anything."

He would have liked to whistle to keep his spirits up, but he didn't dare to. As it was, every little sound he made went echoing round and round, and made him jump.

He went on up to the floor where the room was that had the tower staircase leading from it. He came to the stairway, and stood at the bottom, his heart beating so loudly that he felt sure anyone nearby could hear it!

He stole up the staircase, and felt the shut door. He longed to push it open, but he still didn't know if Brock were behind it, or an enemy. And then, suddenly, he knew!

There came the sound of a sigh, and then a creak as if someone had sat down on a box. "Blow my torch!" said a gloomy voice. "It's no use now – the battery's given out. I can't signal any more."

It was Brock's voice. In delight Peter banged on the door, making poor Brock inside almost jump out of his skin, for he had, of course, no idea at all that Peter was anywhere near. He almost fell off the box.

"Brock!" came Peter's voice. "I'm here. I'm coming. What's happened?" Peter pushed at the door – but alas, it was locked, and wouldn't open. Brock's voice came in excitement from behind the door: "Peter! You old brick! Is the key in the lock?"

"No," said Peter, switching on his torch. "What a blow! I can't get in – and you can't get out."

Brock told him shortly how he had been captured. "And now I'm sitting on a box that may contain half the jewels in the kingdom!" he said. "But I'm a prisoner, and likely to remain one till this man Galli they keep talking about comes along and decides what's to be done with me."

"I'll go back home and get your father to come, and the police," said Peter eagerly. "I don't expect the men will be back tonight."

"Where's Pam?" said Brock. "Fast asleep in bed, I hope!"

"No. She's outside the castle, waiting," said Peter. "She couldn't climb the tree in the dark. She said she'd keep watch in case someone came."

"I say, Peter! I've got an idea!" said Brock suddenly.

"Maybe the other towers have little rooms inside them, with a door like this one. And maybe they all have locks and keys that are the same. Do you think you could go to the tower on this side and see if there's a key in the door of the room there? If there is, bring it back and try it in this lock – it may fit – and open the door!"

"Golly! That's an idea!" cried Peter, and he went down the staircase and made his way round the big stone landing until he came to the end. He went into the room there and found a staircase leading up to the tower above, exactly like the one in the room he had left. Up he went and came to a door.

"And, my goodness, there *is* a key in the lock!" said the boy to himself, in delight. He pulled out the key and made his way back. He fitted it into the lock of Brock's door – and it turned! The lock gave, and the door opened.

"Oh, Peter – what luck!" said Brock, and he squeezed his cousin's arm. "Thanks, old man – you're a brick to rescue me. Now we must go straight down and join Pam – and then I think we ought to rush home and wake up my father. Someone ought to come and see what's in these boxes!"

Down the little stone staircase went the two boys, both in their stockinged feet. They felt tremendously excited, and Peter's hand shook as he held out his torch to show the way. The mystery of Cliff Castle was nearly solved. The secret was in those boxes. Soon Brock's father would come along and open them. Then, maybe, the two men would be caught and everything would be cleared up.

Just as they reached the first landing they had a terrific shock. A great crashing echoed throughout the whole castle, and the two boys jumped so much that they had to stand still. What in the world could the noise be?

CHAPTER ELEVEN

MORE AND MORE EXCITEMENT

The enormous crash came again – and then the boys knew what it was!

"It's somebody banging on that great front door knocker!" cried Peter.

"But who would do that in the middle of the night?" said Brock, amazed.

"Pam, of course," said Peter proudly. "She said she'd watch out – and I expect she's seen someone coming and that's her way of warning us. What a marvellous idea!"

"I say – what a girl she is!" said Brock admiringly. "Well – we'll have to look out. Let's slip down to the kitchen and see if we can get out of that little low door. Maybe the key is on this side."

They ran quietly down the stairs in their stockinged feet – and then paused in horror. In the kitchen, waiting silently, themselves amazed at the noise on the front door, were three men. Two of them Brock had seen before.

The men saw the boys and gave a shout. "Two kids this time!" cried one. "Quick, get them!"

The boys tore into the hall and into the big room where the chimney was that gave on to the secret passage. Brock slammed the door and turned the key in the lock. Then they rushed to the fireplace and climbed quickly up the iron ladder. A heave at the iron ring and the stone moved silently across, showing the way down.

A great noise at the locked door made the boys hurry more than ever. The door would certainly be down very soon, for the lock was sure to be rotten!

It was! It gave way and the door swung open. The three men rushed in and paused. "Surely those kids don't know the secret passage!" cried one of the men in amazement.

"They do!" said another. "Come on – we must get them, somehow, or they'll be away, and tell the police."

They rushed to the fireplace and swarmed up the iron ladder. By this time the boys were at the bottom of the rope ladder, making their way as quickly as they could down the secret stone passage, their hearts beating painfully.

They could hear the men coming after them, and hurried more and more. They came to where the stone passage ended and the earth passage began.

"Hurry, Brock, hurry!" cried Peter. "They are almost on us. Hurry!"

Brock did hurry, but the ground was painful to his stockinged feet. At last the boys came to the small cave and made their way into the larger one. Just as the men got to the small cave the boys forced their way out of the large one, and found themselves on the hillside.

"Up a tree, quick!" whispered Brock. "It's our only chance!"

Peter shinned up a nearby tree, with Brock helping him. Then Brock swung himself up into the dark shadows and both boys lay flat on branches, peering down below, hardly daring to breathe.

It didn't occur to the men that the boys could so quickly have gone up a tree. They thought they had run off into the bushes, and they beat about quickly to find them.

"They'll give it up soon," whispered Brock. He was right. The men soon gave up the search and gathered together. The third man, called Galli, was very angry.

"Fancy letting a couple of kids beat you like this!" he said in disgust. "Now there's only one thing to do – get the stuff out of the tower room at once and find a new hiding place. Go on – get back to the castle and haul the stuff out."

The men went off, the other two muttering angrily to themselves, but they were evidently terrified of Galli, who was the leader.

The men went back up the secret passage. As soon as they were safely out of hearing, the boys slid down the tree into the moonlight and looked at one another excitedly.

"Let's get back home as quickly as we can!" said Peter. "We'll fetch Pam, and run as fast as possible."

"The men will be gone by the time we get Dad and the police here," panted Brock, as they ran up the slope that led to the front of the castle, to find Pam. She saw them coming and jumped out from under a bush.

"Brock! Peter! Oh, how glad I am to see you! Did you hear me crash on the knocker? I saw the three men coming, and they went in at that little low door. I couldn't *think* how to warn you – and I suddenly thought of that great knocker!"

"Pam, you're a marvellous girl!" said Brock, and he threw his arm round his cousin's shoulders and gave her a hug. "Nobody but you would have thought of such an idea! Honestly, I'm proud of you!"

The boys quickly told Pam what had happened to them – and then Brock suddenly fell silent. The other two looked at him.

"What is it, Brock?" asked Peter.

"I've got an idea, but I don't know if it's good or not," said Brock. "Listen – those men are all going back to the tower room, aren't they? Well, do you suppose – do you *possibly* suppose we could get there, too, and wait till they're inside – and then lock them in?"

Peter and Pam stared at Brock. It seemed a mad idea – and yet – suppose, just suppose it could be done!

"The men would never, never guess we were back again," said Peter slowly. "They wouldn't be on the lookout for us. They think we're running off to tell the police. It seems to me that your idea is the only one that might possibly lead to the capture of the men – and the goods, too! Otherwise, by the time we get back here with help, they'll be gone with everything!"

"We'll try it!" said Brock. "Now, look here, Pam – your part in this is to race off by yourself over the fields and wake Daddy and Mother, and tell them everything. Will you do that?"

Pam didn't at all want to do anything of the sort, but she wasn't going to let the boys down. She nodded her head. "I'll go," she said, and she went, running like a little black shadow down the hillside.

"She's a good kid," said Brock, and the two boys turned to go to the castle. They meant to climb up the tree and get in that way. They were sure the little low door would be locked. Up they went and into the dark room. There, on the floor, was the cross in the dust that Peter had made!

"Now quietly!" whispered Brock, as they went down the narrow stone staircase. "The men may be in the kitchen, or the hall."

The boys stole carefully down. There was no one in the kitchen – and no one in the hall. The boys kept to the shadows as they walked.

Suddenly they heard a noise, and Peter clutched Brock by the arm, pulling him into the shadow of a great hall curtain. "It's the men coming out of the chimneyplace," whispered the boy. "They're only just back. It's taken them ages to come up by that steep secret passage. Keep quiet now. We may be able to do something."

The men clattered across the room to the door and then went across the hall to the big staircase, talking in loud voices. It was quite clear that they had no idea at all that the boys were hidden nearby. They went up the stairs, and as soon as they had turned a corner, the boys followed them, so full of excitement that they could hardly breathe!

The three men went on up to the tower room. The boys could hear their voices all the time. They crept after them in their stockinged feet. They had never felt so terribly excited in their lives!

All the men went into the tower room. Peter and Brock stood at the bottom of the little staircase that wound up to the room, and wondered if this was the right moment to go up.

"Better do it now," said Brock, "or they will start to come out again."

Galli, up above, gave orders to the two men. "Take that box first. And hurry up about it!"

There came the sounds of two men swinging a box round to get hold of it.

"Now!" whispered Brock, and the two boys shot up the stairs, one behind the other, breathing fast. They got to the door. The men hadn't heard a sound. By the light of their torches Brock could see two of them lifting one of the boxes, whilst Galli stood by. The boy caught hold of the wooden door, and closed it as quietly as he could. But it made a slight click as the latch went into place. At once Galli noticed it and roared out a warning.

"Look out! There's somebody on the stairs!" He rushed to the door. But Brock had already turned the key in the lock.

Galli hammered on the door in a rage and the stout door shook under his blows.

"Hammer all you like!" shouted Brock exultingly. "You're caught!"

The boys turned to go down the stairs – and then Peter's sharp ears caught something that one of the men said.

"I've got a key to this door! I took it out of the lock

when I shut up that kid. Here, take it, Galli, and undo the door. We'll catch those boys if we have to hunt the castle from top to bottom!"

Peter clutched Brock by the arm. "Did you hear that? They've got the key to this door, Brock! The one that was in the door when they locked you up! Now what are we to do?"

Brock dashed up the stairs again. He switched his torch on to the door, at the same moment as he heard a key being put into the lock from the other side. His torch showed him a big bolt at the top of the door and another at the bottom. Hoping and praying that they would not be too rusty to push into place, the boy took hold of the bottom bolt. He pulled at it, but it stuck badly.

Meantime the men on the other side of the door were trying to turn the key to unlock it. But it was more difficult to do that from inside than outside. Muttering a string of foreign-sounding words, Galli tried to force the key round.

"Let me try the bolt, Brock," whispered Peter, and took Brock's place. But it was no use. He could only move it a little way, it was so rusty.

"Try the top one," said Brock. So Peter stood on tiptoe and tried the one at the top. He was trembling from head to foot, for it was terrible to hear someone doing his best to unlock the door from the inside, whilst he, Peter, was trying with all his might to bolt it from the outside!

"Oh Peter, Peter, won't it move?" groaned Brock, feeling certain that they would be captured if the door was unlocked. Peter suddenly gave a shout, and there was a creaking sound. The rust on the bolt had given way and the bolt had slid slowly into place. The door was bolted!

Almost at the same moment the key turned on the other side and unlocked the door – but it was held by the bolt, and Galli roared with rage as he found that the door would not budge. It gave at the bottom, but the stout bolt at the top held firmly.

The boys were both shaking. They had to sit down on the stairs and lean against one another. Neither boy could have gone down the stairs at that moment. They sat there, close to each other, and heard the three men losing their tempers with one another. They shouted in a strange language, and at times one of them would shake the door with all his strength.

"I hope that top bolt holds," said Peter in a whisper. "Everything in this house is so rotten and old that I wouldn't be surprised if the wretched thing gives way."

"Well, let's try to use the bottom bolt as well then, when the men leave the door alone for a moment," whispered back Brock. "Come on – there's a chance now."

The boys, both together, tried to move the bottom bolt back into place. Peter took Brock's knife and scraped away the rust as best he could. Then they tried again – and to their great joy and relief, the bolt slowly and haltingly slipped into place. Now the door was held at top and bottom, and the boys felt pretty certain that the men could not possibly get out, even if they tried all their strength together on the door.

The men did try once more – and this time they found, of course, that it would not move at the bottom.

"They've fastened the door at the bottom, too, now!"

shouted Galli, and the angry man struck the door with his fists, and kicked at it viciously with his foot.

"Hope he hurts himself!" whispered Brock, who was feeling much better now. He had stopped shaking, and was grinning to himself to think how neatly all the men were boxed up together. "I say, Peter – I rather think we've done a good night's work!"

"I rather think we have, too!" said Peter, and the two boys hugged themselves as they thought of all they had gone through to catch the men.

"I hope Pam gets home safely," said Brock. "I wonder how long it will be before she brings help back. Some time, I expect, because Dad will have to get in touch with the police. Well – I'm quite content to wait here till somebody arrives. I guess we're feeling a bit more comfortable than those three men!"

CHAPTER TWELVE

THE SECRET COMES OUT!

Meantime Pam was speeding across the fields and along the shadowy lanes. Once she had started she no longer felt afraid. She had to bring help to the boys, and that help rested on her swift feet. "Quick, quick!" she kept saying. "I must run like the wind!"

And run like the wind she did. She came to her aunt's house at last, and hammered on the front door, for she did not want to waste time by climbing in at the window. Her uncle awoke at once and came to his window. When he saw Pam standing there in the moonlight he thought he must be dreaming.

"Uncle! Uncle! Let me in, quick!" cried Pam. "There isn't a moment to be lost! The boys are in danger!"

In two minutes Pam was inside the house, sitting on her uncle's knee, pouring out the whole story to him as quickly as she could. He and his wife listened in the utmost amazement. Aunt Hetty could hardly believe the story, but Pam's uncle did at once, and saw that he must act quickly.

"I'll hear all the rest later," he said to the excited little girl. "If those two boys have managed to capture the men as they planned, we must go there at once – and if they haven't managed to, they'll be in the gravest danger. I'll ring up the police now. Hetty, see to Pam. She'd better go back to bed."

But nothing in the world would have persuaded Pam to go back to bed that night! "I'll climb out of the window if you make me go to bed!" she cried. "Oh, Aunt Hetty, I *must* go back to Cliff Castle. I must, I must!"

And, as it turned out, she did, because when her uncle came back from the telephone he said that the police wanted her to go with them to take them to the right room. It wasn't long before a police car roared up to the house with four stout policemen inside!

Pam and her uncle squeezed into the car too, and they set off to Cliff Castle by the road. It was a much longer way than across the fields, but it didn't take very long in the powerful police car.

"Why, look at that light in the sky!" said Pam suddenly, pointing to the east. "What is it, Uncle?"

"It's the dawn coming!" said her uncle, with a laugh. "The night is going. Hasn't it been a long enough night for you, Pam?"

"Yes, it has," said Pam, suddenly feeling glad that the

daylight would soon be there. "I wonder how we can get into the castle, Uncle? There are four ways in – but three of them are almost impossible."

"What are the four ways, Missy?" asked the inspector, who was sitting beside her.

"There's the front door," said Pam, "but the locks and bolts are all rusted, and we couldn't open it. Then there's a little, low door set in the foot of the castle by the kitchen – but that's shut and locked. And there's a secret passage from the bottom of the steep cliff, through the walls of the castle, and up a chimney."

"My word!" said the inspector, startled. "However did you find out all this? I must say you children are pretty daring! What's the fourth way in?"

"It's the way we used first," said Pam. "Up a tree and in at a window. But I'm afraid you're all too big to squeeze in there!"

"We'll break in at the little, low door!" said the inspector with a chuckle. And that is exactly what they did do!

The two boys were still sitting together on the stairs, feeling rather sleepy, watching the dawn put silver fingers in at the slits of window, when they suddenly heard the noise of the police car roaring up to the castle. Then they heard loud blows on the little door far below.

"They're breaking in!" cried Brock, in excitement, and he jumped to his feet, almost falling down the stairway. "They're knocking down that little door. Now they're in – golly, they're here! Pam! Pam! Here we are!"

Pam came tearing up the big staircase, followed by her uncle and the four policemen. She rushed into the room off which the little winding stairway led up to the tower room, shouting as she came.

"Peter! Brock! Did you manage to catch the men? Uncle's here and four policemen!"

"Yes, we've got the men!" shouted Brock, and grinned as he saw Pam's excited face coming round the bend in the stairway. "We've bolted them in well and truly!"

The men had fallen silent when they heard the shouts. They knew perfectly well that everything was up, as far as they were concerned.

"Get away down the stairs, you three children," commanded the inspector, suddenly taking on a new and quite stern voice. The children badly wanted to be in at the finish – but they didn't dare to say a word. They had to go and wait in the room below whilst the police unbolted the door and rushed the three men.

There was a lot of yelling and struggling, but the five men against the three were too strong, and it wasn't long before a sorry procession came down the winding stairway in the charge of three policemen.

"Take them into a room and stay with them till I come," ordered the inspector. Then he beckoned to the three children.

"Come along," he said, "we're going to open those boxes. You deserve to see what's inside, since it was you who really captured the men!"

In the greatest excitement, the children followed the inspector and Brock's father upstairs into the tower room. The great boxes lay there, still unopened.

The inspector had the right tools with him and began to force open the boxes quickly. They were very well fastened indeed, and even when the clasps had been forced back, the ropes cut, and the iron bands severed, there were still the locks to open. But the inspector had marvellous keys for these. "One of these keys will open the locks," he told the watching children. "It's my boast that I've got keys to open any lock in the world!"

The locks of the first box clicked. The inspector threw back the heavy lid. What looked like cotton wool lay on the top. Pam pulled it aside. Then everyone cried out in astonishment and awe – for lying in the box were the most marvellous jewels that the children had ever seen or heard of. Great red rubies shone and glowed in necklaces and tiaras. Brilliant green emeralds winked, and diamonds blazed in the light of the torches that shone down on the jewels.

"I say!" said Brock's father, finding his tongue first. "I say – inspector, these are not ordinary jewels. They are worth a fortune – many fortunes! What are they?"

"Well, it looks to me as if they are the private jewellery of the Princess of Larreeanah," said the inspector. "They were stolen on the steamer, when she fled from her palace in India to this country. It's an amazing story. She had them all put into these boxes and safely fastened in many ways. They were put into the stronghold of the steamer she took. They were apparently guarded night and day – and were taken ashore with her when she landed in this country. But when the boxes were opened at her bank in London, they contained nothing but stones!"

"But how could that be?" said Pam, her eyes opening wide in amazement. "And how are they here, then?"

"Well, I suppose what happened was that one of the guards on the steamer was bribed by some clever thief who knew what was contained in the boxes," said the inspector. "He must have had boxes of exactly the same size and make all ready, filled with stones – probably hidden inside big trunks of his own. At the right moment he must have got into the place where these boxes were stored, exchanged them, and then put these boxes into his own big trunks, and gone ashore safely with them."

"And the poor Princess went off with the boxes of stones!" cried Brock. "Was it that man Galli, do you think?"

"Yes, I should think so," said the inspector, beginning to open another box. "He's very like a famous thief, one of the cleverest we have ever come up against, whom we already want for another daring robbery. He's shaved off his moustache and beard, but I noticed that he had a little finger missing – and so has this thief I was telling you about! My word – look at this!"

The second box was now open, and contained just as amazing treasures as the first. Pam took out a wonderful tiara, rather like a small crown, and put it on.

"Now you're worth about fifty thousand pounds!" said her uncle. "Do you feel grand and important?"

"Oh, very!" said Pam, with a laugh.

"Well, you've every right to feel like that," said the inspector, shutting the first box and locking it. "But not because you're wearing famous jewels. You can feel grand and important because you and your brother and cousin have made it possible for us to recover all this jewellery and to catch the thieves who stole it! At the moment I should say you are the most daring and clever children in the whole kingdom!"

Even Brock blushed at this. All the children felt pleased.

"Well, it didn't seem very clever or daring whilst we were doing it," said Peter honestly. "As a matter of fact, I kept feeling frightened – and I know poor old Pam did."

"It's braver to do a thing if you feel afraid than it is to do it if you don't mind," said the inspector. "I don't know what to do with these boxes. I think I'll handcuff those three men together, send them off in charge of two of my men, and leave the third man here on guard whilst I go and report to Scotland Yard."

"What's Scotland Yard?" said Pam in surprise.

"It's the place where all the head policemen work!" said the inspector, with a sudden grin. "Very important place, too! Well – come along. You children must be tired out."

They went down the stairs. The inspector gave his orders, and the three sullen thieves were handcuffed together, so that two policemen could easily take charge of them. The third one was sent up to guard the tower room.

"I'll send back a car for Galli and the others," said the inspector. "I'll take these children home, and then their uncle can come along with me to the station."

Pam almost fell asleep in the car. She was completely tired out. But the two boys were still excited. They looked out of the car windows at the sun just rising in the eastern sky. It seemed ages and ages since yesterday! Could so much have possibly happened in one night?

Brock's mother made all the children go to bed when they got back. "You look absolutely worn out," she said. "Tell me everything when you wake, Pam. I'll undress you. You are falling asleep as you stand!"

The boys were glad to get into bed now, though it seemed odd to go to bed when the sun was just rising. Brock snuggled down.

"Well, good night," he said to Peter. "I mean, good

morning! What adventures we've had. I'm sorry they're over. I did enjoy solving the mystery of Cliff Castle."

"Yes, we soon found out the secret," said Peter. "But, oh – I'm sorry it's all ended!"

But it hadn't quite ended. The princess of Larreeanah was so overjoyed at the recovery of her jewels that she came herself to see the three adventurous children.

She arrived in a magnificent car, and was wearing some of the jewels. Much to the children's embarrassment, she kissed them all.

They didn't like being kissed by strangers, even if this stranger was a princess – and they made up their minds they weren't going to like her. But they soon changed that idea when they found what she had brought for them in a small van that followed her car!

"Open the door of the van and see what is inside for you!" she said to the three surprised children. Brock pulled open the doors at the back of the van – and all three stared in amazement and awe at the Princess's wonderful present.

"It's a car – a small car just big enough to take the three of us!" said Brock, staring at the marvellous little car inside the van. It was bright red, with yellow bands and yellow spokes to the wheels. The lamps, wind-screen and handles shone like silver.

"It goes by electricity," said the Princess. "I had it made especially for you. You don't have to have a driving licence, of course, because it is listed as a toy car. But actually it is driven just like a real one, has a horn and everything, and goes by electricity, so that you don't need petrol."

"Let's go for a ride in it now!" shouted Peter in excitement. So they pulled out the magnificent little car and got into it. Brock drove it. He pulled a lever, took hold of the steering wheel, and off went the car down the lane with its three excited passengers.

"What a wonderful end to an adventure!" cried Peter. "Didn't I say we'd have real, proper adventures? And wasn't I right?"

Well – he certainly was!

SMUGGLER BEN

CONTENTS

CHAPTER ONE

THE COTTAGE BY THE SEA

Three children got out of a bus and looked around them in excitement. Their mother smiled to see their glowing faces.

"Well, here we are!" she said. "How do you like it?"

"Is this the cottage we're going to live in for four weeks?" said Alec, going up to the little white gate. "Mother! It's perfect!"

The two girls, Hilary and Frances, looked at the small square cottage, and agreed with their brother. Red roses climbed all over the cottage even to the chimneys. The thatched roof came down low over the ground floor windows, and in the thatch itself other little windows jutted out.

"I wonder which is our bedroom," said Hilary, looking up at the roof. "I hope that one is – because it will look out over the sea."

"Well, let's go in and see," said Mother. "Help with the suitcases, Alec. I hope the heavy luggage has already arrived."

They opened the white gate of Sea Cottage and went up the little stone path. It was set with orange marigolds at each side, and hundreds of the bright red-gold flowers looked up at the children as they passed.

The cottage was very small inside. The front door opened straight on to the little sitting room. Beyond was a tiny dark kitchen. To the left was another room, whose walls were covered with bookshelves lined with books. The children stared at them in surprise.

"The man who owns this house is someone who is interested in olden times," said Mother, "so most of these books are about long-ago days, I expect. They belong to Professor Rondel. He said that you might dip into any of the books if you liked, on condition that you put them back very carefully in the right place."

"Well, I don't think *I* shall want to do any dipping into these books!" said Hilary.

"No – dipping in the sea will suit *you* better!" laughed Frances. "Mother, let's see our bedrooms now."

They went upstairs. There were three bedrooms, one very tiny indeed. Two were at the front and one was at the back. A small one and a large one were at the front, and a much bigger one behind.

"I shall have this big one," said Mother. "Then if Daddy comes down there will be plenty of room for him, too. Alec, you can have the tiny room overlooking the sea. And you two girls can have the one next to it."

"That overlooks the sea, too!" said Hilary joyfully. "But, Mother – wouldn't *you* like a room that looks out over the sea? Yours won't."

"I shall see the sea out of this little side window," said Mother, going to it. "And anyway, I shall get a wonderful view of the moors at the back. You know how I love them, especially now when the heather is out."

The children gazed out at the moors ablaze with purple heather. It was really a lovely spot.

"Blue sea in front and purple heather behind," said Alec. "What can anyone want better than that?"

"Well – tea for one thing," said Frances. "I'm most terribly hungry. Mother, could we have something to eat before we do anything?"

"If you like," said Mother. "We can do the unpacking afterwards. Alec, there is a tiny village down the road there, with about two shops and a few fishermen's cottages. Go with the girls and see if you can buy something for tea."

They chattered down the narrow wooden stairway and ran out of the front door and down the path between the marigolds. They went down the sandy road, where blue chicory blossomed by the wayside and red poppies danced.

"Isn't it heavenly!" cried Hilary. "We're at the seaside – and the holidays are just beginning. We've never been to such a lovely little place before. It's much, much nicer than the big places we've been to. I don't want bands and piers and steamers and things. I only want the yellow sands, and big rocky cliffs, and water as blue as this."

"I vote we go down to the beach after tea, when we've helped Mother to unpack," said Alec. "The tide will be going out then. It comes right up to the cliffs now. Look at it splashing high up the rocks!"

The children peered over the edge of the cliff and saw the white spray flying high. It was lovely to watch. The gulls soared above their heads, making laughing cries as they went.

"I would love to be a gull for a little while," said Frances longingly. "Just think how glorious it would be to glide along on the wind like that for ages and ages. Sometimes I dream I'm doing that."

"So do I," said Hilary. "It's a lovely feeling. Well, come on. It's no good standing here when we're getting things for tea. I'm awfully hungry."

"You always are," said Alec. "I never knew such a girl. All right – come on, Frances. We can do all the exploring we want to after tea."

They ran off. Sand got into their shoes, but they liked it. It was all part of the seashore, and there wasn't anything at the sea that they didn't like. They felt very happy.

They came to the village – though really it could hardly be called a village. There were two shops. One was a tiny baker's, which was also the little post office. The other was a general store that sold everything from pokers to strings of sausages. It was a most fascinating shop

"It even sells foreign stamps," said Alec, looking at some packets in the window. "And look – that's a fine boat. I might buy that if I've got enough money."

Hilary went to the baker's. She bought a large crusty loaf, a big cake and some currant buns. She asked for

their butter and jam at the other store. The little old lady who served her smiled at the children.

"So you've come to Sea Cottage, have you?" she said. "Well, I hope you have a good holiday. And mind you come along to see me every day, for I sell sweets, chocolates and ice creams, as well as all the other things you see."

"Oooh!" said Hilary. "Well, we'll certainly come and see you then!"

They had a look at the other little cottages in the village. Fishing nets were drying outside most of them. And one or two of them were being mended. A boy of about Alec's age was mending one. He stared at the children as they passed. They didn't know whether to smile or not.

"He looks a bit fierce, doesn't he?" said Hilary. They looked back at the boy. He did look rather fierce. He was very, very dark, and his face and hands were burnt almost black. He wore an old blue jersey and long trousers, rather ragged, which he had tied up at the ankles. He was barefooted, but beside him were big sea boots.

"I don't think I like him much," said Frances. "He looks rather rough."

"Well, he won't bother *us* much," said Alec. "He's only a fisherboy. Anyway, if he starts to be rough, *I* shall be rough, too – and he won't like that!"

"You wouldn't be nearly as strong as that fisherboy," said Hilary.

"Yes, I would!" said Alec at once.

"No, you wouldn't," said Hilary. "I bet he's got muscles like iron!"

"Shut up, you two," said Alec. "It's too lovely a day

to quarrel. Come on – let's get back home. I want my tea."

They sat in the garden to have their tea. Mother had brought out a table and stools, and the four of them sat there happily, eating big crusty slices of bread and butter and jam, watching the white tops of the blue waves as they swept up the shore.

"The beach looks a bit dangerous for bathing," said Mother. "I'm glad you are all good swimmers. Alec, you must see that you find out what times are best for bathing. Don't let the girls go in if it's dangerous."

"We can just wear swimming costumes, Mother, can't we?" said Alec. "And go barefoot?"

"Well, you won't want to go barefoot on those rocky cliffs, surely!" said Mother. "You can do as you like. But just be sensible, that's all."

"We'll help you to unpack now," said Hilary, getting up.

"Gracious, Hilary – you don't mean to say you've had enough tea yet?" said Alec, pretending to be surprised. "You've only had seven pieces of bread and jam, three pieces of cake and two currant buns!"

Hilary pulled Alec's hair hard and he yelled. Then they all went indoors. Mother said she would clear away the tea when they had gone down to the beach.

In half an hour all the unpacking was done and the children were free to go down to the beach. The tide was now out quite a long way and there was plenty of golden sand to run on.

"Come on!" said Alec impatiently. "Let's go. We won't change into swimming things now, it will waste time. We'll go as we are!"

So off they sped, down the marigold path, through the

white gate, and into the sandy lane. A small path led across the grassy cliff top to where steep steps had been cut in the cliff itself in order that people might get up and down.

"Down we go!" said Alec. "My word – doesn't the sea look grand. I've never seen it so blue in my life!"

CHAPTER TWO

A HORRID BOY – AND A DISAPPOINTMENT

They reached the beach. It was wet from the tide and gleamed brightly as they walked on it. Their feet made little prints on it that faded almost as soon as they were made. Gleaming shells lay here and there, as pink as sunset.

There were big rocks sticking up everywhere, and around them were deep and shallow pools. The children loved paddling in them because they were so warm. They ran down to the edge of the sea and let the white edges of the waves curl over their toes. It was all lovely.

"The fishing boats are out," said Alec, shading his

eyes as he saw the boats setting out on the tide, their white sails gleaming in the sun. "And listen – is that a motorboat?"

It was. One came shooting by at a great pace, and then another. They came from the big seaside town not far off where many trippers went. The children watched them fly past, the white spray flying into the air.

They wandered along by the sea, exploring all the rock pools, picking up shells and splashing in the edge of the water. They saw nobody at all until they rounded a rocky corner of the beach and came to a small cove, well hidden between two jutting-out arms of the cliff.

They heard the sound of whistling, and stopped. Sitting beside a small boat, doing something to it, was the fisherboy they had seen before tea.

He now had on his sea boots, a red fisherman's cap with a tassel hanging down, and a bright red scarf tied round his trousers.

"That's the same boy we saw before," said Alec.

The boy heard the sound of voices on the breeze and looked up. He scowled, and his dark face looked savage. He stood up and looked threateningly towards the three children.

"Well, he looks fiercer than ever," said Hilary, at last. "What's the matter with him, I wonder? He doesn't look at all pleased to see us."

"Let's go on and take no notice of him," said Alec. "He's no right to glare at us like that. We're doing no harm!"

So the three children walked into the hidden cove, not looking at the fisherboy at all. But as soon as they had taken three or four steps, the boy shouted at them loudly.

"Hey, you there! Keep out of this cove!"

The children stopped. "Why should we?" said Alec.

"Because it belongs to me," said the boy. "You keep out of this. It's been my cove for years, and no one's come here. I won't have you trippers coming into it and spoiling it."

"We're *not* trippers!" cried Hilary indignantly. "We're staying at Sea Cottage for a whole month."

"Well, you're trippers for a month then instead of for a day!" said the boy sulkily. "Clear off! I tell you. This is my own place here. I don't want anyone else in it. If you come here I'll set on you and beat you off."

The boy really looked so fierce that the children felt quite frightened. Then out of his belt he took a gleaming knife. That settled things for the two girls. They weren't going to have any quarrel with a savage boy who held such a sharp knife.

But Alec was furious. "How dare you threaten us with a knife!" he shouted. "You're a coward. I haven't a knife or I'd fight you."

"Alec! Come away!" begged Frances, clutching hold of her brother. "Do come away. I think that boy's mad. He looks it anyway."

The boy stood watching them, feeling the sharp edge of his knife with his thumb. His sullen face looked as black as thunder.

Frances and Hilary dragged Alec off round the rocky corner. He struggled with them to get free, and they tore his flannel shirt.

"Now look what you've done!" he cried angrily. "Let me go!"

"Alec, it's seven o'clock already and Mother said we were to be back by then," said Hilary, looking at her watch. "Let's go back. We can settle with that horrid boy another day."

Alec shook himself free and set off home with the girls rather sulkily. He felt that the evening had been spoilt. It had all been so lovely – and now that nasty boy had spoilt everything.

The girls told their mother about the boy, and she was astonished. "Well, he certainly does sound rather mad," she said. "For goodness' sake don't start quarrelling with him. Leave him alone."

"But, Mother, if he won't let us go into the little coves, it's not fair," said Hilary.

Mother laughed. "Don't worry about that!" she said. "There will be plenty of times when he's busy elsewhere, and the places you want to go to will be empty. Sometimes the people who live in a place do resent others coming to stay in it for a while."

"Mother, could we have a boat, do you think?" asked Alec. "It would be such fun."

"I'll go and see about one for you tomorrow," said Mother. "Now it's time you all went to bed. Hilary is yawning so widely that I can almost count her teeth!"

They were all tired. They fell into bed and went to sleep at once, although Hilary badly wanted to lie awake for a time and listen to the lovely noise the sea made outside her window. But she simply couldn't keep her eyes open, and in about half a minute she was as sound asleep as the other two.

It was lovely to wake up in the morning and remember everything. Frances woke first and sat up. She saw the blue sea shining in the distance and she gave Hilary a sharp dig.

"Hilary! Wake up! We're at the seaside!"

Hilary woke with a jump. She sat up, too, and gazed out to the sea, over which white gulls were soaring. She felt so happy that she could hardly speak. Then Alec appeared at the door in his swimming trunks. He had nothing else on at all, and his face was excited.

"I'm going for a dip," he said in a low voice. "Are you coming? Don't wake Mother. It's early."

The girls almost fell out of bed in their excitement. They pulled on swimming costumes, and then crept out of the cottage with Alec.

It was about half-past six. The world looked clean and new. "Just as if it has been freshly washed," said Hilary, sniffing the sharp, salt breeze. "Look at those pink clouds over there! And did you ever see such a clear blue as the sea is this morning. Ooooh – it's cold!"

It *was* cold. The children ran into the water a little way and then stopped and shivered. Alec plunged right under and came up, shaking the drops from his hair. "Come on!" he yelled. "It's gorgeous once you're in!"

The girls were soon right under, and the three of them spent twenty minutes swimming out and back, diving under the water and catching each other's legs, then floating happily on their backs, looking up into the clear morning sky.

"Time to come out," said Alec, at last. "Come on. Race you up the cliff!"

But they had to go slowly up the cliff, for the steps really were very steep. They burst into the cottage to find Mother up and bustling round to get breakfast ready.

At half-past seven they were all having breakfast. Afterwards Mother said she would tidy round the house and then do the shopping. The girls and Alec must make their own beds, just as they did at home.

"When we are down in the village I'll make inquiries about a boat for you," promised Mother, when at last the beds were made, the kitchen and sitting room tidied and set in order. "Now, are we ready? Bring that big basket, Alec. I shall want that."

"Mother, we must buy spades," said Alec. "That sand would be gorgeous to dig in."

"Gracious! Aren't you too big to dig?" said Mother. The children laughed.

"Mother, you're not too big either! Don't you remember how you helped us to dig that simply enormous castle last year, with the big moat round it? It had steps all the way up it and was simply lovely."

They set off joyously, Alec swinging the basket. They did a lot of shopping at the little general store, and the little old lady beamed at them.

"Do you know where I can arrange about hiring a boat for my children?" Mother asked her.

"Well," said the old lady, whose name was Mrs Polsett, "I really don't know. We use all our boats hereabouts, you know. You could ask Samuel. He lives in the cottage over yonder. He's got a small boat as well as a fishing boat. Maybe he'd let the children have it."

So Mother went across to where Samuel was sitting mending a great fishing net. He was an old man with bright blue eyes and a wrinkled face like a shrivelled brown apple. He touched his forehead when Mother spoke to him.

"Have you a boat I could hire for my children?" Mother asked.

Samuel shook his head. "No, Mum," he said. "I have

got one, it's true – but I'm not hiring it out any more. Some boys had it last year, and they lost the oars and made a great hole in the bottom. I lost more money on that there boat than I made."

"Well, I'm sure my three children would be very careful indeed," said Mother, seeing the disappointed faces around her. "Won't you lend it to them for a week and see how they get on? I will pay you well."

"No, thank you kindly, Mum," said Samuel firmly.

"Is there anyone else who has a boat to spare?" said Alec, feeling rather desperate, for he had really set his heart on a boat.

"No one that I know of," said Samuel. "Some of us lost our small boats in a big storm this year, when the sea came right over the cliffs, the waves were so big. Maybe I'll take the children out in my fishing boat if they're well behaved."

"Thank you," said Hilary. But they all looked very disappointed, because going out in somebody else's boat wasn't a bit the same as having their own.

"We'll just go back to old Mrs Polsett's shop and see if she knows of anyone else with a boat," said Mother. So back they went.

But the old lady shook her head.

"The only other person who has a boat – and it's not much of a boat, all patched and mended," she said, "is Smuggler Ben."

"Smuggler Ben!" said Alec. "Is there a smuggler here? Where does he live?"

"Oh, he's not a real smuggler!" said Mrs Polsett, with a laugh. "He's my grandson. But he's just mad on tales of the old-time smugglers, and he likes to pretend he's one. There were smugglers' caves here, you know, somewhere about the beach. I dare say Ben knows them. Nobody else does now."

The children felt terribly excited. Smugglers – and caves! And who was Smuggler Ben? They felt that they would very much like to know him. And he had a boat, too. He would be a fine person to know!

"Is Smuggler Ben grown-up?" asked Alec.

"Bless you, no!" said Mrs Polsett. "He's much the same age as you. Look – there he goes – down the street there!"

The children turned to look. And as soon as they saw the boy, their hearts sank.

"It's the nasty boy with the knife!" said Hilary sadly. "*He* won't lend us his boat."

"Don't you worry about his knife," said old Mrs Polsett. "It's all pretence with him. He's just play-acting most of the time. He always wishes he could have been a smuggler, and he's for ever pretending he is one. There's no harm in him. He's a good boy for work – and when he wants to play, well, let him play as he likes, I say! He doesn't get into mischief like most boys do. He goes off exploring the cliffs, and rows in his boat half the time. But he does keep himself to himself. Shall I ask him if he'll lend you his boat sometimes?"

"No, thank you," said Alec politely. He was sure the boy would refuse rudely, and Alec wasn't going to give him the chance to do that.

They walked back to Sea Cottage. They felt sad about the boat – but their spirits rose as they saw their swimming costumes lying on the grass, bone-dry.

"What about another swim before lunch?" cried Alec. "Come on, Mother. You must come, too!"

So down to the sea they all went again, and by the squeals, shrieks and shouts, four people had a really wonderful time!

—

CHAPTER THREE

HILARY HAS AN ADVENTURE

One evening, after tea, Frances and Alec wanted to go for a long walk. "Coming, Hilary?" they said. Hilary shook her head.

"No," she said. "I'm a bit tired with all my swimming today. I'll take a book and go and sit on the cliff top till you come back."

So Alec went off with Frances, and Hilary took her book and went to find a nice place to sit. She could see miles and miles of restless blue sea from the cliff. It was really marvellous. She walked on the cliff edge towards the east, found a big gorse bush and sat down beside it for shelter. She opened her book.

When she looked up, something nearby caught her eye. It looked like a little-worn path going straight to the ciff edge. "A rabbit path, I suppose," said Hilary to herself. "But fancy the rabbits going right over the steep cliff edge like that! I suppose there must be a hole there that they pop into."

She got up to look – and to her great surprise saw what looked like a narrow, rocky path going down the cliff side, very steep indeed! In a sandy ledge a little way down was the print of a bare foot.

"Well, *someone* has plainly gone down this steep path!" thought Hilary. "I wonder who it was. I wonder where it leads to. I've a good mind to find out!"

She began to go down the path. It really was very steep and rather dangerous. At one extremely dangerous part someone had driven in iron bars and stretched a piece of strong rope from bar to bar. Hilary was glad to get hold of it, for her feet were sliding down by themselves and she was afraid she was going to fall.

When she was about three-quarters of the way down she heard the sound of someone whistling very quietly. She stopped and tried to peer down to see who was on the beach.

"Why, this path leads down to that little cove we saw the other day!" she thought excitedly. "The one where the rude boy was. Oh, I hope he isn't there now!"

He was! He was sitting on his upturned boat, whittling at something with his sharp knife. Hilary turned rather pale when she saw the knife. It was all very well for old Mrs Polsett to say that her grandson was only play-acting – but Hilary was sure that Ben really felt himself to be somebody fierce – and he might act like that, too.

As she stood and watched him, unseen, she saw the

sharp knife slip. The boy gave a cry of pain and clutched his left hand. He had cut it very badly indeed. Blood began to drip on to the sand.

The boy felt in his pocket for something to bind up his hand. But he could find nothing. He pressed the cut together, but it went on bleeding. Hilary was tender-hearted and she couldn't bear to see the boy's face all screwed up in pain, and do nothing about it.

She forgot to be afraid of him. She went down the last piece of cliff and jumped down on the sand. The boy heard her and turned, his face one big scowl. Hilary ran up to him.

She had a big clean handkerchief in her pocket, and she took this out. "I'll tie up your hand for you," she said. "I say – what an *awful* cut! I should howl like anything if I did that to myself."

The boy scowled at her again. "What are you doing here?" he said. "Where are the others?"

"I'm alone," said Hilary. "I found that funny steep path and came down it to see where it led to. And I saw you cut your hand. Give it to me. Come on, Ben – hold it out and let me tie it up. You might bleed to death if you go on like this."

The boy held out his cut hand. "How do you know my name is Ben?" he said in a surly voice.

"Never mind how I know!" said Hilary. "You're Smuggler Ben! What a marvellous name! Don't you wish you really *were* a smuggler? I do! I'm just reading a book about smuggling and it's terribly exciting."

"What book?" asked the boy.

Hilary bound up his hand well, and then showed him the book. "It's all about hidden caves and smugglers coming in at night and things like that," she said. "I'll lend it to you if you like."

The boy stared at her. He couldn't help liking this little girl with her straight eyes and clear, kind little voice. His hand felt much more comfortable now, too. He was grateful to her. He took the book and looked through the pages.

"I'd like to read it after you," he said more graciously. "I can't get enough books. Do you really like smuggling and that kind of thing?"

"Of course," said Hilary. "I like anything adventurous like that. Is it true that there are smugglers' caves along this coast somewhere?"

The boy stopped before he answered. "If I tell you, will you keep it a secret?" he said, at last.

"Well – I could tell the others, couldn't I?" said Hilary. "We all share everything, you know, Alec and Frances and I."

"No, I don't want you to tell anyone," said the boy. "It's my own secret. I wouldn't mind sharing it with you, because you've helped me, and you like smuggling, too. But I don't want the others to know.

"Then don't tell me," said Hilary, disappointed. "You see, it would be mean of me to keep an exciting thing like that from the others. I just couldn't do it. You'd know how I feel if you had brothers and sisters. You just have to share exciting things."

"I haven't got any brothers or sisters," said the boy. "I wish I had. I always play alone. There aren't any boys of my age in our village – only girls, and I don't like girls. They're silly."

"Oh well, if you think that, I'll go," said Hilary, offended. She turned to go, but the boy caught her arm.

"No, don't go. I didn't mean that *you* were silly. I don't think you are. I think you're sensible. Let me tell you one of my secrets."

"Not unless I can share it with the others," said Hilary. "I'm simply longing to know – but I don't want to leave the others out of it."

"Are they as sensible as you are?" asked Ben.

"Of course," said Hilary. "As a matter of fact, Frances, my sister, is nicer than I am. I'm always losing my temper and she doesn't. You can trust us, Ben, really you can."

"Well," said Ben slowly, "I'll let you all into my secret then. I'll show you something that will make your stare! Come here tomorrow, down that little path. I'll be here, and just see if I don't astonish you."

Hilary's eyes shone. She felt excited. She caught hold of Ben's arm and looked at him eagerly.

"You're a sport!" she said. "I like you, Smuggler Ben. Let's all be smugglers, shall we?"

Ben smiled for the first time. His brown face changed completely, and his dark eyes twinkled. "All right," he said. "We'll all be. That would be more fun than playing alone, if I can trust you all not to say a word to any grown-up. They might interfere. And now I'll tell you one little secret – and you can tell the others if you like. I know where the old smugglers' caves are!"

"Ben!" cried Hilary, her eyes shining with excitement. "Do you really? I wondered if you did. Oh, I say, isn't that simply marvellous! Will you show us them tomorrow? Oh, do say you will."

"You wait and see," said Ben. He turned his boat the right way up and dragged it down the beach.

"Where are you going?" called Hilary.

"Back home in my boat," said Ben. "I've got to go out fishing with my uncle tonight. Would you like to come back in my boat with me? It'll save you climbing up that steep path."

"Oh, I'd love to!" said Hilary joyfully. "You know, Ben, we tried and tried to hire a boat of our own, but we couldn't. We were so terribly disappointed. Can I get in? You push her out."

Ben pushed the boat out on to the waves and then got in himself. But when he took the oars he found that his cut hand was far too painful to handle the left oar. He bit his lip and went a little pale under his tan.

"What's the matter?" said Hilary. "Oh, it's your hand. Well, let me take the oars. I can row. Yes, I can, Ben! You'll only make your cut bleed again."

Ben gave up his seat and the girl took the oars. She rowed very well indeed, and the oars cut cleanly into the water. The boat flew along over the waves.

"You don't row badly for a girl," said Ben.

"Well, we live near a river at home," said Hilary, "and we are often out in our uncle's boat. We can all row. So you can guess how disappointed we were when we found that we couldn't get a boat here for ourselves."

Ben was silent for a little while. Then he spoke again. "Well – I don't mind lending you my boat sometimes, if you like. When I'm out fishing, you can have it – but don't you dare to spoil it in any way. I know it's only an old boat, but I love it."

Hilary stopped rowing and looked at Ben in delight. "I say, you really are a brick!" she said. "Do you mean it?"

"I always mean what I say." said Ben gruffly. "You lend me your books – and I'll lend you my boat."

Hilary rowed all round the cliffs until she came to the beach she knew. She rowed inshore and the two got out. She and Ben pulled the boat right up the beach and turned it upside down.

"I must go now," said Ben. "My uncle's waiting for me. See you tomorrow."

He went off, and Hilary turned to go home. At the top of the beach she saw Frances and Alec staring at her in amazement.

"Hilary! Were you with that awful boy in his boat?" cried Frances. "However did you dare?"

"He isn't awful after all," said Hilary. "He's quite nice. He's got wonderful secrets – simply wonderful. And he says we can use his boat when he doesn't want it!"

The other two stared open-mouthed. They simply couldn't believe all this. Why, that boy had threatened them with a knife – he couldn't possibly be nice enough to lend them his boat.

"I'll tell you all about it," said Hilary, as they set off up the cliff path. "You see, I found a little secret way down to that cove we saw – and Ben was there."

She told them the whole story and they listened in silence.

"Things always happen to you, Hilary," said Frances rather enviously. "Well, I must say this is all very exciting. I can hardly wait till tomorrow. Do you really think Smuggler Ben will show us those caves? I wonder where they are? I hope they aren't miles away!"

"Well, we'll see," said Hilary happily. They went home hungry to their supper – and in bed that night each of them dreamt of caves and smugglers and all kinds of exciting things. This holiday promised to be more thrilling than they had imagined.

CHAPTER FOUR

AN EXCITING EVENING

The children told their mother about Ben. She was amused.

"So the fierce little boy has turned out to be quite ordinary after all!" she said. "Well, I must say I'm glad. I didn't very much like to think of a little savage rushing about the shore armed with a sharp knife. I think it's very nice of him to lend you his boat. You had better bring him in to a meal, and then I can see him for myself."

"Oh, thanks, Mother," said Hilary. "I say – do you think we could get ourselves some fishermen's hats, like

Ben wears – and have you got a bright-coloured scarf or sash that you could lend us, Mother? Or three, if you've got them. We're going to play smugglers, and it would be fun to dress up a bit. Ben does. He looks awfully grand in his tasselled hat and sash and big boots."

"Hilary, you don't seriously think I am going to hand you out all my precious scarves, do you?" said Mother. "I'll give you some money to go and buy three cheap hats and scarves with, if you like – and you can all wear your wellingtons if you want big boots. But I draw the line at getting you sharp knives like Ben. Look how even he cut himself today!"

The children were delighted to think they could buy something they could dress up in. The next morning they set off to Mrs Polsett's and asked to see fishermen's hats. She had a few and brought them out. "I knitted them myself," she said. "Here's a red one with a yellow tassel. That would suit you fine, Miss Hilary."

So it did. Hilary pulled it on and swung the tasselled end over her left ear just as she had seen Ben do.

Frances chose a blue one with a red tassel and Alec chose a green one with a brown tassel. Then they bought some very cheap scarves to tie round their waists.

They went back home, pulled on their wellingtons, and put on their hats and sashes.

They looked grand.

Hilary showed them where the little narrow path ran down the steep cliff.

"Goodness," said Alec, peering over the edge. "What a terrifying way down! I feel half-afraid of falling. I'm sure I can never get down those steep bits."

"There's a rope tied there," said Hilary, going down

first. "Come on. Ben will be waiting. I saw his boat out on the water as we came along the cliff."

They all went down the path slowly for fear of falling. When they jumped down the last rocky step into the little cove, they saw Ben there waiting for them, sitting on his little boat. He was dressed just as they were, except that his boots were real sea boots, and he wore trousers tucked well down into them. He didn't move as they came up, nor did he smile.

"Hello, Ben!" said Hilary. "I've brought my brother and sister as you said I could. This is Alec, and this is Frances. I've told them what you said. We're all terribly excited."

"Did you tell them it's all a deep secret?" said Ben, looking at Hilary. "They won't give it away?"

"Of course we won't," said Alec indignantly. "That would spoil all the fun. I say – can we call you Smuggler Ben? It sounds fine."

Ben looked pleased. "Yes, you can," he said. "And remember, I'm the captain. You've got to obey my orders."

"Oh," said Alec, not liking this idea quite so much. "Well – all right. Lead on. Show us your secret."

"You know, don't you, that there really were smugglers here in the old days?" said Ben. "They came up the coast quietly on dark nights, bringing in all kinds of goods. Folk here knew they came, but they were afraid of them. They used to take the goods to the old caves here, and hide them there till they could get rid of them overland."

"And do you really know where the caves are?" said Alec eagerly. "My word, Smuggler Ben – you're a wonder!"

Smuggler Ben smiled and his brown face changed at once. "Come on," he said. "I'll show you something that will surprise you!"

He led the way up the beach to the cliffs at the back. "Now," he said, "the entrance to the old caves is somewhere in this little cove. Before I show you, see if you can find it!"

"In the cove!" cried Hilary. "Oh, I guess we shall soon find it then!"

The three children began to hunt carefully along the rocky cliff. They ran into narrow caves and out again. They came to a big cave, went into that and came out again. It seemed nothing but a large cave, narrowing at the back. There were no more caves after that one, and the children turned in disappointment to Ben.

"You don't mean that these little caves and that one big one are the old smuggling caves do you?" said Hilary. "Because they are just like heaps of other caves we have seen at the seaside."

"No, I don't mean that," said Ben. "Now, you come with me and I'll show you something exciting."

He led them into the big cave. He took them to the right of it and then jumped up to a rocky ledge which was just about shoulder high. In half a moment he had completely disappeared! Hilary felt about up the ledge and called to him in bewilderment.

"Ben! Smuggler Ben! Where have you gone?"

There was no answer. The three children stared up at the ledge. Alec jumped up to it. He felt all along it, up and down and sideways. He simply couldn't imagine where Ben had gone to!

There was a low laugh behind them. The children turned in surprise – and there was Ben, standing at the entrance to the big cave, laughing all over his brown face at their surprise.

"Ben! What happened? Where did you disappear to? And how did you get back to the entrance without us seeing you?" cried Hilary. "It's like magic. Do tell us. Quick!"

"Well, I'll show you," said Ben. "I found it out quite by accident. One day I came into this cave and fell asleep. When I woke up, the tide was high and was already coming into the cave. I was trapped. I couldn't possibly get out, because I knew I'd be dashed against the rocks outside, the sea was so stormy."

"So you climbed up on to this ledge!" cried Hilary.

"Yes, I did," said Ben. "It was the only thing to do. I just hoped and hoped the sea wouldn't fill the cave up completely, or I knew I'd be drowned. Well, I crouched there for ages, the sea getting higher and higher up till it reached the ledge."

"Gracious!" said Frances, shivering. "You must have been afraid."

"I was, rather," said Ben. "Well, I rolled right to the back of the ledge, and put up my hand to catch hold of any bit of jutting-out rock that I could – and instead of knocking against rock, my hand went into space!"

"What do you mean?" said Alec in astonishment.

"Come and see," said Ben, and he took a torch out of his pocket. All the children climbed on to the ledge, and squeezed together there, watching the beam of Ben's torch. He directed it upwards – and then, to their amazement, they saw a perfectly round hole going upwards right at the far corner of the rocky ledge. It didn't look very big.

"See that?" said Ben. "Well, when I felt my hand

going up that hole I slid over to this corner and put my arm right up the hole. And this is what I found."

He shone his torch up the rounded hole in the rock. The three children peered up, one after another.

Driven into the rock were great thick nails, one above the other. "See those?" said Ben. "Well, I reckon they were put there by some old-time smuggler."

"Did you get up the hole?" asked Alec.

"You bet I did!" said Ben. "And pretty quick, too, for the sea was washing inches above the ledge by that time and I was soaked through. I squeezed myself up, got my feet on those nails – they're sort of steps up, you see – and climbed up the hole by feeling for the nails with my feet."

"Where does the hole lead to?" asked Frances in excitement.

"You'd better come and see," said Ben, with a sudden grin. The children asked nothing better than that, and at once Alec put his head up the hole. It was not such a tight fit as he expected. He was easily able to climb up. There were about twenty nails for footholds and then they stopped. There was another ledge to climb out on. The boy dragged himself there, and looked down.

"Can't see a thing!" he called. "Come on up, Smuggler Ben, and bring your torch."

"I'll give Hilary my torch," said Ben. "She can shine it for you up there when she's up, and shine it down for us to climb up by, too. Go on, Hilary."

So Hilary went up next with the torch – and when she shone it around her at the top, she and Alec gave a shout of astonishment.

They were on a ledge near the ceiling of a most enormous cave. It looked almost as big as a church to

"*Real* smugglers have been here!" said Hilary, in a whisper

the children. The floor was of rock, not of sand. Queer lights shone in the walls. They came from the twinkling bits of metal in the rocks.

"Frances! Hurry," cried Hilary. "It's marvellous here."

Soon all four children were standing on the ledge, looking down into the great cave. In it, on the floor, were many boxes of all kinds – small, big, square, oblong. Bits of rope were scattered about, too, and an old broken lantern lay in a corner.

"*Real* smugglers have been here!" said Hilary in a whisper.

"What are you whispering for?" said Alec with a laugh. "Afraid they will hear you?"

"No – but it all seems so mysterious," said Hilary. "Let's get down to the floor of the cave. How do we get there?"

"Jump," said Ben.

So they jumped. They ran to the boxes and opened the lids.

"No good," said Ben. "I've done that long ago. They're quite empty. I often come to play smugglers here when I'm by myself. Isn't it a fine place?"

"Simply marvellous!" said Alec. "Let's all come here and play tomorrow. We can bring candles and something to eat and drink. It would be gorgeous."

"Oooh, yes," said Hilary. So they planned everything in excitement, and then climbed back to the ledge, and down through the hole into the first cave. Out they went into the sunshine. Ben smiled as much as the rest.

"It's fun to share my secret with you," he told the others half-shyly. "It will be grand to play smugglers all together, instead of just by myself. I'll bring some sandwiches tomorrow, and some plums. You bring anything you can, too. It shall be our own secret smugglers' cave – and we're the smugglers!"

CHAPTER FIVE

YET ANOTHER SECRET

The next day the four children met together in the big cave. They felt very thrilled as they climbed up the hole and then jumped down into the smuggler's cave. They had brought candles and food with them, and Alec had bottles of home-made lemonade on his back in a leather bag.

They played smugglers to their hearts' content. Ben ordered them about, and called them "My men", and everyone enjoyed the game thoroughly. At last, Alec sat down on a big box and said he was tired of playing.

"I'd like something to eat," he said. "Let's use this big box for a table."

They set the things out on the table. And then Hilary looked in a puzzled way at the box.

"What's up?" asked Alec, seeing her look.

"Well, I'm just wondering something," said Hilary. "How in the world did the smugglers get this big box up the small round hole to this cave? After all, that hole only just takes us comfortably – surely this box would never have got through it."

Frances and Alec stared at the box. They felt puzzled, too. It was quite certain that no one could have carried such a big box through the hole. They looked at Ben.

"Have you ever thought of that!" Alec asked him.

"Plenty of times," said Ben. "And, what's more, I know the answer!"

"Tell us!" begged Hilary. "Is there another way into this cave?"

Smuggler Ben nodded. "Yes," he said. "I'll show it to you if you like. I just wanted to see if any of my three men were clever enough to think of such a thing. Come on – I'll show you the other way in. Didn't you wonder yesterday how it was that I came back into the other cave after I'd disappeared up the hole?"

He stood up and the others rose, too, all excited. Ben went to the back of the cave. It seemed to the children as if the wall there was quite continuous – but it wasn't. There was a fold in it – and in the fold was a passage! It was wide, but low, and the children had to crouch down almost double to get into it. But almost immediately it rose high and they could stand. Smuggler Ben switched on his torch, and the children saw that the passage was quite short and led into yet another cave. This was small and ran right down to the rocky side of the cliff very steeply, more like a wide passage than a cave.

The children went down the long cave and came to a rocky inlet of water. "When the tide comes in, it sweeps right through this cave," said Ben, "and I reckon that this is where the smugglers brought in their goods – by boat. The boat would be guided into this watery passage at high tide, and beached at the far end, where the tide didn't reach. Then the things could easily be taken into the big cave. The smugglers left a way of escape for themselves down the hole we climbed through from the first cave – you know, where the nails are driven into the rock."

"This gets more and more exciting!" said Alec. "Anything more, Ben? Don't keep it from us. Tell us everything!"

"Well, there is one thing more," said Ben, "but it just beats me. Maybe the four of us together could do something about it though. Come along and I'll show you."

He led them back to the little passage between the big cave and the one they were in. He climbed up the wall a little way and then disappeared. The others followed him.

There was another passage leading off into the darkness there, back into the cliff. Ben shone his torch down it as the others crowded on his heels.

"Let's go up it!" cried Alec excitedly.

"We can't," said Ben, and he shone his torch before him. "The passage walls have fallen in just along there – look!"

So they had. The passage ended in a heap of stones, soil and sand. It was completely blocked up.

"Can't we clear it?" cried Alec.

"Well, we might, as there are so many of us," said

Ben. "I didn't feel like tackling it all by myself, I must say. For one thing I didn't know how far back the passage was blocked. It might have fallen in for a long way."

"I wonder where it leads to," said Alec. "It seems to go straight back. I say – isn't this thrilling!"

"We'll come and dig it out tomorrow," said Hilary, her eyes dancing. "We'll bring our spades – and a sack or something to put the stones and soil in. Then we can drag it away and empty it."

"Be here tomorrow after tea," said Smuggler Ben, laughing. "I'll bring my uncle's big spade. That's a powerful one – it will soon dig away the soil."

So the next day the children crowded into the cave with spades and sacks. They used the ordinary way in, climbing up the hole by the nails and jumping into the cave from the high ledge. Then they made their way into the low passage, and climbed up where the roof rose high, till they came to the blocked-up passage. They went on by the light of their torches and came to the big fall of stones and soil.

"Now, men, to work!" said Smuggler Ben, and the gang set to work with a will. The boys shovelled away the soil and stones, and the girls filled the sacks. Then the boys dragged them down the passage, let them fall into the opening between the two caves, climbed down, dragged the sacks into the large cave and emptied them into a corner. Then back they went again to do some more digging.

"What's the time?" said Alec, at last. "I feel as if we've been working for hours. We mustn't forget that high tide is at half-past seven. We've got to get out before then."

Hilary looked at her watch. "It's all right," she said. "It's only half-past six. We've plenty of time."

"Gracious! Hasn't the time gone slowly!" said Frances in surprise. "Come on – we can do a lot more!"

They went on working, and after a time Ben began to feel rather uncomfortable. "Hilary, what's the time now?" he said. "I'm sure it must be getting near high tide."

Hilary glanced at her watch again. "It's half-past six," she said in surprise.

"But you said that before!" cried Ben. "Has your watch stopped?"

It had! Hilary held it to her ear and cried out in dismay. "Yes! It's stopped. Oh blow! I wonder what the right time is."

"Quick! We'd better go and see how the tide is," said Ben, and he dropped his spade and rushed to the entrance of the blocked-up passage. He dropped down and went into the big cave, and then climbed up to the ledge, and then down by the nail studded hole on to the ledge in the first cave.

But even as he climbed down to the ledge, he felt the wash of water over his foot. "Golly! The tide's almost in!" he yelled. "We're caught! We can't get out!"

He climbed back and stood in the big cave with the others. They looked at him, half-frightened.

"Don't be scared," said Smuggler Ben. "It only means we'll have to wait a few hours till the tide goes down. I hope your mother won't worry."

"She's out tonight," said Alec. "She won't know. Does the water come in here, Ben?"

"Of course not," said Ben. "This cave is too high up.

Well – let's sit down, have some chocolate and a rest, and then, we might as well get on with our job."

Time went on. The boys went to see if the tide was falling, but it was still very high. It was getting dark outside. The boys stood at the end of the long, narrow cave, up which the sea now rushed deeply. And as they stood there, they heard a strange noise coming nearer and nearer.

"Whatever's that?" said Alec in astonishment.

"It sounds like a motorboat," said Ben.

"It can't be," said Alec.

But it was. A small motorboat suddenly loomed out of the darkness and worked itself very carefully up the narrow passage and into the long cave, which was now full of deep water! The boys were at first too startled to move. They heard men and women talking in low voices.

"Is this the place?"

"Yes – step out just there. Wait till the wave goes back. That's it – now step out."

Ben clutched hold of Alec's arm and pulled him silently away, back into the entrance between the caves. Up they went in the blocked passage. The girls called out to them: "What's the tide like?"

"Sh!" said Smuggler Ben, so fiercely that the girls were quite frightened. They stared at Ben with big eyes. The boy told them in a whisper what he and Alec had seen.

"Something's going on," he said mysteriously. "I don't know what. But it makes me suspicious when strange motorboats come to our coasts late at night like this and run into a little-known cave. After all, our country is at war – they may be up to no good, these people. They may be enemies!"

All the children felt a shivery feeling down their backs when Ben said this. Hilary felt that it was just a bit *too* exciting. "What do you mean?" she whispered.

"I don't exactly know," said Ben. "All I know for certain is that it's plain somebody else knows of these caves and plans to use them for something. I don't know what. And it's up to us to find out!"

"Oooh! I wish we could!" said Hilary, at once. "What are we going to do now? Wait here?"

"Alec and I will go down to the beginning of this passage," said Ben. "Maybe the people don't know about it. We'll see if we can hear what they say."

So they crept down to the beginning of the passage and leaned over to listen. Three or four people had now gone into the big cave, but to Ben's great disappointment they were talking in a strange language, and he could not understand a word.

Then came something he *did* understand! One of the women spoke in English. "We will bring them on Thursday night," she said. "When the tide is full."

Another man answered. Then the people went back to their motorboat, and the boys soon heard the whirring of the engine as it made its way carefully out of the long, narrow cave.

"They're using that cave rather like a boathouse," said Ben. "Golly, I wonder how they knew about it. And what are they bringing in on Thursday night?"

"Smuggled goods, do you think?" said Alec, hot with excitement. "People always smuggle things in wartime. Mother said so. They're smugglers, Ben – smugglers of nowadays! And they're using the old smugglers' caves again. I say – isn't this awfully exciting?"

"Yes, it is," said Smuggler Ben. "We'd better come

here on Thursday night, Alec. We'll have to see what happens. We simply must. Can you slip away about midnight, do you think?"

"Of course!" said Alec. "You bet! And the girls, too! We'll all be here! And we'll watch to see exactly what happens. Fancy spying on real smugglers, Ben. What a thrill!"

CHAPTER SIX

A QUEER DISCOVERY

Mother was in by the time the children got back home, and she was very worried indeed about them.

"Mother, it's all right," said Alec, going over to her. "We just got caught by the tide, that's all, playing in caves. But we were quite safe. We just waited till the tide went down."

"Now listen, Alec," said Mother, "this just won't do. I shall forbid you to play in those caves if you get caught another time and worry me like this. I imagined you all drowning or something."

"We're awfully sorry, Mother," said Hilary, putting

her arms round her. "Really, we wouldn't have worried you for anything. Look – my watch stopped at half-past six, and that put us all wrong about the tide."

"Very well," said Mother. "I'll forgive you this time – but I warn you, if you worry me again like this you won't be allowed to set foot in a single cave!"

The next day it poured with rain, which was very disappointing. Alec ran down to the village to see what Ben was doing. The two girls talked excitedly about what had happened the night before.

"Mother says will you come and spend the day with us?" said Alec. "Do come. You'll like Mother, she's a dear."

The two boys went back to Sea Cottage. The girls welcomed them, and Mother shook hands with Ben very politely.

"I'm glad you can come for the day," she said. "You'd better go up to the girls' bedroom and play there. I want the sitting room to do some writing in this morning."

So they all went up to the bedroom above, and sat down to talk. "It's nice of Mother to send us up here," said Hilary. "We can talk in peace. What are our plans for Thursday, Captain?"

"Well, I don't quite know," said Ben slowly. "You see, we've got to be there at midnight, haven't we? – but we simply must be there a good time before that, because of the tide. You see, we can't get into either cave if the tide is up. We'd be dashed to pieces."

The children stared at Smuggler Ben in dismay. None of them had thought of that.

"What time would we have to be there?" asked Alec.

"We'd have to be there about half-past nine, as far as

I can reckon," said Ben. "Can you leave by that time? What would your mother say?"

"Mother wouldn't let us, I'm sure of that," said Hilary in disappointment. "She was so dreadfully worried about us last night. I'm quite sure if we told her what we wanted to do, she would say 'no' at once."

"She isn't in bed by that time, then?" said Ben.

The children shook their heads. All four were puzzled and disappointed. They couldn't think how to get over the difficulty. There was no way out of the cottage except through the sitting room door – and Mother would be in the room, writing or reading, at the time they wanted to go out. "What about getting out of the window?" said Alec, going over to look. But that was quite impossible, too. It was too far to jump, and, anyway, Mother would be sure to hear any noise they made.

"It looks as if I'll have to go alone," said Ben gloomily, "It's funny – I used to like doing everything all by myself, you know – but I don't like it now at all. I want to be with my three men!"

"Oh, Ben – it would be awful thinking of you down in those caves finding out what was happening – and us in our bed, wanting and longing to be with you!" cried Hilary.

"Well, I simply don't know what else to do," said Ben. "If you can't come, you can't. And certainly I wouldn't let you come after your mother had gone to bed, because by that time the tide would be up, and you'd simply be washed away as soon as you set foot on the beach. No – I'll go alone – and I'll come and tell you what's happened the next morning."

The children felt terribly disappointed and gloomy. "Let's go downstairs into the little study place that's lined with books," said Hilary, at last. "I looked into one of the books the other day, and it seemed to be all about this district in the old days. Maybe we might find some bits about smugglers."

Ben brightened up at once. "That would be fine," he said. "I know Professor Rondel was supposed to have a heap of books about this district. He was a funny man – never talked to anyone. I didn't like him."

The children went downstairs. Mother called out to them: "Where are you going?"

"Into the book room," said Hilary, opening the sitting room door. "We may, mayn't we?"

"Yes, but be sure to take care of any book you use, and put it back into its right place," said Mother. They promised this and then went into the little study.

"My word! What hundreds of books!" said Ben in amazement. The walls were lined with them, almost from floor to ceiling. The boy ran his eyes along the shelves. He picked out a book and looked at it.

"Here's a book about the moors behind here," he said. "And maps, too. Look – I've been along here – and crossed that stream just there."

The children looked. "We ought to go for some walks with you over those lovely moors, Ben," said Alec. "I'd like that."

Hilary took down one or two books and looked through them, too, trying to find something exciting to read. She found nothing and put them back. Frances showed her a book on the top shelf.

"Look," she said, "do you think that would be any good? It's called *Old-Time Smugglers' Haunts*."

"It might be interesting," said Hilary, and stood on a chair to get the book. It was big and old and smelt musty. The girl jumped down with it and opened it on the table. The first picture she saw made her cry out.

"Oh, look – here's an old picture of this village! Here are the cliffs – and there are the old, old houses that the fishermen still live in!"

She was quite right. Underneath the picture was written: "A little-known smugglers' haunt. See page 66."

They turned to page sixty-six, and found printed there an account of the caves in the little cove on the beach. "The best-known smuggler of those days was a dark, fiery man named Smuggler Ben," said the book. The children exclaimed in surprise and looked at Ben.

"How funny!" they cried. "Did you know that, Ben?"

"No," said Ben. "My name is really Benjamin, of course, but everyone calls me Ben. I'm dark, too. I wonder if Smuggler Ben was an ancestor of mine – you know, some sort of relation a hundred or more years ago?"

"Quite likely," said Alec. "I wish we could find a picture of him to see if he's like you."

But they couldn't. They turned over the pages of the book and gave it up. But before they shut it Ben took hold of it. He had an idea.

"I wonder if by chance there's a mention of that blocked-up passage," he said. "It would be fun to know where it comes out, wouldn't it?"

He looked carefully through the book. He came again to page sixty-six, and looked at it closely. "Someone has written a note in the margin of this page," he said, holding it up to the light. "It's written in pencil, very faintly. I can hardly make it out."

The children did make it out at last. "For more information, see page 87 of *Days of Smugglers*," the note said. The children looked at one another.

"That would be a book," said Alec, moving to the shelves. "Let's see who can find it first."

Hilary found it. She was always the sharpest of the three. It was a small book, bound in black, and the print was rather faded. She turned to page eighty-seven. The book was all about the district they were staying in, and on page eighty-seven was a description of the old caves. And then came something that excited the children very much. "Read it out, Ben, read it out!" cried Alec. "It's important."

So Ben read it out. "'From a well-hidden opening between two old smugglers' caves is a curious passage, partly natural, partly man-made, probably by the smugglers themselves. This runs steadily upwards through the cliffs, and eventually stops not far from a little stream. A well-hidden hole leads upwards on to the moor. This was probably the way the smugglers used when they took their goods from the caves, over the country.'"

The children stared at one another, trembling with excitement. "So that's where the passage goes to!" said Alec. "My word – if only we could find the other end! Ben, have you any idea at all where it ends?"

"None at all," said Ben. "But it wouldn't be very difficult to find out! We know whereabouts the beginnings of the passage are – and if we follow a more or less straight line inland till we come to a stream on the moors, we might be able to spot the hole!"

"I say! Let's go now, at once, this very minute!" cried Hilary, shouting in her excitement.

"Shut up, silly," said Alec. "Do you want to tell everyone our secrets? It's almost dinnertime. We can't go now. But I vote we go immediately afterwards!"

"Professor Rondel must have known all about those

caves," said Ben thoughtfully. "I suppose he couldn't have anything to do with the strange people we overheard last night? No – that's too far-fetched. But the whole thing is very strange. I do hope we shall be able to find the entrance to the other end of that secret passage."

Mother called the children at that moment. "Dinner!" she cried. "Come along, bookworms, and have a little something to eat."

They were all hungry. They went to wash and make themselves tidy, and then sat down and ate a most enormous meal. Ben liked the children's mother very much. She talked and laughed, and he didn't feel a bit shy of her.

"You know, Alec and the girls really thought you were going after them with that knife of yours," she said.

Ben went red. "I did feel rather fierce that day," he said. "But it's awful when people come and spoil your secret places, isn't it? Now I'm glad they came, because they're the first friends I've ever had. We're having a fine time."

Mother looked out of the window as the children finished up the last of the jam tarts.

"It's clearing up," she said. "I think you all ought to go out. It will be very wet underfoot but you can put on your wellingtons. Why don't you go out on the moors for a change?"

"Oh *yes*, we will!" cried all four children at once. Mother was rather astonished.

"Well, you don't usually welcome any suggestion of walking in the wet," she said. "I believe you've got some sort of secret plan!"

But nobody told her what it was!

CHAPTER SEVEN

GOOD HUNTING

After dinner the children put on their boots and macs. They pulled on their sou'westers, and said goodbye to their mother, and set off.

"Now for a good old hunt," said Ben. "First let's go to the cliff that juts over my little cove. Then we'll try to make out where the passage begins underground and set off from that spot."

It wasn't long before they were over the cove. The wind whipped their faces, and overhead the clouds scudded by. Ben went to about the middle of the cliff over the cove and stood there.

"I should say that the blocked-up passage runs roughly under here," he said. "Now let's think. Does it run quite straight from where it begins? It curves a bit, doesn't it?"

"Yes, but it soon curved back again to the blocked-up part," said Alec eagerly. "So you can count it about straight to there. Let's walk in a straight line from here till we think we've come over the blocked-up bit."

They walked over the cliff inland, foot-deep in purple-heather. Then Ben stopped. "I reckon we must just about be over the blocked-up bit," he said. "Now listen – we've got to look for a stream. There are four of us. We'll all part company and go off in different directions to look for the stream. Give a yell if you find one."

Soon Alec gave a yell. "There's a kind of stream here! It runs along for a little way and then disappears into a sort of little gully. I expect it makes its way down through the cliff somewhere and springs out into the sea. Would this be the stream, do you think?"

Everyone ran to where Alec stood. Ben looked down at the little brown rivulet. It was certainly very small.

"It's been bigger once upon a time," he said, pointing to where the bed was dry and wide. "Maybe this is the one. There doesn't seem to be another, anyway."

"We'll hunt about around here for an opening of some sort," said Alec, his face red with excitement.

They all hunted about, and it was Hilary who found it – quite by accident!

She was walking over the heather, her eyes glancing round for any hole, when her foot went right through into space! She had trodden on what she thought was good solid ground, over which heather grew – but almost at once she sank on one knee as her foot went through some sort of hole!

"I say! My foot's gone through a hole here," she yelled. "Is it the one! It went right through it. I nearly sprained my ankle."

The others came up. Ben pulled Hilary up and then parted the heather to see. Certainly a big hole was there – and certainly it seemed to go down a good way.

The children tugged away at armfuls of heather and soon got the tough roots out. The sides of the hole fell away as they took out the heather. Ben switched his torch on when it was fairly large. There seemed to be quite a big drop down.

"We'd better slide down a rope," he said.

"We haven't got one," said Alec.

"I've got one round my waist," said Ben, and undid a piece of strong rope from under his red belt. A stout gorse bush stood not far off, and Ben wound it round the strong stem at the bottom, pricking himself badly but not seeming to feel it at all.

"I'll go down," he said. He took hold of the rope and lay down on the heather. Then he put his legs into the hole and let himself go, holding tightly to the rope. He slid into the hole, and went a good way down.

"See anything?" yelled Alec.

"Yes. There *is* an underground channel here of some sort!" came Ben's voice, rather muffled. "I believe we're onto the right one. Wait a minute. I'm going to kick away a bit with my feet, and get some of the loose soil away."

After a bit Ben's voice came again, full of excitement.

"Come on down! There's a kind of underground

channel, worn away by water. I reckon a stream must have run here at some time."

One by one the excited children slipped down the rope. They found what Ben had said – a kind of underground channel or tunnel plainly made by water of some kind in far-off days. Ben had his torch and the others had theirs. They switched them on.

Ben led the way. It was a curious path to take. Sometimes the roof was so low that the children had to crouch down, and once they had to go on hands and knees. Ben showed them the marks of tools in places where rocks jutted into the channel.

"Those marks were made by the smugglers, I reckon," he said. "They found this way and made it into a usable passage. They must have found it difficult getting some of their goods along here."

"I expect they unpacked those boxes we saw and carried the goods on their backs in bags or sacks," said Frances, seeing the picture clearly in her mind. "Ooooh – isn't it strange to think that heaps of smugglers have gone up this dark passage carrying smuggled goods years and years ago!"

They went on for a good way and then suddenly came to an impassable bit where the roof had fallen in. They stopped.

"Well, here we are," said Ben, "we've come to the blocked-up part once more. Now the thing is – how far along is it blocked-up – just a few yards, easy to clear – or a quarter of a mile?"

"I don't see how we can tell," said Alec. The four children stood and looked at the fallen stones and soil. It was most annoying to think they could get no farther.

"I know!" said Hilary suddenly. "I know! One of us

"Yes, there *is* an underground channel here of some sort!"

could go in at the other end of the passage and yell. Then, if we can hear anything, we shall know the blockage isn't stretching very far!"

"Good idea, Hilary," said Ben, pleased. "Yes, that really *is* a good idea. I'd better be the one to go because I can go quickly. It'll take me a little time, so you must be patient. I shall yell loudly when I get up to the blocked bit, and then I shall knock on some stones with my spade. We did leave the spades there, didn't we?"

"We did," said Alec. "I say – this is getting awfully exciting, isn't it?"

Ben squeezed past the others and made his way up the channel. He climbed up the rope and sped off over the heather to the cliff side. Down the narrow path he went, and jumped down into the cove.

Meanwhile, the others had sat down in the tunnel, to wait patiently for any noise they might hear.

"It will be terribly disappointing if we don't hear anything," said Frances. They waited and waited. It seemed ages to them.

And then suddenly they heard something! It was Ben's voice, rather muffled and faint, but still quite unmistakable: "Hellooooooooo! Hellooooooooo!"

Then came the sharp noise of a spade on rock: Crack! Crack! Crack!

"Hellooooooooo!" yelled back all three children, wildly excited. "Hellooooooooo!"

"Come – and – join – me!" yelled Ben's voice. "Come – and – join – me!"

"Coming, coming, coming!" shouted Alec, Hilary and Frances, and all three scrambled back up to the entrance of the hole, swarming up the rope like monkeys.

They tore over the heather back to the cliff side and almost fell down the steep path. Down into the cove on the sand – in the big cave – up on to the ledge – up the nail-studded hole – out on the ledge in the enormous cave – down to the rocky floor – over to the passage between the two caves – up the wall – and into the blocked-up passage where Ben was impatiently waiting for them.

"You *have* been quick," he cried. "I say – I could hear your voices quite well. The blocked piece can't stretch very far. Isn't that good? Do you feel able to tackle it hard now? If so, I believe we might clear it."

"I could tackle anything!" said Alec, taking off his mac. "I could tackle the cliff itself!"

Everyone laughed. They were all pleased and excited, and felt able to do anything, no matter how hard it was.

"What's the time?" suddenly said Alec, when they had worked hard for a time, loosening the soil and filling the sacks. "Mother's expecting us in to tea, you know."

"It's quarter-past four already," said Hilary in dismay. "We must stop. But we'll come back after tea."

They sped off to their tea, and Mother had to cut another big plateful of bread and butter because they finished up every bit. Then off they went again, back to their exciting task.

"I say, I say, I say!" suddenly cried Alec, making everyone jump. "I've just thought of something marvellous."

"What?" asked everyone curiously.

"Well – if we can get this passage clear, we can come down it on Thursday night, from outside," said Alec. "We don't need to bother about the tides or anything. We can slip out at half-past eleven, go to the entrance on the moor and come down here and see what's happening!"

"Golly! I never thought of that!" cried Hilary.

Ben grinned. "That's fine," he said. "Yes – you can easily do that. You needn't disturb your mother at all. I think I'd better be here earlier, though, in case those people change their plans and come before they say. Though I don't think they will, because if they come in by motorboat, they'll need high tide to get their boat into the long cave."

The children went on working at the passage. Suddenly Ben gave a shout of joy.

"We're through! My spade went right through into nothing just then! Where's my torch?"

He shone it in front of him, and the children saw that he had spoken the truth. The light of the torch shone beyond into the other side of the passage! There was only a small heap of fallen earth to manage now.

"I think we'll finish this," said Alec, though he knew the girls were tired out. "I can't leave that little bit till tomorrow! You girls can sit down and have a rest. Ben and I can tackle this last bit. It will be easy."

It was. Before another half-hour had gone by, the passage was quite clear, and the children were able to walk up and down it from end to end. They felt pleased with themselves.

"Now we'll have to wait till Thursday," sighed Alec. "Gosh, what a long time it is – a whole day and a night and then another whole day. I simply can't wait!"

But they had to. They met Ben the next day and planned everything. They could hardly go to sleep on Wednesday night, and when Thursday dawned they were all awake as early as the sun.

CHAPTER EIGHT

THURSDAY EVENING

The day seemed very long indeed to the children – but they had a lovely surprise in the afternoon. Their father arrived, and with him he brought their Uncle Ned. Mother rushed to the gate to meet them as soon as she saw them, and the children shouted for joy.

Uncle Ned said he could stay a day or two, and Daddy said he would stay for a whole week.

"Where's Uncle Ned going to sleep?" asked Alec. "In my room?"

In the ordinary way the boy would have been very pleased at the idea of his uncle sleeping in the same room with him – but tonight a grown-up might perhaps spoil things.

"Ned will have to sleep on the sofa in the sitting room," said Mother. "I don't expect he will mind. He's had worse places to sleep in this war!"

Both Daddy and Uncle Ned were in the Army. It was lucky they had leave just when the children were on holiday. They could share a bit of it, too! All the children were delighted.

"I say – how are we going to slip out at half-past eleven tonight if Uncle Ned is sleeping in the sitting room?" said Hilary, when they were alone. "We shall have to be jolly careful not to wake him!"

"Well, there's nothing for it but to creep through to the door," said Alec. "And if he does wake, we'll have to beg him not to tell tales of us."

The night came at last. The children went to bed as usual, but not one of them could go to sleep. They lay waiting for the time to pass, and it passed so slowly that once or twice Hilary thought her watch must have stopped, but it hadn't.

At last half-past eleven came – the time when they had arranged to leave, to go to meet Ben in the passage above the caves. Very quietly the children dressed. They all wore shorts, jerseys, their smugglers' hats, sashes and rubber boots. They stole down the stairs very softly. Not a stair creaked, not a child coughed.

The door of the sitting room was a little open. Alec pushed it a little farther and put his head in. The room was dark. On the sofa Uncle Ned was lying, his regular breathing telling the children that he was asleep.

"He's asleep," whispered Alec, in a low voice. "I'll go

across first and open the door. Then you two step across quietly to me. I'll shut the door after us."

The boy went across the room to the door. He opened it softly. He had already oiled it that day, by Ben's orders, and it made no sound. A streak of moonlight came in.

Silently the three children passed out and Alec shut the door. Just as they were going through the door, their uncle woke. He opened his eyes – and to his very great amazement saw the figures of the three children going quietly out of the open door. Then it shut.

Uncle Ned sat up with a jerk. Could he be dreaming? He opened the door and looked out. No – he wasn't dreaming. There were the three figures hurrying along to the moor in the moonlight. Uncle Ned was more astonished than he had ever been in his life before.

"Now what in the world do these kids think they are doing?" he wondered. "Little monkeys slipping out like this just before midnight. What are they up to? I'll go after them and see. Maybe they'll let me join in their prank, whatever it is. Anyway, Alec oughtn't to take his two sisters out at this time of night!"

Uncle Ned pulled on a mackintosh over his pyjamas and set out down the lane after the children. They had no idea he was some way behind them. They were thrilled because they thought they had got out so easily without being heard!

They got to the hole in the heather and by the light of their torch slid down the rope. Uncle Ned was more and more amazed as he saw one child after another slide down and disappear completely. He didn't know any hole was there, of course. He found it after a time and decided to go down it himself.

Meanwhile, the children were halfway down the passage. There they met Ben, and whispered in excitement to him. "We got out without being seen – though our uncle was sleeping on the sofa near the door! Ben, have you seen or heard anything yet?"

"Not a thing," said Ben. "But they should be here soon, because it's almost midnight and the tide is full."

They all went down to the end of the passage, and jumped down to stand at the end of the long, narrow cave. This was now full of water, and the waves rushed up it continually.

"Easy enough to float any motorboat right in," said Ben. "I wonder what they're bringing."

"Listen!" said Hilary suddenly. "I'm sure I can hear something."

"It's the chug-chug of that motorboat again," whispered Alec, a shiver going down his back. He wasn't frightened, but it was all so exciting he couldn't help trembling. The girls were the same. Their knees shook a little. Only Ben was quite still and fearless.

"Now don't switch your torches on by mistake, for goodness' sake," whispered Ben, as the chugging noise came nearer. "We'll stay here till we see the boat coming into the long channel of this cave then we'll hop up into the passage and listen hard."

The motorboat came nearer and nearer. Then as it nosed gently into the long cave with its deep inlet of water, the engine was shut off.

"Now we must go," said Ben, and the four children turned. They climbed up into the passage above the caves and stood there, listening.

People got out of the motorboat, which was apparently

tied up to some rock. Torches were switched on. Ben, who was leaning over the hole from the passage, counted three people going into the big cave – two men and a woman. One of the men seemed somehow familiar to him, but he was gone too quickly for Ben to take a second look.

"Well, here we are," said a voice from the enormous cave below. "I will leave you food and drink, and you will wait here till it is safe to go inland. You have maps to show you how to go. You know what to do. Do it well. Come back here and the motorboat will fetch you a week from now."

The children listening above could not make out at all what was happening. Who were the people? And what were the two of them to do? Alec pressed hard by Ben to listen better. His foot touched a pebble and set it rolling down into the space between the caves. Before he could stop himself he gave a low cry of annoyance.

There was instant silence in the cave. Then the first voice spoke again very sharply: "What was that? Did you hear anything?"

A wave roared up the narrow cave nearby and made a great noise. Whilst the splashing was going on Ben whispered to Alec: "Move back up the passage, quick! You idiot, they heard you! They'll be looking for us in a minute!"

The children hurried back along the passage as quietly as they could, their hearts beating painfully. And half-way along it they bumped into somebody!

Hilary screamed. Frances almost fainted with fright. Then the somebody took their arms and said:

"Now what in the world are you kids doing here at this time of night?"

"Uncle Ned, oh, Uncle Ned!" said Hilary in a faint

voice. "Oh, it's marvellous to have a grown-up just at this very minute to help us! Uncle Ned, something very strange is going on. Tell him, Alec."

Alec told his astonished uncle very quickly all that had happened. He listened without a word and then spoke in a sharp, stern voice that the children had never heard before.

"They're spies! They've come over from the coast of Ireland. It's just opposite here, you know. Goodness knows what they're going to do – some dirty work, I expect. We've got to stop them. Now let me think. How can we get them? Can they get away from the caves except by motorboat?"

"Only up this passage, until the tide goes down," said Ben. "Sir – listen to me. I could slip down the hole and cast off the motorboat by myself. I know how to start it up. I believe I could do it. Then you could hold this passage, couldn't you, and send Alec and the girls back to get their father. You'd have to get somebody to keep guard outside the cave as soon as the tide goes down, in case they try to escape round the cliffs."

"Leave that to me," said Uncle Ned grimly. "Can you really get away in that motorboat? If you can, you'll take their only means of escape. Well, go and try. Good luck to you. You're a brave lad!"

Ben winked at the others, who were staring at him open-mouthed. Then he slipped along down the passage again until he came to the opening. He stood there listening before he let himself down into the space between the caves. It was plain that the people there had come to the conclusion that the noise they had heard was nothing to worry about, for they were talking together. There was the clink of glasses as the boy dropped down quietly to the floor below the passage.

"They're wishing each other good luck!" said the boy to himself, with a grin. He went to the motorboat, which was gently bobbing up and down as waves ran under it up the inlet of water in the cave. He climbed quietly in. He felt about for the rope that was tied round a rock, and slipped it loose. The next wave took the boat down with it, and as soon as he dared, Ben started up the engine to take her out of the deep channel in the cave.

He was lucky in getting the boat out fairly quickly. As soon as the engine started up, there came a shout from the cave, and Ben knew that the two men there had run to see what was happening. He ducked in case there was any shooting. He guessed that the men would be desperate when they saw their boat going.

He got the boat clear, and swung her out on the water that filled the cove. The boy knew the coast almost blindfold, and soon the little motorboat was chug-chug-chugging across the open sea towards the beach where a little jetty ran out, and where Ben could tie her up. He was filled with glee. It was marvellous to think he had beaten those men – and that woman, too, whoever she was. Spies! Well – now they knew what British boys and girls could do!

He wondered what the others were doing. He felt certain that Alec and the girls were even now speeding up the passage, climbing out through the heather and racing back home to waken their father.

And that is exactly what they *were* doing! They had left their uncle in the passage – and in his hand was his loaded revolver. No one could escape by that passage, even if they knew of it.

"Tell your father what you have told me, and tell him Ben has taken the boat away," he said. "I want men to guard the outer entrance of the caves as soon as the tide goes down. I'll remain here to guard this way of escape. Go quickly!"

CHAPTER NINE

THINGS MOVE QUICKLY

Alec and the two girls left their uncle and stumbled up the dark passage, lighting their way by their small torches. All three were trembling with excitement. It seemed suddenly a very serious thing that was happening. Spies! Who would have thought of that?

They went on up the passage. Soon they came to the place where the roof fell very low indeed, and down they went on their hands and knees to crawl through the low tunnel.

"I don't like that bit much," said Frances, when they were through it. "I shall dream about that! Come on –

we can stand upright again now. Whatever do you suppose Daddy and Mother will say?"

"I can't imagine," said Alec. "All I know is that it's a very lucky thing for us that Daddy and Uncle happened to be here now. Golly – didn't I jump when we bumped into Uncle Ned in this passage!"

"I screamed," said Hilary, rather ashamed of herself. "But honestly I simply couldn't help it. It was awful to bump into somebody strange like that in the darkness. But wasn't I glad when I heard Uncle Ned's voice!"

"Here we are at last," said Alec, as they came to where the rope hung down the hole. "I'll go up first and then give you two girls a hand. Give me a heave, Hilary."

Hilary heaved him up and he climbed the rope quickly, hand over hand, glad that he had been so good at gym at school. You never knew when things would come in useful!

He lay down on the heather and helped the girls up. They stood out on the moor in the moonlight, getting back their breath, for it wasn't easy to haul themselves up the rope.

"Now come on," said Hilary. "We haven't any time to lose. I shouldn't be surprised if those spies know about the passage and make up their minds to try it. We don't want to leave Uncle Ned too long. After all, it's three against one."

They tore over the heather, and came to the sandy lane where Sea Cottage shone in the moonlight. They went in at the open door and made their way to their parents' bedroom. Alec hammered on the door, and then went in.

His father and mother were sitting up in astonishment.

They switched on the light and stared at the three children, all fully dressed as they were.

"What's the meaning of this?" asked their father. But before he could say a word more the three children began to pour out their story. At first their parents could not make out what they were talking about, and their mother made the girls stop talking so that Alec could tell the tale.

"But this is unbelievable!" said their father, dressing as quickly as possible. "Simply unbelievable! Is Ned really down a secret passage, holding three spies at bay? And Ben has gone off with their motorboat? Am I dreaming?"

"No, Daddy, you're not," said Alec. "It's all quite true. We kept everything a secret till tonight, because secrets are such fun. We didn't know that anything serious was up till tonight, really. Are you going to get help?"

"I certainly am," said Daddy. He went to the telephone downstairs and was soon on to the nearest military camp. He spoke to a most surprised commanding officer, who listened in growing amazement.

"So you must send a few men over as quickly as possible," said Daddy. "The children say there are three men in the caves – or rather, two men and one woman – but there may be more, of course – and more may arrive. We can't tell. Hurry, won't you?"

He put down the receiver of the telephone and turned to look at the waiting children. "Now let me see," he said thoughtfully. "I shall want one of you to take me to where Ned is, and I must leave someone behind to guide the soldiers down to the cove. They must be there to guard the entrance to the caves, so that if the spies try to escape by the beach, they will find they can't. Alec, you had better come with me. Frances and Hilary, you can go with Mother and the soldiers, when they come, and show them the way down the cliff and the entrance to the caves. Come along, Alec."

The two set off. Alec talked hard all the way, for there was a great deal to tell. His father listened in growing astonishment. Really, you never knew what children were doing half the time!

"I suppose your mother thought you were playing harmless games of smugglers," he said, "and all the time you were on the track of dangerous spies! Well, well, well!"

"We didn't really know they were spies till tonight," said Alec honestly. "It was all a game at first. Look, Daddy – here's the hole. We have to slide down this rope."

"This really is a weird adventure," said his father, and down the rope he went. Alec followed him. Soon they were standing beside Uncle Ned, who was still in the passage, his revolver in his hand.

"There's been a lot of excited talking," he said in a low voice to his brother, "and I think they've been trying to find a way out. But the tide is still very high, and they daren't walk out on the sand yet. If they don't know of this passage, they won't try it, of course – but we'd better stay here in case they do. When are the soldiers coming?"

"At once," said Daddy. "I've left the two girls behind to guide them down to the cove. Then they will hide, and guard the entrance to the caves, that is as soon as the tide goes down enough."

"Do the spies know you're here, Uncle Ned?" asked Alec, in a low voice.

"No," said his uncle. "They know someone has gone off with their motorboat, but that's all they know. What about creeping down to the end of the passage to see if we can overhear anything? They might drop a few secrets!"

The three of them crept down to the end of the passage, and leaned out over the hole that led down to the space between the two caves. They could hear the waves still washing up the narrow channel in the long cave.

The two men and the woman were talking angrily. "Who could have known we were here? Someone has given the game away! No one but ourselves and the other three knew what we were planning to do."

"Is there no other way out?" said a man's impatient voice, very deep and foreign. "Rondel, you know all these caves and passages – or so you said. How did the old smugglers get their goods away? There must have been a land path they used."

"There was," said the other man. "There is a passage above this cave that leads on to the moors. But as far as I know it is completely blocked up."

"As far as you know!" said the other man, in a scornful voice. "Haven't you found out? What do you suppose you are paid for, Rondel? Aren't you paid for letting us know any well-hidden caves on this coast? Where is this passage? Do you know?"

"Yes, I know," said Rondel. "It's above this one, and the entrance to it is just between this cave and the one we used for the motorboat. We have to climb up a little way. I've never been up it myself, because I heard it was blocked up by a roof-fall years ago. But we can try it and see."

"We'd better get back up the passage a bit," whispered Alec's father. "If they come up here, we may have trouble. Get on to that bit where the big rock juts out and the passage goes round it. We can get behind that and give them a scare. They'll shoot if they see us. I don't want to shoot if I can help it, for I've a feeling they will be more useful alive than dead!"

Very silently the three went back up the passage to where a rock jutted out and the way went round it. They crouched down behind the rock and waited, their torches switched off. Alec heard their breathing and it sounded very loud. But they had to breathe! He wondered if Daddy and Uncle could hear his heart beating, because it seemed to make a very loud thump just then!

Meanwhile, the three spies were trying to find the entrance to the passage. Rondel had a powerful torch, and he soon found the hole that led to the ledge where the secret passage began.

"Here it is!" he said. "Look – we can easily get up there. I'll go first."

Alec heard a scrambling noise as the man climbed up. Then he pulled up the other two. They all switched on their torches and the dark passage was lighted up brightly.

"It seems quite clear," said the other man. "I should think we could escape this way. You go ahead, Rondel. We'll follow. I can't see any sign of it being blocked up, I must say! This is a bit of luck."

They went on up the passage, talking. They went slowly, and Alec and the others could hear their footsteps and voices coming gradually nearer. Alec's heart beat painfully and he kept swallowing something in his throat. The excitement was almost too much for him to bear.

The three spies came almost up to the jutting-out rock. And then they got the shock of their lives! Alec's father spoke in a loud stern voice that made Alec jump.

"Halt! Come another step, and we'll shoot!"

The spies halted at once in a panic. They switched off their torches.

"Who's there?" came Rondel's voice.

Nobody answered. The spies talked together in low voices and decided to go back the way they had come. They were not risking going round that rock! They didn't know how many people were there. It was plain that somebody knew of their plans and meant to capture them.

Alec heard the three making their way quietly back down the passage.

"Daddy! I expect they think the tide will soon be going down and they hope to make their escape by way of the beach," whispered Alec. "I hope the soldiers will be there in time."

"Don't you worry about that!" said his father. "As soon as the tide washes off the beach, it will be full of soldiers."

"I wish I could be there," said Alec longingly. "I don't expect the spies will come up here again."

"Well, you can go and see what's happening if you like," said Daddy. "Your uncle and I will stay here – but you can see if the soldiers have arrived and if the girls are taking them down to the cove."

Alec was delighted. More excitement for him, after all! He went up the passage and swarmed up the rope out of the entrance-hole. He sped over the moor to the cottage.

But no one was there. It was quite empty. "I suppose the soldiers have arrived and Mother and the girls have taken them to the cove," thought Alec. "Yes – there are big wheel-marks in the road – a lorry has been here. Oh – there it is, in the shade of those trees over there. I'd better hurry or I'll miss the fun!"

Off he dashed to the cliff edge, and down the narrow, steep path. Where were the others? Waiting in silence down on the beach? Alec nearly fell down the steep path trying to hurry! What an exciting night!

CHAPTER TEN

THE END OF IT ALL

Just as Alec was scrambling down the steep cliff, he heard the sound of a low voice from the top. "Is that you, Alec?"

Alec stopped. It was Ben's voice. "Ben!" he whispered in excitement. "Come on down. You're just in time. How did you get here?"

Ben scrambled down beside him. "I thought it was you," he said. "I saw you going over the edge of the cliff as I came up the lane. What's happened?"

Alec told him. Ben listened in excitement.

"So they know there's someone in the secret passage,"

he said. "They'll just have to try to escape by the beach then! Well, they'll be overpowered there, no doubt about that. I tied up the motorboat by the jetty, Alec. It's a real beauty – small but very powerful. It's got a lovely engine. Then I raced back to see if I could be in at the end."

"Well, you're just in time," said Alec. "I'm going to hop down on to the beach now and see where the others are."

"Be careful," Ben warned him. "The soldiers won't know it's you, and may take a pot shot at you."

That scared Alec. He stopped before he jumped down on to the sand.

"Well, I think maybe we'd better stay here then," he said. "We can see anything that happens from here, can't we? Look, the tide is going down nicely now. Where do you suppose the others are, Ben?"

"I should think they are somewhere on the rocks that run round the cove," said Ben, looking carefully round. "Look, Alec – there's something shining just over there – see? I guess that's a gun. We can't see the man holding it – but the moonlight just picks out a shiny bit of his gun."

"I hope the girls and Mother are safe," said Alec.

"You may be sure they are," said Ben. "I wonder what the three spies are doing now. I guess they are waiting till the tide is low enough for them to come out."

At that very moment Rondel was looking out of the big cave to see if it was safe to try and escape over the beach. He was not going to try to go up the cliff path, for he felt sure there would be someone at the top. Their only hope lay in slipping round the corner of the cove and making their way up the cliff some way off. Rondel knew the coast by heart, and if he only had the chance he felt certain he could take the others to safety.

The tide was going down rapidly. The sand was very wet and shone in the moonlight. Now and again a big wave swept up the beach, but the power behind it was gone. It could not dash anyone against the rocks now. Rondel turned to his two companions and spoke to them in a low voice.

"Now's our chance. We shall have to try the beach whilst our enemies think the tide is still high. Take hold of Gretel's hand, Otto, in case a wave comes. Follow me. Keep as close to the cliff as possible in case there is a watcher above."

The three of them came silently out of the big cave. Its entrance lay in darkness and they looked like deep black shadows as they moved quietly to the left of the cave. They made their way round the rocks, stopping as a big wave came splashing up the smooth sand. It swept round their feet, but no higher. Then it ran back down the sand again to the sea, and the three moved on once more.

Then a voice rang out in the moonlight: "We have you covered! There is no escape this way! Hands up!"

Rondel had his revolver in his hand in a moment and guns glinted in the hands of the others, too. But they did not know where their enemies were. The rocks lay in black shadows, and no one could be seen.

"There are men all round this cove," said the voice. "You cannot escape. Put your hands up and surrender. Throw your revolvers down, please."

Rondel spoke to the others in a savage voice. He was in a fierce rage, for all his plans were ruined. It seemed as if he were urging the others to fight. But they were wiser than Rondel. The other man threw his revolver down on the sand and put his hands above his head. The woman did the same. They glinted there like large silver shells.

"Hands up, you!" commanded a voice. Rondel shouted something angry in a foreign language and then threw his gun savagely at the nearest rocks. It hit them and the trigger was struck. The revolver went off with a loud explosion that echoed round and round the little cove and made everyone, Rondel as well, jump violently.

"Stand where you are," said a voice. And out from the shadow of the rocks came a soldier in the uniform of an officer. He walked up to the three spies and had a look at them. He felt them all over to see if there were any more weapons hidden about them. There were none.

He called to his men. "Come and take them."

Four men stepped out from the rocks around the cove. Alec and Ben leapt down on to the sand. Mother and the two girls came out from their hiding place in a small cave. Ben ran up to the spies. He peered into the face of one of the men.

"I know who this is!" he cried. "It's Professor Rondel, who lived in Sea Cottage. I've seen him hundreds of times! He didn't have many friends – only two or three men who came to see him sometimes."

"Oh," said the officer, staring with interest at Ben. "Well, we'll be very pleased to know who the two or three men were. You'll be very useful to us, my boy. Now then – quick march! Up the cliff we go and into the lorry! The sooner we get these three into a safe place the better."

Alec's father and uncle appeared at that moment. They had heard the sound of the shot when Rondel's revolver struck the rock and went off, and they had come to see what was happening. Alec ran to them and told them.

"Good work!" said Daddy. "Three spies caught – and maybe the others they work with, too, if Ben can point them out. Good old Smuggler Ben!"

The three spies were put into the lorry and the driver climbed up behind the wheel. The officer saluted and took his place. Then the lorry rumbled off into the moonlit night. The four children watched it go, their eyes shining.

"This is the most thrilling night I've ever had in my life," said Alec, with a sigh. "I don't suppose I'll ever have a more exciting one, however long I live. Golly, my heart did beat fast when we were hiding in the cave. It hurt me."

"Same here," said Hilary. "Oh, Daddy – you didn't guess what you were in for, did you, when you came home yesterday?"

"I certainly didn't," said Daddy, putting his arm round the two girls and pushing them towards the house. "Come along – you'll all be tired out. It must be nearly dawn!"

"Back to Professor Rondel's own house!" said Alec. "Isn't it funny! He got all his information from his books – and we found some of it there, too. We'll show you if you like, Daddy."

"Not tonight," said Daddy firmly. "Tonight – or rather this morning, for it's morning now – you are going to bed, and to sleep. No more excitement, please! You will have plenty again tomorrow, for you'll have to go over to the police and to the military camp to tell all you know."

Well, that was an exciting piece of news, too. The children went indoors, Ben with them, for Mother said he had better share Alec's room for the rest of the night.

Soon all four children were in their beds, feeling certain that they would never, never be able to go to sleep for one moment.

But it wasn't more than two minutes before they were all sound asleep, as Mother saw when she peeped into the two bedrooms. She went to join Daddy and Uncle Ned.

"Well, I'd simply no idea what the children were doing," she told them. "I was very angry with them one night when they came home late because they were caught by the tide when they were exploring those caves. They kept their secret well."

"They're good kids," said Daddy, with a yawn. "Well, let's go to sleep, too. Ned, I hope you'll be able to drop off on the sofa again."

"I could drop off on the kitchen stove, I'm so tired!" said Ned.

Soon the whole household slept soundly, and did not wake even when the sun came slanting in at the windows. They were all tired out.

They had a late breakfast, and the children chattered nineteen to the dozen as they ate porridge and bacon and eggs. It all seemed amazingly wonderful to them now that it was over. They couldn't help feeling rather proud of themselves.

"I must go," said Ben, when he had finished an enormous breakfast. "My uncle is expecting me to go out fishing with him this morning. He'll be angry because I'm late."

But before Ben could go, a messenger on a motorbike

arrived, asking for the four children to go over to the police station at once. The police wanted to know the names of the men with whom Professor Rondel had made friends. This was very important, because unless they knew the names at once, the men might hear of Rondel's capture and fly out of the country.

So off went the four children, and spent a most exciting time telling and retelling their story from the very beginning. The inspector of the police listened carefully, and when everything had been told, and notes taken, he leaned back and looked at the children, his eyes twinkling.

"Well, we have reason to be very grateful to you four smugglers," he said. "We shall probably catch the whole nest of spies operating in this part of the country. We suspected it – but we had no idea who the ringleader was. It was Rondel, of course. He was bringing men and women across from Ireland – spies, of course – and taking them about the country either to get information useful to the enemy, or to wreck valuable buildings. He was using the old smugglers' caves to hide his friends in. We shall comb the whole coast now."

"Can we help you?" asked Ben eagerly. "I know most of the caves, sir. And we can show you Rondel's books, where all the old caves are described. He's got dozens of them."

"Good!" said the inspector. "Well, that's all for today. You will hear from us later. There will be a little reward given to you for services to your country!"

The children filed out, talking excitedly. A little reward! What could it be?

"Sometimes children are given watches as a reward,"

said Alec, thinking of a newspaper report he had read. "We might get a watch each."

"I hope we don't," said Hilary, "because I've already got one – though it doesn't keep very good time."

But the reward wasn't watches. It was something much bigger than that. Can you possibly guess what it was?

It was the little motorboat belonging to the spies! When the children heard the news, they could hardly believe their ears. But it was quite true. There lay the little motorboat, tied up to the jetty, and on board was a police officer with instructions to hand it over to the four children.

"Oh – thank you!" said Alec, hardly able to speak. "Thank you very much. Oh, Ben – oh, Ben – isn't it marvellous!"

It *was* marvellous! It was a beautiful little boat with a magnificent engine. It was called *Otto*.

"That won't do," said Hilary, looking at the name. "We'll have that painted out at once. What shall we call our boat? It must be a very good name – something that will remind us of our adventure!"

"I know – I know!" yelled Alec. "We'll call it *Smuggler Ben*, of course – and good old Ben shall be the captain, and we'll be his crew."

So *Smuggler Ben* the boat was called, and everyone agreed that it was a really good name. The children have a wonderful time in it. You should see them chug-chugging over the sea at top speed, the spray flying high in the air! Aren't they lucky!

ENID BLYTON

Adventure Stories

Mischief at St Rollo's

and

The Children of Kidillin

Illustrated by

Rodney Sutton

Mischief at St Rollo's and *The Children of Kidillin*
were first published separately
in 1947 and 1940 respectively
by T. Werner Laurie Ltd, and Georges Newnes Ltd
First published in the UK in hardback
in 1976 by William Collins Sons & Co. Ltd
and in Armada in 1982

MICHIEF AT ST ROLLO'S

CONTENTS

CHAPTER ONE

A NEW SCHOOL

"I don't want to go to boarding school," said Michael.

"Neither do I," said Janet. "I don't see why we have to, Mother!"

"You are very lucky to be able to go," said Mother. "Especially together! Daddy and I have chosen a mixed school for you – one with boys and girls together, so that both you and Mike can go together, and not be parted. We know how fond you are of one another. It's quite time you went too. I run after you too much. You must learn to stand on your own feet."

Mother went out of the room. The two children stared

at one another. "Well, that's that," said Janet, flipping a pellet of paper at Michael. "We've got to go. But I vote we make our new school sit up a bit!"

"I've heard that you have to work rather hard at St Rollo's," said Mike. "Well, I'm not going to! I'm going to have a good time. I hope we're in the same class."

There was only a year between the two of them, and as Janet was a clever child, she had so far always been in the same form as her brother, who was a year older. They had been to a mixed school ever since they had first started, and although they now had to go away to boarding school, they both felt glad that they were not to be parted, as most brothers and sisters had to be.

The last week of the holidays flew past. Mother took the children to the shops to get them fitted for new clothes.

"We do seem to have to get a lot for our new school," said Janet, with interest. "And are we going to have tuck boxes, Mother, to take back with us?"

"If you're good!" said Mother, with a laugh.

Mother did get them their tuck boxes – one each for them. She put exactly the same in each box – one big currant cake, one big ginger cake, twelve chocolate buns, a tin of toffee and a large bar of chocolate. The children were delighted.

The day came for them to go to their new school. They couldn't help feeling a bit excited, though they felt rather nervous too. Still, they were to go together, and that would be fun. They caught a train to London, and Mother took them to the station from which the school train was to start.

"St Rollo's School," said the big blue label on the

train. "Reserved for St Rollo's School." A great crowd of boys and girls were on the platform, talking and laughing, calling to each other. Some were new, and they looked rather lonely and shy. Janet and Mike kept together, looking eagerly at everyone.

"They look rather nice," said Mike to Janet. "I wonder which will be in our form."

Both boys and girls were in grey, and looked neat and smart. One or two masters and mistresses bustled up and down, talking to parents, and warning the children to take their places. Janet and Mike got into a carriage with several other boys and girls.

"Hallo!" said one, a cheeky-looking boy of about eleven. "You're new, aren't you?"

"Yes," said Mike.

"What's your name?" said the boy, his blue eyes twinkling at Mike and Janet.

"I'm Michael Fairley, and this is my sister Janet," said Mike. "What's your name?"

"I'm Tom Young," said the boy. "I should think you'll be in my form. We have fun. Can you make darts?"

"Paper darts," said Mike. "Of course! Everybody can!"

"Ah, but you should see my new kind," said the boy, and took out a notebook with stiff paper leaves. But just as he was tearing out a sheet the guard blew his whistle, and the train gave a jerk.

"Goodbye, Mother!" yelled Mike and Janet. "Goodbye. We'll write tomorrow!"

"Goodbye, my dears!" called Mother. "Enjoy yourselves and work hard."

The train chuffed out of the station. Now that it was really gone the two children felt a bit lonely. It wasn't going to be very nice not to see Mother and Daddy for some time. Thank goodness they had each other!

Tom looked at them. "Cheer up!" he said. "I felt like that, too, the first time. But you soon get over it. Now just see how I make my new paper darts."

Tom was certainly very clever with his fingers. In a minute or two he had produced a marvellous pointed dart out of paper, which, when it was thrown, flew straight to its mark.

"Better than most darts, don't you think?" said Tom proudly. "I thought that one out last term. The first time I threw one it shot straight at Miss Thomas and landed underneath her collar. I got sent out of the room for that."

Janet and Mike looked at Tom with much respect. All the other children in the carriage laughed.

"Tom's the worst boy in the school," said a rosy-cheeked, fat girl. "Don't take lessons from him – he just doesn't care about anything."

"Is Miss Thomas a mistress?" asked Mike. "Do we have masters *and* mistresses at St Rollo's?"

"Of course," said Tom. "If you're in my form you'll have Miss Thomas for class teacher, but a whole lot of other teachers for special subjects. I can tell you whose classes it's safe to play about in, and whose classes it's best to behave in."

"Well, seeing that you don't behave well in *anybody's* classes, I shouldn't have thought you could have told anyone the difference," said the fat girl.

"Be quiet, Marian," said Tom. "I'm doing the talking in this carriage!"

That was too much for the other children. They fell on Tom and began to pummel him. But he took it all good-humouredly, and pummelled back hard. Mike and Janet watched, laughing. They didn't quite like to join in.

Everyone had sandwiches to eat. They could eat them any time after half past twelve, but not before. Tom produced a watch after a while and looked at it.

"Good!" he said. "It's half past twelve." He undid his packet of sandwiches. Marian looked astonished.

"Tom! It simply *can't* be half past twelve yet," she said. She looked at her wristwatch. "It's only a quarter to."

"Well, your watch must be wrong then," said Tom, and he began to eat his sandwiches. Janet looked at her watch. It certainly was only a quarter to twelve. She felt sure that Tom had put his watch wrong on purpose.

It made the other children feel very hungry to watch Tom eating his ham sandwiches. They began to think it would be a good idea to put their watches fast, too! But just then a master came down the corridor that ran the length of the train. Tom tried to put away his packet of sandwiches, but he was too late.

"Well, Tom," said the master, stopping at the door and looking in. "Can't you wait to get to school before you begin to break the rules?"

"Mr Wills, sir, my watch says five-and-twenty to one?" said Tom, holding out his watch, with an innocent look on his face. "Isn't it five-and-twenty to one?"

"You know quite well it isn't," said Mr Wills. He took

the watch and twisted the hands back. "Put away your lunch and have it when your watch says half-past twelve," he said. Tom gave a look at his watch. Then he looked up with an expression of horror.

"Sir! You've made my watch half an hour slow! That would mean I couldn't start my lunch till one o'clock!"

"Well, well, fancy that!" said Mr Wills. "I wonder which is the more annoying – to have a watch that is fast, or one that is slow, Tom? What a pity! You'll have to eat your lunch half an hour after the others have finished!"

He went out. Tom stared after him gloomily. "I suppose he thinks that's funny," he said.

Tom put away his lunch, for he knew quite well that Mr Wills might be along again at any moment. At half past twelve all the other children took down their lunch packets and undid them eagerly, for they were hungry. Poor Tom had to sit and watch them eat. His watch only said twelve o'clock!

At one, when all the others had finished, he opened his lunch packet again. "Now, of course," he said, "I'm so terribly hungry that ham sandwiches, egg sandwiches, buttered scones with jam, ginger cake, an apple and some chocolate won't nearly do for me!"

The train sped on. It was due to arrive at half past two. When the time came near, Janet and Mike looked out of the windows eagerly. "Can we see St Rollo's from the train?" asked Janet.

"Yes. It's built on a hill," said Marian. "You'll see it out of that window. It's of grey stone and it has towers at each end. In the middle of the building is a big archway. Watch out for it now, you'll soon see it."

The children looked out, and, as Marian had said, they caught sight of their new school. It looked grand!

There it stood on the hill with big towers at each end, built of grey stone. Creeper climbed over most of the walls, and here and there a touch of red showed that when autumn came the walls would glow red with the crimson leaves.

The train slowed down at a little station. Everyone got out. Some big coaches were waiting in the little station yard. Laughing and shouting, the children piled into them. Their luggage was to follow in a van. The masters and mistresses climbed in last of all, and the coaches set off to St Rollo's.

They rumbled up the hill and came to a stop before the big archway. The school looked enormous, now that the children were so close to it. All the boys and girls clambered down from the coaches and went in at a big door.

The two children followed Tom up the stairs to a large and cheerful room, into which the afternoon sun poured. A plump, smooth-cheeked woman was sitting there.

"Hallo, Matron," said Tom, going in. "I've brought two new ones to see you. Are they in my dormitory? I hope they are."

"Well, I'm sorry for them if they are!" said Matron, getting out a big exercise book and turning the pages. "What are their names?"

"Michael and Janet Fairley," said Mike. Matron found their names and ticked them off.

"Yes – Michael is in your dormitory, Tom," she said. "Janet is across the passage with Marian and the girls. I hope they will help you to behave better, not worse. And just remember what I told you last term – if you play any tricks on me this term I'll spank you with my hardest slipper!"

Tom grinned. He took Mike's arm and led him away with Janet. "You'll soon begin to think I'm a bad lot!" he said. "Come on – I'll show you everything."

CHAPTER TWO

SETTLING DOWN

There was plenty to see at St Rollo's. The dormitories were fine big rooms. Each child had a separate cubicle with white curtains to pull around their bed, their dressing-table and small cupboard. The children's luggage was already in the dormitory when they got there.

"We'll unpack later," said Tom. "Look, that will be my bed. And yours can be next to mine, Mike, if I can arrange it. Look – let's pull your trunk into this cubicle, then no one else will take it."

They pulled the trunk across. Then Tom showed Janet her dormitory, across the passage. It was exactly the same as the boys', except that the beds had pink eiderdowns instead of blue. After that, Tom showed them the classrooms, which were fine rooms, all with great windows looking out on the sunny playgrounds.

"This is our classroom if you're in my form," said Tom. Janet and Mike liked the look of it very much.

"I had that desk there at the front, last term," said Tom, pointing to one. "I always try to choose one right at the back – but sooner or later I'm always made to sit at the front. People seem to think that they have to keep an eye on me. Awfully tiresome!"

"I wonder where our desks will be," said Mike.

"Bag two, if you like," said Tom. "Just dump a few books in. Where do you want to sit?"

"I like being near the window, where I can look out," said Mike. "But I'd like to be where I can see you too, Tom!"

"Well, I shall try to bag a desk at the back as usual," said Tom. He took a few books from a bookshelf and dumped them into a desk in the back row by the window. "That can be your desk. That can be Janet's. And this can be mine! All in a row together."

Tom showed them the playgrounds and the hockey fields. He showed them the marvellous gym and the assembly hall where the school met every morning for prayers. He showed them the changing rooms, where they changed for games, and the common rooms where each class met out of school to read, write or play games. Janet and Mike began to feel they would lose their way if they had to find any place by themselves!

"We'll go and unpack now," said Tom. "And then

it'll be teatime. Good! We can all have things out of our tuck boxes today."

They went to their dormitories to unpack. Janet parted from the two boys and went into hers. Marian was there, and she smiled at Janet.

"Hallo," she said. "I saw Tom taking you round. He's kind, but he'll lead you into trouble, if he can! Come and unpack. I'll show you where to put your things. I'm head of this dormitory."

Janet unpacked and stowed away her things into the drawers of the dressing table, and hung her coats in the cupboard. All the other girls were doing the same. Marian called to Janet.

"I say! Do you know any of the others here? That's Audrey near to you. And this is Bertha. And that shrimp is Connie. And here's Doris, who just simply can't help being top of the form, whether she tries or not!"

Doris laughed. She was a clever-looking girl, with large glasses on her nose. "We're all in the same form," she told Janet. "Is your brother in Tom Young's dormitory?"

"Yes," said Janet. "Will he be in my form too?"

"Yes, he will," said Doris. "All the four dormitories on this floor belong to the same form. Miss Thomas is our form mistress. She's nice but pretty strict. Only one person ever gets the better of her – and that's Tom Young! He just simply doesn't care what he does – and he's always bottom. But he's nice."

Meanwhile Mike was also getting to know the boys in his dormitory. Tom was telling him about them.

"See that fellow with the cross-eyes and hooked nose? Well, that's Eric."

Mike looked round for somebody with cross-eyes and a hooked nose, but the boy that Tom pointed to had the straightest brown eyes and nose that Mike had ever seen! The boy grinned.

"I'm Eric," he said. "Don't take any notice of Tom. He thinks he's terribly funny."

Tom took no notice. "See that chap over there in the corner? The one with spots all over his face? That's Fred. He gets spots because he eats too many sweets."

"Shut up!" said Fred. He had one small spot on his chin. He was a big, healthy-looking boy, with bright eyes and red cheeks.

"And this great giant of a chap is George," said Tom, pointing to an undergrown boy with small shoulders. The boy grinned.

"You must have your joke, mustn't you?" he said amiably. "And now Mike what-ever-your-name-is, let me introduce you to the world's greatest clown, the world's greatest idiot, Master Thomas Henry William Young, biggest duffer and dunce, and, by a great effort, the bottom of the form!"

Mike roared with laughter. Tom took it all in good part. He gave George a punch which the boy dodged cleverly.

There was one other boy in the room, but Tom said nothing about him. He was not a pleasant-looking boy. Mike wondered why Tom didn't tell him his name. So he asked for it.

"Who's he?" he said, nodding his head towards the boy, who was unpacking his things with rather a sullen face.

"That's Hugh," said Tom, but he said no more.

Hugh looked up. "Go on, say what you like about me," he said. "The new boy will soon know it, anyway! Be funny at my expense if you want to!"

"I don't want to," said Tom.

"Well, *I'll* tell him then," said the boy. "I'm a cheat! I cheated in the exams last term, and everyone knows it because Tom found it out and gave me away!"

"I didn't give you away." said Tom. "I've told you that before. I saw that you were cheating, and said nothing. But Miss Thomas found out herself. Anyway, let's drop the subject of cheating this term. Cheat all you like. I don't care!"

Tom turned his back on Hugh. Mike felt very awkward. He wished he hadn't asked for the boy's name. Eric began to talk about the summer holidays and all he had done. Soon the others joined in, and when Hugh slipped out of the room no one saw him go.

"It should be about teatime now," said Tom, pulling out his watch. "Golly, no it isn't! Half an hour to go still! My word, what a swizz!"

Just then the tea bell rang loudly, and Tom looked astonished. Mike laughed. "Don't you remember?" he said. "Mr Wills put your watch back half an hour?"

"So he did!" said Tom, looking relieved. He altered his watch again. "Well, come on," he said. "I could eat a mountain if only it was made of cake! Bring your tuck box. What have you got in it? I'll share mine with you if you'll share yours with me. I've got a simply *gorgeous* chocolate cake."

It was fun, that first meal. All the children had brought goodies back in their tuck boxes. They shared with one another, and the most enormous teas were eaten that day! Janet went to sit with Mike, and the two of them gave away part of all their cakes. In exchange they got slices of all kinds of other cakes. By the time they got up from the tea table they couldn't eat another crumb!

"I hope we don't have to have supper!" said Mike. "I feel as if I don't want to eat again for a fortnight. But wasn't it scrumptious!'

The children had to go and see the headmaster and headmistress after tea. Both were grey-haired, and had kindly but rather stern faces. Mike and Janet felt very nervous and could hardly answer the questions they were asked.

"You will both be in the same form at first," said the headmaster, Mr Quentin. "Janet is a year younger, but I hear that she is advanced for her age. You will be in the second form."

"Yes, sir," said the children.

"We work hard at St Rollo's," said Miss Lesley, the headmistress. "But we play hard too. So you should have a good time and enjoy every day of the term. Remember our motto always, won't you: 'Not the least that we dare, but the most that we can!'"

"Yes, we will," said the two children.

"St Rollo's does all it can for its children," said Miss Lesley, "so it's up to you to do all you can for your school, too. You may go."

The children went. "I like the Heads, don't you, Mike?" said Janet. "But I'm a bit afraid of them too. I shouldn't like to be sent to them for punishment."

"I bet Tom has!" said Mike. "Now we've got to go and see Miss Thomas. Come on."

Miss Thomas was in their classroom, making out lists. She looked up as the two children came in.

"Well, Michael; well, Janet!" she said, with a smile. "Finding your way round a bit? It's difficult at first, isn't it? I've got your last reports here, and they are quite good. I hope you will do as well for me as you seem to have done for your last form mistress!"

"We'll try," said the children, liking Miss Thomas's broad smile and brown eyes.

"I'm bad at maths," said Janet.

"And my handwriting is pretty awful," said Michael.

"Well, we'll see what we can do about them," said Miss Thomas. "Now you can go back to the common room with the others. You'll know it by the perfectly terrible noise that comes out of the door!"

The children laughed and went out of the room. "I think I'm going to like St Rollo's awfully," said Janet happily. "Everybody is so nice. The girls in my dorm are fine, Mike. Do you like the boys in yours?"

"Yes, all except a boy called Hugh," said Mike, and he told Janet about the sulky boy. "I say – is this our common room, do you think?"

They had come to an open door, out of which came a medley of noises. A gramophone was going, and someone was singing loudly to it, rather out of tune. Two or thre others were shouting about something and another boy was hammering on the floor, though why, Janet and Mike couldn't imagine. They put their heads in at the door.

"This can't be our common room," said Mike. "The children all look too big."

"Get out of here, tiddlers!" yelled the boy who was

hammering on the floor. "You don't belong here! Find the kindergarten!"

"What cheek!" said Janet indignantly, as they withdrew their heads and walked off down the passage. "Tiddlers, indeed!"

Round the next passage was a noise that was positively deafening. It came from a big room on the left. A wireless was going full tilt, and a gramophone, too, so that neither of them could be heard properly. Four or five children seemed to be having a fight on the floor, and a few others were yelling to them, telling them to "Go it!" and "Stick it!"

A cushion flew through the air and hit Janet on the shoulder. She threw it back. A girl raised her voice dolefully.

"Oh, do shut up! I want to hear the wireless!"

Nobody took any notice. The girl shouted even more loudly: "I say, I WANT TO HEAR THE WIRELESS."

Somebody snapped off the gramophone, and the wireless seemed to boom out even more loudly. There was dance music on it.

"Let's dance!" cried Fred, foxtrotting by, holding a cushion as if it were a partner. "Hallo, Mike, hallo Janet. Where on earth have you been? Come into our quiet, peaceful room, won't you? Don't stand at the door looking like two scared mice."

So into their common room went the two children, at first quite scared of all the noise around them. But gradually they got used to it, and picked out the voices of the boys and girls they knew, talking, shouting and laughing together. It was fun. It felt good to be there all together like a big, happy family. The noise was nice too.

For an hour the noise went on, and then died down as the children became tired. Books were got out, and puzzles. The wireless was turned down a little. The supper bell went, and the children trooped down into the dining hall. The first day was nearly over. A quiet hour after supper, and then bed. Yes – it was going to be nice at St Rollo's!

CHAPTER THREE

A HAPPY TIME

Michael and Janet found things rather strange at first, but after two or three days St Rollo's began to seem quite familiar to them. They knew their way about by then – though poor Janet got quite lost the second day, looking for her classroom!

She opened the door of what she thought was her form room – only to find a class of big boys and girls painting! They sat round the room with their drawing boards in front of them, earnestly drawing or painting a vase of bright leaves.

"Hallo! What do you want?" asked the drawing master.

"I wanted the second form classroom," said Janet, blushing red.

"Oh well, this isn't it," said the master. "Go down the stairs, turn to the right – and it's the first door."

"Thank you," said Janet, thinking how silly she was not to remember what floor her classroom was on. She ran down the stairs, and tried to remember if the drawing master had said turn to the left or to the right.

"I think he said left," said Janet to herself. So to the left she turned and opened the first door there. To her horror, it was the door of the junior mistresses' common room! One or two of them sat there, making out time-tables.

"What is it?" said the nearest one.

"Nothing," said Janet, going red again. "I'm looking for my classroom – the second form. I keep going into the wrong room."

"Oh, you're a new girl, aren't you?" said the mistress, with a laugh. "Well, go along the passage and take the first door on the right."

So at last Janet found her classroom, and was very relieved. But when three or four days had gone by she couldn't imagine how she could have made such a mistake! The school building, big as it was, was beginning to be very familiar to her.

The second form settled down well. Janet and Mike were the only new children in it. Miss Thomas let them keep the desks they had chosen – but she looked with a doubtful eye on Tom, when he sat down at the desk in the back row, next to Janet.

"Oh," she said, "so you've chosen a desk in the back row again, Tom. Do you think it's worthwhile doing that? You know quite well that before a week has gone by you will be told to take a desk out here in front, where I can keep my eye on you."

"Oh, Miss Thomas!" said Tom. "I'm turning over a new leaf this term. Really I am. Let me keep this desk. I'm trying to help the new children, so I'm sitting by them."

"I see," said Miss Thomas, who looked as if she didn't believe a word that Tom said. "Well – I give you not more than a week there, Tom! We'll just see!"

There were a good many children in Mike's form. Mike and Janet soon got to know them all. They were a jolly lot, cheerful and full of fun – except for the boy called Hugh, who hardly spoke to anyone and seemed very sullen.

Tom was a great favourite. He made the silliest jokes, played countless tricks, and yet was always ready to help anyone. The teachers liked him, though they were forever scolding him for his careless work.

"It isn't necessary for you to be bottom of *every* subject, *every* week, is it, Tom?" said Miss Thomas. "I mean – wouldn't you like to give me a nice surprise and be top in something just for once?"

"Oh, Miss Thomas – would it really give you a nice surprise?" said Tom. "Wouldn't it give you a shock, not a surprise! I wouldn't like to give you a shock."

"Considering that you spend half your time thinking out tricks to shock people, that's a foolish remark!" said Miss Thomas. "Now, open your books at page 19."

Janet and Mike found the work to be about the same

as they had been used to. They both had brains, and it was not difficult for them to keep up with the others. In fact, Janet felt sure that, if she tried very hard, she could be top of the form! She had a wonderful memory, and couldn't seem to forget anything she had read or heard. This was a great gift, for it made all lessons easy for her.

Doris, the girl with glasses, was easily top each week. Nothing seemed difficult to her. Even the hot-tempered French master beamed on Doris and praised her – though he seldom praised anyone else. Mike and Janet were quite scared of him.

"Monsieur Crozier looked as if he was going to box my ears this morning!" said Janet to Mike. "Don't you think he did!"

"He will rap your knuckles with a ruler if you give him the slightest chance!" said Tom, with a grin. "He rapped mine so hard last term that I almost jumped out of my skin. I just got back into it in time."

"Idiot!" said Mike. "I bet you had played some sort of trick on him."

"He had," said Fred. "He put white paint on that front lock of his hair – and when Monsieur Crozier exclaimed about it, what do you suppose Tom said?"

"What?" said Janet and Mike together.

"He said, 'Monsieur Crozier, my hair is turning white with the effort of learning the French verbs you have given us this week'," said Fred. "And do you wonder he got his knuckles rapped after that?"

"I'll think out something to make old Monsieur sit up!" said Tom. "You wait and see!"

"Oh, hurry up, then," begged the children around.

A week or two passed by, and Mike and Janet settled

down well. They loved everything. The work was not too difficult for them. The teachers were jolly. Hockey was marvellous. This was played three times a week, and everyone was expected to turn up. Gym was fine too. Mike and Janet were good at this, and enjoyed the half-hours in the big gym with the others.

There were lovely walks around the school. The children were allowed to go for walks by themselves, providing that three or more of them went together. So it was natural that Tom, Mike and Janet should often go together. The other children made up threes too, and went off for an hour or so when they could. It was lovely on the hills around, and already the children were looking for ripe blackberries and peering at the nut trees to see if there were going to be many nuts.

"Doesn't Hugh ever go for a walk?" said Janet once, when she, Mike and Tom had come in from a lovely sunny walk, to find Hugh bent double over a book in a far corner of the common room. He was alone. All the other children were out doing something – either practising hockey on the field, or gardening or walking.

"Well, you have to be at least three to go for a walk," said Tom in a low voice. "And no one ever asks Hugh, of course – and he wouldn't like to ask two others because he'd be pretty certain they'd say No."

"Why does everyone dislike him so?" asked Janet. "He would be quite a nice-looking boy if only he didn't look so surly."

"He was new last term," said Tom. "He's not very clever, but he's an awful swot – mugs up all sorts of things, and always has his nose in a book. Won't join in things, you know. And when he cheated at the exams last term, that was the last straw. Nobody decent wanted to have anything to do with him."

"He can't be very happy," said Janet, who was a kind-hearted girl, willing to be friends with anyone.

"Perhaps he doesn't deserve to be," said Tom.

"But even if you don't deserve to be happy, it must be horrid never to be," argued Janet.

"Oh, don't start being a ministering angel, Janet," said Mike impatiently. "Don't you remember how sorry you were for that spiteful dog next door, who was always being whipped for chasing hens? Well, what happened when you went out of your way to be kind to him, because you thought he must be miserable? He snapped at you, and nearly took your finger off!"

"I know," said Janet. "But that was only because he couldn't understand anyone being kind to him."

"Well, Hugh would certainly snap your head off if you tried any kind words on *him*," said Tom, with a laugh. "Look out – here he comes."

The children fell silent as Hugh got up from his seat and made his way to the door. He had to pass the three on his way, and he looked at them sneeringly.

"Talking about me, I suppose?" he said. "Funny how everyone stops talking when I come near!"

He bumped rudely into Janet as he passed and sent her against the wall. The two boys leapt at Hugh, but he was gone before they could hold him.

"Well, do you feel like going after him and being sweet?" said Tom to Janet. She shook her head. She thought Hugh was horrid. But all the same she was sorry for him.

Mike and Janet wrote long letters to their mother and

father. "We're awfully glad we came to St Rollo's," wrote Mike. "It's such fun to be with boys and girls together, and as Janet is in my form, we are as much together as we ever were. I shouldn't be surprised if she's top one week. The hockey is lovely. I'm good at it. Do send us some chocolate, if you can."

His mother and father smiled at his letters and Janet's. They could see that the two children were happy at the school they had chosen for them and they were glad.

"St Rollo's is fine," wrote Janet. "I *am* glad we came here. We do have fun!"

They certainly did – and they meant to have even more fun very soon!

CHAPTER FOUR

TOM IS UP TO TRICKS

Tom was always up to tricks. He knew all the usual ones, of course – the trick of covering a bit of paper with ink one side, and handing it to someone as if it were a note – and then, when they took it they found their fingers all inky! He knew all the different ways of making paper darts. He knew how to flip a pellet of paper from underneath his desk so that it would land exactly where he wanted it. There was nothing that Tom didn't know, when it came to tricks!

He lasted just four days in his desk at the back. Then Miss Thomas put him well in the front!

"I thought you wouldn't last a week at the back there," she said. "I feel much more comfortable with you just under my eye! Ah – that's better. Now I think you will find it quite difficult to fire off your paper pellets at children who are really trying to work."

The trick that had made Miss Thomas move him had caused the class a good deal of merriment. Miss Thomas had written history questions on the board for the form to answer in writing. Janet was hard at work answering them, for she wanted to get good marks, and Mike was working well too.

Suddenly Janet felt a nudge. She looked up. Tom had already finished answering the questions, though Janet felt certain that he had put "I don't know" to some of them! Tom nodded his head towards the window.

Janet looked there. Just outside was one of the gardeners, hard at work in a bed. He was a large man, red-faced, with a very big nose.

"What about giving old Nosey a shock?" said Tom, opening his desk to speak behind it. Janet nodded gleefully. She didn't know what Tom meant to do, but she was sure it would be funny.

Tom hunted in his desk till he found what he wanted. It was a piece of clay. The boy shut his desk and warmed the clay in his hands below it. It soon became soft and he picked off pieces to make hard pellets.

Janet and Mike watched him. Miss Thomas looked up. "Janet! Michael! Tom! Have you all finished your history questions? Then get out your textbook and learn the list of answers on page 23."

The children got out their books. Tom winked at Janet. He waited until Miss Thomas was standing at

Fred's desk, with her back turned to him, and then, very deftly, he flicked the clay pellet out of the open window with his thumb.

It hit the gardener on the top of his hat. He thought something had fallen on him from above and he stood up, raising his head to the sky, as if he thought it must be raining. Janet gave a muffled giggle.

"Shut up," whispered Tom. He waited till the man had bent down again, and his big nose presented a fine target. Flick! A big pellet flew straight out of the window – and this time it hit the astonished man right on the tip of his nose, with a smart tap.

He stood up straight, rubbing his nose, glaring into the window. But all he saw were bent heads and innocent faces, though one little girl was certainly smiling very broadly to herself. That was Janet, of course. She simply could *not* keep her mouth from smiling!

The gardener muttered something to himself, glared at the bent heads, and bent over his work again. Tom waited his chance and neatly flicked out another pellet. It hit the man smartly on the cheek, and he gave a cry of pain.

All the children looked up. Miss Thomas gazed in surprise at the open window, outside which the gardener was standing.

"Now, look here!" said the angry man, staring in at the window. "Which of you did that? Hitting me in the face with peas or something! Where's your teacher?"

"I'm here," said Miss Thomas. "What is the matter? I don't think any of the children here have been playing tricks. You must have made a mistake. Please don't disturb the class."

"Made a mistake! Do you suppose I don't know when anyone is flicking peas or something at me?" said the gardener. He glared at Janet, who was giggling. "Yes – and that's the girl who did it, too, if you ask *me*! She was giggling to herself before – and I'm pretty certain I saw her doing it."

"That will do, gardener," said Miss Thomas. "I will deal with the matter myself. I am sorry you have been hindered in your work."

She shut down the window. The man went off, grumbling. Miss Thomas looked at Janet, who was very red.

"Kindly leave the gardeners to do their work, Janet," she said in a cold voice. "Bring your things out of your desk, and put them in the empty front one. You had better sit there, I think."

Janet didn't know what to say. She couldn't give Tom away, and if she said she hadn't done it, Miss Thomas would ask who did, and then Tom would get into trouble. So with a lip that quivered, Janet opened her desk and began to get out her things.

Tom spoke up at once. "It wasn't Janet," he said. "I did it. I didn't like the look of the gardener's nose – so I just hit it with a clay pellet or two, Miss Thomas. I'm sure you would have liked to do it yourself, Miss Thomas, if you had seen that big nose out there."

Everyone choked with laughter. Miss Thomas didn't even smile. She looked straight at Tom with cold eyes.

"I hope my manners are better than yours," she said. "If not, I don't know what I should feel inclined to do to you, Tom Young. Bring your things out here, please. You will be under my eye in future."

So, with many soft groans, Tom left his seat at the back beside Janet, and went to the front.

"Oh, what a pity," said Janet, later on, as the class was waiting for Monsieur Crozier to come. "Now you won't be able to do any more tricks, Tom. You're right at the front."

"Goodness, you don't think that will stop Tom, do you?" said Fred. And Fred was right. It didn't!

Monsieur Crozier was not a very good person to play about with, because he had such a hot temper. The class never knew how he was going to take a joke. Sometimes, if Tom or Marian said something sharp, he would throw back his grey head and roar with laughter. Yet at other times he could not see a joke at all, but would fly into a temper.

Few people dared to play tricks on the French master, but Tom, of course, didn't care what he did. One morning, Janet and Mike found him kneeling down in a far corner of the room, behind the teacher's desk. In this corner stood two or three rolled-up maps. Tom was hiding something behind the maps.

"Whatever are you doing?" asked Janet in surprise. Tom grinned.

"Preparing a little surprise packet for dear Monsieur Crozier," he said.

"What is it?" said Mike, peering down.

"Quite simple," said Tom. "Look – I've got two empty cotton reels here – and I've tied thin black thread to each. If you follow the thread you'll see it runs behind this cupboard – behind that bookcase, over the hot water pipe, and up to my desk. Now, what will happen when I pull the threads?"

"The cotton reels will dance in their corner!" giggled Janet, "and Monsieur Crozier won't know what the noise is – because over here is far from where anyone sits! What fun!"

Mike told everyone what was going to happen. It was a small trick but might be very funny. The whole class was thrilled. In the French lesson that day they were to recite their French verbs, which was a very dull thing to do. Now it looked as if the lesson wouldn't be so dull after all.

Monsieur Crozier came into the room, his spectacles on his nose. His thick hair was untidy. It was plain that he had been in a temper with somebody, for it was his habit to ruffle his hair whenever he was angry. It stood up well, and the class smiled to see it.

"*Asseyez-vous!*" rapped out Monsieur Crozier, and the class sat down at once. In clear French sentences the master told them what he expected of them. Each child was to stand in turn and recite the French verb he had been told to learn, and the others were to write them out.

"And this morning I expect *hard work*!" said the French master. "I have had disgraceful work from the third form – disgrrrrrrrraceful! I will not put up with the same thing from you. You understand?"

"Yes, Monsieur Crozier," chanted the class. Monsieur Crozier looked at Tom, who had on a most innocent expression that morning.

"And you, too, will work!" he said. "It is not necessary always to be bottom. If you had no brains I would say 'Ah, the poor boy – he cannot work!' But you have brains and you will not use them. That is bad, very bad."

"Yes, sir," said Tom. Monsieur Crozier gave a grunt and sat down. Fred stood up to recite his verbs. The rest of the class bent over their desks to write them.

They were all listening for Tom to begin his trick. He did nothing at first, but waited until Fred had sat down. There was silence for a moment, whilst the French master marked Fred's name in his book.

Then Tom pulled at the threads which ran to his desk. At once the cotton reels over in the far corner began to jiggle like mad. Jiggle, jiggle, jiggle! they went. Jiggle, jiggle, jiggle!

Monsieur Crozier looked up, puzzled. He didn't quite know where the noise came from. He stared round the quiet class. Everyone's head was bent low, for most of the children were trying to hide their smiles. Janet felt a giggle coming and she shut her mouth hard. She was a terrible giggler. Mike looked at her anxiously. Janet so often gave the game away by exploding into a tremendous laugh.

The noise stopped. Doris stood up to say her verbs. She was quite perfect in them. She sat down. Monsieur Crozier marked her name. Tom pulled at the threads and the cotton reels jerked madly about behind the maps.

"What is that noise?" said the master impatiently, looking round. "Who makes that noise?"

"What noise, sir?" asked Tom innocently. "Is there a noise? I heard an aeroplane pass over just now."

"An aeroplane does not make a noise in this room!" said the master. "It is a jiggling noise. Who is doing it?"

"A jiggling noise, sir?" said Mike, looking surprised. "What sort of jiggling noise? My desk is a bit wobbly, sir – perhaps it's that you heard?"

Mike wobbled his desk and made a terrific noise. Everyone laughed.

"Enough!" cried Monsieur Crozier, rapidly losing his temper. "It is not your desk I mean. Silence! We will listen for the noise together."

There was a dead silence. Tom did not pull the threads. There was no noise at all.

But as soon as Eric was standing up, reciting his verbs in his soft voice, Tom jerked hard at his threads, and the reels did a kind of foxtrot behind the maps, sounding quite loud on the boards.

"There is that noise again!" said the master angrily. "Silence, Eric. Listen!"

Tom could not resist making the reels dance again as everyone listened. Jiggle-jiggle-jiggle-tap-tap-tap-jiggle-jiggle they went, and the class began to giggle.

"It comes from behind those maps," said the French master, puzzled. "It is very strange."

"Mice, perhaps, sir," said Mike. Tom flashed him a grin. Mike was playing up well.

The French master did not like mice. He stared at the maps, annoyed. He did not see how the noise could possibly be a trick, for the maps were far from any child's desk.

"Shall I see, sir?" asked Tom, getting up. "I don't mind mice a bit. I think Mike may be right, sir. It certainly does sound like a mouse caught behind there. Shall I look, sir?"

Now, what Tom thought he would do was to look

behind the maps, pocket the reels quickly after pulling the threads away, and then announce that there was no mouse there. But when he got to the corner, he couldn't resist carrying the trick a bit further.

"I'll pretend there really *is* a mouse!" he thought. "That'll give the class a real bit of fun!"

So, when he knelt down and fiddled about behind the maps, pulling away the threads and getting hold of the cotton reels, he suddenly gave a yell that made everyone jump, even the French master.

"It's a mouse! It's a mouse! Come here, you beastly thing! Sir, it's a mouse!"

The class knew perfectly well it wasn't. Janet gave a loud, explosive giggle that she tried hastily to turn into a cough. Even the surly Hugh smiled.

Tom knocked over all the maps, pretending to get the mouse. Then he made it seem as if the little creature had run into the classroom, and he jumped and bounded after the imaginary mouse, crawling under desks and nearly pulling a small table on top of him. The whole class exploded into a gale of laughter that drowned Monsieur Crozier's angry voice.

"Come here, you!" yelled Tom, thoroughly enjoying himself. "Ah – got you! No, I haven't! Just touched your tail. Ah, there you are again. Whoops! Nearly got you that time. What a mouse! Oh, what a mouse! Whoops, there you go again!"

Mike got out of his desk to join him. The two boys capered about on hands and knees and nearly drove Monsieur Crozier mad. He hammered on his desk. But it was quite impossible for the class to be silent. They laughed till their sides ached.

And in the middle of it all Miss Thomas walked in, furious! She had been taking the class next door, and could not imagine what all the noise was. She had felt certain that no teacher was with the second form. She stopped in surprise when she saw Monsieur Crozier there, red in the face with fury.

The class stopped giggling when they saw Miss Thomas. She had a way of giving out rather unpleasant punishments, and the class somehow felt that she would not readily believe in their mouse.

"I'm sorry, Monsieur Crozier," said Miss Thomas. "I thought you couldn't be here."

"Miss Thomas, I dislike your class," said Monsieur Crozier, quite as ready to fly into a temper with Miss Thomas as with the children. "They are ill-disciplined, ill-behaved, ill-mannered. See how they chase a mouse round your classroom! Ah, the bad children!"

"A mouse!" said Miss Thomas, in the utmost surprise. "But how could that be? There are no mice in the school. The school cats see to that. Has anyone got a tame mouse then?"

"No, Miss Thomas," chorused the children together.

"We heard a noise behind the maps," began Tom – but Miss Thomas silenced him with a look.

"Oh, you did, did you?" she said. "You may as well know that I don't believe in your mouse, Tom. I will speak to you all at the beginning of the next lesson. Pardon me for coming in like this, Monsieur Crozier. I apologize also for my class."

The class felt a little subdued. The French master glared at them, and proceeded to give them so much homework that they would have groaned if they had dared. Tom got a rap on his knuckles when he opened his mouth to protest. After that, he said no more. Monsieur Crozier was dangerous when he got as far as knuckle-rapping.

Miss Thomas was very sarcastic about the whole affair when she next saw her class. She flatly refused to believe in the mouse, but instead, asked who had gone to examine the noise in the corner.

"I did," said Tom, who always owned up to anything, quite fearlessly.

"I thought so," said Miss Thomas. "Well, you will write me an essay, four pages long, on the habits of mice, Tom. Give it to me this evening."

"But Miss Thomas," began Tom, "you know it's the hockey match this afternoon, and we're all watching it, and after tea there's a concert."

"That doesn't interest me at all," said Miss Thomas. "What interest me intensely at the moment are the habits of mice, and that being so, I insist on having that essay by seven o'clock. Not another word, Tom, unless you also want to write me an essay on, let us say, cotton reels. I am not quite so innocent as Monsieur Crozier."

After that there was no more to be said. Mike and Janet gave up watching the hockey match in order to help Tom with his essay. Mike looked up the habits of mice, and Janet looked up the spelling of the words. With many groans and sighs Tom managed to write four pages in his largest handwriting by seven o'clock. "It *is* decent of you to help," he said gratefully.

"Well, we shared the fun, didn't we?" said Mike. "So we must share the punishment too!"

CHAPTER FIVE

AN EXCITING IDEA

In the middle of that term Mike's birthday came. He was very much looking forward to it because he knew he would have plenty of presents sent to him, and he hoped his mother would let him have a fine birthday cake.

"I hope it won't be broken in pieces before it arrives," he said to Janet. "You know, Fred had a birthday last term, and he said his cake came in crumbs, and they had to eat it with a spoon. I'd better warn Mother to pack it very carefully."

But Mother didn't risk packing one. She wrote to Mike and told him to order himself a cake from the big cake shop in the town nearby. "And if you would like to give a small party to your own special friends, do so," she said. "You can order what you like in the way of food and drink and tell the shop to send me the bill. I can trust you not to be too extravagant, I know. Have a good time, and be sure your birthday cake has lots of icing on."

Mike was delighted. He showed the letter to Tom. "Isn't Mother decent?" he said. "Can you come down to the town with Janet and me today, Tom, and help me to order things?"

"You're not going to ask all the boys and girls in the class to share your party, are you?" said Tom. "You know, that would cost your mother a small fortune."

"Would it?" said Mike. "Well – what shall I do, then? How shall I choose people without making the ones left out feel hurt?"

"Well, if I were you, I'd just ask the boys in your own dormitory, and the girls in Janet's," said Tom. "That will be quite enough children."

"Yes, that's a good idea," said Mike, pleased. "I wish we could have our party in a separate room, so that the others we haven't asked won't have to see us eating the birthday cake and the other things. That would make me feel rather mean."

"Well, listen," said Tom, looking excited. "Why not have a midnight feast? We haven't had one for two terms. It's about time we did."

"A midnight feast!" said Janet, her eyes nearly popping out of her head. "Oooh, that would be marvellous. I've read about them in books. Oh Mike, *do* let's have your party in the middle of the night. Do, do!"

Mike didn't need much pressing. He was just as keen on the idea as Janet and Tom! The three of them began to talk excitedly about what they would do.

"Shall we have it in one of our dormitories?" said Janet. "Either yours or mine, Mike?"

"No," said Tom at once. "Mr Wills sleeps in the room next to ours – and Miss Thomas sleeps in the room next to yours, Janet. Either of them might hear us making a noise and come and find us."

"We needn't make a noise," said Janet. "We could just eat and drink."

"Janet! You couldn't possibly last an hour or two without going off into one of your giggling fits, you know you couldn't," said Mike. "And you make an awful noise with your first giggle. It's like an explosion."

"I know," said Janet. "I can't help it. I smother it till I almost burst – and then it comes out all of a sudden. Well – if we don't have the feast in one of our dormitories, where *shall* we have it?"

They all thought hard. Then Tom gave a grin. "I know the very place. What about the gardeners' shed?"

"The gardeners' shed!" said Mike and Janet together. "But why there?"

"Well, because it's out of the school and we can make a noise," said Tom. "And because it's not far from the little side door we use when we go to the playing fields. We can easily slip down and open it to go out. And also, it would be a fine place to store the food in. We can put it into boxes and cover them with sacks."

"Yes – it does sound rather good," said Mike. "It would be marvellous to be out of the school building, because I'm sure we'd make a noise."

"Last time we had a midnight feast, we had it in a dormitory," said Tom. "And in the middle someone dropped a ginger beer bottle. We got so frightened at the noise that we all hopped into bed, and the feast was spoilt. If we hold ours in the shed, we shan't be afraid of anyone coming. Let's!"

So it was decided to hold it there. Then the next excitement was going down to the town to buy the food.

They went to the big cake shop first. Mike said what he wanted. "I want a big birthday cake made," he said. "Enough for about twelve people, please. And I want it to be covered with pink icing, and written on it in white I'd like 'A happy birthday'. Can you do that?"

"Certainly," said the shopgirl, and wrote down Mike's name, and his mother's address, so that she might send her the bill. Then Mike turned to the others. "What else shall we have?" he said. "You help me to choose."

So Janet and Tom obligingly helped him, and between them they chose chocolate cakes, biscuits, shortbread and currant buns. Then they went to the grocer and asked for tinned sweetened milk, which everyone loved, sardines, tinned pineapple, and bottles of ginger beer.

The shop promised to pack up the goods and have them ready for the children to collect on the morning of Mike's birthday. The children meant to go down immediately after morning school and fetch the things.

They felt very excited. Janet and Mike counted up the cakes and things they had ordered and felt sure they had bought enough to feed everyone very well indeed.

"And now we'll have to ask everyone," said Mike happily. "Isn't it fun to invite people, Janet?"

"I'll ask the girls in my dorm tonight," said Janet.

"The rest of the class won't be there then, so they won't know. I vote we don't tell anyone except our guests that we're going to have a feast. We don't want it to get to the ears of any of the teachers. Tell the boys in your dorm to keep it quiet, Mike."

"Right," said Mike. Then he frowned. "I say, Janet," he said, "what about Hugh? Are we to ask him?"

Janet stared at Mike. She didn't know what to say. "Well, I suppose we'd better," she said at last. "It would be rather awful to leave him out as he belongs to your dormitory. No one likes him – but still he'd feel simply awful if he knew we were having a feast and he hadn't been asked."

"All right," said Mike. "I'll ask him. But he's such a surly fellow that he'll be an awful wet blanket."

Tom agreed that Hugh must be asked too. "I don't want him," he said, "but, after all, he belongs to our dorm, and it would make him feel pretty dreadful to be left out when everyone else is going."

So Mike quite meant to ask Hugh too. But then, something happened to make him change his mind. It had to do with Tom, and it happened in Mr Wills' class.

Mr Wills was taking maths with the second form. Tom was bored. He hated maths, and seldom got a sum right. Mr Wills had almost given him up. So long as Tom sat quietly at his desk and didn't disturb the others, Mr Wills left him in peace. But if Tom got up to any tricks Mr Wills pounced on him.

Tom usually behaved himself in the maths class, for he respected Mr Wills, and knew that he would stand no nonsense. But that morning he was restless. He had slept very well the night before and was so full of beans that he could hardly sit still. He had prepared a trick for the French master in the next lesson, and was longing to play it.

The trick was one of his string tricks. He was marvellous at those. He had slipped into the classroom before school that morning and had neatly tied strong yellow thread to the pegs that held the blackboard on its easel. A jerk at the thread, and a peg would come out – and down would crash the blackboard!

Tom looked at Mr Wills. Mr Wills caught his eye and frowned. "Get on, Tom," he said. "Don't slack so. If you can't get a sum right, get it wrong. Then, at least, I shall know you've been doing something!"

"Yes, Mr Wills," said Tom meekly. He scribbled down a few figures that meant nothing at all. His hand itched to pull away the peg. As his desk was at the front, he could easily leap forward and pick up the peg before Mr Wills could see that string was tied to it.

"It's a bit dangerous to try it on with Mr Wills," thought Tom. "But I'm so bored, I must do something!"

He turned round and caught Mike's eye. Mike winked. Tom winked back, then he winked twice with each eye in turn. That was his signal to Mike that a trick was about to be played! Mike nudged Janet. They both looked up eagerly. Hugh caught their eager looks and wondered what was up. He guessed that Tom was about to play a trick and he watched him.

Mr Wills was at the back of the room, looking at Bertha's work. Tom jerked his thread. The peg of the easel flew out – one side of the blackboard slipped down – and then it fell with a resounding crash on the floor, making everyone jump violently. Mike and Janet knew what had happened, and they tried not to laugh. Hugh also saw what had happened. Before anyone could do anything Tom was out of his desk in a flash, and had picked up the blackboard and peg and set them back in place. He wondered whether or not to remove the threads, but decided he would risk it again.

"Thank you, Tom," said Mr Wills, who hadn't for a moment guessed that it was a trick. "Get on with your work, everybody."

Most of the children guessed that it was Tom up to his tricks again. They watched to see if it would happen once more. Mr Wills went to see Hugh's work. He had done most of his sums wrong, and the master grumbled at him.

"You haven't been trying! What have you been thinking of to put down this sum like that? No one else in the class has so many sums wrong!"

Hugh flushed. He always hated being grumbled at in front of anyone. "I'm sure Tom has more sums wrong than I have," he said, in a low voice.

At that moment Tom jerked the two pegs neatly out of the easel, and the board fell suddenly, with an even greater crash than before. Everyone giggled, and Janet gave one of her explosions. The noise she made caused the children to laugh even more loudly.

"What's the matter with the board this morning?" said Mr Wills irritably.

"I should think Tom has something to do with it," said Hugh spitefully. "You'll find he hasn't got a single sum right – and has given all his attention to our blackboard instead. I have at least been working!"

There was a silence. Mr Wills went to the blackboard.

He examined the pegs. But they now had no thread on them, for Tom had slipped it off and it was safely in his pockets.

But not very safely, after all! Mr Wills turned to Tom. "Just turn out your pockets, please," he ordered. Tom obeyed promptly – and there on the desk lay the telltale yellow thread, still with the little slipknots at one end.

"I'll see you after the class, Tom," said Mr Wills. "I can't make you do good work – but I can at least stop you from preventing the others from working. You should know by now that I don't stand any nonsense in my classes."

"Yes, sir," said Tom, dolefully.

"Maths is a most important subject," went on Mr Wills. "Some of the children here are working for scholarships and it is necessary they should get on well this term. If you disturb my classes once more I shall refuse to have you in them."

"Yes, sir," said Tom again, going red. Mr Wills had a very rough tongue. When the master had turned his back on the class to write something on the now steady blackboard, Tom turned round to get the comfort of a look from Mike and Janet. They nodded at him – and then Tom caught sight of Hugh's face.

Hugh wore a spiteful grin on his face. He was pleased to have got Tom into trouble.

"Sneak!" whispered Mike to Hugh.

"*Silence!*" said Mr Wills, not turning round. Mike said no more, but gave Hugh a look that said all his tongue longed to say!

"Wait till after school!" said the look. "Just wait till after school."

CHAPTER SIX

MIDNIGHT FEAST!

Tom got a tremendous scolding after the class, and entered the French class four minutes late, with a very red face. Monsieur Crozier looked at him in surprise.

"And why are you late?" he said. "It is not the custom to walk into my classes after they have started."

"Please, sir, I'm sorry," said Tom, "but Mr Wills was talking to me."

The French master guessed that Tom had been up for a scolding, and he said no more. Tom was very subdued that lesson. Mr Wills had said some cutting things to him, and the boy felt rather ashamed of himself. It was all very well to play tricks and have a good time – but there *was* work to do as well! So he sat like a lamb in the French class, and really listened to the lesson.

After school, Mike, Janet and Fred went after Hugh. "Sneak!" said Mike furiously. "What did you want to go and give Tom away for?"

"Why shouldn't I?" said Hugh. "He sneaked on me last term."

"No, he didn't," said Mike. "He says he didn't – and you know as well as anybody that Tom's truthful. He doesn't tell lies. You're a beastly sneak!"

"Oh, shut up," said Hugh rudely, and walked off. But the others walked after him, telling him all kinds of truthful but horrid things about himself. Hugh went into a music room to practise and banged the door on them. He even turned the key in the lock.

"He really is a spiteful sneak," said Janet. "Mike, you're surely not going to ask him to our feast now, are you?"

"You bet I'm not," said Mike. "As if I'd have a sneaky creature like that on my birthday night! No fear!"

"Well, we'll ask all the others, and we'll warn them not to say a word to Hugh," said Janet. So they asked everyone else – Fred, Eric, small George, Marian, Bertha, Connie, Audrey and Doris. With Mike, Janet and Tom there would be eleven children altogether.

"And don't say a single word to anyone outside our dormitories," said Mike. "And don't say anything to Hugh, either. He's such a sneak that I'm not asking him. I'm sure if he got to know we were having a feast he'd prowl round and then tell about it! So, not a word, mind!"

Mike's birthday came. He had a lot of cards and many presents. A good deal of it was money and he meant to spend it in the holidays. His mother and father sent him a new paintbox and pencil box with his name on them. His grandfather wrote to say that he had bought him a new bicycle. Janet gave him a box of writing paper and stamps. The others gave him small presents, pencils, rubbers, sweets and so on. Mike was very happy.

"After school, we'll pop down with baskets and get all those things," he said. "We'd better ask one or two of the others to come too. We'll never be able to carry all the stuff ourselves."

So Fred and Marian came too, and the five set off with giggles and talk. They came back with all the food and drink, and undid the birthday cake in the gardeners' shed. It was simply marvellous.

"A happy birthday" was written across it, and the pink icing was thick and not too hard. It was a fine big cake. The children were delighted. Mike put it carefully back into its box.

The gardeners' shed was a big place. It was piled with boxes, tools, pots, wood and so on. Actually it was not much used, for the gardeners had another, smaller shed they preferred, and they used the big shed mostly as a storehouse. The children soon found a good hiding place for their food and drink.

There was an enormous old crate, made of wood, at the back of the shed. They put everything into this and then put a board on top. On the board they piled rows of flowerpots.

"There," said Mike. "I don't think anyone would guess what is under those pots! Now, let's arrange what we're going to sit on."

There were plenty of boxes and big flower pots. The children pulled them out and arranged them to sit on. "We shall have to pin sacks across the windows," said Mike. "Else the light of our candles will be seen."

"Better do that this evening," said Tom. "It might make people suspicious if they came by and saw sacks across the windows."

So they left the windows uncurtained. There was nothing else they could do except smuggle in a few mugs and plates and spoons. Janet said she could do this with Marian. She knew where the school crockery was kept, and she could easily slip into the big cupboard after crafts that afternoon and get what was needed. They could wash it after the feast and put it back again.

"I think that's everything," said Mike happily. "I say – this is going to be fun, isn't it! Golly, I can hardly wait till tonight!"

"I'll wake the girls in my dorm," said Janet, "and you wake the boys, Mike. Don't wake Hugh by mistake, though!"

Everything went off as planned. Janet fell asleep, but awoke just before midnight. She switched on her torch and looked at her watch. Five minutes to twelve! She slipped out of bed, put on shoes, stockings, vest, under her nightdress, and jersey over it. Then her dressing gown on top. She woke the other girls one by one, shaking them and whispering into their ears.

"It's time! Wake up! The midnight feast is about to begin!"

The girls awoke, and sat up, thrilled. They began to put on vests and jerseys too. Meanwhile the boys were doing the same thing. Mike had awoken them all, except, of course, Hugh, and in silence they were dressing. They did not dare to whisper, as the girls could, because they were afraid of waking Hugh.

They all crept out of the dormitory, and found the six girls waiting for them in the passage outside. Janet was trying to stop her giggles.

"For goodness' sake don't do one of your explosions till we're out in the shed," said Mike anxiously. So Janet bit her lips together and waited. They all went down the stairs and out of the little side door. Then across to the big shed. Mike opened the door and everyone filed in. Once the door was shut, the children felt safe and began to talk in loud whispers.

Mike and Tom quickly put sacks across the three windows, and then lit three candles. Their wavering light made strange shadows in the shed, and everything looked rather mysterious and exciting. The other children watched Mike and Tom go to the box at the back and lift off the flowerpots arranged there.

And then out came the good things to eat and drink! How the children gaped for joy to see them! They all felt terribly hungry, and were pleased to see so much to eat and drink.

Mike set the birthday cake down on a big box. All the children crowded round to look at it. They thought it was marvellous. "We'll cut it the very last thing," said Mike. "And don't forget to wish, everybody, because it's a birthday cake!"

They made a start on sardines and cake. It was a lovely mixture. Then they went on to currant buns and biscuits, pineapple and tinned milk. They chattered in low voices and giggled to their hearts' content. When

Fred fell off his box and upset tinned, sticky milk all over himself, there was a gale of laughter. Fred looked so funny with his legs in the air, and milk dripping all over him!

"Sh! Sh!" said Mike. "Honestly, we'll wake up the whole school! Shut up, Janet! Your giggles make everyone worse still. You just make me want to giggle myself."

"This is the best feast we've ever had," said Tom, helping himself to a large piece of chocolate cake. "Any more ginger pop, Mike?"

"Yes," said Mike. "Help yourself – and now, what about cutting the grand birthday cake?"

"It looks big enough for the whole school," giggled Marian. "I say – I wish Hugh knew what he was missing! Wouldn't he be wild! I expect he is still sound asleep in his bed."

But Hugh wasn't! He had woken at about half past twelve, and had turned over to go to sleep again.

And then something strange had struck him. There was something missing in the dormitory. It was quite dark there and the boy could see nothing. But he lay there, half-asleep, wondering what was missing.

Then suddenly he knew. There was no steady breathing to be heard. There was no sound at all. Hugh sat up, alarmed. Why was nobody breathing? That was the usual sound to be heard at night, if anyone woke up. What had happened?

Hugh switched on his torch and got out of bed. He looked round the curtains that separated his cubicle from the next boy's. The bed was empty!

Hugh looked at all the beds. Every one was empty. Then the boy guessed in a flash what was happening.

"It's Mike's birthday – and he's having a midnight party somewhere. The beast! He's asked everyone else, and not me! I bet Janet's dormitory is empty too."

He slipped out to see. It was as he had guessed – quite empty. All the beds were bare, their coverings turned back. The boy felt angry and hurt. They might have asked him! It was hateful to be left out like this.

"I'm always left out of everything!" he thought, hot tears pricking his eyelids. "Always! Do they think it will make me behave any better to them if they treat me like this? How I hate them! I'll jolly well spoil their feast for them. That will serve them right!"

CHAPTER SEVEN

A SHOCK FOR THE FEASTERS

Hugh wondered how to spoil the feast. Should he go and knock on Mr Wills' door and tell him that the dormitories were empty? No – Mr Wills didn't look too kindly on telltales. Well, then, he had better find out where the children were feasting and spoil it for them.

He looked out of the window, and by a chance he caught sight of a tiny flicker outside. It came from a corner of the big window of the shed. The sack didn't quite cover the glass. Hugh stood and looked at it, wondering where the light came from.

"It's from the big shed," he thought. "So that's where they're feasting. I'll go down and find out!"

Down he went, out of the door, which the children had left open, and into the yard. He went across to the shed, and at once heard the sounds of laughter and whispering inside. He put his eye to the place in the window where the light showed, and saw the scene inside. It was a very merry one.

Empty bottles of ginger beer lay around. Empty tins stood here and there, and crumbs were all over the place. It was plain that the two dormitories had had a marvellous time. Hugh's heart burned in him. He felt so angry and so miserable that he could almost have gone into the shed and fought every child there!

But he didn't do that. He knew it would be no use. Instead, he took up a large stone and crashed it on to the window! The glass broke at once, with a very loud noise. All the children inside the shed jumped up in fright, their cake falling from their fingers.

"What's that?" said Mike in a panic. "The window is broken. Who did it?"

There was another crash as the second window broke under Hugh's stone. The children were now really afraid. They simply couldn't imagine what was happening.

"The noise will wake everyone up!" cried Mike, in a loud whisper. "Quick, we'd better get back to our dormitories. Leave everything. There isn't time to clear up."

Hugh didn't wait to break the third window. He had seen a light spring up in Mr Wills' room above and he knew the master would be out to see what was happening before another minute had gone by. So he sped lightly up the stairs, and was in his bed before the door of Mr Wills' room opened.

The eleven children opened the door of the shed and fled into the school. They went up the stairs and into the passage where their dormitories were – and just as they were passing Mr Wills' door it opened! Mr Wills stood there in his dressing gown, staring in amazement at the procession of white-faced children slipping by.

"What are you doing?" he asked. "What was all that noise?"

The children didn't wait to answer. They fled into their rooms and hopped into bed, half-dressed as they were, shoes and all. Mr Wills went into the boys' dormitory, switched on the light and looked sternly round. He pulled back the curtains from those cubicles that had them drawn around, and spoke angrily.

"What is the meaning of this? Where have you been? Answer me!"

Nobody answered. The boys were really frightened. Hugh's bed was nearest to Mr Wills, and the master took hold of Hugh's shoulder, shaking him upright.

"You, boy! Answer me! What have you been doing?"

"Sir, I've been in bed all the evening," said Hugh truthfully. "I don't know what the others have been doing. I wasn't with them."

Mr Wills glared round at the other beds. "I can see that you are half-dressed," he said in an icy voice. "Get out and undress and then get back into bed. I shall want an explanation of this in the morning. You can tell the girls when you see them, that I shall want them too. It seems to me that this is something the Heads should know about. Now then – quick – out of bed and undress!"

The boys, all but Hugh, got out of bed and took off their jerseys and other things. Mr Wills told Hugh to get out of bed too.

"But I'm not half-dressed," said Hugh. "I've only got my pyjamas on, sir. I wasn't with the others."

But Mr Wills wasn't believing anyone at all that night. He made Hugh get out too, and saw that he was in his pyjamas as he said. He did not notice one thing – and that was that Hugh had his shoes on! But Mike noticed it.

He was puzzled. Why should Hugh have his shoes on in bed? That was a funny thing to do, surely. And then the boy suddenly guessed the reason.

"Hugh woke up – saw the beds were empty – put on his shoes and slipped down to find us. It was he who broke the windows, the beast! He's got us all into this trouble!"

But he said nothing then. He would tell the others in the morning. He slipped back into bed and tried to go to sleep.

All the eleven children were worried when the morning came. They couldn't imagine what Mr Wills was going to do. They soon found out. Mr Wills had gone to the two Heads, and it was they that the children were to see, not Mr Wills. This was worse than ever!

"You will go now," said Mr Wills, after prayers were over. "I don't want to hear any explanations from you. You can tell those to the Heads. But I may as well tell you that I went down into the shed last night and found the remains of your feast, the candles burning – and the windows smashed. I understand the feast part – but why you should smash the windows is beyond me. I am ashamed of you all."

"We didn't smash . . ." began Mike. But Mr Wills wouldn't listen to a word. He waved them all away. Hugh had to go, too, although he kept saying that he hadn't been with the others. Mike had told the others what he suspected about Hugh, and every boy and girl looked at him with disgust and dislike.

They went to see the Heads. Their knees shook, and Bertha began to cry. Even Janet felt the tears coming. All the children were tired, and some of them had eaten too much and didn't feel well.

The Heads looked stern. They asked a few questions, and then made Tom tell the whole story.

"I can understand your wanting to have some sort of a party on Michael's birthday," said Miss Lesley, "but to end it by smashing windows is disgusting behaviour. It shows a great lack of self-control."

"I think it was Hugh who broke the windows," said Mike, not able to keep it back any longer. "We wouldn't have done that, Miss Lesley. For one thing we would have been afraid of being caught if we did that – it made such a noise. But, you see, we left Hugh out of the party – and I think that out of spite he smashed the windows to give us a shock, and to make sure we would be caught."

"Did you do that, Hugh?" asked the headmaster, looking at the red-faced boy.

"No, sir," said Hugh, in a low voice. "I was in bed asleep. I don't know anything about it."

"Well, then, why was it you had your shoes on in bed

when Mr Wills made you get out last night?" burst out Tom. "Mike saw them!"

Hugh said nothing, but looked obstinate. He meant to stick to his story, no matter what was said.

The punishment was very just. "As you have missed almost a night's sleep, you will all go to bed an hour earlier for a week," said Miss Lesley.

"And you will please pay for the mending of the windows," said the headmaster. "You too, Hugh. I am not going to go into the matter of how the windows got broken – but I think Michael is speaking the truth when he says that he would not have thought of smashing windows because of the noise. All the same, you will all twelve of you share the cost of mending the windows. I will deduct it from your pocket money."

"And please remember, children, that although it is good to have fun, you are sent here to work and to learn things that will help you to earn your living later on," said Miss Lesley. "There are some of you here working for scholarships, and you will not be able to win them if you behave like this."

The children went out, feeling very miserable. It was hateful to go to bed early – earlier even than the first formers. And they felt bitter about the payment for the windows, because they themselves had not broken them.

"Though if we hadn't held the feast, the windows wouldn't have been broken," said Mike. "So in a way it was because of us they got smashed. But I know it was Hugh who did it, out of spite. Let's not say a word to him. Let's send him to Coventry and be as beastly as we can."

So Hugh had a very bad time. He was snubbed by the

whole of his class. The first and third formers joined in too, and nobody ever spoke a word to him, unless it was a whispered, "Sneak! Telltale! Sneak!" which made him feel worse than if he had not been spoken to.

He worried very much over the whole thing. It was awful to have no friends, terrible to be treated as if he were a snake. He knew it was stupid and wrong to have broken the windows like that. He had done it in a fit of spiteful temper, and now it couldn't be undone.

He couldn't sleep at night. He rose the next day looking white and tired. He couldn't do his work, and the teachers scolded him, for he was one of the children who were going in for the scholarship. He couldn't remember what he had learnt, and although he spent hours doing his prep, he got poor marks for it.

Hugh knew that he must win the scholarship, for his parents were not well-off and needed help with his schooling. He had brothers and a sister who were very clever, and who had won many scholarships between them. Hugh didn't want to let his family down. He mustn't be the only one who couldn't do anything.

"The worst of it is, I haven't got good brains, as they have," thought the boy, as he tried to learn a list of history dates. "Everything is hard to me. It's easy to them. Daddy and Mother don't realize that. They think I must be as clever as the rest of the family, and I'm not. So they get angry with me when I'm not top of my form, though, goodness knows, I swot hard enough and try to be."

The children all paid between them for the windows. They were mended and the remains of the feast were cleared away. The week went by, and the period for going to bed early passed by too. The children began to forget about the feast and its unfortunate ending. But they didn't forget their dislike for Hugh.

"I shan't speak a word to him for the rest of the term," said Fred. And the others said the same. Only Janet felt sorry for the boy, and noticed how white and miserable he looked. But she had to be loyal to the others, and so she said nothing to him too, and looked away whenever he came near.

"I can't stick this!" Hugh thought to himself. "I simply can't. I wish I could run away! I wish I was old enough to join a ship and go to sea. I hate school!"

CHAPTER EIGHT

A SHOCK FOR TOM – AND ONE FOR HUGH

The days slipped by, and each one was full of interest. Janet and Mike liked their work, and loved their play. They loved being friends with Tom, and they liked all the others in their form except Hugh.

The great excitement now was crafts. The boys were doing carpentry, and the things they were making were really beginning to take shape. The girls were doing raffia-work and were weaving some really lovely baskets. Janet couldn't help gloating over the basket she was making. It was a big workbasket for her mother, in every bright colour Janet could use. Mike was making a very fine pipe rack for his father.

But the finest thing of all that was being made in the carpentry class was Tom's. The boy was mad on ships, and he had made a beautiful model. He was now doing the rigging, and the slender masts were beginning to look very fine indeed, set with snowy sails and fine thread instead of ropes.

There were wide windowsills in the craft and carpentry room, and on these the children set out their work, so that any other form could see what they were doing. They all took a deep interest in what the others were making. Tom's ship was greatly admired and the boy was really proud of it.

"I think this is the only class you really work in, Tom, isn't it?" the woodwork master said, bending over Tom's model. "My word, if you worked half as hard in the other classes as you do in mine, you would certainly never be bottom. You're an intelligent boy – yes, very intelligent – and you can use your brains well when you want to."

Tom flushed with pleasure. He gazed at his beautiful ship and his heart swelled with pride as he thought of how it would look on his mantelpiece at home, when it was quite finished. It was almost finished now – he was soon going to paint it. He hoped there would be time to begin the painting that afternoon.

But there wasn't. "Put your things away," said the master. "Hurry, Fred. You mustn't be late for your next class."

The children cleared up, and put their models on the

wide windowsills. The master opened the windows to let in fresh air, and then gave the order to file out to the children's own classroom, two floors below. The craft rooms were at the top of the school, lovely big light rooms, with plenty of sun and air.

The next lesson was geography. Miss Thomas wanted a map that was not in the corner and told Hugh to go and get it from one of the cupboards on the top landing. The children stood up to answer questions whilst Hugh was gone.

In the middle of the questions, something curious happened. A whitish object suddenly fell quickly past the schoolroom windows and landed with a dull thud on the stone path by the bed. The children looked round in interest. What could it have been? Not a bird, surely?

Mike was next to the window. He peeped out to see what it was – and then he gave a cry of dismay.

"What's the matter?" asked the teacher, startled.

"Oh, Miss Thomas – it looks as if Tom's lovely ship is lying broken on the path outside," said Mike. Tom darted to the window. He gave a wail of dismay.

"It *is* my ship! Somebody has pushed it off the windowsill, and it's smashed. All the rigging is spoilt! The masts are broken!"

The boy's voice trembled, for he had really loved his ship. He had spent so many hours making it. It had been very nearly perfect.

There was a silence in the room. Everyone was shocked, and felt very sorry for Tom. In the middle of the silence the door opened and Hugh came in, carrying the map.

At once the same thought flashed into everyone's mind. Hugh had been to the top of the school to get the map – the cupboard was opposite the woodwork room – and Hugh had slipped in and pushed Tom's ship out of the window to smash it!

"You did it!" shouted Mike. Hugh looked astonished.

"Did what?" he asked.

"Smashed Tom's ship!" cried half a dozen voices.

"I don't know what you're talking about," said Hugh, really puzzled.

"That will do," said Miss Thomas. "Tom, go and collect your sip. It may not be so badly damaged as you think. Hugh, sit down. Do you know anything about the ship?"

"Not a thing," said Hugh. "The door of the woodwork room was shut when I went to get the map."

"Storyteller!" whispered half a dozen children.

"Silence!" rapped out Miss Thomas. She was worried. She knew that Tom had been hated by Hugh ever since last term, and she feared that the boy really had smashed up the ship. She made up her mind to find out about it from Hugh himself, after the lesson. She felt sure she would know if the boy were telling her the truth or not, once she really began to question him.

But it was not Miss Thomas that Hugh feared. It was the children! As soon as morning school was over they surrounded him and accused him bitterly, calling him every name they could think of.

"I didn't do it, I didn't do it," said Hugh, pushing away the hands that held him. "Don't pin everything on to me simply because I have done one or two mean things. I didn't do that. *I* liked Tom's ship, too."

But nobody believed him. They gave the boy a very bad time and by the time that six o'clock came, Hugh was so battered by the children's looks and tongues that he crept up to his dormitory to be by himself. Then the tears came and he sobbed to himself, ashamed because he could not stop.

"I'm going away," he said. "I can't stay here now. I'm going home. Daddy and Mother will be angry with me, but I won't come back here. I can't do anything right. I didn't smash that lovely ship. I liked it just as much as the others did."

He began to stuff some of his clothes into a small case. He hardly knew what he was doing. He knew there was a train at a quarter to seven. He would catch that.

The other children wondered where he was. "Good thing for him he's not here," said Fred. "I've thought of a few more names to call him, the horrid beast!"

They were all in their common room, discussing the affair. Tom's ship stood on the mantelpiece, looking very sorry for itself. The woodwork master came to see it.

"It's not as bad as it might be," he said cheerfully. "Just a bit dented here. Those masts can easily be renewed, and you can do the rigging again. You're good at that. Cheer up, Tom!"

The master went out. "All very well for him to talk like that," said Tom gloomily. "But it isn't his ship. I don't feel the same about it now it's spoilt."

There came a knock at the common room door. It was such a timid, faint knock that at first none of the children heard it. Then it came again, a little louder.

"There's someone knocking at the door," said Audrey, in astonishment, for no one ever knocked at their door.

"Come in!" yelled the whole form. The door opened

and a first former looked in. It was a small boy, with a very white, scared face.

"Hallo, Pete, what's up!" said Fred.

"I w-w-w-want to speak to T-t-t-tom," stammered the small boy, whose knees were knocking together in fright.

"Well, here I am," said Tom. "Don't look so scared. I shan't eat you!"

The small boy opened and shut his mouth like a fish, but not another word came out. The children began to giggle.

"Peter, whatever's the matter?" cried Janet. "Has somebody frightened you?"

"N-n-n-no," stammered Pete. "I want to tell Tom something. But I'm afraid to."

"What is it?" asked Tom kindly. He was always kind to the younger ones, and they all liked him. "What have you been doing? Breaking windows or something?"

"No, Tom – m-m-m-much worse than that," said the boy, looking at Tom with big, scared eyes. "It's – it's about your lovely ship. That ship there," and he pointed to the mantelpiece.

"Well, what about it?" said Tom, thinking that Pete was going to tell him how he had seen Hugh push it out of the window.

"Oh, Tom, it was my fault it got broken!" wailed the little boy, breaking into loud sobs. "I was in the woodwork room with Dick Dennison, and we were fooling about. And I fell against the windowsill – and – and – "

"Go on," said Tom.

"I put out my hand to save myself," sobbed Pete, "and it struck your lovely ship – and sent it toppling out of the open window. I was so frightened, Tom."

There was a long silence after this speech. So Hugh hadn't anything to do with the ship, after all! No wonder he had denied it so vigorously. All the children stared at the white-faced Pete.

"I d-d-d-didn't dare to tell anyone," went on the small boy. "Dick swore he wouldn't tell either. But then we heard that you had accused Hugh of doing it – and we knew we couldn't do anything but come and own up. So I came because it was me that pushed it out – quite by accident, Tom."

"I see," said Tom slowly. He looked at the scared boy and gave him a kindly push. "All right. Don't worry. You did right to come and tell me. Come straight away another time you do anything – you see, we've done an injustice to somebody else – and that's not good. Go along back to your common room. I daresay I can manage to mend the ship all right."

The small boy gave Tom a grateful look out of tearful eyes, and shot out of the room at top speed. He tore back to his common room, feeling as if a great load had been taken off his heart.

When he had gone, the children looked at one another. "Well, it wasn't Hugh after all," said Janet, saying what everyone else was thinking.

"No," said Tom. "It wasn't. And I called him a good many beastly names. For once they were unjust. And I hate injustice."

Everyone felt uncomfortable. "Well, anyway, he's done things just as horrid," said Fred. "It's no wonder we thought it was him. Especially as he just happened to be by the woodwork room at the time."

"Yes," said Mike. "That was unlucky for him. What are we going to do about it?"

Nobody said anything. Nobody wanted to apologize to Hugh. Tom stared out of the window.

"We've got to do something," he said. "Where is he? We'd better find him and get him here, and then tell him we made a mistake. We were ready enough to be beastly – now we must be ready to be sorry."

"I'll go and find him," said Janet. She had remembered Hugh's startled face as the others had suddenly accused him when he had come into the room carrying the map. She thought, too, of his miserable look when they had all pressed round him after tea, calling him horrid names. They had been unjust. Hugh had done many mean things – but not that one. Janet suddenly wanted to say she was sorry.

She sped into the classroom. Hugh wasn't there. She ran to the gym. He wasn't there either. She looked into each music room, and in the library, where Hugh often went to choose books. But he was nowhere to be found.

"Where can he be?" thought the little girl. "He can't be out. His clothes are hanging up. What has he done with himself?"

She thought of the dormitory. She ran up the stairs, and met Hugh just coming out, carrying a bag, with the marks of tears still on his face. She ran up to him.

"Hugh! Where have you been? What are you doing with that bag? Listen, we want you to come downstairs."

"No, you don't," said Hugh. "None of you want me. I'm going home."

"Hugh! What do you mean?" cried Janet, in alarm.

"Oh, Hugh, listen. We know who broke Tom's ship. It was little Pete. He pushed it out of the window by accident! Don't go home, Hugh. Come down and hear what we have to say!"

CHAPTER NINE

THINGS ARE CLEARED UP!

But Hugh pushed past Janet roughly. He did not mean to change his mind. Janet was scared. It seemed a dreadful thing to her that Hugh should run away because of the unkindness he had received from his class. She caught hold of the boy and tried to pull him back into the dormitory.

"Don't," said Hugh. "Let me go. You're just as bad as the others, Janet. It's no good your trying to stop me now."

"Oh, do listen to me, Hugh," said Janet. "Just listen for half a minute. Pete came and owned up about the ship. He pushed it out of the window when he was fooling about. And now you can't think how sorry we are that we accused you."

Hugh went back into the dormitory, and sat on the bed. "Well," he said bitterly, "you may feel pretty awful about it – but just think how I feel always to have you thinking horrid things about me, and calling me names, and turning away when you meet me. And think how I felt when I woke up the other night and found everyone had gone to a midnight feast – except me! *You've* never been left out of anything. Everyone likes you. You don't know what it's like to be miserable."

Janet took Hugh's cold hand. She was very troubled. "Hugh," she said, "we did mean to ask you to our feast. Mike and Tom and I planned that we would. We didn't want you to be left out."

"Well, why didn't you ask me then?" demanded Hugh. "It would have made all the difference in the world to me if only you had. I'd have felt terribly happy. As it was you made me lose my temper and do something horrid and spiteful. I've been ashamed of it ever since. I spoilt your feast – and got you all into trouble. I wanted to do that, I know – but all the same I've been ashamed. And now that I'm going to run away, I want you to tell the others something for me."

"What?" asked Janet, almost in tears.

"Tell them I *did* break the windows, of course," said Hugh, "and tell them that I want to pay for them. They had to pay a share – well, give them this money and let them share it out between them. I wanted to do that before, only I kept saying I hadn't broken the windows, so I couldn't very well offer to pay, could I? But now I can."

Hugh got out his leather purse and took out some silver. He counted it and gave it to Janet. "There you are," he said. "I can't do much to put right what I did, but I can at least do this. Now goodbye, Janet, I'm going."

"No, don't go, Hugh, please don't," said Janet, her voice trembling. "Please come down and let us all tell you we're sorry. Don't go."

But Hugh shook off her hand and went quickly down the stairs, carrying his little bag. Janet flew down to the common room, tears in her eyes and the money in her hand. She burst in at the door, and everyone turned to see what she had to say.

"I found him," said Janet. "He's – he's running away. Isn't it dreadful? He says he's ashamed of himself now for breaking the windows, and he's given me the money to give you, to pay for the whole amount. And oh Mike, oh Tom, somehow I can understand now why he broke those windows – he was so miserable at being left out!"

"I do wish we hadn't accused him unjustly," began Fred. "It's an awful pity he cheated last term like that. He seemed quite a decent chap till then – but somehow we got it into our heads after that that he was a dreadful boy and we didn't really give him a chance."

"Look here – I'm going after him," said Tom suddenly. "If the Heads get to know about this, we'll all get into awful trouble, and goodness knows what will happen to Hugh. What's the time? Half past six? I can catch him then, before he gets on the train."

He ran out of the school building and went to the shed

where Mr Wills' bicycle was kept. He wheeled it out and jumped on it. He didn't stop to light the lamp. Down the drive he went and out of the great school gates.

He pedalled fast, for it was quite a way to the station. He kept his eyes open for Hugh, but it was not until he had almost come to the station that he saw the boy. Hugh was running fast. He had been running all the way, because he had been so afraid of missing the train.

Tom rode up close to him, jumped off the bicycle, clutched Hugh's arm and pulled him to the side of the road. He threw the bicycle against the hedge, and then dragged the astonished boy into a nearby field.

"What's up? Oh, it's you, Tom! Let me go. I'm going home."

"No, you're not," said Tom. "Not until you hear what I've got to say, anyway. Listen, Hugh. We're ashamed of ourselves. We really are. It's true you've been pretty beastly and spiteful – but it was partly because of us. I mean, we made you behave like that. I see that now. If we'd behaved differently you might have, too. You were a decent chap till the end of last term. We all liked you."

"I know," said Hugh, in a low voice. "I was happy till then. Then I cheated. I know there's no excuse for cheating – but I had a reason for my cheating. It seemed a good reason to me then, but I see it wasn't now."

"Somehow or other I had to pass that exam," said Hugh. "All my brothers and my sister are clever and pass exams and win scholarships, and my father said I mustn't let the family down. I must pass mine too. Well, I'm not really clever. That is why I have to swot so hard, and never have time to play and go for walks as the rest of you do. So, as I was afraid I'd not pass the exam, I cheated a bit. And you gave me away."

"I didn't," said Tom. "I saw you'd cheated, but I didn't give you away. Why don't you believe that? Miss Thomas found it out."

"Do you swear you didn't give me away?" said Hugh.

"I swear I didn't!" said Tom. "You've never known me to sneak, have you, or to tell lies? I do a lot of silly things and play the fool, but I don't do mean things."

"All right. I believe you," said Hugh. "But I can't tell you how the thought of that cheating, and knowing that you all knew it, weighed on my mind. You see, I'm not really a cheat."

"I see," said Tom. "It's really your parents' fault for trying to drive you too hard. You're silly. You should tell them."

"I'm going to," said Hugh. "That's one thing I'm going home to say now. And I've been so miserable this term that what brains I have won't work at all! So it's no good me trying for the scholarship anyhow. Somehow things aren't fair. There's you with brains, and you don't bother to use them. There's clever Janet and Mike, and they fool about and don't really try to be top when they could. And there's me, with poor brains, doing my very best and getting nowhere."

Tom suddenly felt terribly ashamed of all his fooling and playing. He felt ashamed of making Mike and Janet do bad work too, for they none of them really tried their hardest. He bit his lip and stared into the darkness.

"I've done as much wrong as you have," he said at last. "You cheated because you hadn't got good enough brains – and I've wasted my good brains and not used them. So I've cheated too, in another way. I never thought of it like that before. Hugh, come back with me. Let's start again. It's all been a stupid mistake. Look – give us a chance to show you we're sorry, won't you?"

"You didn't give *me* a chance," said Hugh.

"I know. So you can feel awfully generous if you will give *us* a chance!" said Tom. "And look here – I'm not going to waste my good brains any more and cheat the teachers out of what I could really do if I tried – I'm going to work hard. I'll help you, if you'll help me. I don't know how to work hard, but you can show me – and I'll help you with my brains. See?"

Just then a loud whistle came from the station and then a train puffed out. Hugh looked at the shower of sparks coming from the funnel.

"Well, the train's gone," he said. "So I can't go with it. I'll have to come back with you. Let me sleep over it and see how I feel in the morning. I don't want to see any of you again tonight. I should feel awkward. If I make up my mind I can begin all over again, I'll nod at you when we get up – and just let's all act as if nothing had happened. I can't stand any more of this sort of thing. I simply *must* work if I'm going to enter for that scholarship."

The two boys went back together. Hugh went straight upstairs to his dormitory, telling Tom to say that he didn't want any supper. But before he went, Hugh held out his hand.

There was a warm handshake between the two of them and then Tom went soberly back to the common room, wondering what to say. The children crowded round him and Tom explained what had happened.

When they heard what Hugh had said about how he was expected to do as well as his brothers and sister, and how he knew he hadn't good enough brains, they were silent. They knew then why Hugh had swotted so much. They even understood why he had been tempted to cheat. Every child knew how horrid it was to disappoint parents or let their family down.

"Well, let's hope he'll make up his mind to stay," said Tom. "And listen – I feel quite a bit ashamed of *my* behaviour too. My parents pay for me to learn things here, and I never try at all – except in woodwork. I just fool about the whole time, and make you laugh. Well, from now on, I'm going to do a spot of work. And so are you, Mike and Janet. You've neither of you been top once this term, and you could easily be near it, and give Doris a shock!"

"All right," said Janet, who had been thinking quite a lot too, that night. "I'll work. Miss Thomas said today she would give me a bad report because I've not been doing my best. I don't want that. Mike will work too. We always do the same."

Hugh was asleep when the children went up to bed. For the first night for a long time he was at peace, and slept calmly without worrying. Things had been cleared up. He was happier.

In the morning the boys got up when the bell went. Tom heard Hugh whistling softly to himself as he dressed, and he was glad. Then a head was put round Tom's curtains, and Tom saw Hugh's face. It was all smiles, and looked quite different from usual.

Tom stared at the smiling head. It nodded violently up and down and disappeared. Tom felt glad. Hugh was doing the sensible thing – starting all over again, and giving the others a chance to do the same thing!

And what a change there was for Hugh that morning when the boys and girls met in their common room! He was one of them now, not an outcast – and everyone felt much happier because of it.

CHAPTER TEN

END OF TERM

Miss Thomas and the other teachers had a pleasant shock that week. For the first time since he had been at St Rollo's Tom began to work! The teachers simply couldn't understand it. Not only Tom worked, though – Mike and Janet did too.

"Something's happened that we don't know about," said Miss Thomas to Mr Wills. "And do you notice how much happier that boy Hugh looks? It seems as if the others have decided to be nicer to him. It's funny how Tom seems to have made friends with him all of a sudden. They even seem to be working together!"

So they were. They did their prep together, and learnt many things from each other. Tom's quick brains were useful at understanding many things that Hugh's slow brains did not take in – and Hugh's ability for really getting down to things, once he understood them, was a fine example for the rather lazy Tom.

"You make a good team," said Miss Thomas approvingly. "I am pleased with you both. Tom, I think it would be a good idea to move you away from that front desk, and put you beside Hugh. You can help one another quite a lot."

"Oooh, good," said Tom, his eyes gleaming. "It does rather cramp my style, Miss Thomas, to be under your eye all the time, you know."

The class laughed. They had been surprised at Tom's sudden change of mind regarding his work. But they were afraid that he might no longer fool about as he used to do. He always caused so much amusement – it would be sad if he no longer thought of his amazing tricks.

"Don't worry," said Tom, when Mike told him this. "I shall break out at times. I can't stop thinking of tricks even if I'm using my brains for my work too!"

He kept his word, and played one or two laughable tricks on poor Monsieur Crozier, nearly driving him mad. Tom provided him with a pen on his desk, which on being pressed for writing, sent out a stream of water from its end. The French master was so angry that he threw the blackboard chalk down on the floor and stamped on it.

This thrilled the class immensely, and was talked of for a long time. In fact, that term, on the whole, was a very exciting one indeed. Mike and Janet got quite a shock when they realized that holidays would begin in a week's time!

"Oh! Fancy the term being so nearly over!" said Janet dolefully.

"Gracious, Janet, don't you want to be home for Christmas?" said Marian.

"Yes, of course," said Janet. "But it's such fun being at St Rollo's. Think of the things that have happened this term!"

Miss Thomas overheard her. She smiled. "Shall I tell you what is the most surprising thing that has happened?" she said.

"What?" asked the children, crowding round. Miss Thomas held the list of marks for the last week in her hand. She held it up.

"Well, for the first time this term Tom Young isn't bottom!" she said. "I couldn't believe my eyes when I added up the marks – in fact I added them all up again to make sure. And it's true – he actually isn't bottom. Really, the world must be coming to an end!"

Everyone roared with laughter. Tom went red. He was pleased.

"I suppose I'm next to bottom, though," he said, with a twinkle.

"Not even that!" said Miss Thomas. "You are sixth from the top – simply amazing. And Hugh has gone up too – he is seventh. And as for Mike and Janet – well, wonders will never cease! They tie for second place, only two marks behind Doris!"

Mike, Janet, Tom and Hugh were delighted. It really

was nice to find that good work so soon showed results. Hugh took Tom's arm.

"I can't tell you how you've helped me," he said. "Not only in my work – in other ways too. I feel quite different."

The children thought that Hugh looked different too. He smiled and laughed and joked with the others, and went for walks as they did. Who would have thought that things could possibly have turned out like that, after all?

The term came quickly to an end. There were concerts and craft exhibitions – and, not quite so pleasant, exams as well! All the children became excited at the thought of Christmas, pantomimes, presents and parties, and the teachers had to make allowances for very high spirits.

The last day came. There was a terrific noise everywhere, as packing went on in each dormitory, and boys and girls rushed up and down the stairs, looking for pencil boxes, books, boots, shoes and other things. There were collisions everywhere, and squeals of laughter as things rolled down the stairs with a clatter.

"I suppose all this noise is necessary," sighed Mr Wills, stepping aside to avoid somebody's football, which was bouncing down the stairs all by itself, accompanied above by a gale of laughter.

"Goodness – how glad I shall be to say goodbye to all you hooligans! What a pity to think you are coming back next term!"

"Oh no, sir – we're glad!" shouted Mike, rushing down after the football. "We love the holidays – but it will be grand to come back to St Rollo's!"

Goodbyes were said all round. Some of the children were going home by train, some by car.

"Good!" said Janet. "We don't need to say goodbye till we get to London. Look – there's our coach at the door. Come on!"

They piled into the big coach, with about twenty other children. It set off to the station. The children looked back at the big grey building.

"Goodbye St Rollo's," said Mike. "See you next term. Goodbye! Goodbye!"

THE CHILDREN OF KIDILLIN

CONTENTS

CHAPTER ONE

THE MEETING OF THE FOUR COUSINS

Two children and a dog raced down to the village sweet shop in excitement. They opened the little door of Mrs MacPherson's shop and went inside.

"Good morning," said Mrs MacPherson, in her soft Scottish voice. "You look excited, the two of you."

"We are," said Sandy, a tall boy with a jolly, freckled face. "We've got our English cousins coming to live with us till the war's over! We've never even seen them!"

"They're about the same age as we are," said Jeanie, Sandy's sister. "One's called Tom, and the other's called Sheila. They live in London, but their parents want them to go somewhere safe till the war's over. They're coming to-morrow!"

"So we've come down to get some of your bull's-eye peppermints for them," said Sandy.

"And will they do lessons with Miss Mitchell, your governess?" asked Mrs MacPherson, getting down her big jar of peppermint humbugs. "It will be right nice company for you."

"It's to be hoped the town children don't find it dull down here," said Mrs MacPherson, handing over a fat bag of sweets. Sandy and Jeanie stared at her in surprise.

"*Dull*!" said Jeanie, quite crossly. "How could anyone find Kidillin dull? There's the river that rushes through Kidillin, and the hills around, and away yonder the sea!"

"Ay, but there's no cinema for twelve miles, and only three shops, not a train for ten miles, and no buses!" said Mrs MacPherson. "And what will town children do without those, I should like to know?"

The two children left the little shop. They gazed into the two other shops of Kidillin – which were general stores, and sold most things – and then made their way home again, each sucking a peppermint.

Sandy and Jeanie were really indignant at the thought that anyone could be bored with Kidillin. They loved their quiet Scottish life, they loved Kidillin House, their home, and enjoyed their lessons with Miss Mitchell, their old governess. They knew every inch of the hills about their home, they knew the flowers that grew there, the birds and the animals that lived there, and every cottager within miles.

Sandy and Jeanie were to drive to the nearest town to

meet their cousins the next day. So, with Miss Mitchell driving the horse, they set off. It was a long way, but the autumn day was bright and sunny, and the mountains that rose up around were beautiful. The children sang as they went, and the clip-clop of the horse's feet was a pleasant sound to hear.

The train came in as they arrived at the station. Sandy and Jeanie almost fell out of the trap as they heard its whistle. They rushed through the little gate and on to the platform.

And there stood a boy and girl, with a pile of luggage around them – and a dog on a lead!

"Hallo!" cried Sandy. "Are you Tom and Sheila?"

"Yes," said the boy. "I suppose you are Sandy and Jeanie? This is our dog, Paddy. We hope you don't mind us bringing him – but we couldn't, we really *couldn't* leave him behind!"

"Well, I hope he gets on all right with *our* dog," said Sandy doubtfully. "Mack is rather a jealous sort of dog. Come on. We've got the trap outside. The porter will bring out your luggage."

The four children, the dog and a porter went out to Miss Mitchell. She shook hands with Tom and Sheila, thought that Sheila was very pretty, but far too pale, and that Tom was too tall for his age. But they had nice manners, and she liked the look of them.

"Welcome to Scotland, my new pupils!" said Miss Mitchell. "Get in – dear me, is that your dog? I hope he won't fight Mack."

It looked very much as if Paddy would certainly fight Mack! The two dogs growled, bared their teeth and strained hard at their leads. Their hair rose on their necks and they looked most ferocious.

"What an unfriendly dog Mack is," said Tom. This was not at all the right thing to say. Sandy looked angry.

"You mean, what an unfriendly dog your Paddy is," he said. "Our Mack would have been pleased enough to see him if he hadn't growled like that."

"Mack can come up on the front seat with me," said Miss Mitchell hastily. She didn't want the cousins to quarrel within the first five minutes of their meeting.

"Then I shall drive," said Sandy at once. He wasn't going to sit behind in the trap and talk politely to a boy who was rude about Mack.

"Can you drive this trap yourself?" said Sheila in surprise.

"Of course," said Sandy. "I've driven it since I was four." He thought Sheila was rather a nice girl – but Jeanie didn't! Jeanie thought Sheila was too dressed-up for anything!

"How does she think she's going to walk on the hills in *those* shoes?" thought Jeanie scornfully, looking at Sheila's pretty shoes. "And what a fussy dress! All those frills and ribbons! But I like Tom. He's nice and tall."

They drove home. Miss Mitchell did most of the talking, and asked the two London children all about the home they had left. They answered politely, looking round at the countryside all the time.

"Doesn't it all look awfully big, Sheila," said Tom. "Look at those mountains! Oh – what a funny little village! What is it called?"

"It is Kidillin," said Jeanie. "We live not far away, at

Kidillin House. Look – you can see it above those trees there."

Sheila and Tom looked at the plain, rather ugly stone house set on the hillside. They did not like the look of it at all. When they had gone to stay with their uncle in the English countryside the year before, they had lived in a lovely old thatched cottage, cosy and friendly – but this old stone house looked so cold and stern.

"I hope the war will soon be over!" said Tom, who really meant that he hoped he wouldn't have to stay very long at Kidillin. Sandy and Jeanie knew quite well what he was really thinking, and they were hurt and angry.

"They are as unfriendly as their dog!" whispered Jeanie to Sandy, as they jumped down from the cart. "I'm not going to like them a bit."

"I wish we were at home!" whispered Sheila to Tom, as they went up the steps to the front door. "It's going to be horrid, being here!"

CHAPTER TWO

THE OLD COTTAGE ON THE HILLSIDE

For the first few days things were very difficult for all four children, and for the two dogs as well. They were even more difficult for poor Miss Mitchell! Sandy and Jeanie never quarrelled – but now she had four children who bickered and squabbled all day long!

As for the dogs, they had to be kept well apart, for they each seemed to wish to tear the other to pieces! They had to take it in turns to be tied up so that they could not fly at one another all day long.

"And really, I'm wishing I could tie up the children too," Miss Mitchell said to Sandy's mother. "For they're like the dogs – just ready to fly at one another's throats all day long!"

Mrs MacLaren laughed. "Give them time to settle down to each other," she said. "And you'd better begin lessons again tomorrow, Miss Mitchell – that will keep them out of mischief a bit."

Sandy and Jeanie had been showing off to Tom and Sheila. They had taken them for a long walk, up a difficult mountain, where a good deal of rough climbing had to be done. The English children had panted and puffed, and poor Sheila's shoes were no use at all for such walking.

"Can't we have a rest again?" asked Sheila at last. "I'm so tired. This is a dreadful place for walking. I'd much rather walk in the park!"

"In the *park*!" said Sandy scornfully. "What, when there's fine country like this, and soft heather to your feet! And look at the view there – you can see the sea!"

The four children sat down. Far away they could see the blue glimmer of the sea, and could hear very faintly the shrill cry of the circling gulls. Tom was so tired that he only gave the view a moment's look, and then lay down on his back. "Phew, I'm tired!" he said. "I vote we go back."

"But we're not yet at the burn we want to show you," said Jeanie. Sheila giggled.

"It does sound so funny for a stream to be called a *burn*!" she said. "It sounds as if something was on fire – going to see the *burn*!"

"The bur-r-r-rn, not the *burn*," said Sandy, sounding the R in burn. "Can't you talk properly?"

"We can talk just as well as *you*!" said Tom, vexed, and then off they went, squabbling again!

Mack, who was with the children, barked when he heard them quarrelling. He wanted someone to quarrel with too! But Paddy was at home, tied up, much to Tom's annoyance.

"Be quiet," said Tom to Mack. "I can't hear myself speak when you begin that noise. Where are you going, Sandy? I want to rest a bit more."

"There'll be no time to finish the walk if you lie there any longer," said Sandy. "This is the fourth time we've stopped for you – a lazy lot of folk you Londoners must be!"

"All right. Then we'll *be* lazy!" said Tom angrily. "You and Jeanie go on, and Sheila and I will stay here till you come back – and you can go and find your wonderful bur-r-r-r-rn yourself!"

"Oh do come, Tom," begged Jeanie. "It really is a strange sight to see. The water comes pouring out of a hole in the hillside – just as if somebody had turned a tap on!"

"Well, don't you go rushing up the mountain so quickly then," said Tom, getting up. "I'm sure you're just showing off! I bet you and Jeanie don't go so fast when you're alone! You're just trying to make us feel silly."

Jeanie went red. It was quite true – she and Sandy had planned together to take the two Londoners for a stiff walk up the mountains, going at a fast pace, just to show them what Scots children could do. And now Tom had guessed what she and Sandy had planned.

"Oh come on," said Sandy impatiently. They all went

up the steep, heathery slope, rounded a big crag, and then slipped and slid on a stony stretch that scratched Sheila's shoes to bits!

Suddenly there was a rumble of thunder round the mountain. Tom looked up anxiously. "I say! Is there going to be a storm?" he said. "Sheila always gets a cold if she gets soaked. Is there anywhere to shelter?"

"There's an old tumbledown hut not far from here," said Sandy. "Come on – run!"

The rain began to fall. The four children and the dog ran full pelt over the heather – up another slope, round a group of windblown pine trees – and there, in front of them, tucked into the mountainside, was an old, tumble-down cottage!

The children rushed to the door, flung it open and ran inside. They shook themselves like dogs, and the rain flew off their clothes, just as it was flying off Mack's coat. Then Sandy gave a cry of surprise.

"I say! Somebody lives here! Look!"

The children looked around the little stone house. It was roughly furnished with chairs, a table and two camp beds. An oil stove stood in a corner, and something was cooking on it.

"Funny!" said Jeanie, staring round. "Nobody's here at all – and yet there's something cooking on the stove."

"Perhaps there's someone in the tiny room at the back," said Sandy, and he pushed open the door and looked inside. The boy stopped in the greatest surprise. Nobody was there – nobody at all – but the whole room seemed full of a strange-looking machine, that had knobs and handles, valves and levers on it. Sandy was just going to tell Tom to come and see, when he heard footsteps.

He shut the door of the little room quickly, just as the door of the house swung open, and a fat man came in. He was so astonished when he saw the children that he couldn't say a word. He stood and gaped at them in amazement. Then he turned a purple-red and caught Tom by the shoulder.

He made strange noises, and pushed the boy out of the door so roughly that he almost fell. He was just about to do the same to Jeanie when Sandy stepped up and stopped him. The boy stood there in his kilt, glowering at the angry man.

"Don't you dare touch my sister!" he said. "What's up with you? There was a storm coming on, and we came in here out of the rain. We didn't know anyone lived here – it's always been empty before. We'll go if you don't want to give us shelter!"

There was the sound of footsteps again and another man came into the house, looking dismayed and astonished. He began to roar at the children.

"What are you doing here? Clear out! If you come here again I'll set my dog on you!"

The children stumbled out of the old hut in a fright. The second man caught hold of Tom and shook him. "Did you go into the room at the back?" he demanded. "Did you? Go on, answer me! If you've come to steal anything, you'll be sorry."

"Of course we haven't come to steal anything!" said Tom indignantly. "No, I didn't go into any room at all except the one you found us in – I didn't even know there *was* another room! So keep your silly secrets to yourself!"

The man made as if he would rush at him, but Mack somehow got in between, and tripped the man over. He sat up nursing his ankle, looking as black as thunder.

"Loose the dog, Carl!" he yelled. "Loose the dog."

"Come on," said Sandy at once. "It's a big brute of a dog. I can see it over there. It would eat Mack up!"

The four children flew down the path in the rain. No dog came after them. The rain poured down, and Tom looked anxiously at Sheila again. "We really shall have to shelter somewhere," he said. "Sheila is getting soaked and I promised Mother I'd look after her."

"There's an overhanging rock by the burn we wanted to show you," said Sandy, stopping. "But it's rather near that old hut. Still, the men won't see us there, and they'll think we've gone home frightened, anyway. Come on!"

Sandy led the way. In a few minutes they came within sound of rushing water, and then Tom saw a great craggy rock. They went towards it, and were soon crouching under it out of the rain.

"This is the burn, or stream we wanted to show you," said Sandy. "Look – it gushes out of the hole in this rock – isn't it odd? It comes from the heart of the mountain – we always think it's very strange."

It *was* strange. There was a large, uneven hole in one side of the great rock, and from it poured a clear stream of water that fell down the mountainside in a little gully it had made for itself. On and on it went down the mountain until, near the bottom, it joined the rushing River Spelter.

"Jeanie and I have climbed down beside this water all the way from this stone to the river," said Sandy proudly. "It's very difficult to do that. We had to take a rope with us to get down at some places, because the burn becomes a waterfall at times!"

Tom was very interested in the torrent that poured out of the hole in the rock. He went close up to it and peered into the hole, whose mouth was almost hidden by the spate of water.

"Does this water get less when there are no rains?" he asked. Sandy nodded. "Yes," he said, "it's very full now, for we've had heavy rains the last week or two. Wouldn't it be exciting to crawl through that hole, when the water was less, and see where it led to!"

"Where does the River Spelter rise?" asked Tom. "In this same mountain?"

"Nobody knows," said Sandy. Tom looked astonished.

"But hasn't anyone followed it up to see?" he asked.

"No," said Sandy with a laugh. "It's like this burn here – it suddenly flows out of the mountain, and no one has ever dared to seek its source, for it would mean swimming against a strong current, in pitch black darkness, underwater! And who would care to do that!"

"How funny," said Tom thoughtfully. "This is a more exciting place than I thought – springs that gush out of rocks, and rivers that come from underground homes – and strange men that live in secret tumbledown huts!"

"Let's start home again now," said Sandy, suddenly remembering the two men and their dog. "It's stopped raining. Tom, remind me to tell you something when we get back."

Down the mountain they went – and poor Sheila

quickly decided that it was far worse to go down steep slopes than to go *up* them! She was tired out when at last they reached Kidillin House.

"Oh Sandy, you shouldn't have taken Tom and Sheila so far," said Miss Mitchell, when she saw Sheila's white, tired face. "And look – the child's soaked through!"

Sandy and Jeanie were ashamed of themselves when they saw that Sheila really was too tired even to eat. They went to tie up Mack, and to let Paddy loose.

"Anyway, we've shown Tom and Sheila what sillies they are when it comes to walking and climbing!" said Sandy. "Oh – where's Tom? I wanted to tell him something!"

He found Tom groaning as he took off his boots. "My poor feet!" he said. "You're a wretch, Sandy – you wait till I find something I can do better than you!"

"Tom," said Sandy. "Listen. I peeped inside the back room of that old tumbledown hut – and do you know, there was a whole lot of machinery there. I don't know what it was – I've never seen anything like it before. Whatever do you think those men keep it there for? Seems funny, doesn't it, in a place like this?"

Tom sat up with a jerk. "Some sort of *machinery*!" he said in amazement. "What, in that old hut on that desolate mountainside, where there are only a few sheep? How would they get machinery there? There's no road."

"There's a rough road the other side of the mountain," said Sandy. "Easy enough to go over the top, and get down to the path that way – and there's a good motor road a bit farther down the other side, too."

Tom whistled. His eyes grew bright. "I wonder if

we've hit on something peculiar!" he said. "We'll tell your father, and see what he says. Perhaps those two men are spies!"

"Don't be silly," said Sandy. "What would spies do here, among the mountains? There's nothing to spy on! Anyway, my father is away now."

"All right, Mr Know-all," said Tom. "But we might as well tell your father when he comes back, all the same!"

CHAPTER THREE

A CHAPTER OF QUARRELS

The next day the children began lessons with Miss Mitchell. Tom was most disgusted.

"Have I got to learn from a woman?" he said. "I've been used to going to a boys' school. I don't want to learn from a woman."

"Well, Sandy does," said Mrs MacLaren with a laugh. "And he's a pretty hefty boy, isn't he? There is no school here, you see, and until the war is over Sandy must stay at home."

So Tom and Sheila joined Sandy and Jeanie in the schoolroom with Miss Mitchell – and they soon found a way of paying back the two Scottish children for the long walk of the day before! Tom was far ahead of Sandy in arithmetic, and Sheila's writing was beautiful – quite different from Jeanie's scrawl.

"Good gracious! Is that as far as you've got in arithmetic!" said Tom, looking at Sandy's book. "I did those sums *years* ago! You *are* a baby!"

Sandy scowled down at his book. He knew he was not good at arithmetic. Miss Mitchell had struggled with him for years.

"Go to your place, Tom," said Miss Mitchell briskly. "Everybody isn't the same. Some are good at one thing and some are good at another. We'll see if your geography is as good as your arithmetic! Perhaps it isn't!"

But it was! Tom was a clever boy, and Sheila was a sharp little girl, who read easily and beautifully, and who wrote as well as Miss Mitchell herself.

"I can see that Sheila and I are going to be the top of the class!" said Tom slyly to Sandy, as they went out at eleven o'clock for a break in their lessons. "You may be able to beat us at climbing mountains, Sandy – but we'll beat you at lessons! Why, Jeanie writes like a baby!"

"I *don't*!" said Jeanie, almost in tears.

"Yes, you do," said Sheila. "Why, at home even the *first* class could write better than you can! And you don't even know your twelve times table yet!"

This was quite true. Jeanie did not like lessons, and she had never troubled to try really hard to learn all her tables. Poor Miss Mitchell had been in despair over her many times.

But Jeanie was not going to have her English cousins laughing at her. She made up her mind to learn all her tables perfectly as soon as she could. This was hard for her, because Jeanie would not usually spend any of her playtime doing anything but climbing the hills, swimming in the river, and driving round the lanes in the pony-trap.

Secretly Miss Mitchell was pleased that Tom and Sheila were ahead of Jeanie and Sandy. Now perhaps her two pupils would feel ashamed, and would work much harder.

"And it won't do Tom and Sheila any harm to find that they can't do the walking and climbing that our two can," thought Miss Mitchell. "After a few quarrels they will all settle down and be happy together."

The two dogs eyed one another and tried to boast to one another in their own way. Paddy could do plenty of tricks, and whenever he wanted a biscuit he sat up on his hind legs in a comical way. Then Tom would put a biscuit on his nose, and say, "Trust, Paddy, trust!"

Paddy would not eat the biscuit until Tom said "Paid for!" Then he would toss the biscuit into the air, catch it, and gobble it up.

Mack watched this trick scornfully. *He* wasn't going to do any tricks for *his* food! Not he! If he wanted anything extra he'd go out and catch a rabbit. He was very proud of the fact that he could run as fast as a rabbit, and had three times brought a rabbit home to Sandy. Could Paddy do that? Mack barked to Paddy and asked him.

Paddy didn't answer. He lay curled up by Tom's feet, his eyes on Mack, ready to fly at him if he came any nearer. Mack whined scornfully, and then got up. He meant to show Paddy what he could do.

"Woof?" he said. Paddy got up too. He knew that Mack wanted him to go out with him, and though he was still on his guard, he thought it would be fun to go into the hills with this dog, who knew the way about.

"Look at that!" said Sandy in surprise. "That's the first time that Paddy has gone with Mack without flying at him."

The two dogs trotted out of doors, Paddy a good way behind. He could see the tiniest wag in Mack's tail and so he trusted him – but if that wag stopped, then Paddy was ready to pounce on him!

Out of the corner of his eye Mack saw Paddy's tail too. He could see the tiniest wag there also. Good. As long as that little wag was there, Mack knew that Paddy would not fling himself on him.

So, each watching the other carefully, the dogs went out on the hills. And then Mack began to show off to Paddy. He spied a rabbit under a bush and gave chase. The rabbit tore down a burrow. Mack started up another one and that went down a burrow too. Then Paddy started up a young rabbit, but it was away and up the hill before he had even seen which way it went!

"Woof! Watch me!" barked Mack, and he tore after a big rabbit so fast that he snapped at its white bobtail before it could get down a burrow. Mack walked back to Paddy, with the bit of white fluff still in his mouth.

Paddy turned his head away, pretending not to look, and then began to scratch himself. *He* wasn't going to tell this boastful dog that he thought it was jolly clever to catch a rabbit's tail – though secretly he couldn't help admiring Mack very much for his speed and strength.

After he had scratched himself well, he got up and trotted back to the house.

"I'm tired of this silly game," his tail seemed to say to Mack. Mack followed him in, disappointed. Paddy waited till both dogs were in the room, and then he stood on his hind legs and shut the door! This was another of his tricks, and people always thought it was very clever.

"Goodness! Did you see Paddy shut the door?" said Jeanie, quite astonished. "Mack! *You* can't do that, old boy! You'd better learn!"

Mack was angry. He growled. What! Here he had just been smart enough to catch a rabbit's tail – and now this silly dog had shut the door and been praised for a stupid thing like *that* – and Sheila was giving him a biscuit for his cleverness! Well, why didn't Sandy give *him* a biscuit for his smartness with rabbits?

And so both the dogs and the children were angry with the others' boasting, and would not be friends. Out of doors the Scottish cousins were far and away better than the English pair, and could run faster, jump higher and climb farther – but indoors Tom and Sheila shone. Their lessons were done more quickly and better than their cousins', and they could learn anything by heart in a few minutes.

"It takes me half an hour to learn this bit of poetry," grumbled Sandy. He was bent over "Horatius keeps the Bridge." He liked the story in it, but it was so difficult to learn.

"How slow you are!" laughed Tom. "It took me just five minutes. I can say it straight off now – listen!"

"Oh be quiet, you boaster!" growled Sandy, putting

his hands over his ears. "I wish you'd never come! You make Miss Mitchell think that Jeanie and I are as stupid as sheep, and she's always scolding us."

There was silence. Tom and Sheila said nothing at all. Sandy began to feel uncomfortable. He looked up. Tom had gone very red, and Sheila looked as if she was going to cry.

Tom got up and spoke stiffly. "I'm sorry you wish we'd never come. We didn't think we were as bad as all that. But seeing that you have said what you really thought, I'll also say what *I* think. I wish we had never come too. Sheila and I have done our best to keep up with you in your walking and climbing because we didn't want you to think we were weak and feeble. But we are not used to mountains and it would have been kinder of you if you'd let us go a bit slower at first. However, I suppose that's too much to expect."

"And *I'd* like to say something too!" burst out Sheila. "You're always boasting about your wonderful mountains and the brown bur-r-rns, and the purple heather-r-r-r – but we would rather have the things we know. We'd like to see the big London buses we love, and our tall policemen, and to see the trains. We'd like to see more people about, and to go in the parks and play with our own friends at the games we know. It's p-p-p-perfectly horrid b-b-being here – and I w-w-w-want my m-m-m-mother!"

She burst into tears. Jeanie was horrified. Had they really been as unkind as all that? She ran over to Sheila and tried to put her arms round her cousin. But Sheila pushed her away fiercely. Tom went over and hugged his sister.

"Cheer up," he said. "When the war's over we'll go back home. Sandy and Jeanie will be glad to be rid of us then – but we'll make the best of it till we go."

Sandy wanted to say a lot of things but he couldn't say a word. He was ashamed of himself. After all, his cousins were his guests. How *could* he have said to them that he wished they had never come? What would his mother and father say if they knew? Scottish people were famous for the welcome they gave to friends.

Tom thought that Sandy was sulking, and he looked at him in disgust. "I'm sorry Sheila and I are a bit more forward in our lessons than you," he said. "But we can't help that any more than you can help knowing your old mountains better than we do. Sheila, do stop crying. Here comes Aunt Jessie."

Jeanie looked up in alarm. If Mother came in and wanted to know why Sheila was crying and found out – my goodness, there would be trouble! She and Sandy would be sent to bed at once, and have nothing but bread and water!

Sheila stopped crying at once. She bent her head over her book. Tom went to his place and began to mutter his poetry to himself – so when Mother came into the room she saw four children all working hard, and did not know that two of them were ashamed and frightened, that one was angry and hurt and the fourth one was very miserable and homesick.

She looked round. "What, still doing lessons!" she said.

"It's some poetry Miss Mitchell gave us to learn before she went out," explained Tom. "We've nearly finished."

"Well, finish it this evening," said Mother. "It's half past two now, and a lovely day. Would you all like to take your tea out somewhere on the hills, and have a picnic? You won't be able to do it much longer, when the mists come down."

"Oh yes, Mother, do let's have a picnic!" cried Jeanie, flinging down her book. She always loved a picnic. "We'll go and find some blackberries."

"Very well," said Mother. "Go and get ready and I'll pack up your tea."

She went out. Jeanie spoke to Sheila. "It was nice of you not to let Mother see you were crying," she said. Sheila said nothing. She looked miserably at Jeanie. She did not want to climb mountains for a picnic. But there was no help for it. It was such a hilly country that sooner or later you had to climb, no matter in what direction you went!

The girls went to their room. Jeanie pulled out some comfortable old shoes and took them to Sheila. "Look," she said. "Wear these, Sheila. They are old and strong, much better for climbing than the shoes you wear. Mother is getting some strong shoes for you next time she goes into the town."

They fitted Sheila well. Jeanie gave her an old tammy instead of a straw hat. Then they went downstairs to find the boys.

Sandy still hadn't said a word to Tom. He just couldn't. He always found it very difficult to say he was sorry about anything. But he found a good stick and handed it to Tom, knowing that it would make climbing a good deal easier.

Tom took it – but he put it in a corner of the room when Sandy was not looking! He would dearly have loved to take it, but he wasn't going to have Sandy thinking he needed a stick, like an old man! Jeanie saw him put the stick away and she went to Sandy.

"Sandy!" she whispered. "Tom would like the stick, I know, and so would Sheila – but they won't have them if they think we don't take them too. So let's take one each, and then the others won't mind."

This was rather clever of Jeanie! For as soon as Tom saw that Jeanie and Sandy had also found sticks for themselves he at once went to take his from the corner where he had put it! After all, if his cousins used a stick, there was no reason why he shouldn't as well!

They set off. They allowed both dogs to come, for although they were still not good friends the two dogs put up with one another better now. Tom and Sandy carried a bag each on their backs, full of the picnic things.

"I say! Let's go up to that funny old hut again, and see if those two men are still there!" said Tom, who always liked an adventure. "I'd like to peep into that back room if I could, and find that machine that Sandy saw."

"But isn't that too far?" said Jeanie, anxious to show that she could consider others. Tom shook his head stoutly. He was beginning to get used to the hills now.

"I can help Sheila over the bad bits," he said, "and now that she's got strong shoes on, and a good stick, she'll be all right, won't you, Sheila?"

"Yes," said Sheila bravely – though her heart sank at the thought of the long climb again.

"All right then," said Sandy. "We'll go up to the hut and see what we can find!"

CHAPTER FOUR

A WALK AND A SURPRISE

They set off. Sheila did not find the climb so hard as she thought. She was getting used to walking in the hilly country now, and besides, Jeanie's shoes were well-made for climbing and were very comfortable. So Sheila walked well, and began to enjoy herself.

"We'll have our tea when we get to that clump of birch trees," said Jeanie, when they had climbed for some time. "There's a marvellous view from there. We can see the steamers going by, it's such a clear day!"

So, when they reached the birches, they all sat down and undid the picnic bags. There were tomato sandwiches, hard-boiled eggs, with a screw of salt to dip them into, brown bread and butter, buttered scones and some fine currant cake. The children ate hungrily, and looked far away to where the sea shone blue in the autumn sunshine.

"There goes a steamer!" said Jeanie, pointing to where a grey steamer slid over the water. "And there's another."

"Over there is where the *Yelland* went down," said Sandy, pointing to the east. "And not far from it the *Harding* was torpedoed too. I hope those steamers that we are watching now will be all right."

"Of course they will," said Tom lazily. "I bet there's no submarine round about here!"

Jeanie cleared up the litter and packed the bits of paper back into the bags. Her mother was always very strict about litter, and it had to be brought back and burnt, never left lying about.

"Well, what about creeping up to see if we can spot what's in that back room?" said Tom, getting up. "I'm well rested now. What about you, Sheila?"

"Sheila can stay here with me," said Jeanie, quickly. "I don't want to go any farther today. We'll wait here till you come back."

Sheila looked at Jeanie gratefully. She was tired, and did not really want to go any farther – but she would not have said so for anything!

Sandy looked at Jeanie in amazement, and was just going to tease her for being lazy, when his sister winked quickly at him. That wink said as plainly as anything "Sheila's tired but won't say so – so I'll pretend I am, and then she won't mind staying here."

"All right, Jeanie," said Sandy. "Tom and I will go – and we'll take the two dogs."

So off went the two boys, each with his stick, though Sandy kept forgetting to use his, and tucked it under his arm. Tom was glad to have the help of his, though, and it made a great difference to the climb.

When they had almost come in sight of the old cottage, Tom stopped. "I think one of us had better stay here a few minutes with the dogs," he said. "The other can creep through the heather and find out whether the men are about – and that dog they spoke of. *I* don't want to be a dog's dinner!"

"All right," said Sandy. "Take the dogs, Tom. I'll go. I know the way better than you do."

So Tom held the two dogs, and Sandy wriggled through the heather silently until he came in sight of the old cottage. No one seemed to be about. The door was shut. No dog barked.

Sandy wriggled closer. Not a sound was to be heard. No smoke came from the chimney. Sandy suddenly got up and ran to the old cottage. He peered in at the front window. The place was empty, though the furniture was still there.

It only took the boy a minute or two to make sure that no one, man or dog, was about. He ran to the edge of the heather and whistled to Tom. Up he came with the two dogs.

"There's no one here," said Sandy. "We'll go in and I'll show you that funny machinery with all its knobs and handles and things."

The tried the door. It was locked! Sandy put his hefty

shoulder to it and pushed – but the lock was good and strong and would not give an inch.

"They've put a new lock on it," said the boy in disappointment. "It never used to have a lock at all. Well, let's go and look in through the back window."

They went round to the back of the cottage. But there they had a surprise!

"They've boarded up the window inside!" said Sandy in amazement. "We can't see a thing! Not a thing! Oh blow! I did want to show you what was in that little room, Tom."

"It's funny," said Tom thoughtfully, rubbing his chin and frowning. "Why should they do that? It means that the machinery, whatever it is, is still in there, and they've boarded it up in case we come back and spy around. I do wish we could get into the house."

But it was no good wishing. The door was locked and bolted, the one front window was fastened tightly, and the back one was boarded up so well that not even a chink was left for peeping.

"Well, we can't see anything, that's certain," said Tom. "Let's go and have a look at that stream coming out of the hillside through that rock, Sandy. I'd like to see that again."

The boys went there. The water still poured out of the curious hole – but there was not so much of it as before.

"That's because we haven't had so much rain this week," explained Sandy. Tom nodded. He went to the hole and peered into it. "If the water goes down much more we could easily get in there," he said. "I'd love to see where that water comes from. I read a book written

He peered in through the front window

by a Frenchman, Sandy, who explored heaps of underground streams and caves in France, and crawled through holes like that."

"What did he find?" asked Sandy, interested.

"He found wonderful caves and underground halls and pits, and he found where some mysterious rivers had their beginnings," said Tom. "I'll show you the book when we get home. You know, if only we could get past that spring pouring out from the rock, we might find extraordinary caverns where no foot had ever trodden before!"

Tom was getting excited. His eyes shone, and he made Sandy feel thrilled too. "Might there be a cave or something in this mountain then?" he asked.

"There might be heaps," said Tom. "And maybe somewhere in this great mountain is the beginning of the River Spelter. You told me that it comes out from underground and that no one knows where it rises."

Sandy's eyes shone now. This was the most exciting thing he had ever heard of. "Tom, we *must* explore this," he said. "We must! If only these men weren't here – they will send us away if they see us. I wish I knew what they were up to."

"So do I," said Tom. "When your father comes back, we'll tell him about them, Sandy, and about the peculiar machinery they've hidden in that back room."

A rabbit suddenly appeared on the hillside and looked cheekily at the two dogs, who were sitting quietly by the boys. At once both Paddy and Mack barked loudly and tore at the rabbit.

It did a strange thing. It shot up the hillside, leapt over the boys, and then disappeared into a burrow just beside the spring that gushed from the rock. And then Paddy did an even stranger thing!

He shot after the rabbit – but was stopped by the water. He leapt right over the water, saw the hole in the rock through which the spring flowed – and shot into the hole! He thought the rabbit had gone there!

He didn't come out. He disappeared completely. The two boys gaped at one another, and then Tom called his dog sharply.

"Paddy! Paddy! Come here!"

No Paddy came. Only a frightened whining could be heard from inside the hole. Paddy must have got right through the water and be sitting somewhere beyond.

"Paddy! Come out!" cried Tom anxiously. "You got in – so you can get out! Come on now!"

But Paddy was terrified. The noise of the water inside the rock was tremendous, and the dog was terribly afraid. He had managed to scramble to a rocky shelf above the flow of the spring, and was sitting there, trembling. He could hardly hear the shouts of his master, because of the noise the water made.

"*Now* what are we to do?" said Tom, in dismay. "He's right inside that rock. Paddy! PADDY, you idiot!"

But Paddy did not appear. Sandy looked worried. They must get the dog somehow.

Tom looked at Sandy. "Well, I suppose he will come out sometime," he said. "Had we better wait any longer? The girls will be getting worried."

"We can't leave your dog," said Sandy. He knew that Tom loved Paddy as much as he loved Mack. Mack was looking astonished. He could not imagine where Paddy had gone!

Sandy climbed up to the rock, and looked into the hole. The rushing water wetted him, and spray flew into his face.

"I believe I could wriggle through the water today," he said. "It's not very deep and not very strong. I could find old Paddy and push him out for you."

"Oh no, Sandy," said Tom. "You'd get soaked, and you might hurt yourself. You don't know what's behind that spring!"

Sandy was stripping off his clothes. He grinned at Tom. "I don't mind if I *do* get soaked now," he said. "I'll just hang myself out to dry, if I do!"

CHAPTER FIVE

A RESCUE AND A STRANGE DISCOVERY

Sandy climbed right up to the hole again, and then began to push himself into it. It was more than big enough for his body. As he wriggled, the cold water soaked him, and sometimes his face was under the surface, so that he had to hold his breath. His body blocked up the light that came in from the hole, and everything looked black as night. It was very weird and strange.

He felt about as he went through the hole. It widened almost at once, behind the opening, and became higher and more spacious. The water became shallower too.

Sandy sat up in the water, and felt about with his hand. He felt the rocky ceiling a little above him, and on one side was a rocky shelf. His hand touched wet hair!

"Paddy!" he cried. "You poor thing! Go on out of the hole, you silly!"

His voice was almost drowned in the sound of the rushing water around him, but Paddy heard it and was comforted. He jumped down into the water beside Sandy. Sandy pushed him towards the hole.

Paddy was taken by the swirl of the water and lost his balance. The water took him like a floating log and he was rushed to the opening, struggling with all his feet. He shot out with the spring, and fell at Tom's feet.

Tom was delighted. He picked up the wet dog and hugged him, and then Paddy struggled down to shake the water from his hair. Mack came up and sniffed him in astonishment.

"Been swimming?" he seemed to say. "What an extraordinary idea!"

Sandy was still in the rocky hole. He was getting used to the darkness now. He sat up on the shelf where he had found Paddy, and felt about with his hands. Then he made his way a little farther up the stream. The rocky ceiling got quickly higher – and then Sandy found himself in a great cave, at the bottom of which the stream rushed along with a noise that echoed all around. It was so dark that Sandy could hardly see the shape of the cave. He only sensed that it rose high and was wide and spacious. He was filled with astonishment and excitement, and went back to tell Tom.

But meanwhile something was happening outside! Tom had heard voices, and, peeping round the bend, he had seen in the distance the two men returning to their cottage! With them was a large dog.

Tom called in through the hole. "Sandy! Sandy! Quick! Come back!"

Sandy was already coming back. He sat down in the water when the ceiling fell low, and then, as it became lower still, the boy had to lie full length in the water, and wriggle along like that, the stream sometimes going right over his face. He got to the opening at last, and Tom helped him down.

"Sandy! Hurry! The men are back!" whispered Tom. "They've got a dog too, and he may hear us at any moment. Put on your things quickly."

Sandy tried to be quick. But his body was cold from the icy water, and he could not make his hands pull on his things quickly over his wet body. He shook and shivered with the cold, and Tom did his best to help him to dress.

He was just getting on his coat when the men's dog came sniffing round the corner! When he saw the boys and the dogs he stood still, and the fur on his neck rose high with rage! He barked loudly.

"Quick!" said Tom to Sandy. "We must go. Let's go down this way and maybe the men won't see us!"

So the two boys hurried round a bend, where bracken grew tall, and began to make their way through it. The dog still barked loudly, and the two men came running to him.

"What is it? Who is it?" cried one of them. "Go on, find him, find him!"

The fat man shouted something too, but the boys could not understand what he said. They were creeping down the hillside, glad that the men had not yet seen them. But the dog heard them, and came bounding after them.

"Now we're done for!" groaned Tom, as he saw the big dog leaping down towards them. He grasped his stick firmly. But someone else stood before him! It was Paddy, his wet fur bristling, and his throat almost bursting with fierce growls. Mack joined him, his teeth bared. Side by side the two dogs glared at the enemy, who, when he saw two of them, stopped still and considered. He was bigger than either – but they were two!

The men were following their dog. "Come on, Tom," whispered Sandy. "Let the dogs settle it for us. We must get back to the girls quickly."

They wriggled through the bracken and heather, slid down a stony slope unseen, and then made their way to where the girls were waiting anxiously. The boys had been a very long time.

"Sh!" said Sandy, as Jeanie opened her mouth to shout a welcome. And just as he said that a tremendous noise broke out – a noise of barking and howling and whining and yelping and growling and snarling!

"Good gracious!" said Jeanie, starting up. "Are the dogs fighting?"

"Yes – fighting a big dog together!" said Sandy. "Come on, we must go whilst the dogs are keeping off the men. They haven't seen us yet and we don't want them to."

"But will the dogs be all right?" panted Sheila as they ran down the hillside.

"Of course!" said Sandy. "Our Mack is more than a

match for two other dogs, and I reckon your Paddy is too!"

The children stopped when they reached a big gorse bush, and sat down behind it, panting. They were safe there, for an old shepherd's shelter was nearby, and Loorie, the shepherd, was pottering about in the distance. In a few hurried words the boys told the girls all that had happened.

Tom stared when Sandy told of the cave behind the rock where the spring gushed out. "I was right then!" he cried. "I say, what fun! We must go and explore that when we get a chance. If only those men weren't there."

"Perhaps they won't be there long, once my father hears about them," said Sandy grimly. "I think they are spies of some sort. I guess the police would like to see what is in their back room too!"

"I wish those dogs would come back," said Sheila, looking worried, for she hated to think that Paddy might be bitten by the big dog.

No sooner had she spoken than the two dogs appeared, looking extremely pleased with themselves! Paddy's right ear was bleeding, and Mack's left ear looked the worse for wear – but otherwise they seemed quite all right.

They trotted up to the children together, and sat down, looking proud and pleased. Mack licked Paddy's ear. Paddy sniffed in a friendly way at Mack and then, putting out a paw, pawed him as if he wanted a game.

"Why, they're good friends now!" cried Jeanie in surprise. "They like each other!"

Tom and Sandy looked at one another. Jeanie looked at Sheila.

"It's time *we* were friends too," said Tom, with a red

face. "Thanks, Sandy, for rescuing Paddy from that hole. It was jolly good of you – getting into that icy cold water and wriggling up a narrow rocky hole. You're a good friend."

"So are you," said Sandy. "I'm sorry for what I said. I didn't mean it. I was only mad because you were better at arithmetic than I was. I'm glad you came, really."

"Shake!" said Tom, with a laugh, and he held out his hand to Sandy. "We're friends now, and we'll stick by each other, won't we – just like the two dogs!"

The girls stared at the boys, glad to see that they were friends now. Jeanie held out her hand to Sheila. She would have liked to hug her, but she thought it looked grander to shake hands like the boys. Sheila solemnly shook her hand, and then they all began to laugh.

CHAPTER SIX

A DISAPPOINTMENT – AND A PICNIC

Things began to happen quickly after that exciting day. For one thing Captain MacLaren, Sandy's father, returned home on forty-eight hours' leave, and the children and Mrs MacLaren told him about the mysterious men in the old cottage on the mountain.

Captain MacLaren was astonished and puzzled. He was inclined to think that Sandy was making too much of the curious "machinery" he had seen in the back room. However, when he heard that one man had called the other "Carl," he decided that he had better tell the police.

"Carl is a German name," he said. "I can't imagine why German spies could possibly want to hide themselves away on such a lonely hillside, but you never know! They may be up to something odd. I'll ring up the police."

He did so – and two solemn Scots policemen came riding out to Kidillin House on their bicycles, with large notebooks and stumpy pencils to take down all the children said.

"We'll go up to the cottage and investigate, Captain," said the sergeant, shutting his notebook with a snap. "It's a wee bit unlikely we'll be finding anything to make a noise about, but we'll go."

They knew where the cottage was, and they set off to find it that afternoon. The children were very much excited. Miss Mitchell could hardly get them to do any sums, French or history at all. Even her star pupil, Tom, made all kinds of silly mistakes, and when he said that there were 240 shillings in a pound, instead of 240 pence, the governess put down her pencil in despair.

"This won't do," she said. "You are not thinking of what you are doing. What *are* you thinking of?"

But the four children wouldn't tell her! They were thinking of the exciting cave that Sandy had discovered behind the stream! They hadn't said a word about this to the grown-ups, because they were afraid that if they did they might be forbidden to explore it – and how could they bear to promise such a thing?

"We'll tell Mother as soon as we know exactly what's behind that hole," said Sandy. "We'll take our torches, and we'll explore properly. We might find strange cave pictures done by men hundreds of years ago! We might find old stone arrowheads and all kinds of exciting things!"

Sandy had been reading Tom's book. This book told of the true adventures of a Frenchman in underground caves and rivers, and of all the wonderful pictures he had found drawn on the walls and ceilings of the hidden caves. Sandy was simply longing to do some exploring himself now.

Miss Mitchell decided that it was no use doing any more lessons until the policemen came back from the old cottage. She was feeling a bit excited herself, and guessed what the children's feelings must be like. So she told them to shut their books, and go to do some gardening. Sandy and Jeanie each had their own gardens, and Tom and Sheila had been given a patch too.

"It is time to dig up your old beans and to cut down your summer plants, Sandy," said Miss Mitchell. "Tom, you can help the gardener to sweep up the leaves. Sheila, you can help Jeanie to get down the beanpoles."

The children ran off, shouting in joy. From the garden they would be able to see the policemen when they came down from the mountain.

"They'll have the two spies with them!" said Sandy.

"Yes, and maybe they'll be handcuffed together," said Tom, sweeping up the leaves as if they were spies! "I wonder if they'll make the dog a prisoner too!"

"I guess our two dogs gave him a rough time!" said Jeanie. She looked at Mack and Paddy, who were tearing round and round after each other. Jeanie had treated their ears well, and they were almost healed already. She was very good with animals. "They're jolly good friends now!" said Jeanie, pleased. "I'm glad we don't have to tie up first one and then another."

"I wonder how the police will get that machinery down the mountain," said Tom, stopping his sweeping for a moment.

"Same way as it was got up, I expect!" said Sandy. "On somebody's back! I expect it was taken up in pieces from the road the other side of the mountain."

"Look!" said Sheila suddenly. "Here come the policemen! Aunt! Uncle! Miss Mitchell! Here come the policemen."

In great excitement the children ran to the gate. But to their disappointment they saw that the two policemen coming down the hillside were alone. The men were not with them!

"I wonder why," said Tom.

"Perhaps they weren't there," suggested Jeanie.

The policemen came up to Kidillin House and smiled as the children rained questions on them. Only when Captain MacLaren came out to see them did they say what had happened.

"Yes, sir, there are two men there all right," said the sergeant. "They say that they left London because of their fear of air raids, and took that little cottage for safety. I asked them to let me look all over it – and there's no machinery of any sort there. I think yon boy of yours must have imagined it. There's no place round the old cottage where they could hide anything either."

"I *didn't* imagine it!" cried Sandy. "I didn't!"

"Did any of the others see it?" asked the sergeant, looking at Tom, Sheila and Jeanie.

"No," they said. "But we saw the windows boarded up!"

"They say they did that for the blackout," said the second policeman. "They've curtains for the front room but none for the back."

"Pooh! As if they'd bother to blackout windows that look right on to the mountain behind!" said Tom, scornfully. "All a made-up tale!"

"One man is deaf and dumb," said the sergeant. "We got all the talk from the dark man."

That made the children stare even more. Both Tom and Sandy had heard the *two* men talking. Why then did one pretend to be deaf and dumb?

The policemen jumped on to their bicycles and rode off, saluting the captain. The children gathered together in a corner of the garden and began to talk.

"What have they done with the machinery?"

"Why did one pretend to be dumb?"

"What a stupid reason for boarding up the window!"

"I guess I know why one pretended to be dumb! I bet he talks English with a German accent! I bet if he answered the policeman's questions, he would give himself away at once!" This was Tom speaking, and the others listened to him.

"Yes, that's it!" went on the excited boy. "He's the one called Carl – he's a German all right. It's an old trick to pretend to be dumb if you don't want to give yourself away!"

"And they guessed we might tell the police so they hid their machinery quickly," said Sandy. "But didn't have time to unboard the windows."

"That's it," said Tom. There was a silence, whilst they all thought quickly.

"Golly! I think I know!" cried Tom, in such an excited voice that they all jumped. "They've taken it to pieces, and managed somehow to get it into the cave behind the stream! That's what they've done. Somehow or other they must have known about that cave."

"It would be easy enough to do that, if the two of them worked together," said Sandy, thinking hard. "They could wrap the pieces in oiled cloth, tie them to ropes – and then one man could climb back to the cave and pull up the rope whenever the other man tied the packets on to it. It is sure to have been able to take to pieces, that machine – how else could they have got it up to the cottage so secretly?"

"We've hit on their secret all right," said Tom, and his face glowed. "*Now* what we've got to do is quite simple."

"What's that?" asked all the others.

"Why, all we've got to do is to go up to the cottage, lie low till the men go shopping or something, and then explore that cave again," said Tom. "If we find the machinery is there, we'll know we're right, and we can slip down to the police at once!"

"Oh good!" said Sandy. "The girls could keep watch for us, Tom, and you and I could take our swimming trunks and wriggle through the hole together."

"Is there time today?" wondered Tom looking, at his watch. But there wasn't. It was a nuisance, because all the children were longing to go on with their big adventure – and now they would have to wait till the next day!

Fortunately for them the next day was Saturday. They begged their governess to let them take their lunch on the hills. Mrs MacLaren had gone to the town to see her husband off once more, and Miss Mitchell was in charge.

"Very well," said Miss Mitchell. "I think I'll come with you today. I've nothing much to do."

The children stared at one another in dismay. If Miss Mitchell came they couldn't do anything! They could not think of a single reason to give her to stop her coming.

"I'll go and ask Cook to get a good lunch ready," said Miss Mitchell, bustling out to the kitchen. "I'll pack it up nicely into the picnic bags."

"Well, isn't that awful!" said Sheila, as the governess went out of the room. "What *can* we do to stop her coming?"

They thought and thought – but it was no good. She would have to come!

"Well, listen," said Tom at last. "After we have had our picnic, you two girls can stay with Miss Mitchell, and Sandy and I will slip off to explore again. That's the only thing we can do."

"But we wanted to come too!" wailed Sheila.

"Well, you can't!" said Tom. "Now for goodness' sake don't make a fuss, Sheila, or Miss Mitchell will begin to think something's up!"

But Miss Mitchell didn't guess anything at all. She packed up the lunch, gave it to the two boys to carry on their backs, and soon they were all ready to start.

"Got your torch, Sandy?" whispered Tom.

"Yes," whispered back Sandy. "And I've got my swimming trunks on under my clothes too!"

They all set off. They climbed up the sunny hillside, chattering and laughing, picking blackberries as they went. Miss Mitchell was glad to see them all such good friends now, even the two dogs! They chased rabbits, real and imaginary, all the time, and once Paddy got so far down a hole that he had to be pulled out by Tom.

The boys made their way towards the cottage. Miss Mitchell was not sure she wanted to go there.

"Those men won't like us spying around," she said. "They probably guess that it is you children who had the police sent up there."

"Well, we'll not go too near," said Sandy. "What about having our lunch here, Miss Mitchell? There's a beautiful view for you to look at."

Miss Mitchell knew the view well. It was the same one that the children had looked at before, when they watched the steamers going by, far away on the blue sea. They all sat down, glad of a rest.

"There's a steamer," said Tom.

"Yes," said Miss Mitchell, looking at it through the pair of field glasses she had brought. "I hope it won't be sunk. Those coastal steamers should go in convoys, but they won't be bothered – and two were sunk the other day."

"What were they?" asked Sandy. "The *Yelland* and the *Harding*, do you mean?"

"No, two others have been sunk since then," said Miss Mitchell. "By a submarine too – so there must be one lurking about somewhere."

The children looked at the little steamer slipping slowly along, and hoped that it would not be sunk. Miss Mitchell opened the picnic bags and handed out ham sandwiches, tomatoes, hard-boiled eggs, apples, jam tarts and ginger buns.

"Oooooh! What a gorgeous picnic!" said Sheila, who was rapidly getting as big an appetite as her Scottish cousins. There was creamy milk to drink too. The dogs had one large biscuit each and little bits of ham that the children pulled from their sandwiches. Everybody was very happy.

"Goodness me, the sun's hot!" said Miss Mitchell, after they had all eaten as much as they could. "You had better have a little rest before we go on – we really can't climb higher, on top of our enormous lunch!"

She lay back on the warm heather and put her hat over her eyes. The children sat as still as mice. The same thought came into everyone's head. Would Miss Mitchell go to sleep?

For five minutes nobody said a single word. Even the dogs lay quiet. Then Jeanie gave a little cough. Miss Mitchell didn't stir. Jeanie spoke in a low voice. "Miss Mitchell!"

No answer from Miss Mitchell. Jeanie leaned over her governess, and lifted Miss Mitchell's hat up gently so that she could see if the governess was really asleep.

Her eyes were fast shut and she was breathing deeply. Jeanie nodded to the others. Very quietly they got up from the heather, shaking their fingers at the two dogs to warn them to be quiet. They climbed up higher, rounded a bend in the hillside, and then began to giggle.

"Good!" said Tom, at last. "We've got away nicely. Now come on quickly, everyone. We haven't a minute to lose!"

They climbed quickly towards the old cottage, keeping

a good lookout as they went. Would the two men be about? Would they be able to do any exploring? They all felt tremendously excited, and their hearts beat loudly and fast.

CHAPTER SEVEN

MISS MITCHELL IS VERY CROSS

Slowly and quietly the children crept over the heather that surrounded the cottage. Mack and Paddy crept with them, joining in what they thought was some new game.

No one was about. The dog was not to be seen either. "I'll just creep over to the cottage and see what I can see!" whispered Sandy. So off he went, running quietly to the hut. He peeped cautiously in at a window – and then drew back very quickly indeed.

He came back to the others. "The two men are there," he whispered. "But they are sound asleep, like Miss Mitchell! This must be a sleepy afternoon! Come on –

we'll go to the underground burn, and see if we can get into the cave and look round before the men wake up."

In great delight the four children crept quietly off to where the big rock jutted out, through which the water fell down the mountainside. But when they came in sight of it, what a shock they got!

Tied up outside the rock was the big dog!

The children stopped in dismay. Tom pushed them back, afraid that the dog would see or hear them. They stared at one another, half-frightened.

"It's no good trying any exploring this afternoon!" said Tom, frowning in disappointment. "Absolutely no good at all. But it shows one thing plainly – they're afraid we may guess their hiding place and explore it – so they've put the dog there to guard it!"

"Well, we can't possibly get past that big brute," said Sandy. "I wonder now if there are any signs of trampling round about the burn there, Tom. If they've hidden anything in that cave, they'd have to stand around the rock a good bit, and the footmarks would show. I've a good mind to creep nearer and see."

"No, let me," said Tom at once. He always liked to be the one to do things if he could – and Sandy had done the exploring last time! Tom felt it was his turn.

"Tom! Come back!" whispered Sandy, as Tom crept forward on hands and knees. "I can go much more quietly than you!"

But Tom would not turn back. It was a pity he didn't – for suddenly he knelt on a dry twig which cracked in two like a pistol shot!

The dog, lying quietly by the rock, raised up its head at once and then leapt to its feet, sniffing the air. Tom crouched flat – but the dog saw him. It began to bark loudly, and the mountainside rang and echoed with its loud voice.

"Quick! Get down the slope, back to Miss Mitchell!" said Sandy. "Those men will be out in a minute!"

Sandy was right. The two men woke up at once when they heard the barking of the dog. The door of the cottage opened and out they ran. One of them shouted loudly. "What is it, Digger, what is it?"

Then he saw the children disappearing down the hillside and with a cry of rage he followed them. "Loose the dog!" he yelled to the other man. The children tore away as fast as they could, slipping and sliding as they went.

The dog was loosed – but as soon as he was faced once more by the two dogs who had beaten him the other day he dropped his tail and refused to go after the children. The man beat him, but it was no use. Digger was afraid of Mack and Paddy.

But the first man was not afraid of anything! He plunged down the hillside after the children, and just as they reached the place where they had left Miss Mitchell, he caught them up.

Miss Mitchell awoke in a hurry when she heard such a noise of scrambling and shouting. She sat up and looked round. The children ran up to her – and the man came up in a rage.

"What are these children doing here?" he shouted. "I tell you, I'll whip them all if they come spying round here. Can't a man be left in peace?"

"I don't know what you are talking about," said Miss Mitchell firmly. "We came up on the hills for a picnic, and we have as much right here as you have. Please go away at once, or I will report you to the police."

The man glared at Miss Mitchell. He began to shout again, but when Miss Mitchell repeated that she would certainly tell the police of his threats to her children, he muttered something and went back up the hillside.

Miss Mitchell was very angry with them. "So you slipped off up to the cottage when I was having a little nap, did you?" she scolded. "Now you see what has happened! You have made enough trouble for those two men already by telling made-up tales about them – and now you go prowling round their cottage again! You will promise me not to go there again."

The children looked at one another in dismay. Just what they hoped wouldn't happen!

"Very well," said Sandy sulkily. "I promise not to go to the cottage again."

"So do I," said Tom. The girls promised too. Miss Mitchell gathered up the picnic things, and said that they must all return home. She really was very cross.

"Miss Mitchell, those weren't made-up tales," said Sandy, as they went down the mountainside. "You shouldn't say that. You know we speak the truth."

"I don't want to hear any more about it," said the governess. "It is most unpleasant to have a man roaring and shouting at us like that, because of your stupid behaviour. You know quite well that I would not have allowed you to go to the cottage if you had asked me."

Miss Mitchell was cross all that day. But the next day was better, and the children went to church glad that Miss Mitchell seemed to have forgotten about the day before. She had not told their mother about them, so that was good.

When they came out of church there was half an hour before lunch. In the distance the children saw Loorie, the old shepherd. Sandy was fond of him, and asked Miss Mitchell if they might go and talk to him.

Loorie was treating a sheep that had a bad leg. He nodded to the children, and smiled at Tom and Sheila when Sandy explained that they were his cousins.

"This is an easy time of year for you, isn't it, Loorie?" asked Sandy.

"Oh aye," said the old man, rubbing the sheep's leg with some horrid-smelling black ointment. "The winter's the busy time, when the lambing's on."

He went on to tell Tom and Sheila of all the happenings of the year. The two town children listened in great interest. They could hardly understand the Scottish words the old man used, but they loved to hear them.

"Did you lose any lambs this year, Loorie?" asked Sandy.

"Aye, laddie, I lost too many," said Loorie. "And do you ken where I lost them? Down the old pothole on the mountain up there!"

"What old pothole?" asked Tom, puzzled.

"Oh, it's a strange place," explained Sandy. "There's a big hole up there, that goes down for ever so far. The sheep sometimes fall into it and they can never be got out."

"It's funny to sit by the hole," said Jeanie. "You can hear a rushing sound always coming up it."

"Folks do say that's the River Spelter," said Loorie,

setting the sheep on its legs again. "Aye, folks say a mighty lot of things."

"The Spelter!" said Tom, surprised. "Why, do you mean that the Spelter goes under the pothole you're talking about?"

"Maybe it does and maybe it doesn't," said the old shepherd, closing his tin of ointment. "There's funny things in the mountains. Don't you go taking the lasses near that pothole, now, Master Sandy!"

"There's Miss Mitchell calling," said Sandy hurriedly, for he saw by Tom's face that his cousin was longing to go to visit the pothole! "Goodbye, Loorie. We'll see you again soon."

As they ran back to Miss Mitchell, Tom panted out some questions. "Where's the pothole! Is it anywhere near the underground stream? Do you suppose that's the Spelter that runs beneath the pothole, or our stream?"

Sandy didn't know at all. But he knew quite well that before that day was out, Tom would want to go and explore the pothole! Sandy wanted to as well.

"I can't think why I didn't remember the pothole before," thought the boy. "I suppose it was because I've known about it all my life and never thought anything about it!"

CHAPTER EIGHT

DOWN THE POTHOLE

That afternoon the four children and the dogs set off to the pothole. They had talked about it excitedly, and Tom felt sure that if there was water at the bottom, it might be the very same stream that poured out of the hole in the rock. If it was, they could get down the hole and follow it up – and maybe come to the cave from behind.

"And then we can see if the spies have hidden their things there!" cried Sandy. "We didn't think there could be another way in – but there may be! What a good thing we had that talk to old Loorie this morning."

They took a good many things with them that afternoon. Both boys had strong ropes tied round their waists. All of them had torches, and Tom had matches and a candle too.

"You see," he explained, "if the air is bad, we can tell it by lighting a candle. If the candle flickers a lot and goes out, we shall know the air is too bad for us. Then we shall have to go back."

They also had towels with them, because Tom thought they might have to undress and wade through water. They could leave their towels by the pothole and dry themselves when they came back. They all felt excited and important. They were out to catch spies, and to find out their secrets!

Sandy took them round the mountain, in the opposite direction to the one they usually went, and at last brought them to the pothole.

It certainly was a very strange place. It looked like a wide pit, overgrown with heather and brambles – but Sandy explained that when they climbed down into this pit-like dell, they would come to the real pothole, a much narrower pit at one side of the dell.

They climbed down into the dell, and Sandy took them to one side. He kicked away some branches, and there below them was the pothole!

"Loorie must have put those branches across to stop the sheep from falling in," said Sandy. "Now just sit beside this hole and listen."

The four of them sat beside the strange hole. It was not very big, not more than a metre wide, and curious bits of blue slate stuck out all around it. The children peered down into the hole, but it was like looking down into an endless well. They could see nothing but blackness.

But they could hear a most mysterious noise coming up to them! It was like the sound of the wind in the trees, but louder and weirder.

"Yes – that's water rushing along all right," said Tom, sitting up again, his face red with excitement. "But it sounds to me a bigger noise than our little stream could make. It sounds more like the River Spelter rushing along in the heart of the mountain, down to where it flows out at the foot, in the village of Kidillin!"

"Could we possibly get down there?" asked Sandy doubtfully. "Would our ropes be long enough? We don't want any accidents! I don't know how we'd be rescued!"

Tom flashed his torch down the hole. "Look!" he said. "Do you see down there, Sandy – about two metres down? There's a sort of rocky shelf. Well, we may find that all the way down there are these rocky bits to help us. If we have a rope firmly round our waists so that we can't fall, we'll be all right. I'll go down first."

"No, you won't," said Sandy. "I'm better used to climbing. Don't forget that it was you who cracked that twig yesterday and gave warning to the dog. If it had been I who was creeping along, the dog would never have known."

Tom looked angry. Then the frown went from his face and he nodded. "All right," he said. "Perhaps it would be best if you went. You're good at this sort of thing and I've never done it before."

"The girls are not to come," said Sandy. "Not today, at any rate. It looks more dangerous than I thought, and anyway, we'll want someone to look after the ropes for us. We will tie the ends to a tree, and the girls can watch that they don't slip."

Neither of the girls made any objection to being left at the top. Both of them thought the pothole looked horrid! They were quite content to let the boys try it first!

They all felt really excited. Sandy tied the ends of their two strong ropes to the trunk of a stout pine tree. He and Tom knotted the other ends round their waists as firmly as they could. Now, even if they fell, their ropes would hold them, and the girls could pull them up in safety!

Sandy went down the pothole first. He let himself slip down to the rocky ledge some way down. His feet caught on it with a jerk. His hands felt about for something to hold.

"Are you all right, Sandy?" asked Tom, flashing his torch down the hole.

"Yes," said Sandy. "I'm feeling to see if there's somewhere to put my feet farther down." Sandy was as good as a cat at climbing. He soon found a small ledge for his right foot, and then another for his left.

Bits of slate, stone and soil broke away as he slowly climbed downwards, and fell far below him. The pothole did not go straight down, but curved a little now and again, so that it was not so difficult as Sandy had expected to climb down.

"Come on, Tom!" he called. "If you're careful where to put your feet, it's not too difficult."

Tom began his climb down too. He found it far more difficult than Sandy, for he was not so used to climbing. His feet slithered and slipped, and he cut his hands when he clutched at stones and earth.

The girls at the top were holding on to the boys' ropes, letting them out gradually. Tom's rope jerked and pulled, but Sandy's rope went down smoothly.

As Sandy went down farther and farther, the noise of rushing water became louder and louder until he could not even hear his own voice when he called to Tom. Tom was kicking out so many stones and bits of earth that they fell round poor Sandy like a hailstorm!

"Stop kicking at the sides of the hole!" yelled Sandy. But Tom couldn't help it. Sandy wished he had put on a hat, to stop the pebbles from hitting his head – but soon, at a bend in the hole, he became free of the "hailstorm", and went downwards comfortably.

It was the first part that was so steep and difficult. It was easier farther down, for rocky ledges stuck out everywhere, making it almost like climbing down a ladder.

The noise of the water was deafening. Sandy thought it was so near that he might step into it at any moment. So he switched on his torch and looked downwards. The black water gleamed up at him, topped with white spray where it flowed over jutting rocks. It was farther down than he had thought.

As he climbed down to the water, the hole widened tremendously, and became a cave. Sandy jumped down beside the shouting river, and stood there, half-frightened, half-delighted.

It was a strange sight, that underground river! It flowed along between rocky walls, black, strong and noisy. It entered the cave by a low tunnel, which was filled to the roof with the water. The river flowed in a rocky bed and entered another black tunnel just near

Sandy – but it did not fill this tunnel to the roof. Sandy flashed his torch into the tunnel, and saw that for some way, at any rate, the roof was fairly high, about up to his head.

There was a rattle of stones about him, and Tom came sliding down the walls of the pothole at a great speed! He had missed his footing and fallen! But he had not far to fall, and fortunately for him, his rope was only just long enough to take him beside Sandy, and it pulled him up with a jerk, before he fell into the water.

"Steady on!" said Sandy. "You *are* in a hurry!"

"Phew!" said Tom, loosening the rope a little round his waist. "That wasn't very pleasant. I'm glad I was fairly near the bottom. My word, the rope did give my waist an awful pull! I say, Sandy! What a marvellous sight this is!"

"The underground world!" said Sandy, flashing his torch around. "Look at that black rushing river, Tom! We've got to wade down that, through that tunnel – see?"

"Oooh!" said Tom. "Where do you suppose it goes to?"

"That's what we've got to find out," said Sandy. "I think myself that away up that other tunnel there is the source of the Spelter. It probably begins in a collection of springs all running to the same rocky bed in the mountain, and then rushing down together as a river. But really it's not more than a fast stream here, though it makes enough noise for a river!"

"That's because it is underground, and the echoes are weird," said Tom. "Also, it is going downhill at a good rate, not flowing gently in an even bed. How deep do you suppose it is, Sandy?"

"We'll have to find out!" said Sandy, beginning to undress. "Hurry up! Got your torch with you? Well, bring it, and bring the oilskin bag too, in case we have to swim, and need something waterproof to put our torches in. I've got the candles and matches."

CHAPTER NINE

IN THE HEART OF THE MOUNTAIN

Both boys stood in their swimming trunks. They shivered, for the air was cold. Sandy put one leg into the rushing stream. The water was icy!

"Oooh!" said Sandy, drawing back his leg quickly! "It's mighty cold, Tom. Just hang on to me a minute, will you, so that I can feel how deep the water is."

Tom held on to his arms. Sandy slipped a foot into the water again. He went in over his knee, and right up to his waist! Then he felt a solid rocky bottom, and stood up, grinning.

"It's all right!" he said. "Only up to my waist, Tom. Come on in and we'll explore the tunnel."

Tom got into the water, and then the two boys began to wade along the noisy stream. It went gradually downwards, and once there was quite a steep drop, making a small waterfall. The boys had to help one another down. It was very cold, for the water was really icy. They were both shivering, and yet felt hot with excitement.

The roof of the tunnel kept about head or shoulder-high. Once the tunnel widened out again into a small cave, and the boys climbed out of the water and did some violent exercises to warm themselves.

They got back into the water again. It suddenly got narrow and deeper. Deeper and deeper it got until the two boys had to swim. And then the tunnel roof dipped down and almost reached the surface of the water!

"*Now* what are we to do?" said Tom, in dismay.

"Put your torch into its oilskin bag, to begin with," said Sandy, putting his into the bag, next to the candle and box of matches. "Then it won't get wet. If you'll just wait here for me, Tom, I'll swim underwater a little way and see if the roof rises farther on."

"Well, for goodness' sake be careful," said Tom, in alarm. "I hope you've got enough breath to swim under the water *and* back, if the roof doesn't rise! The water may flow for a long way touching the roof."

"If it does, we can go no farther," said Sandy. "Don't worry about *me*! I can swim under water for at least a minute!"

He took a deep breath, plunged under the water, and swam hard. He bobbed his head up, but found that the rocky ceiling still touched the stream. He went on a little way, and then, when he was nearly bursting for breath, he found that the roof lifted, and he could stand with his head out of the water.

He took another deep breath and went back for Tom. "It's all right," he gasped, coming up beside him. "You need to take a jolly good breath though. Take one now and come along quickly."

Tom began to splutter under the water before he could stick his head up into the air once more and breathe. Sandy couldn't help laughing at him, and Tom was very indignant.

"Just stop laughing!" he said to Sandy. "I was nearly drowned!"

"Oh no you weren't," giggled Sandy. "I could easily have pulled you through, Tom. Come on – the next bit is easy. We can swim or wade. Let's swim and get warm."

So they swam along in the deep black water for some way – and then the tunnel widened out into a great underground hall. It was a spooky place. Strange stones gleamed in the light of their torches. Phosphorescent streaks shone in the rocky walls, and here and there curious things hung down from the ceiling rather like icicles.

"Ooh, isn't it weird?" whispered Tom – and at once his whisper came back to him in strange echoes. "Isn't it weird, isn't it weird – weird – weird?" The whole placed seemed to be full of his whispering.

"It's magnificent!" said Sandy, revelling in the strangeness of it. "See how those stones gleam? I wonder if they're valuable. And look at the shining streaks in that granite-like wall! I say, Tom, think, perhaps we are the very first people to stand in this big underground hall!"

The underground river split into three in the big cavern. One lot of water went downwards into the steep tunnel, one wandered off to the other end of the cavern, and the third entered a smaller tunnel, and ran gently along it as far as Sandy could see.

"We'll follow this second one that goes to the other end of the cave," said Sandy. "We needn't wade in it – we can walk beside it. Come on."

So they walked beside it, and found that it wandered through a narrow archway into yet another cave – and there they saw a strange sight.

The water stopped there and formed a great underground lake, whose waters gleamed purple, green and blue by the light of the boys' torches. The lake was moved by quiet ripples. Tom and Sandy stood gazing at it.

"Isn't it marvellous?" whispered Tom, and again his whisper ran all round and came back to him in dozens of echoes.

Sandy suddenly got out the candle and lighted it. The flame flickered violently and almost went out.

"The air's bad in this cave!" cried Sandy. "Come back to the other, where the rushing water is! Quick!"

He and Tom left the strange lake, and ran back to the great, shining hall. The air felt much purer at once and the boys took big breaths of it. The candle now burnt steadily.

"For some reason the air isn't good yonder," said Sandy. "Well, we can't go *that* way! There's only one way left – and that's to wade down that tunnel over there. Maybe it's the right one!"

"We'll hope so," said Tom, doing some more exercises, and jumping up and down. "Come on, Sandy. In we go!"

So into the water they went once more. How cold it was again! The tunnel was quite high above the water, and the stream itself was shallow, only up to their knees. It was quite easy to get along.

They waded along for a long way, their torches lighting up the tunnel. And then a very surprising thing happened.

They heard the murmur of voices! Tom and Sandy listened in the greatest astonishment. Perhaps it was the noise of the stream? Or strange echoes?

They went on again, and came out into a small cave through which the stream flowed quite placidly. And there they heard the voices again!

Then suddenly the voices stopped, and an even stranger sound came. It was the sound of somebody playing an organ!

CHAPTER TEN

A VERY STRANGE DISCOVERY

Sandy clutched hold of Tom, for the sound crept into every corner of the cave, and filled it full. They were drowned in music!

It went on and on and then stopped. No further noise came, either of voices or music. The boys flashed their torches into each other's faces and looked at one another in amazement.

"An organ! In the heart of the mountain!" said Tom, in an amazed whisper. "Didn't it sound wonderful?"

"Come on – let's get out of this cave and see what's in the next one!" whispered Sandy. "Maybe there's an underground church here, with somebody playing the organ!"

The boys crept along, one behind the other. They suddenly saw a light shining through a rugged opening in the cave. It came from a cave beyond. Sandy peeped round to see what it was.

A lantern swung from a rope in the roof of a cave. It was a large cave, and in it were the two men who lived in the old cottage! They were crouched over the machinery that Sandy had seen in the back room!

Sandy clutched Tom's hand, and his heart leapt and beat fast. So they had actually come to the cave behind the gushing spring that fell from the hole in the rock!

They could hardly believe their good luck! They squeezed each other's hand, and wished that the men would go away from the machinery, whatever it was, so that they might see what it was.

"I wish they'd go back to the cottage," whispered Sandy – and at once his whisper ran round and round and sounded like a lot of snakes hissing! The men looked up in alarm.

"What was that noise?" said one.

The second man answered in a language that Sandy knew was German. He wasn't deaf and dumb then! Sandy rejoiced. They *were* spies, he felt quite sure. But how could he make them go away, so that he and Tom could examine the cave properly.

Sandy had an idea. He suddenly began to make the most dreadful moaning noises imaginable, like a dog in pain. He made Tom jump – but the two men jumped even more. They sprang up and looked round fearfully.

"Ooooh, ah, ooh-ooh-ah, wee-oo, wee-oo, waaaah!"

wailed Sandy. The echoes sent the groaning noise round and round the cave, gathering together and becoming louder and louder till the whole place was full of the wildest moaning and wailing you could imagine!

The men shouted something in fear. They ran to the stream, jumped into it, waded in the water till they got to the rock through which it flowed, and then wriggled out of the hole, down to the ground below, on the sunny hillside. They had never in their lives been so terrified.

Tom and Sandy screamed with laughter. They held on to one another, and laughed till they could laugh no more. And the echoes of their laughter ran all around them till it seemed as if the whole place must be full of laughing imps.

"Come on – let's have a look round now," said Sandy at last. They ran into the men's cave – and then Tom saw what the "machinery" was!

"It's a wireless transmitter!" he cried. "I've seen one before. These men can send out wireless messages as well as receive them – and oh, Sandy, that's what they've been doing, the wretches! As soon as they see the steamers pass on the sea in the distance, they send a wireless message to some submarine lurking nearby, and the submarine torpedoes the steamers!"

"Oh! So that's why there have been so many steamers sunk round our coast," said Sandy, his eyes flashing in anger. "The hateful scoundrels! I'm going to smash their set, anyway!"

Before Tom could stop Sandy, the raging boy picked up a stone and smashed it into the centre of the transmitter. "You won't sink any *more* steamers!" he cried.

"Good," said Tom. "Now let's wriggle to the hole where the stream gushes out, Sandy, and see if the men are anywhere near. If they're not, we could wriggle out, and go back to the girls overground. I really don't fancy going all the way back underground!"

"Nor do I," said Sandy. "It would be much quicker if we got out here, went up to the top of the mountain, and climbed down from there to where the girls are waiting."

"Fancy, Sandy – we've been right through the mountain!" said Tom. "I guess no boy has ever had such an adventure as we've had before!"

"Come on," said Sandy. "I'll go first."

He was soon at the mouth of the hole. He peered out – but there was no one about at all, not even the big dog. "I bet the men have run into the cottage, taken the dog to guard them, and locked the door!" called back Sandy.

"Well, your wails and groans were enough to make anyone jump out of their skin!" said Tom. "I got an awful scare myself, Sandy!"

The two boys wriggled out of the hole, soaked again by the rushing water. But once they stood in the warm sun they forgot their shivers and danced for glee.

"Come on!" said Sandy. "No time to lose! The climb will make us as warm as can be!"

Off they went, climbing up the mountainside, revelling in the feel of the warm heather. The sun shone down and very soon they were as warm as toast – too warm, in fact, for Tom began to puff and pant like an engine!

They went over the top at last, sparing a moment to look back at the magnificent view. Far away they could see the blue sea, with a small steamer on it. "The submarine can't be told about *you*!" said Sandy. "Come on, Tom."

On they went. Tom followed Sandy, for Sandy knew every inch of the way. Down the other side they went, scrambling in their swimming trunks over the heather. And presently in the distance, they saw the blue frocks of the two girls.

Sheila was bending anxiously over the pothole, wishing the boys would come back. It was so long now since they had gone down the hole. She almost fell down it herself when she heard Sandy's shout behind her.

"Hallo! Here we are!"

The girls leapt to their feet and looked round in amazement. They were so surprised that they couldn't say a word. Then Jeanie spoke.

"How *did* you get out of the pothole?" she gasped. "Sheila and I have been sitting here for hours, watching – and now you suddenly appear!"

"It's a long story," said Sandy, "but a very surprising one. Listen!"

He sat down on the heather and he and Tom told how they had made their way through the heart of the mountain, wading and swimming in the river, and how they had found the strange underground lake, and had taken the right turning to the cave behind the spring. When they told about the men, and how Sandy had frightened them with his groans and wails, the girls flung themselves backwards and squealed with laughter.

"And now we know the secret of why our steamers on this coast are so easily sunk," finished Sandy. "It's because of those two traitors and their wireless. Well, I smashed that! And now the best thing we can do is to go back home and get the police again!"

"What about our clothes?" asked Tom.

"They can wait," said Sandy. "We'll get them from the pothole sometime. We ought to go and get the police before the men discover that I've broken their wireless, and escape!"

"Come on then!" cried the girls, jumping up, "We're ready!"

And down the hillside they all tore, the two boys in their swimming trunks, with their oilskin bags still hanging round their necks!

CHAPTER ELEVEN

THE HUNT FOR THE TWO SPIES

Miss Mitchell jumped in surprise when the four children rushed into the garden where she was busy cutting flowers – the boys in their swimming trunks, and the girls squealing with excitement.

"Miss Mitchell! Miss Mitchell! We've found out all about the two spies!"

"Miss Mitchell! We've been down the pothole!"

"Miss Mitchell! We know how those steamers were sunk!"

"Miss Mitchell! Can we phone the police? Listen, do listen!"

So Miss Mitchell listened, and could hardly believe her ears when the children told her such an extraordinary tale.

"You dared to go down that pothole!" she gasped. "Oh, you naughty boys! Oh, I can't believe all this, I really can't."

Mrs MacLaren came home at that moment, and the children streamed to meet her, shouting their news. Mrs MacLaren went pale when she heard how Sandy and Tom had actually climbed down the dangerous pothole.

"Well, you certainly won't do *that* again!" she said firmly. "You might have killed yourselves!"

"But, Mother, our clothes are still down there," said Sandy. "We'll have to get them."

"You are far more important to me than your clothes," said Mrs MacLaren. "On no account are you to go potholing again! And now – I think I must certainly ring up the police."

The children clustered round the phone whilst Mrs MacLaren rang for the police station. They were so excited that they couldn't keep still!

"Do sit down," begged Miss Mitchell. "How *can* your mother phone when you are jigging about like grasshoppers!"

Mrs MacLaren told the sergeant what the children had discovered. When the sergeant heard that Sandy had smashed the spies' wireless with a stone, he roared with laughter.

"Ah, he's a bonny lad, yon boy of yours!" he said into the phone. "He didn't wait for us to see if that wireless was really doing bad work – he smashed it himself! Well, Mrs MacLaren, I'm fine and obliged to your children for doing such good work for us. This is a serious matter, and I must get on to our headquarters now, and take my orders. I'll be along at Kidillin House in a wee while!"

Mrs MacLaren put the phone down and turned to tell the children. "Can we go with the police, Mother? Oh do let us!" begged Sandy. "After all, we did find out everything ourselves. And if those men have escaped, by any chance, we would have to show the police how to squeeze in through the rock where the spring gushes out."

"Very well," said Mrs MacLaren. "But go and put some clothes on quickly, and then come down and eat something. You must be very hungry after all these adventures."

"Well, so I am!" said Jeanie, in surprise. "But I was so excited that I didn't think of it till you spoke about it, Mother."

"I'm jolly hungry too, Aunt Jessie!" said Tom. "Come on, Sandy, let's put on jeans and jerseys, then we'll have time for something to eat before the police come."

The children expected to see only the constable and the sergeant – and they were immensely surprised when a large black car roared up the drive to Kidillin House, with *six* policemen inside!

"Good old police!" said Sheila, watching the men jump out of the car. "I love our London policemen, they're so tall and kind – but these police look even taller and stronger! I guess they won't stand any nonsense from the spies!"

An inspector was with the police – a stern-looking man, with the sharpest eyes Sandy had ever seen. He beckoned to Sandy and the boy went to him proudly.

"These spies may know they have been discovered, isn't that so?" asked the police. "They have only to go into their cave to see their wireless smashed, and they would know that someone had guessed their secret."

"Yes, sir," said Sandy. "So I suggest that half your men go in the car to the other side of the mountain, and go up the slope there – it's a pretty rough road, but the car will do it all right – and the other half come with us up *this* side. Then if the spies try to escape the other way, they will be caught."

"Good idea," said the inspector. He gave some sharp orders, and three of the men got into the car and roared away again. When they came to the village of Kidillin, they would take the road that led around the foot of the mountain and would then go up the other side.

"Come on," said the inspector, and he and the children and two policemen went up the hillside. The dogs, of course, went too, madly excited. Sandy said he could quiet them at any moment, and to show that he could, he held up his finger and called "Quiet!" At once the two dogs stopped their yelping and lay down flat. The inspector nodded.

"All right," he said. "Come along."

They trooped up the mountainside. When they came fairly near the old cottage, the children had a great disappointment. The inspector forbade them to come any farther!

"These men may be dangerous," he said. "You will stay here till I say you may move."

"But, please, sir," began Sandy.

"Obey orders!" said the inspector, in a sharp voice.

The children stood where they were at once, and the three men went on. The dogs stood quietly by Sandy.

It seemed ages before the children heard anything more. Then they saw one of the policemen coming down the heather towards them.

"The men are gone!" he said. "Our men the other side didn't meet them, and we've seen no sign of them. Either they've escaped us, or they're hiding somewhere on the hill. They've left their dog though. We've captured it, and it's tied to a tree. Don't let your two go near it."

The children looked at one another in dismay and disappointment. "So they've escaped after all!" said Tom. "Well, what about us showing you where their wireless is? We might as well do that whilst we're here."

So the two boys took the six policemen to the hole in the rock, where the water gushed out. Two of the men squeezed through after Sandy and Tom, who once more got soaked! But they didn't care! Adventures like this didn't happen every day!

The men looked in amazement at the "machinery" in the cave. "What a wonderful set," said one of the policemen, who knew all about wireless. "My word! No wonder we've had our steamers sunk here – these spies had only to watch them passing and send a wireless message to the waiting submarine. We'll catch that submarine soon, or my name isn't Jock!"

"It's a strange sort of place, this," said the other policeman, looking round.

Sandy startled the policeman very much by suddenly clutching his arm and saying "Sh"!

"Don't do that!" said the man, scared. "What's up?"

"I heard something over yonder," said Sandy,

pointing to the back of the cave. "I say – I believe the spies are hiding in the mountain itself! I'm sure I heard a voice back there!"

The policeman whistled. "Why didn't we think of that before! Come on, then – we'll hunt them out. Do you know the way?"

"Yes," said Sandy. "There's another cave behind this, and then a tunnel through which a shallow stream runs, and then a great underground hall, with a strange lake shining in a separate cavern."

"Goodness!" said the policeman, staring at Sandy in surprise. "Well, come on, there's no time to lose."

They followed Sandy into the next cave. The boy lit the way with his torch. Then they all waded up the stream in the dark rocky tunnel, and came out into the enormous underground hall.

And at the other end of the great cavern they heard the sound of footfalls, as the two spies groped about, using a torch that was almost finished.

"Give yourselves up!" shouted the first policeman, and his voice echoed round thunderously. The spies put out their light and ran, stumbling and scrambling, into the cave where the underground lake shone mysteriously. Sandy remembered that the air was bad there.

He told the policeman. They put on their own torches and groped their way to the cave of the lake. The air was so bad there that the two spies, after breathing it for a minute or two, had fallen to the ground, quite stupefied.

The policemen tied handerkerchiefs round their mouths and noses, and ran in. In a moment they had dragged the two men out of the lake cave and, whilst they were still drowsy, had quickly handcuffed them. Now they could not escape!

Sandy and Tom were dancing about in excitement. The spies were caught! Their wireless was smashed! Things were too marvellous for words!

It took them some time to squeeze out of the hole in the rock, with two handcuffed men, but at last they were all out. The surprise on the inspector's face outside was comical to see!

"They were in there, sir," said a policeman, jerking his head towards the caves. "My word, sir, you should see inside that mountain! It's a marvellous place."

But the inspector was more interested in the capture of the spies. Each of them was handcuffed to a policeman, and down the hill they all came, policemen, spies, children – and dogs! The big dog belonging to the men was taken over the hill by one policeman, to the car left on the road below. Mack and Paddy had barked that they would eat him up, and looked as if they would too!

"So the spies' dog had better go by car!" said the inspector, smiling for the first time.

CHAPTER TWELVE

THE END OF THE ADVENTURE

What an exciting evening the children had, telling their mother and Miss Mitchell all that had happened! Captain MacLaren came too, on twenty-four hour's leave, for the police had phoned to him, and he felt he must go and hear what had happened.

"It's a great thing, you know, catching those two spies," he said. "It means we'll probably get the submarine out there that's been damaging our shipping – for we'll send out a false message, and ask it to get in a certain position to sink a ship – but our aeroplanes will be there to sink the submarine instead!"

"Could we explore the inside of the mountain again, please, Uncle!" asked Tom.

"Not unless I am with you," said Captain MacLaren firmly. "I promise you that when I get any good leave, and can come home for two or three weeks, or when the war is over, we'll all go down there exploring together. But you must certainly not explore any more by yourselves. Also, the winter will soon be here, and the rains and snow will swell that underground lake, and the streams, and will fill the caves and tunnels almost to their roofs. It will be too dangerous."

"Uncle, when we *do* explore the heart of the mountain with you, we could find out if the river there *is* the beginning of the Spelter," said Tom, eagerly. "We could throw something into it there – and watch to see if what we throw in comes out at the foot of the mountain where the river rushes!"

"We could," said Captain MacLaren, "and we will! We'll have a wonderful time together, and discover all kinds of strange things!"

"But we shall never have *quite* such an exciting time again as we've had this last week or two," said Sandy. "I couldn't have done it without Tom. I'm jolly glad he and Sheila came to live with us!"

"So am I!" said Tom. "I'm proud of my Scottish cousins, Uncle Andy!"

"And I'm proud of my English nephew and niece!" said the Captain, clapping Tom on the back. He looked at them with a twinkle in his eye. "I *did* hear that you couldn't bear one another at one time," he said, "and that you and the dogs were all fighting together!"

"Yes, that's true," said Sandy, going red. "But we're

all good friends now. Mack! You like old Paddy, don't you?"

Mack and Paddy were lying down side by side. At Sandy's words Mack sat up, cocked his ears, and then licked Paddy on the nose with his red tongue!

"There you are!" said Sandy, pleased. "That shows you what good friends they are! But I shan't lick Tom's nose to show he's *my* friend!"

Everybody laughed, and then Miss Mitchell spoke.

"I wonder what's happening to those two spies," she said. And at that very moment the telephone rang. It was the inspector, who had called up the Captain to tell him the latest news.

"One of the men is a famous spy," he said. "We've had our eye on him for years, and he disappeared when war broke out. We are thankful to have caught him!"

"I should think so!" said the Captain. "What a bit of luck! It's difficult to round up all these spies – they're so clever at disappearing!"

"Well, sir, they won't do any more disappearing – except into prison!" chuckled the inspector. "And now there's another bit of news, sir – I don't know if you've heard it?"

"I've heard nothing," said the Captain. "What's the second piece of news, Inspector?"

"It's about that submarine, sir. We've spotted it – and we've damaged it so that it couldn't sink itself properly."

"Good work!" cried the Captain in jòy. "That *is* a fine bit of news!"

"We've captured the submarine," went on the inspector, "and we've taken all the crew prisoners."

"What have you done with the submarine?" asked the

Captain, whilst all the children crowded round him in excitement, trying to guess all that was said at the other end of the telephone.

"The submarine is being towed to Port Riggy," said the inspector, "and if the children would like to come over and see it next week, we'll be very pleased to take them over it, to show them what they've helped to capture!"

"What does he say, what does he say?" cried Sandy. "Quick, tell us, Father!"

"Oh, he just wants to know if you'd like to go over to Port Riggy next week, and see the submarine you helped to capture!" said the Captain, smiling round at the four eager faces.

"Who said we should never have such an exciting time as we've been having!" yelled Tom, dancing round like a clumsy bear. "Golly! Think of going over a submarine! Miss Mitchell – you'll have to give us a day's holiday next week, won't you!"

"Oh, it depends on how hard you work," said Miss Mitchell, with a wicked twinkle in her eye.

And my goodness, how hard those four children are working now! They couldn't possibly miss going over to Port Riggy to see that submarine, could they?

The Enid Blyton Trust for Children

We hope you have enjoyed the adventures of the children in this book. Please think for a moment about those children who are too ill to do the exciting things you and your friends do.

Help them by sending a donation, large or small to the ENID BLYTON TRUST FOR CHILDREN. The Trust will use all your gifts to help children who are sick or handicapped and need to be made happy and comfortable.

Please send your postal orders or cheques to:

The Enid Blyton Trust for Children,
3rd Floor
New South Wales House
15 Adam Street
London WC2N 6AA

Thank you very much for your help.

Other titles by
Enid Blyton
in Armada

Mystery Stories	£2.25	☐
Adventure Stories	£2.25	☐
The Mystery That Never Was	£2.25	☐
The Treasure Hunters	£2.25	☐
Six Cousins at Mistletoe Farm	£2.25	☐
Six Cousins Again	£2.25	☐
The Children at Green Meadows	£2.25	☐
Adventures on Willow Farm	£2.25	☐
The Boy Next Door	£2.25	☐
Shadow the Sheepdog	£2.25	☐